Expanding Cracks

Expanding Cracks

Into the Void: Book Two

Ben Pick

To my friends and family, who taught me the most worthwhile lessons in life.

CONTENTS

CONTENTS

CONTENTS

Derek

For the umpteenth time in who knows how many days, Derek Something forced his brain to remember he wasn't dead.

I have a name. It's not Something... it's... Fen!

I've been in here for too long. It's messing with my head.

This void was purgatory by any standard definition, like a dark ocean spreading in every conceivable direction. All it lacked were the souls of the wandering dead. A dull glow lit this place from its inner source, never providing enough light to see clearly.

Typically, looking down from great heights arose a sense of nausea. Not here. With no ground in sight, the darkness beyond his feet might as well be up. His sense of balance certainly didn't care, either.

Thick, open textbooks drifted beside his head, with papers attached to clipboards and crumpled wads of wrong answers. The collective mess floated on nothing, aided by the weightlessness of this place.

"This is all your fault," he told his homework, to break the utter silence. He stared at the jumble of words and symbols on the page. For every sentence his sponge-like mind absorbed, he felt another memory drip from his ears. His mind should spring back to normal once he left this in-between place and returned to the real world.

Emphasis on *should.*

I'll solve one more homework question, then I'll take a break.

The chemical equation he wrote for the final answer looked balanced. He used it to calculate the remaining values and clapped the AP Chemistry book shut in victory.

As a reward, he shoved his entire arm into the backpack, wriggling it between books and folders, feeling for his prize.

I can make up for the five years—no, the five weeks—that I lost.

I think I lost. Uncertainty crept into the voice in his head.

"I'm not crazy, right?" he muttered.

You're the one debating with yourself.

A tiny crinkling sound indicated his search wasn't in vain. His hand clasped an energy bar. He tore it open and inhaled it in a single bite.

Rumbling pains reminded him that his stomach was empty and as vast as the void he was in.

Checking one of the two borrowed stopwatches from his pocket, the numbers read thirteen hours, eleven minutes, and twenty-five seconds.

That's too short. I've been in the void for much longer.

After counting to ten, the stopwatch remained at the same numbers: thirteen hours, eleven minutes, and twenty-five seconds glowed on the display.

Time was blending, folding back on itself.

His eyelids sank as he waited for the numbers to change.

He collected the sheets of scratch paper and textbooks and placed them in his backpack lest they float away while he took a nap. Carrying all his completed homework, his backpack acted as a lifeline, binding him to reality. He slid it over one shoulder, the metal ends of the straps clanking against the hard plaster cast covering his forearm.

Dull aches from his broken arm sent twinging sensations along his muscles as his backpack nestled in the nook between his head and shoulder. Little better than sleeping on a brick, he found some comfort in the hard support of the stiff makeshift pillow. He could sleep for as long as he wanted in the void with no time passing in the real world, in essence, napping for free.

Releasing a long breath, his buoyant muscles loosened.

As slumber fast approached, he vowed to continue the search for the other version of himself when he woke.

I'll find the Derek who was lost somewhere in this void.

A rolling sensation snapped him awake. Like standing on a capsized boat caught on the steep tides of a summer storm, the void tossed him about, sending him in deeper.

His arms flailed in vain to grasp something—anything.

The panic rising in him was washed away by the nothingness of the void as his mind failed to hold the fragments of increasingly hazy thoughts.

Emergency Broadcast

Rachel

With a wave of his hand, Mr. DeSantos, the band director, began the first piece of Rachel Mason's Friday morning class. She readied her drumsticks above her snare drum as the woodwind instruments opened with a soft, simplified version of the piece's overall theme. Brass horns layered on top, building a solid base from a lower octave.

Highland View High School's band room was not the best for acoustics. Sounds struck the green-and-gold-painted concrete walls and glass windows at odd angles. The music they created in the large room also rebounded off the metal-grated lockers used to hold student instruments. Today's practice pieces were more for reinforcing fundamentals than perfecting their upcoming performances. The more difficult songs would be better rehearsed in the auditorium, where sound panels magnified nuances often drowned out by louder sections.

One. Two. Three. Four. Rachel counted the four-beat measure, synchronizing with the pace set by the band director. She tightened her grip on her worn, hickory drumsticks. A good number of nicks and chips ran along the otherwise smooth wood in her hands. She held their oval tips an inch above her snare drum.

Two. Two. Three. Four. Music enraptured her, washing over her, a warm decades-old blanket smelling of budding tulips.

Three. Two. Three. Four. Rachel manifested her power.

Quarter and sixteenth notes appeared translucent over the ends of the playing instruments. Even without triggering her ability to see the interlocking patterns within the sounds, the music told her where to come in. All the musicians worked together to improve the collective symphony.

Standing in the first percussion position to Rachel's third, Lauren's hands twitched above her snare. Though unfair for Rachel to consider anyone short when she failed to pass the five-foot mark, Lauren wasn't much taller. She hunched over her drum, her still-wet blond hair sagging over her narrow peaches-and-cream face like a mop.

A full beat too early, Lauren burst into the tapping rhythm. Rachel flinched at the clash, beginning her entrance with the other snare drums on time. Heedless of the missed cue, Lauren continued to charge ahead, expanding the rift across the instruments. The trumpet player closest to her picked up their pace, cascading the disruption across more and more sections. Those following the shifting tempo collided headlong with everyone else at the correct pace.

The music memorized, Rachel's eyes never left the band director's baton, which cut the air in precise motions. His other hand waved and pointed to the baton to bring half the band back to his tempo. He scanned the room, searching for the problem. Whenever he got an instrument to slow to the correct time, another followed Lauren and sped up in its place.

Mr. DeSantos gave up fighting for control and waved his baton in a circle, bringing everyone to a stop. He never lost his composure. With a calm smile, he uttered one word: "Enough."

The room fell silent and braced for more instructions.

He straightened his purple polka-dotted tie, sent askew by his exaggerated gestures during the song. Mr. DeSantos's narrow dark eyes glanced over the snare drums, passing Rachel and moving on. Affronted that he didn't stare at or single out Lauren for her mistake, Rachel knew it would do no good to shame her publicly. The band director's meaty arms rose and started a four-count beat.

"Watch for my signal, and don't jump the entrance. Once more, with feeling."

Rachel's stomach spun, muting other sounds as it twisted her insides. Symphonic Band was her first class, so it was too early to be hungry for lunch. The disjointed sensation nearly made her miss the cues. Lauren deferred to Rachel, letting her make the first move, then loudly joined after Rachel began. Together, they played the piece as written. All the while, Rachel's attention pulled her elsewhere.

Like tuning an instrument, slight variances in matching pitches created jarring wobbles. She kept looking across the band, seeking the sounds penetrating her ears and making her nauseous.

At the end of the song, the music stopped, yet the warbled noise continued. A low thrum settled at the base of her skull.

Altering her perceptions and triggering her ability, the world expanded into music. Her classmates whispered back and forth in the brief interlude without instructions. Though too far to hear their words, musical notes hovered near each person, less clear than when she saw the notes leaving their instruments.

Beyond the glass windows, musical notes danced far in the distance. The pull of someone using their abilities drew her toward the window. To reach Rachel in the band room, they must be much closer than the notes appeared to be—or tossing around some serious firepower.

The power dispersed. Rachel hoped her friends were done messing around. Though this couldn't be Tracy or Derek. Burdened by mountains of missed schoolwork, they needed days of climbing to catch up to their classmates, and her two friends had *better* be in their first class.

"Take it from the top." Mr. DeSantos's voice ripped Rachel from the distraction. Dexterous fingers spun her drumsticks in a circle and brought them to a standstill above her snare drum's head, ready to play.

They played through Francis McBeth's "Masque" two more times to ensure it stuck with their muscle memories. When Lauren held her nerves in check, Rachel had to admit she played admirably, befitting her temporary lead position. Aided by the percussion's solid backbone, Rachel's classmates created a beautiful work of art.

As the last notes faded, Mr. DeSantos tapped his baton against the music stand. "Thanks to your improved performance, I think you deserve a reward. I'll end a few minutes early to give you a chance to relax before your next class. Keep practicing every night for our first winter concert a week from Saturday, and don't forget the encore show the Saturday after."

Mr. DeSantos unrolled his sleeves and strode to his office at the back of the room. Halfway there, he paused, adding an afterthought. "Since the first concert is over Thanksgiving break, I'll be opening the band room all day for anyone who wants to get in any last-minute practice."

Rachel collected and organized her music, placing it and her drumsticks in her backpack. The fastest wind players had only removed the reeds from their mouthpieces, to say nothing of the various complex instrument parts they still needed to disassemble and store.

She propped against a storage locker for instruments. The desire to crawl inside and catch up on desperately overdue shut-eye was overpowering.

Rachel angled herself so the metal locker pinched skin through her shirt. The pain kept her awake for another minute. Opening her copy of *Macbeth* to the red ribbon bookmark, she took out her English assignment's accompanying review questions. Scribbling a couple of sentences on how Macbeth was frustrated with Banquo, Rachel hoped her answer was adequate. She pulled a Tracy maneuver and threw in some SAT words to make it sound like she gave the assignment more thought than she did.

Another homework task passably finished, she calculated her upcoming weekend down to the minute, starting with this afternoon. Balancing the amount of time to tackle the growing list of overdue homework against Mr. Marshal's Saturday and Sunday all-day superpower training sessions was an exponentially daunting task. Returning to a normal social life was nothing more than a wistful dream.

A shadow fell across Rachel. Though it didn't block too much light, the source of the shadow had no intention of letting Rachel catch up on her schoolwork in peace.

"Thank you," said Lauren.

Rachel fought to keep her voice free of irritation. "For what?"

"For not challenging me to your old first snare spot since you've been back."

"Too much turmoil in our percussion section gives the heartbeat of the band an arrhythmia," replied Rachel.

For all her faults, Lauren assumed the leadership role of first snare as well as anyone. She didn't ask for Rachel to go missing for a month. Nor was it Lauren's fault Rachel had also lost her drum major position in marching band. There was no point in being mad at Lauren.

Lauren's eyebrows furrowed. "These songs have a lot of tricky parts. I'm working extra hard to get them right."

"I'm giving you until next semester to figure it out. The first week of school in the new year, consider your position open to the best player when I challenge you." *That's assuming I don't get lost thousands of years in the past again.*

"Sounds more than fair."

When Lauren didn't move on, Rachel asked, "Was there anything else?"

Biting her lip, Lauren leaned closer. "Thank you for saving me last Sunday," she whispered.

Rachel clapped her book shut, hoping to startle Lauren into making sense. "What?"

Lauren's words stretched longer and longer. "Some D.C. asshole used the shoulder to pass me in the merge lane and swerved toward my car. They would have shaved half my MINI Cooper. Instead, their car jerked to the opposite side. If it wasn't you, then Derek or one of the other monster slayers saved my life."

Derek better not be controlling traffic again. Louis was stuck with physical therapy from the crash Derek caused when he last moved a car with his power. Besides, Sunday was their second day of Mr. Marshal's weekend training, and no one skipped.

Rachel met Lauren's eager eyes. "Sounds like you got lucky. We don't use our powers to do every good deed. Plus, moving cars isn't in my power set."

Lauren winked. "Sure."

Buzzing coursed from Rachel's backpack.

Smartphones around the room made monotone robotic wails, an AI army on the march. "Emergency. Emergency. Large creature spotted near Rabbit Run and Cedar Street. To those in the immediate vicinity: evacuate and find shelter."

Her classmates lowered their instruments mid-disassembly into their laps. Whole bodies shifted to stare at Rachel. Her eyes cast over the room, making contact with her peers, people she had known for a decade.

Reverent looks ranged from Lauren's intrigue to outright fear in the face of the French horn player. The room collectively held its breath, awaiting Rachel's reaction.

"Translation: monster attack. Thanks, *fortissimo* alert system," Rachel muttered to herself. The local government had cobbled together this noisy mess of an alert in the week since her battle with the Beast. "Think this is a drill?" she asked the person who happened to be closest.

Lauren shifted her feet, eyeing the exit doors on opposite sides of the room and likely not knowing which to choose. "I hope so. I snuck out of this class and caught sight of the bear monster from a second-floor window. That thing you fought scared me shitless. I can't handle another one."

Rachel hoped the alarm was some kind of mistake. Her trembling heart beat faster with each set of eyes falling on her. This class size was nothing compared to the number of high school football fans who watched her perform as the drum major during the halftime shows. During those games, though, she moved through a well-rehearsed routine, supported by the collective audience's encouragement and her marching band brothers and sisters.

Used to. She sighed. *That's another band position I've lost.*

Here, trapped in this band room, everyone was staring at her, into her, through her.

They looked to Rachel for guidance, deferring to her wisdom when she felt no more competent than anyone else.

Maybe Tracy had the right idea by using music to catalyze her abilities. Blocking out the world to use her powers seemed like a prerequisite to doing what the human body was not intended to handle. *Aspects*, Rachel mentally corrected, *not powers*. Learning to master these Aspects began with using their proper name.

The attention gave her a strong desire to disappear into thin air, leaving only the sound of a snap. Too bad that wasn't one of her abilities. She was, however, capable of the next best thing: speed. She opened the Aspect's gate and let the rush of power flow through her.

Acutely aware of the blood coursing in her veins, steady breaths became another part of the symphony that was Rachel. She felt each inhale and exhale of her classmates and the individual popping sounds of clasps being latched to shut instrument cases.

Mr. DeSantos rolled in his chair from his office and over the carpet, his voice booming as he asked Rachel, "Are you going to help? Rabbit Run is a good mile from here. Need a ride?"

One. Two. Three. Four. Counting in four beat measures, Rachel shifted her powers, closing one Aspect's gate and opening another. *Two. Two. Three. Four.* What she imagined as an internal metronome accelerated its beats per minute to be faster than those around her. *Three. Two. Three. Four.*

Speeding thumps of her heart settled into a regular rhythm. "No thanks. My powers can get me there faster."

Not wanting to arrive to battle exhausted, she held back a full-blown sprint and power walked to the door. Her classmates' eyes followed too slowly to keep up. They might as well be walls for how little they moved as they reached for their phones to get a video of her.

Her dark hair's ringlets bounced, more so the faster she walked. Small though it was, changing her hairstyle was the biggest sense of control she took since the world declared her a hero. Her dyed blue tips within the mix of hair bobbed across her vision.

In her power walk to the school's front entrance, she approached another student staring at a hall map. As fast as Rachel was going, this student leaned into Rachel's path, anticipating her movements at a regular speed. Pivoting on one heel to avoid a crash, Rachel slid on the smooth linoleum tiles and lost her footing.

Her classmate caught Rachel in her arms, bracing her back leg for Rachel's excess momentum, and brought her to a complete halt. Unsurprisingly, Rachel's eye level met her classmate's shoulder. She was used to that. What she wasn't used to was how solid this student was. The girl loosened her grip on Rachel.

Her forest-green eyes returned Rachel's stare. Armed with boots, jeans, and a bright blue T-shirt, she didn't match the rest of the student body dressed in fall colors. The shirt revealed a toned frame and definition in her arms. Her hairband held most of her blond hair in place, and her bangs draped around her eyes.

Her classmate hadn't reacted to Rachel's display of power, not even the typical eyebrow raise in shock and awe. "Which way is the Advanced Placement Chemistry class with..." She checked a printed sheet of paper. "Mr... ah... Sprog? This maze has me turned about, and my orientation ended early."

Rachel pointed to the science wing. "Go back the way you came and take the sharp left at the junction. The first period is more or less over, so you're better off going straight to your second."

Recognition flashed on her classmate's face. "It's you! Has something gone fubar? Are you running to stop another monster?"

"Gotta go." She had already wasted too much time. Rachel returned to her power-augmented speed and sprinted to do battle against the Beast. She must have been no more than a blur to this stranger as she used her power to race down the hall and out the school's main entrance.

Biting winds slammed the metal door shut behind her. Taking ragged breaths, she acclimated to the November air, then sprinted ahead.

Her shirt pressed flat against her stomach and slapped her sides. Wind at these speeds meant the air might as well be a pool of Vermont maple syrup. Slowing herself, while still moving faster than humanly possible, Rachel conserved power for the fight.

The shortcut through the neighboring construction site revealed rubble where model houses had stood, courtesy of the Beast. A week since Rachel and her friends fought that giant bear, the construction site remained a disaster zone. Running through under-construction buildings, the Beast collapsed them haphazardly before Rachel and her friends arrived to defend their home. Glass crunched beneath her feet. She picked her way around sharp metal beams and scrap plywood. Crumbling concrete streets shifted under her steps.

Recalling how the monster's ink-black insides dripped from its body after dropping out of the sky brought her to a standstill. Derek had convinced her that thing was subdued and defeated. The warning blaring from her phone proved otherwise.

Shivering from more than the brisk cold, Rachel looked longingly back at her school. Derek or Ri Ur Tol or someone else could handle this emergency problem. Her Aspect of speed was better suited for a retreat than combat.

No one would know if she left... Rising fears begged her to run and not stop until she was hundreds of miles beyond the horizon and the monster's reach.

But she steeled her resolve with the hard fact that people relied on her to protect them, from classmates to friends to John.

In the dead-end cul-de-sac, Rachel leaned her head back and exhaled as much nervous energy as possible with a long groan.

She sprinted toward the monster's last known location, rustling up her courage despite the nagging voice inside shouting at her to flee in the opposite direction.

2

Escaped Shadow

Tracy

Dew-tipped grass smoldered under the footsteps of the human silhouette made of shadow. To call it human-shaped was a stretch. It had legs and arms connected to a rough body and a head, though the form shifted, making the number of limbs difficult to count. Extra arms and legs sprouted and dispersed like wisps of fog pelted by rain.

Tracy Wayfield fought to suppress her shudder of pure terror. When she had last faced the shadow monster inside the void, one of its arms had been as long as a city block. The creature in front of her was no larger than three people meshed into one. *That doesn't make it any less deadly*, she mentally chided herself.

Behind the shadow monster, a jagged line hovering in the air sealed. The bright burst of pink hues surrounding the closed portal to the void winked from existence, trapping the shadow monster in Tracy's world.

Sweat seeped from her palms as she noticed the creature's steps carving a trail of dead grass from its now-closed misshapen portal. A mere scratch from this thing once left her incapacitated for a day. Yet she decided to face it all over again when her phone alert sounded, their county's desperate attempt to seem in control in the wake of last week's monster attack. Meanwhile, if she drove thirty minutes in any direction, most people didn't believe in monsters or powers. They claimed it was an elaborate stunt by those desperate for attention.

I know better.

The shadow passed through the chain-link fence surrounding the community park's baseball outfield. Metal corroded and melted at the creature's touch.

The park was abandoned on the early November day. No dogs fetched tennis balls. No kids played baseball. No one was present to watch her die.

Smoke evaporated from whatever passed for its skin, reacting to no longer being within the void. Its form shrank, yet not fast enough.

"You can't be here," she uttered.

There was no mouth for it to respond. Tracy imagined the shadow howling at her. The being's blank expression made the face-less terror worse. Tracy forgot how to scream.

She once watched this shadow dismember ancient warriors by the dozens. Worse, Tracy's final images of those battle-hardened men and women who survived touching the shadow were of them writhing on the ground. In a stroke of reckless stupidity, she and her friends risked their lives to reenter the void and seal that entrance. They barely evaded the shadow to return to their rightful present.

Now, as Tracy turned to run away, a familiar blur passed by her side, bringing a breeze in her wake.

Rachel's here!

Coming to a stop, her blue and brown springs of hair bounced and stilled.

Rachel ran a lap around the monster and the park so quickly that Tracy needed to unfocus her eyes to follow her movement. Upon returning, she reported, "I can see where its trail appeared from nowhere, and there's no sign of an open portal." Rachel leaned her toes against the sidewalk's curb, stretching her calves like this was a running workout, not a fight for their lives. "Phew. This little thing is what's setting off the emergency alarms? I thought we had to fight the Beast all over again."

No longer squaring against the monster alone, Tracy kept her feet in place and didn't run for shelter. "The Beast was nothing. Remember what the shadows did to people who got too close, and look at how its touch siphoned life from the grass."

"It's a lot smaller now."

Short on monster-slaying ideas, Tracy's mouth kept running ahead while her brain sought a strategy. "Where's the rest of our support?"

The shadow swiped its long arm toward them. Rachel accelerated and dragged Tracy back, saving her from being dismembered. "No idea."

"We need all of us playing together for this gig's performance."

Tracy threw her headphones over her ears and sank into her playlist, specially chosen for kicking ass. Guitar riffs unlocked inner gates, flushing power through her veins while her heart beat in time with the melody. Along with the power came the itch of her long-healed battle wound which left no scar.

No longer a mere discomfort, her pain burst open like dead skin from a third-degree sunburn, where the more power she pulled, the deeper the burning sensation reached. She cracked her knuckles rather than cry out. Hearing the series of pops from grinding bones eased the nerves buried within her forearm.

Rachel cringed. "Did you pick up that bad habit from Flint's primitive people?" She sprinted ahead, throwing sticks and stones at the shadow to deteriorate it faster.

Too focused on her power, Tracy didn't respond. Soil and grass rippled beneath their feet, material for her to reshape using her power. Tracy sank into a knee-deep ditch. She reformed the ground, making it snake upward to form a metallic skeletal structure over her arms. Gathering more material from the earth, she transmuted it into motors to reinforce her joints. Tracy covered her creation with metal sheets. Her muscles shook from the exertion as she examined the robotic arms flexing above her shoulders. Lacking individual fingers, they ended in punching glove fists.

The shadow swung its arms at Rachel. She ran beyond its range each time, distracting it for the precious seconds Tracy needed.

Motors whirred and gears spun into motion, bringing her into striking range. Winding her fist back, Tracy sprung a one-two punch. Her mechanical arms passed right through the shadow. Like grasping a cloud, the creature offered no resistance.

Tar-colored smoke clung to the disintegrating mechanical arms where they touched the shadow.

Tracy's thumbs pressed the trigger buttons of her fail-safes, and the heavy metal structure ejected, narrowly avoiding the contaminated surfaces from coming in contact with her skin.

Rachel's ongoing attack placed her right under one of the falling mechanical arms. She sped up, passing within an inch of the evaporating creation. Off balance, Rachel tripped, sliding to a halt and sending up clumps of grass.

The two of them were within the creature's reach, and Rachel was at its mercy.

"Hey!" Tracy shouted, waving her arms in the air.

Her plan worked perfectly. Black wisps stretched for her instead of Rachel—but too fast. Tracy's left arm lifted to meet the shadow with a will of its own.

Snap. Someone grabbed her shoulder.

Snap. Tracy was instantly fifty feet from where she'd been standing.

Snap. In the distance, a lean young woman appeared next to Rachel.

Snap. The two of them were next to Tracy.

The shadow monster spun, looking for someone to attack.

Rachel got to her feet. "Thanks for the save, Ri Ur Tol."

Long jet-black hair settled when Ri Ur Tol stopped teleporting about the battlefield. Her hands rested over a pair of knives strapped to her belt. Alert brown eyes studied the monster and the park, instantly absorbing details that would take Tracy minutes or hours to observe. Tensed leg muscles gave the impression Ri Ur Tol was a lioness waiting for the moment to pounce on her prey's neck, assuming the shadow had one.

They held the monster at bay. Whenever it attacked one of them, Ri Ur Tol teleported them behind it.

"We hunt together again." Ri Ur Tol spared a moment to smile at Tracy and Rachel. Then her gaze locked on the shadow. Hatred flashed within those deep brown eyes. Not even when fighting the Beast did she show this much animosity. "Today, I take revenge for the blood of my people this shadow spilled, a creature so evil, stars don't shine upon it."

Tracy stepped back from Ri Ur Tol's rictus smile.

"Did you learn English?" Rachel asked, unafraid of the warrior's conviction. "I think that's the first time I've heard your voice without a translator."

Ri Ur Tol didn't turn when she answered. "A little."

Tracy wracked her brain for ways to hurt this creature. While Ri Ur Tol teleported Tracy around the shadow monster's punch, she hurled another pillar of earth at it. This slow method of causing it to evaporate was the best strategy Tracy came up with. "Where's Derek? We need another powerhouse who can hit that thing without touching it."

Ri Ur Tol shook her head. "Focus on the hunt, not missing hunters."

Two metal chains spun horizontally through the shadow's middle, splitting it in half. The gap in the shadow's chest reformed, making the creature whole again, if a little smaller.

The man who had swung the chains was wearing a plaid long-sleeved shirt with jeans. Thankfully, Flint wore a different shirt than he had last weekend. The man from the past behaved as expected in issues of hygiene, where he considered them to be, at best, suggestions.

The shadow lunged for Flint, catching his chains. It pulled Flint forward. Tracy launched a pillar from the ground and severed its hands before it split Flint open and consumed him.

Flint jumped back and retreated, smoke clinging to the chains dispersed before eating the metal to nothing.

The ends of Flint's chains spun in circles, gathering momentum, and whistling in what could only be called hunger.

Tracy had a better idea to scatter the shadow into insubstantial smoke. Gathering all the nearby material for her transmutation, Tracy and the two others closest to her sank to their waists in the resulting crater.

Hardened soil bent to her will to clamp shut around the shadow, appearing like the jaws of a giant rising from the ground to capture their foe.

Falling to one knee, Tracy panted, drained by entombing the creature from the void.

Flint's twin metal chains sailed where the shadow stood as Tracy's enclosed container formed around it. The chains collided with her soil prison, crumbling an entire side.

"What the hell? I had it contained!" she gasped at Flint.

Flint's raised voice was strained as he spun the chains again. "I hurt it, and I was mid-swing when you acted."

The shadow eased through the cracked soil wall, shifting its shape and reforming in front of them. Its long arm clubbed Tracy's soil construct to free itself faster. Her efforts to encase the shadow weren't completely wasted. Evaporating smoke stained the enclosing soil, destroying more of her creation, but shrinking the shadow's body all the while.

As more of the shadow slid free, it solidified into a long arm ending in serrated claws, which looked like they might saw her in half as an afterthought. The shadow monster sliced into the ground in front of her as she rolled to the side. It pulled back for another lunge.

"Help me, Ri!" Tracy yelled, her limbs unwilling to stand.

Ri Ur Tol grabbed Tracy by the shirt, not bothering to lift her, and held Rachel's hand. *Snap.* They were behind Flint, his chains whirling dangerously.

"Together. Or. Not. At. All." Ri Ur Tol's words came out unevenly, as though she were not fully certain of their meaning.

"My chains can tear it apart," said Flint, whose magic enhanced his speech to the point he spoke their language without inflections of an accent.

Ri Ur Tol shook her head. "Too slow." She pointed at Tracy. "Feed Tracy magic to bury it with her creations."

Rachel and Ri Ur Tol placed their hands on Tracy's shoulders. Power flowed from them until they fell beside Tracy on the ground, their bodies too weak to stand.

"Join," said Ri Ur Tol to the outlier.

The shadow drifted closer. Flint looked at the three of them. He stopped swinging the chains and wrapped them around his arms, much as he had done with leather bindings when Tracy first met the strange man. Glancing into the distance, he shook his head. "We will not run. I'll spare what I can."

Now that he was closer, Tracy saw Flint's chains were layered on top of more wrappings. No longer leather, they appeared to be thin cloth bandages. These allowed his fingers more flexibility.

Flint's heavy hand dropped onto her head. A rocket launched her metaphorically into the clouds from the power he shared.

Flint dropped to his knees, arms curled against his body, his face stuck in a grimace.

Everyone was immobile as the shadow monster closed in.

Within five feet, it launched with its killing touch.

Tracy unleashed her power.

The ground materialized into a wall, severing the tip of the shadowy arm. It fell, smoking and evaporating. Tracy formed pillars of earth to strike the shadow from all angles.

She shifted the ground beneath them into a platform, moving her and her friends from danger.

Soil sprang to form another wall of her earth prison to trap the shadow monster. And another wall. And another, forming a series of prisons around the creature.

Vision clouding and clutching her burning arm, Tracy created more soil walls on top of the mess. Inhaling gasping breaths, she counted to ten.

One by one, her friends picked themselves up off the ground. Tracy limped to the multilayered boxes she'd formed.

With the last of her power, she collapsed the walls onto the creature. A ball of blackness, the last vestige from the shadow, disintegrated.

Pockmarks littered the field from the creature's steps, though the park was mostly intact.

Tracy teetered, her eyelids sinking. Rachel was there in an instant to hold her up.

"You did amazing," Rachel said.

"Thanks." Tracy opened her eyes long enough to glance around the smoldering park. "Think we're now on work release from school to go into the monster-hunting business? I hope my teachers won't mind if I sleep the rest of the day."

Rachel scrunched her face. "You can. I'll cover for you at school, considering how much more effort you put into this fight." She forced out a bitter laugh. "It's going to suck paying attention in my afternoon classes after fighting for my life. I can't miss any more days, though."

Tracy yawned. "I owe you one. See you at Mr. Marshal's training facility. I'll head there after I get in a nap."

"With the monster... done, where is Derek?" asked Ri Ur Tol.

"No idea," Flint said. "I do not sense any other magic being used nearby."

Tracy was ready to pass out on the spot when her perceptions shifted. It felt as though she blacked out for a second, and the world carried on, the same jolt as when waking from dreams of falling off of tree branches.

A thrum vibrated in the stringed tendons of her arm where the shadow monster once marked her, turning today's sweet victory into a hollow taste on her tongue.

They had done nothing to stop the being in the void.
The creature made of shadow was still alive.

3

Drowning on Land

Tracy

Tracy sat in her room at Mr. Marshal's training facility, listening to her Music Appreciation homework. The overdue assignments were as much a means to distract her from thinking about the shadow monster as they were an attempt to catch up on missed schoolwork.

Her noise-canceling headphones brought the smooth cymbal work to life. She remembered listening to the drum solo at some point in this semester's course, though she lacked the context to identify the song for the assigned schoolwork.

She clawed at an itch within her forearm, but nothing eased the discomfort. To distract her mind, she ran her fingers over the metallic desk. This desk Mr. Marshal provided was functional, if simplistic, but the rest of her room made up for its basic design. Using her powers, Tracy had formed the furniture for her room at the training facility, like a fuzzy rug, dresser, mirror, nightstand, and plenty of band posters to cover chrome-colored walls. The entertainment system went a smidge overboard, but her neighbors, Rachel and Nicole, had yet to complain. Without much downtime to blow out the speakers, her friends' ears were saved.

Half gym, half laboratory, half dormitory, all mansion, Mr. Marshal's training facility was unexpected. This was her second weekend stay, and the sense of wonder had yet to abate.

The previous weekend, her first here, she spent recuperating from the Beast, when not draining her powers in ever more elaborate displays to gauge her strength.

The training facility wasn't living up to its name, given how Mr. Marshal delayed another Saturday morning's planned workouts until this afternoon. Though she did need more time to recover from the lingering effects of yesterday's battle with the shadow monster. She used the extra hours to climb out of the deep grave of homework before next week's new material buried her alive. Exploring the confines of her weekend getaway dropped to the bottom of her list of priorities. Once she finished some homework, she would be ready to map the rooms in the facility.

How Mr. Marshal purchased the building intended for a summer camp of the future was anyone's guess. They might as well be on a moon colony, given the isolated space they were allowed to roam. The nearly two-hour drive to the mountains rewarded them with at least a hundred acres of untamed woodlands to cut loose with their powers.

Though more kind to trees than Derek and her training regimens in his backyard, a few had still fallen to errant explosions or a mechanized punch from devices she created.

Remembering her schoolwork, Tracy ran through the list of jazz musicians and failed to recall the artist she was listening to. Her itching arm consumed other thoughts, overpowering the music in her headphones.

She transmuted the spot into concrete to soothe the sensations beneath her skin. Her nerve endings couldn't irritate her if she re-made them into something nonliving. Immediately disgusted by the lack of sensation, she reversed the change in her forearm to match her unblemished arm.

But the change didn't take completely. Her arm appeared different, harder, and a fraction of a shade whiter. She brought her forearm to her eye and saw a slight bumpy texture covering her skin, which appeared to be more than goosebumps.

She cradled her arm, scared that her unchecked powers had caused permanent damage.

Minutes passed as she waited for her heart to slow or her arm to dissolve.

When nothing happened, she calmed a bit. At least she still had an arm.

Tracy turned her attention back to the Music Appreciation answer sheet, but her brain still drew a blank on the artist's name. She threw the headphones at stacked piles of overdue homework. "I can't concentrate!"

Burying her head in her hands, Tracy massaged her temples. She reached for another stack of papers, shifting to make headway on her Calculus II homework. She was getting nowhere fast and considered asking Rachel for help, though her teacher might be on a different lesson.

Sounds of retching carried from outside Tracy's closed door, followed by a sickening slap like a cup of Jell-O thrown at a wall. Tracy's empty stomach danced. Before she could cover her ears in noise-canceling technology and pretend she heard nothing, the sounds permeated through her door again.

With a resigned sigh, Tracy investigated.

She stepped into thick slippers and pushed the electronic panel to open the door and dim her lights. The hallway matched her bedroom's motif, with hospital-clean floors made of the same shiny alloy as the walls. Tracy once made the mistake of letting her bare feet touch the cold metal. Now when wandering the halls, she always kept her feet covered.

The highly sterilized spaceship-on-its-maiden-voyage style presented by the walls lacked flavor. There were no painted walls or glued wallpaper flowers as decoration.

She ran toward the sounds and found Ri Ur Tol outside her bedroom door, surrounded by a puddle of water. Tracy nearly slipped as she came to a stop.

Ri Ur Tol was on the floor; drenched clothes clung to her body. She coughed, spitting out more water than Tracy thought possible. Light from a flashlight on the ground cast each of her heaving motions onto the wall. Her face was clenched in a pained expression with each cough.

Tracy patted Ri Ur Tol's back to ease the air into her lungs and expel any lingering trapped water. "What happened to you?"

Breathing seemed too much of a struggle for Ri Ur Tol to waste air speaking. Tracy supported her weight and got her moving to her friend's room. After a few steps, Ri Ur Tol could walk on her own, though she still didn't say a word.

Tracy was tempted to block Ri Ur Tol's path, forcing her to explain what happened. One look at the warrior's driven stare and Tracy changed her mind. Short by modern standards, Ri Ur Tol was of average height in the era she belonged. More than that, she was well-toned, befitting her people. Tracy didn't want to get on the wrong side of her. Worse, Ri Ur Tol might give extra training exercises if Tracy pressed too hard.

The metallic door to Ri Ur Tol's room slid open to reveal four unadorned walls, a bare desk, and a perfectly made bed. Tracy opened the thick window halfway, even though it allowed the biting fall air to enter. Beside the desk rested a rack holding dozens of daggers that varied in size. A sharpening stone rested on the floor. The stone remained vigilant, waiting to taste the next blade's edge.

"We need to get you a poster or something to fix this dismal atmosphere you're living in." Tracy gestured in disgust. "That'll be my goal for today, after you tell me why you're soaking wet."

With another cough, Ri Ur Tol spoke, her words sounding raw as they left her throat. "Leave me be."

"No. I owe you, considering you've already saved my life several times."

"Then make me a tool to breathe underwater."

"Huh?"

"You created my translator. Use your magic and find a way."

"That won't be easy. Challenge accepted," Tracy said with a smirk.

Ri Ur Tol faced the window, her bright eyes dulled against the natural light flowing into the room.

Sensing Ri Ur Tol's disappointment, Tracy amended, "I meant it won't be easy to invent the tech we need. I have an idea or two to improve scuba gear. Otherwise, you'll have to carry oxygen tanks."

"You are not as selfish as I thought."

Tracy held an index finger above her lips. "Shhhh. Don't tell anyone. Let me see what I can create here."

Ri Ur Tol sat on the floor and braced herself against the bed. She seemed curious rather than being a back seat driver eager to tell Tracy how to use her powers. Ri Ur Tol's presence was not unwanted, pleasant almost, a reminder someone was there to patch Tracy up if this exploded.

Music flowed from Tracy's phone. The top of her playlist started with lighthearted pop, taking a few tracks to build up to more intense songs. She scratched the bumpy skin on her forearm, shrugging aside the itch she worked so hard to scrub from her body. Her fingernails broke skin but did nothing to soothe what felt like a worm tunneling where she couldn't reach.

Intrigued by the challenge of transmuting a machine that didn't exist, Tracy clenched her fist to crack her knuckles. She closed her eyes and visualized how the key components fit and worked in unison. The mouthpiece would need to filter oxygen from the water, much like fish gills.

She pulled the metallic material from the wall of Ri Ur Tol's room, though not enough to dig a hole to the other side. What formed in her hands was an elongated cone with two small cylinders protruding from either side. It was better suited for a birthday party hat than a breathing apparatus. The device crumbled in her hands when she took her first breath.

Sculpting the existing material, Tracy made Creation 2.0. This one retained the long, conical shape of her first failed attempt.

"Come on, Tracy," she chided herself. "Who the hell are these for, Toucan Sam?"

"Who's Toucan Sam? I'm the one who needs to breathe underwater."

"He's from a sugar-blasted breakfast cereal, which you are healthier not being introduced to."

Tracy put on her mask. The gap over her mouth let in some oxygen when she breathed, though not nearly enough. Sucking in more air caused the mouthpiece to collapse on itself. Panic set in as the device covered her mouth and blocked fresh air.

Ri Ur Tol snatched the device from Tracy's face, ripping several hairs from the top of her head. "I'm fine. I'm fine," Tracy gasped.

Still, Ri Ur Tol ensured Tracy had no problems breathing before allowing her to continue.

Having found her morning's calling, Tracy spent hours refining her creations in better and better iterations. Ri Ur Tol changed her clothes and stood idly by, studying Tracy's growing pile of failed transmutations.

With her last attempt before lunch, Tracy shoved the device over her mouth and was surprised it worked. Air flowed through the sides and the mouthpiece felt solid. It seemed ready to test in a controlled underwater experiment.

She sank into the chair and wiped her forehead. "I need a break. Ready for lunch?"

Previously still as a marble statue, Ri Ur Tol moved. "I, too, need food from this morning's endeavor."

Tracy pounced on the opening. "Care to tell me more about where you went and what tried to drown you? It might improve the breathing tool to know exactly how you want to use it."

"No." Ri Ur Tol opened her door and led Tracy out.

Together they traveled down the lonely hallway. Outside, their bedrooms appeared identical, except for the name tags on the electric panels attached to each door.

Turning before the foyer, Tracy ran her hand over the keypad to the dining room. The light went green and the door slid sideways, receding into the wall.

Smells of cheese and greasy goodness caused her stomach to grumble.

The large oval room contained a matching oval table. Stacks of warm pizza boxes stood in the center of the table, enough for a dozen people. Tracy placed the boxes in front of the empty seats. Roasted coffee beans invaded her nostrils, a steady reminder of her missed weekly Saturday morning trek to the bagel shop.

Not bothering with a filter for her thoughts, Tracy said, "Remind me to convince Mr. Marshal to bring an oven and refrigerator so we can cook healthier meals. I don't want to survive on a diet of pizzas. Otherwise, I'll have to make a few holes in the wall to create basic appliances with my powers."

At her side, Ri Ur Tol said, "Convince Mr. Marshal to bring in an oven and refrigerator because you don't want to survive on a diet of pizzas."

A slice of pepperoni pizza fell from Tracy's hands. "Was that a joke?"

Ri Ur Tol's face remained expressionless, neither confirming nor denying whether she had gained a sense of humor.

The door slid open. With bags under her eyes and eyelids sinking lower and lower, Rachel meandered straight to the coffeepot. "Ah, sweet nectar, how I missed thee."

Rachel emitted a howling yawn, so contagious it forced Tracy to yawn too. Rachel hadn't bothered to change from loose-fitting pajamas, hiding much of her in their baggy folds.

"You've seen better days," said Tracy.

Rachel's eyes closed, swallowing any harsh comment. "Cramming days of schoolwork into an hour of time relative to you will have that effect. I took a brief nap, but I'm still exhausted and my powers are spent *before* training. " Rachel let out a long sigh. "After my morning study session, I only finished a few assignments."

"Must be nice to have the power to alter time. I'm way behind on all things school-related." Tracy read her friend's face, adding, "I mean, that's rough. Have something to eat."

Tracy extended her plate, offering a slice of pepperoni pizza. Seeing Rachel practically drooling, Tracy was tempted to pull back, knowing she risked losing an arm.

Rachel accelerated, downing a pizza in the time it took Tracy to blink. She released an appreciative, "Mmmmm."

Tracy grabbed a new slice for herself. "Aren't you bored with pizza again?"

"By the stars," injected Ri Ur Tol, holding her own slice of pepperoni, "I never tire of your time's delicacies."

Rachel nodded, reaching for another serving. "Why are you complaining? This has all the major food groups. There's even a veggie somewhere in there."

"Our meals need variety," said Tracy. "If Mr. Marshal can't do it, I'll volunteer to cook. These carbs will sit like a rock in my stomach throughout today's workout."

"It has much more flavor than those weird protein bars he gives us for breakfast."

Tracy looked in distaste at the cabinet where boxes of unmarked, barely edible blocks were stored. *They provided the energy to sprint and use powers all morning, but at what cost?* The bars had the flavor of glue and consistency of sawdust.

"How are our friends back home?" Tracy asked.

"They missed you last night. Obviously, they understand that taking out a shadow monster is a reasonable excuse to miss a night of gaming."

Rachel went into a riveting rendition of her greatest victories over John and Louis. A pang of regret settled in Tracy's gut over failing to go out due to her own exhaustion. No wonder Rachel craved coffee.

Flint entered the dining room, his hawkish eyes piercing the four corners with a dedication that made Tracy believe assassins were lying in wait. His tan cheeks looked much healthier and smoother than when they first met, and his face was covered in a gritty, dirt-caked beard.

He'd tied his golden hair in what he claimed was a warrior's style but looked like a ponytail. *Maybe he was right to live in the wilds for however many years he did in the ancient past if it gave his hair that sheen.* Tracy didn't want to think of the hundreds of dollars she wasted to perform a similar feat.

The man's blue flannel shirt strained to the material's limit, stretching over tiny chains outlined by the fabric. Despite the bulk, he moved quietly, the sounds dampened by his thick clothes.

He took an entire box of pepperoni pizza without a complaint about the food options.

Tracy didn't know what to make of the strange man from the past, nor how to feel about the young woman who walked in after him.

Nicole Felcos jumped into the kitchen, her legs and arms moving in sync with what must be some rhythm in her head, parts of which she hummed. Her medium-length red hair radiated the sun's warmth on this cool autumn day, even in the enclosed room. Nicole's magenta glasses sat comfortably on her small, sharp nose. Tracy's dimensionally challenged friend sniffed the air and followed the smells of the brewed coffee. Nicole poured a cup, inhaling its steaming aroma, and exhaled into a broad smile.

Where Rachel's dour morning demeanor reminded Tracy of how little quality sleep she got last night, Nicole's smile gave her the means to face the day.

An unsettling churning squirmed in Tracy's gut. For the hundredth time this week, she reminded herself this wasn't the Nicole she grew up with. Tracy never kissed *this* Nicole on her last evening before Nicole and her family moved to Colorado. This Nicole was clearly better off without the desperate attempt to steal her from her then-girlfriend Allerie. Joining them from an alternate reality, this Nicole spat in the face of infinite possibilities.

Nicole leaned over Ri Ur Tol to grab a slice of pizza, invading her personal space. "Sorry I wasn't at yesterday's showdown with the shadow monster," said Nicole. "I'm days from being combat ready. I won't miss your next fight."

Ri Ur Tol's face was absent of Nicole's enthusiasm. "I decide when you hunt with us."

"Any word from Derek?" Mr. Marshal's sudden appearance in the doorway made Tracy jump.

Her guidance counselor-turned-super-powered coach had his gray hair hanging loosely to his neck. Mr. Marshal seemed to want to make a relatable impression with his casual plain T-shirt and jeans. He didn't have to try for anything. He gave Derek superpowers, who, in turn, gave them to Tracy. Through the transitive property, the secret to Tracy's success in life came from him. The fact she knew virtually nothing about the middle-aged man with ancient eyes didn't matter, so long as he never reclaimed these powers.

Tracy wiped pizza oil from her lips. "I texted. Still no answer from the lazy ass. He probably burned out from some harebrained alone time training and is still sleeping it off."

"When did you last see him?" Mr. Marshal's bushy eyebrows carried the earnestness of a grandfather eagerly awaiting news of Tracy's day. His timeless face might have been anywhere from forty to sixty. Tracy could never be sure.

"Yesterday," Tracy answered without thinking. Then she remembered he wasn't at school before the shadow monster arrived. "Actually, Thursday afternoon."

"What if he's doing something important? Shouldn't we trust him?" asked Nicole, her hand covering her mouth as she chewed.

Ri Ur Tol shook her head. "Fighting together is always stronger than fighting alone."

Tracy wasn't one to miss an opportunity. "Want me to skip today's training to drive to his house and drag him back here?"

Mr. Marshal didn't so much as smile. "No."

"Looks like he ditched your training after one weekend," Rachel said.

"Will you follow through with reabsorbing his powers for missing training?" Tracy asked, edging her way to the door. These powers were theirs. Derek deserved a warning that part of him was about to be ripped out.

"If I have to," said Mr. Marshal. "Though I thought you would have realized the waste in doing so. Alone, I would not have been able to defeat the monsters you have. After lighting the spark of Derek's power, and he in two of you, your combined potential exceeded mine a long time ago." Mr. Marshal spun a virtual knob on the room's control screen. A heavy panel that comprised the entire wall slid to the side, exposing the thick glass window.

Much-needed color flooded the otherwise monochrome room. Golden sunlight reflected off beautiful yellows, oranges, and reds of fallen leaves or those holding fast to their trees. Brown tree trunks spread hundreds of yards into the forest, extending farther than Tracy could see.

Resting along the side of a small mountain, this mansion appeared to be riding the waves of the woodlands.

Ruining the moment, Mr. Marshal spoke. "Finish eating and prepare for the afternoon. Today's training begins in thirty minutes. For those who can tell time, get the others to the front porch by then."

"Why do you keep pushing us until our bodies crash?" Rachel asked.

Mr. Marshal's gaze passed over each of them. "I'm not pushing you hard enough. Monsters are coming."

Knowing better than to go for her usual sarcastic remark, Tracy went with, "From where?"

"The void."

Ri Ur Tol chimed in. "Are they like the shadow monster we faced in the park?"

"Worse."

Tracy rubbed her hands together to rekindle the warmth that seeped from the room. "Well, shit."

"My sentiments as well," said Mr. Marshal. "Which is why we need to find one of our resident hard hitters—Derek. Ri Ur Tol is right; without all of us together, we will be ripped apart."

4

Bearings

Derek

Derek Fen crawled from the opening in time and space onto the rough pavement. The portal to the void sealed with a *whoosh* of sucking air.

A fourteen-sided star had seared itself into his mind when he formed the exit from the void. It faded to nothing as he dispersed the power of multiple combined Aspects. Derek's aching lungs gasped, choking as though this were the first time the organs were used. His body was recoiling from being in the void for so long and from pulling in so much power to escape.

A thud and clatter violently rattled his eardrums, the sound of his backpack dropping from heavy arms too tired to carry their burdens. The impacts continued ringing like a string rupturing, starting with a powerful twang which settled into a high-pitched whine. Bright orange sunlight assaulted his eyes, forcing them shut. Moss and muck from the riverbank below piqued his nostrils. That and the choking poison of a discarded cigarette carried to him from somewhere on the bridge's pedestrian path.

He curled into the fetal position, accepting the compounding weaknesses of his mind and body, allowing sleep to overtake him.

Loud footsteps and heaving breaths of a jogger moved as far from Derek as possible on the narrow path, waking him. They must not have seen him exit from the now sealed portal, meaning to the pedestrian, he was any other stranger.

Emitting a full-bellied yawn, he tested each limb to be certain no part of himself was left in the far reaches of the world between worlds.

Two hands? Derek moved dull limbs hanging on either side, feeling tiny hairs along his arm sway with the motions. *Check.*

One arm still broken? He knocked on the cast over his forearm, which reverberated the impact. *Check.*

Two feet? Standing was too much. The effort spread aches through both legs. *Check.*

He stretched his shoulder, the lingering thin scar shifting as he moved. He used it as a reminder of the first time he traveled into the past and its many dangers.

Derek rubbed his face, dragging his hand from thick eyebrows down the steep incline of his nose, and finally brushing over hints of hair sprouting from his chin. "And here I thought I had been gone long enough to grow a wizard's beard."

He combed his fingers through untidy hair. For all his time spent in the void, it didn't feel longer.

Venturing to open his eyes a fraction, he adjusted to the world that now overwhelmed his senses until it came into focus. The last rays of crimson daylight rested on the rusted chain-link fence of the bridge. Suburbs of Washington, D.C. never looked so vibrant under the setting sun. Remaining daylight settled on windshields, making each car appear alive with an inner flame.

Major repairs to the bridge's guardrails and fence were complete, sparing potential safety risks of a careless walker falling onto the highway or river below. His eyes traced the parallel gouges along the pedestrian path's concrete. These morbid claw marks were a reminder of the first time his Beast attacked him.

The river reflected the image of the bridge Derek crouched on. Redirected flows of water passed through a crater. Plants had not reclaimed the battle scar since he subdued his Beast and disturbed this peaceful marsh with his exploding punch. He massaged his broken arm, easing the growing discomfort spreading along his muscles bound within the cast.

Derek retrieved a pair of stopwatches from each pocket and clicked their stop buttons.

A minute shy of twenty hours on the display of one didn't feel right. Between sleeping and homework, Derek was certain he survived in the void for several days, if not weeks.

He checked the backup stopwatch. It had timed out at 99:99:99, a more reasonable number, though it left him at a loss.

Neither stopwatch felt accurate.

He'd finished most of his missed AP Chemistry and English homework inside the void, leaving his brain fried. Between reading the material, rereading it, and going back for a third read, not to mention the time needed to solve the assigned problems, it seemed weeks had passed in the half-light of the void.

The final nap, when he was too exhausted to continue, nearly unmade him. Currents of the void had dragged him to ocean-like depths and squeezed him in a blanket of bone-crushing pressure.

It took nothing less than every collective memory of home to return to the shallows of the void. He shut down his terrifying thoughts of being lost, endlessly floating across the landscape of nothingness.

The shadow monster had been waiting at the doorway he used to enter the void. Derek skewed his path from where the monster hovered and punched a new exit. Doing so meant he had arrived at this unknown point—past, future, or otherwise—from when he left.

He turned on his phone, worried about how much time he may have lost. Aside from searching for clues to the location of the alternate-world version of himself, he went into the void to cheat at life. He was going to be pissed if his brilliant solution caused him to fall further behind on schoolwork.

Phew. Only two days.

A brisk breeze chilled his exposed legs. The weather, which could have passed for summer heat when he left, had dropped by a good twenty degrees. The cold ate right through his cotton long-sleeved shirt and shorts.

Sore and stiff, his broken arm had not seemed right since Tracy's abilities tripled its size and then shrank it back to normal. It tingled, residual effects of the broken bones acting as his personal barometer alert for damp air. The region's humidity was like too many needles puncturing his skin, meaning an evening shower was heading his way now.

Hunger pains from returning to the world of the living forced Derek to heave his weight onto his feet and stand. Haze covered his vision, further perturbed by the shining car lights of those stuck on the highway beneath the bridge. Risking collapsing in the head rush, he bent and collected his belongings. Derek opened his stuffed backpack and rifled through it to ensure he hadn't left his AP Chemistry textbook or completed *Hamlet* paper in the void.

He reached for the sword hilt strapped to his backpack with his uninjured hand. He followed the grip up to the blade, where the edge ended abruptly half a finger's length from the guard. Fragmented during the fight with his Beast, the severed blade was useless as a weapon, though holding it still made the world come to life. An influx of power traveled from the sword into him. The stored power recuperated a small amount of what he had spent opening the portal from the void.

Lifting the backpack over one shoulder threw him off balance, so he used a delicate telekinetic push to stabilize and stand upright.

Derek wrapped the blade in a towel from his backpack. The bundle was too large to fit in his backpack, so he shoved it in the gap between his back and backpack to avoid drawing too much suspicion.

Buzzing in his pocket went off from a slew of messages. Progressively more passive-aggressive texts from Tracy, concerned messages from Rachel and his parents, and even missed calls and voicemails. Derek started messaging them all back, apologizing for missing the fight.

Derek's stomach grumbled. He weighed his options and decided on gelatos at the Cold Snap. The thought of running into its owners, his friend Louis's parents, made his stomach drop, but he needed to see a friendly face, and they were the closest.

Walking down the bridge's pedestrian path spit him into the shopping center. He picked up the pace in front of the gym, cringing at the memory of the day he had quit his job there.

A slight nudging inside craved to return to the days before these powers, where he worried about nothing more than homework, exams, and staying awake at a menial, minimum-wage job.

Drops of water sprinkled his head and shoulders. Derek hurried to shelter, his stomach driving him to food.

Large blue lettering tipped with painted plaster icicles announced the Cold Snap's location to the world. Arguably a tad too much, it gave the impression of the quaint store having survived the latest Washington, D.C. Snowpocalypse.

The doorbell chimed when Derek entered. Mrs. Delfino smiled and waved. Hunger gave Derek tunnel vision as he approached. Unlike the last time he saw her, Mrs. Delfino's eyes were no longer downcast. Her average build bounded up from the seat behind the counter with catlike dexterity.

When she got a good look at Derek, her expression shifted to one of concern. "Are you all right? You look half starved." Applying fresh gloves, she sped through the motions to scoop him a double cup of birthday cake gelato. "It's the sugariest flavor we have for our local hero. Eat. Eat," she beckoned.

Derek couldn't meet her gaze. When he finally looked at her, Derek saw her son's matching honey-colored eyes as he hung upside down, suspended in the car Derek flipped with his mind. "How's Louis today?"

Mrs. Delfino beamed an award-winning smile. "Frank is picking him up from physical therapy. He's been steadily improving but is still a little nervous about driving alone."

Without knowing what to say or trusting his tongue to speak, Derek paid for the cone, despite Mrs. Delfino insisting he didn't have to.

Chilly sweetness slid over his taste buds, summoning tears. The stark contrast between feeling nothing within the void and the white-and-blue-streaked birthday cake-flavored gelato left Derek reeling. If he had savored better desserts in his lifetime, they were forgotten. As far as he knew, this was the single greatest meal in the world.

Hunger momentarily abated, Derek noticed the other occupant of the shop. With an AP Chemistry book open and notes strewn across the table, John Brooks was too enraptured to notice Derek. An elastic black workout shirt clung to John's skin, highlighting every muscle. Blond locks tinged with brown crowded his forehead and steadily approached his eyes. His head spun from the book to messy notes and back again.

Derek walked over and stood behind John, not knowing what to say.

Without looking up from his schoolwork, John said, "Shouldn't you be at that training place all weekend with Rachel and Tracy?"

"Yeah. I lost track of time and missed it." Peering over John's shoulder, Derek said, "The last molecule in that chemical equation should be a four, not two. Want some help on the rest of it?"

"How on Earth did you finish all the previous assignments to understand this material?"

Derek snapped his fingers. "Got it on your first guess. I wasn't on Earth."

John turned around to look at Derek. He arched an eyebrow, judging Derek wordlessly.

"Shit." Raising his hands in defense, Derek braced for the verbal assault. "Right, you didn't want me using my powers. Fine, I admit I used them and went into the void to study. I needed to regain the month I lost in school while traveling through time."

"You don't have to account for every time you use your powers or ask for permission. My threat to expose you is pointless since everyone knows what you can do."

Derek released a breath he didn't realize he was holding. "Do you really not care that I admitted to being in another dimension?"

"Is that where you've been since Friday? I noticed you weren't in Mr. Sprog's class. Then the shadow monster attacked, and the rest of us spent the morning crammed in the gymnasium. I assumed you were playing at being a hero to defend us."

Picturing his friends and classmates waiting, uncertain if their end was imminent, a knot formed in Derek's throat, making it difficult to breathe. John deserved a better friend than Derek, one who didn't abandon his post protecting their home to get ahead in school.

Grasping for a new topic, Derek blurted the first thing that surfaced in his head. "How are you and Rachel doing? Taking her to that Snow Ball dance?"

"Won't it be lame?"

"Probably, but it'll be a good chance for all five of us to get together and for me to dust off my dance moves."

That elicited an unenthusiastic laugh. "Are you really so desperate to hang out?"

"It's either that or bowling if we want to go anywhere in this town after 8 p.m. Tracy doubled my score last time. I prefer something closer to home than a trip to Bethesda's bowling alley."

John opened a half-filled plastic bottle and spat in it.

Derek's face scrunched in revulsion. "Why are you cutting water weight if you're not wrestling this season?"

John shook his disgusting spit bottle at Derek, reveling in how it forced Derek to turn. "Weigh-ins are in an hour, and I was allowed back on the team. I've got to ditch this water weight."

"That's great!" Derek nearly dropped the last bite of his ice cream to clap. "But I thought your coach never bent the rules."

Shrugging, John said, "Given the recent disasters, there were a lot of accommodations for the season. Coach made an exception so I could rejoin the team."

Derek clapped John's back. "Good for you! What time is your match?"

"I don't want you there." Before Derek found the words to convey his confusion, John continued. "Remember the last football game we watched together? I'm surprised that's still recorded as a win, when anyone who reviews the footage can witness your cheating."

Derek wanted to hit himself to remove the guilt sinking in his chest. "Fair point and noted. I was careless when I first grasped these powers. I'd never do anything like that again."

"You could have broken that guy on the other team's leg. I'm glad you didn't think to put up a telekinetic wall. Otherwise, he might have gone home with a concussion."

"I paid for the mountain of mistakes, almost giving up my life to undo the worst of them."

John faced Derek, his eyes shifting pointedly from Derek to Mrs. Delfino behind the counter. "Where does crippling Louis fit among the 'worst of them'?"

Unable to suppress his wince, Derek replied, "He's been doing better."

"*Better.* Sure. Don't worry. I haven't told Louis or his family what you did. There's no point in hurting them more."

"Thanks. I didn't mean for my powers to erupt and throw his car."

"All the more reason I don't want you at my matches. I'll avoid even the perception of cheating with your telekinesis, so there won't be any doubts when I win State—alone." John returned to the Chemistry problems, cross-referencing handwritten notes with tabbed textbook pages.

Edging away from his bristling friend, Derek made his way to the exit. There was no counterpoint to plead in his defense.

So much for my warm welcome home.

5

Respite

Derek

Coming around the last bend of his driveway, Derek slowed to a walk. Orange and maroon leaves fluttered over the paved road. He jumped on one, feeling the crinkling under his shoes.

His barn-turned-house emerged from behind oak trees, which had shed most of their leaves. Wood panels shielded the house's outside, giving it the impression of belonging to this forest, as though sprung from a tiny seed decades ago. The solar panels on the roof and floor-to-ceiling windows gave away that the building was not some strange natural plant.

Harvested pawpaw fruit trees stretched to the edge of the woods. Every year, his family had to fight encroaching flora from consuming their home and these crops, a Maryland staple.

Cast against the dark sky, lights inside beckoned. Like a fishbowl, the ground floor's large windows showcased his older sister in the kitchen. Steam rose from a pot on the stove while she wrangled meat frying in a pan. The sight made a tiny amount of drool slip from the side of his mouth.

His trash heap on wheels wasn't here; it was in the shop getting repaired. After the fight with his Beast, he'd come home to find his car even more dilapidated than usual. Its driver's side airbag was deployed and deflated, and broken glass of the destroyed windshield littered the front seats and his driveway.

This damage was intentional, a stalling tactic against his Beast.

The morning his Beast attacked was chaotic, starting with his choice to run away from home after he abused his powers and smashed a door into his dad. Derek's dad put himself further in harm's way by driving Derek's car into his Beast, giving Derek time to escape to his friends. Without his dad's gamble, Derek would not have survived the day.

He clutched his chest to ease the bottomless pit as each mistake made using his powers dug deeper inside. When he had punched his bedroom door, he had felt invincible, as though his problems burned to ash like the scorch mark his fist left. Until his dying day, he would never forget the noxious scent of burning paint and wood. Nor would he forget seeing his dad flattened beneath the door Derek launched in frustration, not realizing his dad was on the other side.

Despite their yelling match, which led to Derek's outburst, his dad had rammed Derek's car into the giant monster to stall it from chasing Derek.

While Derek fought for his life against his Beast, his dad fought his own battle in the hospital due to the car crash. Hell, that day, both Fens were probably in the same emergency room without knowing it. He hoped they got a family discount or earned a stamp on some tracking card. Maybe by his fifth emergency room visit, he'd get one free.

Derek eased open the side door of his house's addition and entered through the den.

His sister was waiting, hands on her hips. With the prominent nose Olivia shared with their dad nestled between her glare, she mimicked his disappointed look. "Dad came home from the hospital this afternoon."

Derek stepped around her toward the stairs and his bedroom to avoid another guilt trip.

She gripped his arm. Though not physically restraining, it brought Derek to a standstill while she spoke. "Not that you would know, since you were too busy to visit."

"How could I face him after I sent him to the hospital?"

"Considering dad saved your life, the least you could do was ditch training to welcome him home. We didn't know if you survived Friday's attack against the shadow monster. There were fewer witnesses this time, and most of their reports conflicted. Not that the bear-monster attack the week before was any better. I was stuck watching shaky cam footage of you fighting that house-sized monster."

"You're in luck. I wasn't there fighting the shadow monster."

"We didn't know that. I assumed you went to training after the monster attack. You didn't tell us anything."

Struggling to keep his tears from falling, a few drops got loose. He had been a terrible son, a terrible friend, and a terrible student for Mr. Marshal's training. Putting schoolwork and finding the other Derek as his top priority meant the rest of his life rotted.

Derek removed his backpack, placing it and the broken sword in the coat closet. "How was I supposed to plan for dad's early return?"

"It's called a smartphone."

"Cell signals haven't figured out how to broadcast to a separate dimension, yet," Derek bit back. "Hopefully, next time I go into the void, there will be a tower set up and I'll get reception."

Olivia's questioning glare settled. The next thing Derek knew, she wrapped him in a tight hug. "Keep coming back safe to us, 'kay?"

Derek returned her hug. "I'm sorry I made you worry. I needed to bring someone lost in the void home to... his family. He's still out there, so I'll keep looking. I also had a month's worth of school assignments to catch up on. I thought I could control the void to return the moment I left."

A piercing alarm sounded. Olivia raced to the stove, the smell of burned meat flowing across the kitchen.

Olivia switched off the burner and waved a towel over the smoke detector until the alarm stopped.

Derek's dad walked in from his study room to open a window, letting out the heat and smoke filling the room. He moved stiffly, holding his back. Never one to be overweight, a belly peaked from beneath the stretched fabric of his shirt.

How has he gained so much weight in a week to be noticeable?

That would not be the first thing he said to his dad since the day of their argument. Derek chose the easier person to talk to and faced his sister.

"I don't think chicken is supposed to be black."

Olivia flipped him off. "All right, Master Chef, you want to cook?"

She scraped the outermost layer of chicken to salvage the meal while daring Derek to comment under her glare. Despite the smell of charred meat, Derek licked his lips in anticipation of satisfying the hunger the void left in his stomach. The earlier gelato held him over as a snack, yet he needed a feast.

Their dad sat on a stool at the kitchen counter, staring at unfiltered moonlight encroaching from a wall of windows.

Purple bruises on his dad's forehead had faded to off-green and yellow. He scratched his arms where more yellow-tinged bruising marred his skin.

Derek opened his mouth to speak. Words eluded him, to say nothing of the gnawing, compounding guilt which kept him from visiting the hospital this past week.

"The doctors said I was in good enough health," his dad explained. "They let me come home a day earlier than expected. How was your latest adventure? The local news says you and your friends were incredible and stopped another monster. My son, the hero!"

Derek let out a long sigh. "I wasn't there. I had a promise to keep."

His dad's face fell. "You also promised me you'd stop skipping school. Except, they called your mom to say you weren't there on Friday. Isn't that why you decided to only train on weekends?"

The power to open a portal to the past, future, and nowhere offered a solution to all his problems, except Derek's foolproof plan had blown up in his face. "I thought I could make up all my homework by studying in the void. I'm scrambling to improve my grades to get into a good college. I already missed the early decision deadline on account of being lost in time."

"Are you still interested in bioengineering?"

"It's a little late for course correction."

"Not at all. You're eighteen; your life is far from over and easy enough to change. I care more about you finding what inspires you and leads to a fulfilling career. Don't let me or anyone else influence your decision. These powers of yours opened doors neither of us imagined. Why not ease back into your life and consider exploring yourself for a year after high school instead of jumping into college?"

"Tracy gave me the same advice." A snort escaped Derek. "I'm terrified to live in a world where she's the voice of reason. Once I take the missed exams from when I was stuck in time, I'll be mostly on track."

"Great, but that's still not a good enough reason to skip a day of school. I doubt colleges value truancy."

"This was a one-time field test while I still had the courage to travel into the void. That shortcut's closed since the shadow monster is waiting right on the other side. I wasn't expecting it and narrowly avoided it seeing me. I can't press my luck again without a solid plan."

His dad glanced at Olivia for help, who shook her head. They were never going to understand Derek's challenges, and he lacked the willpower to explain.

Luckily, his dad changed tactics. "On the bright side, they gave us matching casts."

With big clomping steps down their stairs, the smallest person in their home made the most noise as his mom entered the kitchen. She spoke at Derek's chest height.

"Your injuries aren't jokes. That horrid creature might have killed you two."

Derek set the placemats and silverware to keep his hands active, rather than quake under her stern glare accentuated by green-rimmed glasses. "My Beast won't bother us anymore. We have an all-new monster to worry about."

"No, you don't. You're not worrying about any other monsters."

"Yes, I do, and I'm sorry about how I acted that morning." Derek licked his lips, choosing his words. "My Beast came from me. It was a part of me cleaved from the whole, a part filled with raw emotions I'm afraid to admit exist."

Before Derek could continue, his dad interrupted. "I don't care where it came from. I care about you."

Derek melted. He had never been so proud to be his father's son. "Thank you for being so brave. I need to train to control my powers so that others won't be hurt by my mistakes again, or remove myself from the equation altogether."

"That's nonsense." His mom wagged her finger at him. "Train if you have to, but you are not removing yourself from anything."

This was a losing battle, and Derek's fortitude was failing in the wake of their three gazes, ranging from curious to stern to earnest. "How's the riveting life of a rocket scientist?"

His mom's face brightened. "Much more interesting now that my son proved the existence of multiple dimensions. When your dad returns to the lab, we're going to test a slew of new theories, and I need my best technician."

A light cough came from his dad. "That might not be soon."

Unspoken looks passed between his parents. His dad's face turned a fraction of a hair, signaling his mom with the slightest shake of his head.

Interjecting over the settling dead air, Derek added, "Aside from my schoolwork, I went into the void to find another dimension's version of me who was lost because of my mistake."

"Another you?" his parents asked in unison once they got control of their dropped jaws.

"Long story short: I need to search the void for the other version of me."

"I know I'm going to regret this," began Olivia. "What if you brought someone with a stronger tie to this other you, like Other Nicole?"

"I don't think 'Other Nicole' is the right way of putting it. How do you even know about her?"

"Well, I am a genius. That and Tracy's been keeping me informed when you leave your family out of the loop."

His dad's index finger bounced in the air as though he were badly calculating the tip at a restaurant. "Wait, hold on. Are there two Nicoles running around in our world?"

"I'm sure there are countless Nicoles. If you mean, is there a dimension-hopping version of one of my oldest friends? Yes. By the way, on her Earth, she stayed here on the East Coast."

His mom rubbed her forehead.

His dad wrapped an arm over her shoulder, holding her close. "That's a lot... Are you bringing either Nicole to the Snow Ball?"

"The Nicoles aren't interchangeable and I'm not our world's Nicole's type. As for Other Nicole, she's dating the lost Derek." Derek shook his head to make sense of the various people he kept track of. "It's all too confusing for me to think about now. How do you even know about the school dance?"

"There was an email from the school asking for volunteers to—"

Derek's breath caught. "You didn't!"

His dad held his neutral face for precious seconds, skyrocketing Derek's heart rate, then he cracked a smile. "I decided against embarrassing you for one night."

Olivia handed Derek a filled plate, the charred coating of chicken scraped from the surface to reveal edible meat. "Why don't we pick this up in the dining room? I'm starving."

His dad passed his food to Derek. "I'm not hungry. I had a snack when I got home."

Derek balanced his two dinner plates, careful not to drop a morsel.

Olivia flicked her head at their dad's back when their parents entered the dining room. Her message was received.

Derek paused halfway to the set table, tallying the details, from the lack of appetite, back pain, and swollen stomach. Their dad was lulling them into a false sense of security. The old man tried to hide them, yet the cancer symptoms showed through.

One thing was clear for Derek: whatever schedule Tracy planned for human transmutations, they were bumping it up to save his dad and repair Louis's body.

6

Worship

Rachel

Rachel tapped the sides of the steering wheel in her parked white Audi, staring at students passing beneath the bright red archway of her school's side entrance, waiting for Monday morning to start.

Catching herself in the rearview mirror, she started her new morning credo. "No monster will attack today. This will be another typical day of senior year." An uncontrolled yawn ended her pep talk.

Long chimes of the first bell announced the day was starting, yet leaving the car meant suffering through the stares of her classmates. Some were subtle. Most weren't. Last Friday's monster attack, the second in a week, was sure to make the problem worse.

She refused to be another Derek, hiding from problems until they attacked as a physical Beast. Her powers, however, presented unique solutions to what life lay at her feet.

One student held open the door for those behind her. Rachel ramped up her powers, covering the distance from her car to the door in less than a second. Weaving between her classmates who moved at the speed of a wall, Rachel got to the band corridor without incident. She was careful not to touch anyone and risk launching them into a locker.

A three-foot-wide paper snowflake hung on the band room door, a poster to promote the upcoming dance. Thanksgiving was around the corner, yet the school administration wanted to summon winter blizzards with an aptly named Snow Ball. The dance was scheduled for the second week of December when temperatures were bound to be in the forties and well above freezing. Still, a dance was a dance.

Wild visions of John planning some elaborate scheme to ask her to the dance fluttered across her thoughts. She'd give her boyfriend another day to work up the courage to ask her, otherwise she intended to ask him.

In Symphonic Band, they ran through the upcoming concert pieces. Clarinets in the front row craned their necks around to face Rachel. Not even Mr. DeSantos was above staring at her when sweeping his eyes across the sections.

Rachel's hands moved on autopilot. Her eyes drooped halfway through the first song, leaving her on the verge of falling asleep while standing. Late nights catching up on homework, weekends spent training, and fighting the shadow monster were taking their toll on her body.

Tracy pulled Rachel out of her stupor in their second period, Music Appreciation. "Did you really lose your percussion spot to Lauren?"

Rachel couldn't face Tracy. Her words made it seem like she was sinking into the ground. "Yeah. Missing a month of practice made it official. I'm third to her first position."

"Want me to work with you to get us back into drumming shape?"

Rachel raised a quizzical eyebrow in judgment. "I thought you stopped playing when you quit the band."

"Hey now! I'm not classically trained like you, but you're wrong if you think I'm done with drums because I left my band. I practice when I can... though it has been a while."

Rachel wrestled over what to say, hurt by what she knew was true. "Lauren's earned it, and I promised not to challenge her until next semester."

Seeing disappointment flash over Tracy's face, Rachel added, "I would be in for a jam session this week, though."

Without bothering to think or breathe, Tracy said, "I'm in!"

The class stopped at Tracy's shout. Her classmates leaned closer to hear more. Rachel wanted to shrink, to hide, to run, and not stop until she was far away from their prying eyes.

Tracy patted Rachel's hand and stood, rattling off the tale of their recent conquest over the shadow monster. Rachel closed her eyes and breathed slowly in and out, feeling her pulse return to normal.

Thankfully, Tracy stole the spotlight. Rachel stopped listening when her friend referred to herself as a hero for the third retelling of Friday's battle for the entire class.

Taking her seat in AP Physics, Rachel saw a familiar face sitting next to her, one she couldn't place. The girl's blond hair highlighted her intense green eyes. Recognizing the look of being sized up, Rachel's classmate appeared more inquisitive than judgmental. The green and brown camo pants made her stand out in the classroom setting, well removed from any forest.

"I know you," Rachel said more bluntly than she intended.

That extracted a half smile from the newcomer. "You abandoned me in the hallway on my first day." Wiping an imaginary tear from her eye, she continued, "Lost and alone, I fought a roaming herd of freshmen to hold on to my boots."

"Sorry. I never got your name."

"It's Melissa Kim, and trust me, I understand. I heard about the Charlie Foxtrot you handled that morning."

"The Charlie what now?"

Melissa's eyes widened, and her breath caught before settling instantly. "The mess with that smog thing. How did you prevent any human casualties?"

"Between the time of day and the phone alerts, no one was in the park when we fought the shadow. In the earlier fight with the Beast, I ran like crazy to save everyone. Another one of our friends helped me by warping people out of some tough spots."

Melissa's eager expression encouraged Rachel to go on, but Rachel had no interest in being like Tracy. "To be honest, saving everyone from the first monster came at a cost that left us too drained and forced us to make a desperate gamble to survive."

Tapping on her tablet, Mrs. Strata began class by projecting the lesson's material onto the larger screen. Sporting a blue blazer and tan pants, Rachel's teacher looked more prepared for a corporate cubicle than this classroom. She explained the formulas for determining objects in motion with quick precision, waiting for struggling students.

During pauses in Mrs. Strata's sentences, Rachel used her abilities to speed herself up. The added time allowed her to consider the few facts she knew about Aspects, as though through study, she might break them into fundamental equations like any other physics problem.

With one Aspect, she saw the world through sound, another let her feel the thoughts of others. Maybe those were related. Too many unknowns left her understanding of her powers like a wedge of Swiss cheese rife with holes.

She adjusted her internal metronome, applying the Aspect she used as frequently as breathing. The world slowed around her as she thought at inhuman speeds.

Crossing these three Aspects once left her blind for an entire night. She had not made that mistake again since then, becoming familiar with closing one Aspect before using another. Derek ignored reason, crossing many Aspects to rip apart barriers leading to other universes and times. Considering the devastation of the void or traveling through time, a different combination may have led to the disastrous creation of his Beast.

"Suppose we have a *student* running at thirty meters per second." Mrs. Strata's voice penetrated Rachel's thoughts. Bracing for the inevitable, Rachel lowered her head onto her desk as Mr. Strata continued, "Yes, that is running at thirty meters per second. This isn't your average student. Those outside our county may think it's a hoax, but I saw the monster firsthand. Trust me, this student is a hero to defeat that monster with her friends. She's at it again, leaping from a thirty-degree angle over another monster to rescue a student. What is the tallest invading monster she can leap over?"

Without raising her head, Rachel knew every eye in the class fell on her. Inner heat turned her ears red, and she froze. Hero worship was one thing; adding her into physics equations was absurd. What next? Was her calc class going to use L'Hôpital's Rule to solve some random function as Rachel's speed approached infinity?

To her credit, Mrs. Strata's explanation was thorough, breaking the initial velocity into X and Y vectors. "By assuming other forces are negligible, this problem becomes simple."

Tony raised his hand for a moment, calling out his question when Mrs. Strata didn't immediately notice him. "What if those other forces, like wind resistance, create a noticeable impact?"

Rachel never understood why Derek and Tracy complained so much about Tony. He seemed likable, and his poignant question animated their teacher's face more than the cup of coffee she sipped between slides.

But for fear of drawing more attention, Rachel would have asked the same thing. The answer to this question might help her understand why moving at faster speeds felt like running through water. As though trapped in a nightmare, the faster she forced her sturdy legs to move, the heavier they became until she slowed her internal metronome.

Mrs. Strata cleared the screen to draw a new diagram of a stick figure falling. Arrows pointed above and below the hapless victim who jumped without a parachute. "Air resistance is the complex force proportional to velocity squared. It reaches a maximum when equal to the weight, at which point acceleration is zero and velocity remains constant."

"Until this person comes to a stop by meeting the ground," Tony called out.

"Correct," said Mrs. Strata. "This is a taste of the complicated problems you can expect to solve in college courses."

When the bell to end the period rang, Rachel's growling stomach appreciated being in Group A's first lunch shift.

Mrs. Strata hovered over Rachel's shoulder as she packed to race to food. With a groaning sigh, Rachel braced for the question she knew was coming. All her other teachers had kept her aside to discuss how to finish the semester following the month-long black hole in her studies. "I need one more day to complete the homework you assigned three weeks ago. I can have it ready for you at our after-school lesson tomorrow."

"Take your time, so long as you're prepared for final exams."

"I'll catch up over the two extra days off this week for fall break." Rachel tried to move around her teacher.

Mrs. Strata adjusted to block Rachel's exit. "Can I study you and your friends? What you can do presents unfathomable ways to revolutionize the field of physics."

"We aren't science experiments."

"Of course, of course. That being said, this is a once-in-a-lifetime opportunity." Eager eyes shone with the brightness of the sun.

"The three of us already spend every afternoon with our teachers on makeup lessons." Unwilling to outright dash Mrs. Strata's ambitions, Rachel added, "We'll see."

Not getting the hint, her teacher said, "I look forward to it."

* * *

Rachel sat at one of the dozens of long tables inside the cafeteria built to house hundreds, currently filled beyond capacity. Bright daylight lit the room from the glass windows of the back wall. On warmer days when the doors remained open, the windows made the cafeteria feel like a blended mix of outside weather.

Louis Delfino moved his crutches aside to give her more room. He regarded Rachel's triple platter of fully loaded half-smokes with a raised eyebrow. His perfect teeth shone in his smiling greeting, hinting at a return to his pre-car crash self. Over the weekend, the hard cast over his arm had been downgraded to a soft brace. To expose as much of his olive-colored skin as possible, he had rolled his long-sleeved shirt almost to his shoulders. Hard plastic mesh still reinforced his broken leg.

Louis watched her watching him, patting his leg. "This mint-chocolate chip of a cast is ready to come off in two more weeks."

"Great!" Rachel took a large bite of her lunch, careful not to drip the cheesy mess onto her clothes. "Has Tracy talked to you about her idea to fix the problem faster?"

Well into his second pudding container, Louis eyed his salami sandwich with suspicion. "That's a big old empty gallon bucket of no on that one. What's her idea?"

Derek plopped into the seat next to Louis, mindful not to brush any of their injured limbs, and asked, "How do you handle the unbearable itches?"

"A twelve-inch ruler can work wonders to reach the right spots."

Derek munched on potato chips like a loud machine gnashing glass, metal, and fireworks. Every crunch sent a twinge through Rachel and Louis.

Rachel talked over Derek's chewing. "The rest of us survived Friday's ordeal, no thanks to you. But if I were you, I'd smooth everything over with Tracy as soon as you can."

Offering half a grunt, Derek said, "She seemed all right in AP Chem this morning."

Louis blew bubbles into his boxed Yoo-hoo. "I'm not surprised you missed the signals broadcasting your way."

"You're no expert on women," Derek replied.

"I never claimed to be."

"I don't either, do I?"

Rachel accelerated herself to have the time to breathe deeply, seeking calm. She counted to one hundred, then slowed to normal. "You don't. When she wasn't gloating, Tracy spent Music Appreciation venting to me." Looking over the two of them, she added, "Take it from me; she's pissed."

Derek's alarm softened into concern. "How have you been feeling after the fight?"

For the first time in over a decade, I slept with the light on. "Like I said, we survived. Aside from suffering with us, I don't know what difference you would have made. I keep seeing the shadow monster around every dark corner."

The other students leaned their heads toward Rachel's table to catch glimmers of the conversation. Those were the same expressions the mall rent-a-cop held as he found reason after reason to follow her when she was shopping for a fun dress. None of them believed she possessed the basic right to live in peace, let alone without scrutiny.

These weren't the faces of Saturday afternoon football fans. Cheering crowds raised her up without question. Here, classmates sought the spark that made Rachel and her friends special.

"Everyone is looking at us," she whispered between bites. "They think we're in the middle of the greatest conversation of the decade."

"Let them," said Derek. "People think what they want."

Louis helped himself to one of Derek's potato chips. "You saved us from a monster invasion twice."

Rachel sighed. "That's not really what happened. They were separate attacks, not an invasion."

Derek pushed the bag of chips in front of Louis when he reached for it again. "Our powers are a part of us. Either people will get used to the new us, or they won't."

Those classmates Rachel made eye contact with suddenly found an interest in their fingernails or the surface of their tables. "That's an entitled way to see the world."

"True. On the other hand, my friends' opinions are the only ones which matter to me. We don't have the power to sway the masses, so worrying about what they think is a waste of time. Besides, if things get bad," Derek added with a twisted smile, "I'll go into the past and unmake our present."

That set off a few yelps from eavesdroppers.

"Kidding. I'm joking for all of you listening in," Derek said to placate Louis and the rest.

Good thing these people don't know how close he came to fulfilling that promise. I still don't know why the present isn't altered from our trip to the past.

Lost in her thoughts, Rachel absentmindedly finished her meal at high speed. Derek and Louis fell silent, staring at her, their eyes locked on her empty trays.

Rather than wait to hear their jaws hit the floor, she explained, "My metabolism has sped up, and I need a ton of food to put my stomach to sleep."

"When you bought three lunches, I didn't think you'd gobble them all up," Louis said.

Derek leaned in, lowering his voice. "Did Mr. Marshal give you a serious workout this weekend?" Pity showed across his face.

"What were you doing with Mr. Marshal?" whispered Louis.

"Nothing weird," Rachel replied. "He's training us to improve our Aspects."

"Is Mr. Marshal a secret superhero or something?"

"Possibly. He knocked Tracy on her ass when she tried to use an Aspect on him."

The bell rang as she looked longingly at the food line. Unless she used her power to steal the food, a midafternoon snack wasn't happening today. Group B was on the way to lunch, and fourth period was calling. Rachel left her friends to join the swelling press of student bodies transitioning between lunch and class.

A mass of people blocked the hallway on the way to her locker. Rachel used her size to slip in the spaces between those larger than her.

At the center, Allerie Lorana stood opposite Tracy. Allerie leaned over to one of her friends beside her and whispered loud enough for everyone to hear, "Looks like our resident freak went and dyed her hair. I hear your powers let you be whatever you want, and yet you choose to be," Allerie gestured at Tracy up and down with a smirk, "you."

Rachel admired the green tinges Tracy added to the ends of her brunette hair. Tracy casually highlighted the change by running her fingernails through her long hair. Only Rachel noticed how tightly Tracy clenched her arm as though in pain. "We're back to this? So soon after I saved your life?" Tracy asked.

Allerie's expression softened for a fraction of a second, and then it returned to disdain. "I would have been fine without your help."

"Well, next time I'll let a giant bear monster burn you to a crisp, or should I transmute you into a slug for fun?"

Allerie took a step back, her eyes flashing for an instant in apparent fright. Then her nose scrunched as if she smelled seeping sewage. "Not everyone needs ogres like you interfering in their lives."

Allerie opened her mouth to expand on her insult, except Rachel had heard enough. She accelerated, running around the circle to push at the backs of Allerie's knees.

Returning to a spot within the crowd, Rachel slowed, watching the drama queen fall on her angry face. Instead of squaring down her enemy or adding witty banter, Tracy's head moved around, settling in Rachel's direction. Tracy's eyes narrowed.

Rachel hurried to her locker. She swapped out the morning books and folders for those needed for her afternoon classes. Slamming her locker shut, Rachel jumped at the figure standing beside her.

"What you did will lead to retaliation, probably against Tracy and not you," said John. He didn't bother to kiss her hello, offering condescension instead. "Everyone knows you just used your powers to hurt Allerie."

Rachel remained defiant. "I won't stand by and let one of our friends be bullied. Especially when Allerie was baiting Tracy to hit her."

"Allerie's slurs shouldn't be allowed, but there has to be a better way to handle the situation. I'll convince Allerie to stop harassing Tracy instead of using force and tripping her like you did."

"I—"

"Being so free with your powers leads to trouble," interrupted John.

She reached for his hand, but he was already walking to lunch. To Rachel's disappointment, he didn't so much as peck her on the cheek for comfort before leaving.

Rachel passed through fourth period in a daze, barely taking any notes.

Tracy was waiting outside their fifth class, Computer Science. "I didn't need your help. I have bigger shadow-sized problems to worry about than Allerie."

They took their seats next to each other as their teacher, Ms. Whistler, gave them a ten-question quiz, jolting Rachel awake. She was stuck answering B for everything, as she couldn't figure out how to write the basic if-else statements to solve the problems.

Rachel submitted her quiz. Her cheeks burned, and she felt as though lava rumbled inside her for all the answers she knew she got wrong.

Tracy grasped Rachel's hand. "We need a moment," she told their teacher as she submitted her quiz. "It's superpowered business."

Ms. Whistler looked nervous as she nodded. "Of course. If you needed to leave before the quiz, you should have said so. Be sure to study the quiz topic later."

"Thanks. We'll be back soon." Tracy led Rachel into the hall.

When they were alone, Tracy stared into Rachel's eyes. "Spill it. What's wrong? You looked so upset in there."

An avalanche knocked loose inside Rachel. All she could do to stop tears from falling was speak faster. "Teachers are squeezing me to make up the assignments I missed. Even with my powers, I'm too far behind. I haven't slept more than an hour all week. Our friend group is hanging together by a thread. I can't. I. Just. Can't."

"Breathe."

"There are too many pieces of our lives to pick up and fix. We missed too much."

Without warning, Rachel was caught in a tight hug. "I'm sorry for calling you out earlier. Allerie has a way of setting me off, which no one else should have to deal with. Life is a lot, but I know you can handle any monster-sized problem it throws at you. I've seen it."

Tracy's embrace brought iron resolve billowing within Rachel. She *would* make up all her missed schoolwork over this week's Thanksgiving break.

Tracy let go, holding her at arm's length. "We do this together, friends to the end of time."

Lacking flair, Tracy's words resonated, giving Rachel the courage to face an army of teachers and overdue assignments.

When they returned, Ms. Whistler was holding Tracy's phone. "This kept going off in your backpack. Normally, I'd keep phones one day for every interruption, but I accidentally read one of your texts as it flashed on the screen. I'm sorry. It appeared, and I couldn't unsee it."

Tracy's phone chimed again. Her face paled as she read the latest message. "Rachel, the shadow's back in the park. We need to go. *Now.*"

7

Red Light

Derek

Derek stood over the wide hole in the park's sidewalk. The concrete path appeared to have been scooped out, as well as the soil beneath. Seven large parallel lines were cut from the concrete leading to the empty space.

The mild odor of smoldering embers lingered from where the portal to the void had partially opened.

Most people in the park stayed clear of Louis, Tracy, John, and Derek. Some strangers had their cameras out, snapping pictures and recording videos. If any of them hoped to capture the next monster attack, they were about to be disappointed.

Rachel slowed from a running blur to a stop in front of them. "I did another pass, and there's no sign of any monster or portal. You good here?"

Tracy nodded at Rachel, patting her shoulder. "Don't worry. It looks like the shadow didn't fully make it through, so please don't be late for band practice."

"Let me know if you need my help and I'll come back. Hey Louis, are you coming?"

Louis shook his head and pointed to his phone. "A tear in the world feels more important than Jazz Band practice, plus I still have an hour before I need to be there. We start later than you all."

Rachel threw him a quizzical look. "Are you going to be ready for our competition?"

Louis held up his arm, still encased in a brace. "With this on, my practice schedule is limited."

Rachel's shoulders sank. "I'm sorry."

Tracy waved goodbye to Rachel. "Get going and have fun at band. We got it from here."

Rachel nodded and was gone in a second as she raced back to their school.

"Can I see the video again?" Derek asked Louis.

"Sure." Louis handed over his phone. They watched a shaky recording of a broken line appearing above the sidewalk. Flashes of light spewed from the errant bursts of energy. The shadow punctured the portal to the void with its giant seven fingered hand. Each finger ended in deadly claws which scraped the sidewalk, cutting through it.

The opening to the void twisted and bent as though alive. The shadow retreated back into the void as the crack blinked from existence.

John crouched to touch where the shadow tried to breach into their world, then seemed to think better of it and stood.

"Someone posted this an hour ago," said Louis. "As the resident kings and queens of weird, what does it mean?"

Derek held back darkening thoughts. "Nothing good."

"The video didn't catch how the portal opened," said John. He faced Derek with a sneer. "Could it have been that monster you created that ran rampant on the other side of this neighborhood?"

"My Beast? Doubtful. It seemed afraid of the void. Someone would have seen it if it had shown up." Derek paused. "Wait, how do you know I created it?"

John looked away and shrugged. "Rachel told me all about it."

Tracy put force into her words. "I'm sure she told you those details in confidence. I doubt she'd want you to throw them back at Derek."

John let out a heavy sigh. "I wouldn't have, except Derek let it live when he had a chance to stop it once and for all."

"It's a part of me, one I can still sense out there. Even if it weren't, it's a living being. I had no right to kill it."

John held up his hands to show he meant no harm. "That's perfectly fine, so long as it doesn't come back to attack us. With how little you know about it, letting it live seems like a big risk."

Tracy moved her hand along the claw marks cut into the ground. She held her hand close to hide how much she shook. "The Beast is old news. What are we doing about the shadow monster?"

Derek's brain tossed around the small number of details he knew. "You fought one of those shadow monsters in this park before. Think the location is connected?"

Tracy's entire body shuddered. "Like the exits from the void are easier to make in places where they've already been opened?"

"That could be it." Details sifted in Derek's head until he settled on another nugget of truth. "Last time, how'd you get here before Rachel to face the shadow monster?" he asked Tracy.

Chewing on her lip, Tracy admitted, "I drove to school but didn't have the patience to go in. I came to this park looking for a reason not to skip. My grades are already blown for the semester. I had no motivation to show up after a stressful week."

Louis let out a tiny yelp.

The sounds of high-pitched screeching tires made Derek look up with hesitation, worried he was about to watch a car crash happen. A car sped through a red light, swerving between a runner and an oncoming car that had slammed on its brakes. The runner shouted curses at the car's wake amid several other cars all honking at the illegal maneuver.

John clicked his tongue at the car speeding off. "You should have stopped that, Derek."

Too scared of what he might unleash, Derek didn't even consider it. "Is this a test to see if I'll abuse my power?"

"Multiple people were almost hit by someone breaking the law in front of us."

Derek studied John, looking for signs of sarcasm or that this was a bad joke. "Louis is standing right here. You should know why me stopping a moving car is a terrible idea."

"As someone with powers, you have a responsibility to use them to prevent people from being hurt."

Derek defended himself. "No one was hurt."

Louis shook his head to clear the shock. "That was pure luck, and what about the next time somebody blatantly runs a red light?"

"There are too many terrible drivers for me to stop them all."

"I'm not looking for a fight," started John. "If you have powers and someone's in danger nearby, then you should throw yourself into the line of fire to save them."

Derek had to admit John had a point. He clapped Tracy's shoulder. "That's what we'll do to combat the shadow: Hero Watches! We keep an eye out for trouble in the neighborhood and look for portals to the void."

Tracy groaned. "So I have another after-school activity to deal with?"

"That's a great idea," exclaimed John.

"Not with all the schoolwork I need to catch up on," countered Tracy. "I'll be up all night to redo Mr. Sprog's latest lab answers for partial credit. Not to mention the latest asshole comment he made in today's class. He's been out of control toward Derek and me since discovering we have powers."

Louis's concern amounted to a raised eyebrow. "What did he say?"

Tracy looked up at the sky as though answers were written on a cloud. "I can't exactly remember... It was definitely insulting. Derek, can you remember?"

Drawing back on Mr. Sprog's class felt like grasping fog. The material Mr. Sprog taught was there, but the specifics of their teacher's words were lost. "Strange. It was this morning. I remember you being pissed, but I can't picture his face when he said it. John, can you remember?"

John shook his head. "Sorry. With my training programs stepping up, all the classes before lunch are a blur."

"One thing at a time, then," Louis cut in. "Why not rotate people for these Hero Watches so no one gets overwhelmed?"

"That makes sense," Derek agreed.

John rested his arm on Derek's shoulders. "The portal is closed and I don't see any monsters attacking now. I'm all caught up on school and training, so want to do a night of games at my place?"

A sense of hope rose from deep inside Derek as he looked at each of his friends. "Hell yeah!"

"I'm in," said Louis.

Tracy glanced back at the hole in the sidewalk, fear flashing over her features. "You three have fun. I still have plenty of homework to handle."

8

Harmonized Lives

Tracy

Tracy scrambled for an answer in Tuesday's first class. She skimmed her notes, hoping for something to click in her head after her teacher had called on her.

"Fe_2O_3 is ferrous oxide," Tracy guessed.

Her AP Chemistry teacher, Mr. Sprog, let out a disappointed *hmph* sound. "Interesting theory. Now tell me why you are wrong."

There was no reason for Mr. Sprog to be such a dick. His stiff manner was so unlike the harsh but fair Mr. Sprog from the start of the semester. Everything else in the room was the same, from the classroom's black laminated tables for labs to the cabinets filled with glass graduated cylinders. Even the projector screen connected to Mr. Sprog's laptop was the same. The difference was that since Tracy and Derek had revealed their powers, Mr. Sprog directed all his ire at them.

Tracy braced for the knockout punch from her classmate, Allerie. Instead of a thinly veiled insult, Allerie's attention was buried in her notes, too busy to care about Tracy.

Tracy glanced at her own rushed notes, pushing them over the late assignment she was scrambling to work through while Mr. Sprog had been talking. Her suffix explanations on top of the pile were reversed from the on-screen content, with "-ous" and "-ic" trading places. "Ferric Oxide."

Mr. Sprog clapped his hands. "Correct, Ms. Wayfield. Please remember, students are best educated when they save homework for home."

"You said something rude like that to me yesterday too. Why are you punishing me?"

Mr. Sprog strode between desks, hands clasped behind his back, a doctor making rounds. Given his newfound demeanor, this doctor was more likely to insult patients than cure them. "I am sure you are aware of the significant number of your additional responsibilities as our local *protector*. I am ensuring you are prepared to handle them inside and outside the classroom."

"Of course I'm prepared. I'm your top student in this class and my powers have nothing to do with you."

"Were. Past tense. Your falling grades are proof these burdens are hindering you."

Tracy curled her fists under her desk, lacking a rebuttal that wouldn't send her straight to detention for a record number of curses.

Mr. Sprog stopped behind the adjacent Derek, Mr. Sprog's other superpowered victim. "Mr. Fen, what is the chemical formula for lead sulfate?"

"Pb... S... O... I don't know the rest." Derek's head lowered, his hand curling into a fist beneath the desk. He muttered so softly only Tracy heard, "This was easy when I had all the time in the world."

"What was that?" Mr. Sprog's garlic-based lunch invaded Tracy's airspace.

"PbSO$_4$." The new girl saved Derek. She didn't raise her hand to be called on, preferring a more direct method.

Mr. Sprog spread his arms in front of him, palms facing upward to form his standard stance. He looked at her like a statue staring at a pigeon resting on it. "Correct, except I was asking Mr. Fen, not you, Ms... I'm sorry, can you remind me of your name again?"

"I'm Melissa, no 'Ms.'"

"In the future, refrain from answering for others."

"I knew the answer, though."

Mr. Sprog returned to the front of the room, the corners of his mouth twitching in repressed fury as he resumed the lesson.

The blond-haired transfer student's athletic build caught Tracy's eye. The presence Melissa exuded impressed Tracy. Anyone willing to stand up to a teacher in a room full of students was worthy of admiration. She was sorry for where the new girl was placed. Stuck in the worst seat, Melissa shared a table with Allerie and Tony.

Too soon, the bell rang. Tracy swallowed, counting the hours remaining until school ended, and for once, she wished to extend the day.

She nibbled on her hair while packing the spiral notebook and pens. The follicles tasted the same as every other time she gave in to this bad habit, despite the green coloring at the ends of her hair. She was disappointed there wasn't a hint of candy apple artificial flavoring.

Using her powers to tinge her hair green had been easy. She practiced it all night to ensure she got it right. The concept should be the same for more complicated bodily changes, like repairing broken bones. Still, she kept inventing new worst-case scenarios for how she would fail Louis. She looked at Derek, wanting his support, yet held back from confiding in him. His cautious nagging would talk her out of it faster than she could transmute an outer layer of Louis's skin.

Tracy approached the front of the room, handing the completed homework to Mr. Sprog. He flipped the stapled pages, looking for what wasn't there. "You are missing two more sheets for assignments nine and ten."

"All the other teachers gave us extensions, considering we took out two monsters. Why can't you?" Tracy blurted out.

"I am not other teachers." A cry of frustration was rising in Tracy's throat. Before she yelled at her teacher, he smiled. "Very well. You may submit the overdue work on Monday after our fall break—for half credit."

Biting her tongue, Tracy moved to the side. Derek and John had formed a line to speak with Mr. Sprog. Derek handed in his homework, much thicker than the stack of papers Tracy had submitted.

"Mr. Fen, I've been meaning to ask, who was the young man who fought alongside you last week?"

Derek paused. "Young man?"

Mr. Sprog sifted through the stack of papers. They might as well have been discussing the weather. "The same one who hurled lightning and bought you a chance to flee from your bear monster. More recently, he swung chains to dissipate the shadow being."

"You mean Flint? Aren't you the same age?"

Mr. Sprog stared at the ceiling. "Flint? Odd, he does not seem like merely a 'Flint.'"

"He goes by Flint, but his name is Aelaphus."

"That is an uncommon name," Mr. Sprog mused, not really speaking to Derek anymore.

Seeing Rachel waiting in the hallway, Tracy left Derek and John to Mr. Sprog's whims.

Tracy made it halfway to the door when Tony stepped in front of her to lean an elbow on her shoulder. As his phone flashed, he formed devil horns with his fingers, capturing physical evidence of her glaring daggers at him.

"Cool selfie. Thanks," he said, unapologetic for leaving an imprint on her retinas. "That magic you do is pretty awesome."

"Don't flash that in my eyes again." Tracy pushed Tony off, giving him a shove for good measure. The sizable bulk she felt as he slunk off surprised her.

Before jumping into the past, she hadn't looked at him closely. The month had been more than kind to Tony. Gone was the scrawny kid who seemed ready to lawyer up when trouble was thrown his way. The biceps she brushed were about to put John's sculpted body to shame. Too bad Tracy wasn't one to be attracted to overpowering brawn. No amount of a shiny new outer shell could fully disguise the guy she despised.

Derek left the classroom, waving at her as he hurried down the hall.

"Who's that teacher John's talking to? I've never had a class with him," Rachel asked Tracy, peering into the room Derek had left.

"Mr. Sprog."

"His tempo is different from everyone else."

"There you go with your tempo stuff again. What are you even talking about?"

"It's hard to describe how my powers let me observe the world. Let's say everyone else in this room is near enough to a 4/4-time signature at sixty beats per minute. He seems to set a comparatively allegro pace, at a brisk eighty beats per minute."

"So, he's faster? Is that how you see the Nicole from the other Earth?"

"No. She's more like our same tempo at a different key signature."

"Okay..."

"The one other person I've seen with a tempo so far from the norm is Mr. Marshal, though he's not as drastic. His beats per minute hover at about seventy. I think Flint had an abnormal tempo, too, but I try not to look at him with my powers since I caught a glimpse beneath his arm bindings."

"Is he covered in scars or open wounds?"

"Worse. Hands were reaching for his heart from the gaps in his bindings. They weren't there in real life, only visible using my powers."

"Creepy. Well, you didn't know any of this tempo stuff about our teacher, so what brought you to the science wing before Music Appreciation?"

Rachel's arms folded over her chest, staring into the open doorway. "I'm looking for John."

John and Mr. Sprog were hissing at one another, quietly yelling without raising their voices. Like stray cats, they circled, waiting to pounce.

John stormed out of the classroom, his fuming expression turning his sharp jawline into a series of more severe angles. John's entire demeanor melted at the sight of Rachel, returning his features to their standard handsome form.

"WanttogototheSnowBallwithme?" Rachel spoke so quickly, the whole sentence felt like a single word.

"Oh." John's eyebrows jumped up his forehead. Stars formed and collapsed in the pause which passed. "Of course!" His hand rubbed the back of his neck. "I didn't think you wanted to go."

"We missed Homecoming. That means the next dance is at the top of my list to attend." Rachel pressed up against John, kissing him while classmates moved around them. Tracy looked away, so as not to stare. When the pair came up for air, Rachel said, "You've seemed so distracted since I've returned to the present. I wanted to make sure nothing was wrong and that we were still in sync."

Tiptoeing as quietly as she could, Tracy left for Music Appreciation to give the two lovers some privacy. She owed Rachel for providing a much needed distraction. Classmates swam up and downstream in the overcrowded halls, leaving her lost to her wandering thoughts. Her abilities were the means to heal her friend. Louis had already been permanently scarred by Derek's loss of control.

Tracy hoped she was different, hoped she proved to be more capable.

Once she finished her after-school makeup calc lesson, she would face the truth.

9

Healing Hands

Tracy

Louis hopped toward Tracy's car, supported by the crutches bearing the brunt of his weight. He left the unassuming office building where she knew he'd spent the last hour in physical therapy busting his ass.

She unlocked the doors, but stayed seated. Louis would get frustrated if she helped him into the car.

Louis tossed his crutches in the back and winced as he collapsed into the passenger seat. With his brow beaded with sweat, her friend appeared to be the ghost of Louis.

So much for the recovery process.

Tracy drove to her house, wishing to stretch those final minutes of the drive until she had to work with her powers.

"It's not too late to reconsider." She hated how her voice wavered.

Louis's empty eyes regarded her. Drained of physical strength, he looked too tired for false promises. "What are the odds this will work?"

"Eighty percent," Tracy suggested. Caving, she amended her guess. "Seventy percent?" She patted Louis's arm cast. "It has to be above fifty."

"I'm going to go insane if I have to repeat the physical therapy for my foot once it's free of the cast." Louis shook his head. Drops of sweat from his hair sprinkled the car's dashboard. "Let's do it before I lose my nerve."

Too soon, Tracy pulled up to her house. Its boxed design looked like three separate pieces of concrete, wood, and stone had been smashed together. Her mother's architectural masterpiece, Tracy's house always felt more impractical than unique.

Windows on the ground floor exposed the kitchen and living room on either side of the house, separated by the red front door. With the lights on, her house became a giant misshapen lantern to ward against the shadows.

The two-car garage was missing both vehicles. Her parents were still at work, leaving Tracy to reign over the house and use her powers at will. Both mother and father were aware of her gifts. Once most of planet Earth had heard about her fight with the monsters, there was no hiding the truth from them. Though encouraging, her parents couldn't hide the fear in their eyes or quakes in their voices when she was in the room. They treated her like a grenade with the pin yanked, wanting to hold the delicate lever down one moment and toss her away the next.

Her front door unlocked automatically once she was close enough for her devices to connect to her home base's Wi-Fi. The Geofence was one of many technical marvels that made her house smarter than most people.

Louis did a good job keeping pace, his feet and crutches landing on the stone pathway instead of the gravel gaps.

She opened the front door to find a smaller-sized, male version of her running into the room, ambushing them. Victor tapped his foot, eager as a puppy. "What are you two doing?"

Broad-shouldered and with a deepening voice, her freshman brother had all the markings of an oncoming growth spurt to take after their tall mother. Victor's mild facial features were lengthening, losing his squeezable baby cheeks. Brown shaggy hair hung loosely, needing to be trimmed and styled. He seemed to be growing it out with no end in sight.

"Nothing. Going to the basement," Tracy told her little brother.

"I've known you and Louis long enough to know you aren't hooking up. Are you doing powers stuff?"

Louis stoked the flames of Victor's excited face. "That's right. It's go time."

"Can I watch?"

"No," replied Tracy.

"Come on," Victor pleaded. "The parental units left their credit card. I'll order delivery from your favorite Greek place."

"There's hope for you yet." Tracy's mouth watered at the mere thought of honey-dipped baklava. "Order me the usual and add an extra Gyro Platter for lunch tomorrow."

"I'll have the Trio Platter," said Louis.

"On it." Victor raced to place the order on his phone. These powers weren't half bad. She might turn her brother into a decent person through steady bribes of demonstrating her transmutations.

"Fine. You can watch," said Tracy pointedly, staring into her brother's eyes, "but you have to be quiet when I'm using my powers. What I'm doing is dangerous."

"Maybe this isn't the best idea," mused Louis.

There was her chance for an easy out. "I don't want to push you. Do you want me to go ahead?"

Louis left the question hanging on the air. Eventually, he closed his eyes as he answered, "Yes."

Tracy left her shoes at the front door and helped Louis hobble down to the basement. Once there, she removed her socks, curling her toes into the soft, blue carpet fibers. She pulled a box of scrap metal closer, her collected material for practicing her transmutations at home.

Running a finger over her pride and joy disturbed a layer of dust. She'd spent years acquiring all the pieces of her drum set. With its high and mid toms, floor tom, snare, hi-hat, crash cymbal, and a ride cymbal, this was one comfortable throne. To her family's utter delight, when Derek revealed his abilities and flipped her world on its head, her drum practice fell largely to the wayside.

La-Z-Boy chairs that went near horizontal were perfectly spaced in front of the home theater. Since her parents updated the surround sound system, the setup put every movie theater within a thirty-mile radius to shame. Her movie buff parents spared no expense to create the ideal setup for family movie nights. Between their work picking up and Tracy's newfound powers, not to mention the month she disappeared to the past, movie nights were of a bygone era in the Wayfield household.

Tracy promised herself to get the family together for a post-Thanksgiving day of relaxation and do nothing but watch movies.

Louis eyed her full drum set. "Are you still playing in your band?"

Tracy held the drumsticks, twirling them in her hands. She tapped out a quick rhythm. Her music flowed more naturally than breathing and eased the tense knots she held inside. Falling back on the familiar steadied her thoughts to the transmutation task ahead. Tracy replaced the drumsticks in their holster and ran her fingers on the grooved wood. "No. Once I learned about Derek's powers, and later got my own, I sacrificed my dream of playing in a band to spend more time learning about these powers."

Tracy couldn't help looking longingly at her drumsticks, remembering when her biggest concern was finding a gig for her band to play.

"Food is on its way." Victor interrupted. He whirled around the bottom of the stairs to slide next to Louis. "What superpowered awesome sauce do you have for us today?"

Tracy stretched her arms out and popped her knuckles in preparation to astonish her audience.

Connecting her phone to the surround sound speakers, she set the mood with a classical hit from the late 1700s, as performed by the Baltimore Symphony Orchestra. Blended contradictions sounded all around, calming Tracy's racing heart. Given how Mozart's "Jupiter" was his final composed symphony, she hoped that didn't bode poorly for her evening's endeavor.

Tracy sat cross-legged, facing Louis. Tentatively, she reached for the teal mesh cast over his leg. Fingers raced across the surface, pressing between the open spaces to touch Louis's skin. She forced herself to think of him in terms of components.

Much like sensing the complexities within concrete or forged iron swords of the ancient past, she worked her powers to sense his underlying pieces and discover how they combined into the whole. A warm, tingling buzz greeted her fingertips as she delved past outer layers and into contracting muscles. Ever so slowly, she worked her senses inside, searching for the imperfections in muscles and bones.

Spongy new bone had filled in the diagonal gap between the separated edges, hinting at the large scope of the original break. These pieces had all but hardened into what appeared to be swollen bone pressing into muscle, the source of his pain and instability.

Cringing as she prodded deeper beneath his skin, Louis uttered, "Ow! Go easy on me."

"Sorry. I'm trying. There's no manual for my powers." Tracy transmuted the extra knobs of bone into air, drawing it from Louis's body like any other material. Time slipped by as she remodeled the remaining bone to prevent it from pressing into the surrounding muscles.

Tracy wiped lines of sweat dripping from her forehead.

Through his clenched jaw, Louis asked, "Are you almost done?"

"Just finishing with your leg." Tracy studied her transmutation work for faults. She withdrew and sank backward onto the carpet, breathing deeply. "You didn't deserve to be in that car accident. I'm fixing the problem."

"And if Derek could take it back, he would."

Tracy froze, hoping she had misheard. "You knew?"

"From the moment I woke up upside down, hanging by my seat belt." He studied Tracy, holding no malice in his eyes' sweet honey color. "Seeing the guilt on his face told me he was involved somehow. When I watched the police footage of him fighting the Beast, it answered every question I had about my accident."

A great weight welled up in Tracy's chest. Lest it eat away her insides, she shared her burden. "In the name of honesty, fixing you is important, but this is practice for a bigger challenge."

Louis opened his mouth to comment but waited for Tracy to continue before inevitably chewing her out.

"I used my body to practice for you and am using your body to practice for healing Derek's dad."

Louis tensed. "His cancer is back?"

Unable to bring herself to speak, she nodded.

"Wait, you tested this on yourself first?" Louis's voice raised an entire octave by the end of his question, shock plastered on his face.

"Don't sound so surprised, jerkface. I care what happens to you."

"Must be because of my dashing good looks and sense of humor."

At the sound of a ringing doorbell, Victor hopped to his feet. "Whatever you have to tell yourself when you go to sleep at night, Louis," he said, racing from the room.

Victor returned with dinner. Louis helped himself to the lamb strips from his platter. Meanwhile, Tracy shoveled both entrees into her mouth to replenish the energy she'd burned in her precision transmutations. Too soon, she went back to work. The horizontal break in Louis's arm was mostly healed as opposed to the long diagonal line she found in his leg bone.

As she probed inside his arm, Louis's expression made it look like someone had squeezed lemon juice into his eyes. She transmuted the extra bone fragments into air and removed them from inside her friend.

She checked her work, looking for mistakes—particularly any sharp edges that would puncture muscle and negate her healing efforts.

Tracy withdrew her hands from Louis's arm. "According to my WebMD studies, you should be all better. Keep walking with the crutches and don't lift weights until getting checked out by a doctor."

Victor looked back and forth between Tracy and Louis. "That was boring. There was nothing to see except a lot of hand-holding."

"It's over?" Louis asked.

"As far as I can tell, yes." Tracy leaned back, sinking slightly into the carpet.

Louis wiggled his fingers and played an imaginary saxophone. "Sweet! I've been more or less benched in Jazz Band, but now I'm back sooner than I thought!"

"You should take it easy. This is the first time I've done something like this."

"Sure, sure," Louis muttered too quickly.

Tracy sipped mouthfuls of water to ease the sense of dehydration on her tongue. She fought the oncoming nap to recuperate so she wouldn't collapse on the spot.

Louis stood, walking to get another spoonful of juicy lamb strips without using the crutches, testing his repaired leg. He looked to be on the verge of jumping for joy.

Filling the peaceful meal with noise, Louis asked, "How was Nicole there fighting that bear monster with you?

"That Nicole wasn't the one we grew up with." An itch formed in Tracy's throat. She pushed through to not feel the weight of her words. "I miss our Nicole so much. It's difficult to look at the other Nicole, knowing she barely knows me. Although, I like how she's different, but familiar, kind of like when you hear your favorite song performed by a different band."

"Like, as in like-like?"

A glimmer of pain built in her chest for an instant at the thought of being with Nicole. Tracy shook her head to clear it, but still cherished the thought. "I'm not her type, given how she plunged into an alternate world on the chance to rescue Derek."

Louis dropped his fork onto the carpet, his mouth hanging open. "Derek did what?"

Tracy automatically picked up the fork, cleaning her floor with a napkin before a stain set. "*Other* Derek," she told her stunned friend. "Long story short, there's another version of Derek lost in the void."

"That's terrible. I can't imagine more than one Derek."

"Apparently, neither could the universe. Having the pair collide in the void sent us to an alternate Earth and him cascading into the unknown. That's why our Derek went into the void: to look for clues."

"At what point will our Derek die from a guilt overdose?"

Tracy's sarcastic laugh carried a sour aftertaste. "He's acting all kinds of stupid to fix what he caused and bring the other Derek back. I would give up that mountain of gold again to find someone worth leaving my home dimension to find."

"Hold the mint-chocolate chip. You gave up a mountain of gold?"

"I have a lot to fill you in on from when I explored the past. My kitchen is stocked with ice cream if you want to hear all about it."

10

Family Meal

Rachel

Rachel lowered her pencil, unable to concentrate on her homework. Tormenting her nose for hours, smells of turkey wafted from the oven up the stairs and through the gap in her bedroom door. It carried the best versions of home, reminding her of pure warmth and peace.

That is until her mom's lungs blasted her voice to all corners of the house without losing a decibel. "Rachel, please come down and set the—"

Rachel shifted her perceptions, using her powers to speed into the wide hallway, which spread out from her bedroom toward her parents' bedroom and office. She slid down the banister and past her mom at the foot of the stairs. In the eerie stillness offered by her speed powers, her mom appeared to be a strong-willed marble statue, an inescapable force meant to last for centuries.

"—taaaaeeeee—" Imani Mason continued, unaware of Rachel making her way to the kitchen.

Her mom's high cheekbones and smooth skin reminded Rachel of the features she inherited. Imani's engaging brown eyes had a way of making you feel like the only person in the room when she talked to you.

To get back to studying sooner, Rachel maintained her powers to enhance her speed and power walked about her home. She opened modern-styled cabinet drawers for the fancy, spotless cloth placemats while forcing herself to ignore tantalizing aromas from homemade stuffing. Her dad, Darnell Mason, sifted the final spices over his cooling masterpiece on top of the shiny marble counter. She raced into the well-lit dining room and lay the cloth across the table.

"—buuuuuuuulllllllll," her mom finished.

On her second speedy pass for silverware, Rachel gave in, sneaking a spoonful of a cooling dessert. She delighted in the simple perfection of her dad's sweet potato casserole. Cinnamon lit every sensor in her nose and made her mouth water. The gooey marshmallow topping rounded the flavoring, an ever-present reminder to pace herself during the meal so she wouldn't get full before eating the fall treat.

Rachel set the glasses and made another loop around the table to adjust the settings, slowing herself back to normal. Bent forward and panting in the open dining room, she told her mom, still at the foot of the stairs, "Done."

No surprise registered on her mom's face at the blatant use of powers or the slight gusts of wind circling the house in Rachel's wake. Her parents had adapted to this new normal in record time, mostly by putting any piece of paper under heavy objects so they wouldn't blow away.

Rachel caught her breath on the floor next to her black and brown German shepherd, Max. Peeling his wide eyes from the gas stove, the lovable fluffball's tail was wagging. He raised his prematurely gray muzzle, hoping for a few scratches behind the ears. Of course, she obliged.

Her dad took a grindstone to his best cutting knife, going through the motions she'd seen Ri Ur Tol do dozens of times. The diminutive man's stature explained why Rachel never broke the five-foot height marker. His face was as clean-shaven as the top of his head, the sheen of which reminded her of a brass instrument.

"There's nothing wrong with living life at its intended pace," her dad said from the side of his mouth.

"I have too much to get done and never enough time," countered Rachel.

Since he was wholly focused on carving the twenty-pound turkey, Rachel rescued the used gravy-stirring spoon before it made it safely to the dishwasher and rewarded her good boy for being a good boy. Sloppy wet smacking sounds told Rachel that Max had found the hidden utensil behind her back and out of her dad's view.

"The laziest dog in the world will keep begging for more if you encourage him like that," her dad admonished.

"How can you say no to that face?" Rachel rubbed her dog's belly. "Doggo's earned an extra snack or two, haven't you, Max?"

Rachel brought dinner into the dining room, organizing the trays of stuffing, stuffed portobello mushrooms, cornbread, and roasted carrot and beet salad on the trivets.

She and her mom settled into their seats. Rachel's foot tapped the carpet, her eyes ravenously following the turkey with the eagerness of one tormented by the smells of it being cooked all day. She licked her lips in anticipation.

This amount of food for the three of them typically lasted for two weeks. It was so much, in fact, her family always agreed to wait a full year before thinking about turkey again. Factoring in her powers, Rachel guessed leftovers might stretch for a week, helped along by the fact she was spending the rest of the long weekend at training. Otherwise, the multi-course meal would have been gone in two days, tops. A pang of guilt gave her pause that she could eat so much of her family's food so fast.

To offset the monstrous proportions of their meal, her Lawful Good parents were dropping off a separate thirty-five-pound frozen turkey to a nearby homeless shelter. The shelter accepted donations to feed everyone in the coming winter months. That was why the Mason family had their Thanksgiving meals at one in the afternoon.

Her dad entered the room with the turkey and gravy. "Are you ready for finals and college prep amid the hassle of saving the world?"

The meal hadn't officially started yet, and they were already prodding her with questions about school. Rachel added more to her plate, planning to save herself from answering by filling her mouth with food. "There are too many assignments for me to make up, so I don't know how to deal with life right now."

"You'll find a way to finish all your schoolwork," Rachel's mom said.

Rachel gritted her teeth, feeling her blood rising at the unhelpful rhetoric. "Maybe. Unless I catch up quick, I won't be presenting myself at my best to my top-pick school. It will already be tight for me to meet the application deadline."

Her dad submerged his turkey in an ocean of gravy. "If you don't get into Virginia Tech, your second favorite will be perfect for you."

Her mom took a different approach to gravy, spreading one drop on her plate to be used for dipping both slices of turkey. "Stay positive, and you'll do well in any electrical engineering program."

Rachel's fingers tensed into misshapen bird claws. "That's easy for you to say. You've been taking apart toasters and telephones for the past half century with grandpa. Whenever I visit him, he still shows me that picture of you with a screwdriver in your hand before you learned to walk. I don't want that."

"I never wanted to pressure you into a career path," her mom said in her deliberate parenting voice Rachel hated. "Engineering is what you told us you wanted to study."

"What will you study instead?" asked her dad.

"Since coming back from the past, my teachers have been so unbelievably understanding with every makeup lesson after school, and it's really made a difference for me. I want to do that for students too, but on a regular basis, not just when they're behind in their work." *My teachers have shown more passion in two weeks than you ever have for your drone jobs.* "I want to teach."

"With your grades, you can succeed at anything."

"Argh!" A piece of beet flew from Rachel's mouth. "GPAs do a terrible job at showing the effort I put in. My easiest class showers me with an A, while I have to study physics daily to limp to my B-. It won't be so simple to just get into any program."

Her mom hesitated, shifting her gaze to Rachel's dad. A silent cue floated between them. "You're an inspiring young woman, and you'd make a brilliant teacher."

"Speaking of inspiring, your mom and I rearranged our schedules to attend your concert on Saturday."

Rachel's half-eaten bite of turkey dropped from her fork. "Right. Crap. I need to be in two places at once or skip training."

Sensing the tension in the room, her parents fell into more superficial topics of conversation. In her head, Rachel walked through all possibilities for managing school, training, and life. There was no way to achieve a balance; she was bailing water on a sinking rowboat.

* * *

"My parents are the worst!" Rachel shouted.

"I agree," John said in his deadpan voice. "Your supportive parents sound like awful people."

Rachel lifted her hand from the soft grass they sat on to squeeze John's hand. Stars above gazed down at them, envious of their contact. "You know what I mean."

John lowered his plate of the Mason's reheated sweet potato casserole and wrapped his free arm around her shoulders, soothing her tight muscles. "I do," he whispered. "Your parents would rather lift you up so you can soar than have you stand next to them on the ground."

Another pinprick of a bright dot came into view in the night sky, fighting against the light pollution from her house and the heated pool. Rachel checked her watch, her feet bouncing nervously at realizing the time. At best, they had another thirty minutes before her parents came home from the shelter.

"Are powers worth this struggle?" John asked, interrupting her thoughts.

"Given how I use them to protect everyone I care about, there's no question in my mind."

"Aren't these powers causing all your problems?"

"Abilities aren't without drawbacks, yet the benefits vastly outweigh the tolls on my body. No one else on the planet experiences what I do when I open the Aspect to raise my speed."

"Fine, you have a handle on your abilities," John started and stopped. "What about Derek? Or Tracy? Admit it, your life wouldn't be half as stressful if not for your adventures across time."

"My life for the near future is climbing out of the hole that missing five weeks created. Without that journey, we would never have survived the Beast."

Ripping noises came from the ground as John yanked a handful of grass and tossed it into the air. The green blades scattered, some falling quickly and others spinning and landing on her back porch. "Have you heard what people think you, Derek, and the rest are doing? Reports come in daily of miraculous saves from impending car crashes up and down the 495 Beltway."

"I've been too busy to catch any news, and it can't be Derek or any of the others. Should I be concerned with how much you're thinking about Derek while we're together?"

Hopping to his feet, John yanked another fistful of grass. "Fine. I'll focus on you and even help expand your training." Gesturing at his fist, he said, "Every time you catch a piece of grass, you get a kiss from me. Whenever one touches the ground, I get a kiss from you."

Rachel couldn't help but smile. She stood and pressed her lips against John's sealed mouth. Comfort spread from where their lips met, sinking into the rest of her. Her heart didn't beat at a humming-bird pace as it did the first time she kissed him, all wrapped up in nerves and errant thoughts. This kiss set a steadier beat. Their world might fall apart, but together she and John would face it. Kissing him was like basking under the sun on a frigid day, a moment of pure fire when all else dimmed. "You're lucky you're cute."

John leaned back, one hand folded around her waist. "Cute? Not hot or dashing or distractingly sexy?"

"Don't push it."

John tossed the green stems of grass over his shoulder.

She watched them fall, each blade of grass representing the fluttering seconds between now and when she needed to leave for this weekend's training.

Rachel pulled John closer. She stood on her toes to kiss him, ignoring the rest of his silly game.

11

Tradition

Tracy

Tracy's jacket saved her from the shrill wind wailing across the bridge. Ri Ur Tol refused to shiver under her own jacket, though Tracy doubted her friend had ever experienced a climate that dropped below sub-tropical heat.

They walked laps from the shopping center on one side of the bridge to the construction site on the other. As the Cold Snap was closed so Louis's family could eat together, she paced to help her think. That, and to work off her third helping of gravy-drenched turkey.

She was surprised none of her other friends had driven to the shopping center's parking lot after Thanksgiving dinner, congregating here out of habit. She half expected Louis to unlock the Cold Snap's door and turn on the lights for her.

Unlike her friends, the police were out in numbers. Several cop cars barricaded the road, stopping every vehicle passing by the shopping center and forcing the drivers to take a breathalyzer test. For once, she appreciated the intention behind the police's presence.

Midway through their second pass over the highway, Ri Ur Tol asked, "Do your people normally eat their own weight at the end of every harvest? I have never eaten such an over-indulgent meal in all my nineteen harvests."

"Thanksgiving is a time-honored tradition of excess. Be glad we'll be training tomorrow and missing the other tradition, Black Friday. Although I would like to see how you fare in the holiday rush."

Ri Ur Tol patted her stomach. "One tradition is fine for me. I won't need to eat again until the next new moon."

"You should feel honored. This home-cooked meal is one of the rare days my parents go all out with baking instead of ordering in food."

"What is next for your culture's celebrations?"

"Normally, we stare at the television to watch games. We have that to look forward to when you feel like heading back to my house." Tracy ran a hand over the new cement used to fill in the deep grooves the Beast scratched into the structure during its first attack. The lingering discoloration proved not all scars fully heal. "I do have a confession. There were ulterior motives for inviting you to Thanksgiving dinner. I survived fighting with the shadow in the park thanks to luck. The shadow monster is still in the void, and I know it will find a way into this world. Help me form a plan to defeat it."

"Why me?"

"You're resourceful and stunningly intelligent in a fight."

Ri Ur Tol blushed, or it might have been the cold tingeing her cheeks. "We know the creature cannot withstand living in this world. It fades with everything we've seen it come in contact with." Ri Ur Tol met Tracy's eyes. "You can reform this world into objects to attack it and turn it into smoke faster, making you our prime defense against the shadow."

"You're saying we need to protect me?" Tracy asked, her frown deepening. "I like your plan, but it's not much more than we had already."

Ri Ur Tol grunted. "I am warming up. What does the shadow desire?"

"I never got the chance to ask when it was trying to kill me."

Ri Ur Tol's glare forced Tracy to bite back her wit. "All creatures have desires."

"It did grab some of your people when it momentarily escaped the void in the past," Tracy added, trying to help.

"The creature lunged for you as well in the park. Perhaps it intends to eat the living."

Sharp wailing sirens alerted Tracy to the excitement on the highway below. Speeding from the shopping center, a sports car weaved between traffic, trailed by multiple police cars. Free of the long row of slow cars, the fleeing vehicle had nothing but open road to speed up further and increase the gap ahead of the police. They were going to get away.

Light reflected oddly on the highway concrete for a fraction of a second. The sports car wobbled as it passed over the spot, skidding into the adjacent lane. Screeching tires fought for traction, marring the road with rubber marks. The driver regained control of the car, except rather than continue speeding ahead, they slowed and pulled onto the shoulder.

A middle-aged man stepped out of their vehicle, near enough to Tracy and Ri Ur Tol above on the bridge to see his unsteady crooked gait.

Tracy clicked *tut-tut* sounds. "This is one of the worst days of the year for drunk driving."

The man got on his knees with his hands behind his head and the cop roughly handcuffed him, driving him to the ground.

"They really hate it when you leave your car," Tracy explained.

"I am glad he gave up without a fight." Ri Ur Tol returned the knives in her hands into the folds of her jacket. "I have been forced to remove men and women behaving in odd manners after celebrating more than they could handle."

The man's shouts smoothed from disoriented rabble to coherent anger. On the walk to the back of the police car, his footfalls were even and not stumbling as they had been when he first stepped from his car. All signs of inebriation he showed had vanished within a minute.

Tracy looked at the spot where she had seen the glint on the highway that caused the speeding car to swerve. The road looked normal now. This night may be cold, but it was above freezing. Ice appearing and disappearing in seconds was impossible, not without the aid of a power.

She scanned behind every tree below, uncertain whether she wanted to find someone or was terrified of crossing paths with another person who possessed powers.

No one stood out in the poorly lit area as she hurried back to her car, dragging Ri Ur Tol by the hand.

12

Questions and Favors

Derek

Untamed underbrush threatened to swallow a poorly tied sneaker as Derek's sluggish feet trudged forward. Morning sunlight shone past empty treetop canopies, baking his skin beneath his long-sleeved shirt. Sweat formed on his chest, tempting him to remove his outer layer. Though doing so would blind him for a fraction of a second and leave him open to an attack.

His stomach stretched and contracted, settling back to normal after last night's Thanksgiving dinner.

Towering trees filling this forest appeared as soulless pillars, their spirits disappearing as leaves fell, to return in spring. In their place, bare trunks held a hundred years of secrets within their bark.

He listened for crunching from piles of dried fallen orange and brown foliage, waiting for a sound to reveal his sparring partner's position. Instead, he heard a woodpecker searching for nutritious bugs by hammering its beak into a tree.

Earthen aromas of dew-soaked moss carried hints of the forest he grew up in, albeit a much older, distant cousin.

Separated from his home by a two-hour drive, if one disregarded speed limits, this forest might have once stretched all the way to his backyard. On a clear summer day, he could catch hints of this mountain range from the tallest buildings in Bethesda.

Spinning Sharpie markers crossed his vision.

Self-preservation took over.

Derek threw a mental fist, sending the markers sideways.

"HEY!" he shouted to no one visible. "You aimed at my face."

Soft humming gave away her position. Derek almost imagined Nicole's head bobbing up and down while she psyched herself up to attack with an improvised tune.

Nicole leaped from behind a stunted oak tree, her body angled like an action hero. She threw another marker halfway through her dramatic dive.

Derek jumped aside from the wild throws. The motion sent his sling-wrapped arm banging into his chest.

"You're getting better," he encouraged.

She tapped the bridge of her nose. "My accuracy's gotten much better without these glasses. Your Nicole was right to switch to contacts."

"Now, all you need to work on is not broadcasting your hiding spot by singing."

"You have your methods, and I have mine."

"Practice your methods so they don't give away your position."

Nicole brushed leaves and dirt from her spandex fighting outfit, which Tracy crafted for her. The brown, red, and orange camouflage pattern hid her well when she remained still. She pulled a pointy red leaf from her hair, which matched its color, and added, "There's no point in practicing against you if you half-ass it. I'm nowhere near Ri Ur Tol's skill, and you subdued her when she tried to slit Tracy's throat back in the ancient past."

"She wasn't expecting me to be awake, or to have powers. Besides, Tracy was her target, not me. I wouldn't last a minute with her in a fair fight."

"Still, our matches are over the instant you use your abilities."

Derek quelled rising nerves, which had distracted him all morning. He suppressed his powers to prevent from using them while fueled with this much stress. Otherwise he would be feeding his Beast. His hand slid to the hilt of the broken sword strapped to his back, using it to siphon his excess power. Useless as a fighting weapon, it craved more power, finding new life as a battery for a rainy day.

"Neither of us would learn a thing if I won by overusing my gifts. Minus that last throw, your aim is improving, and I'm getting a better sense of preventing bodily harm." He raised his sling to emphasize his point.

Snap.

Ri Ur Tol appeared in front of him, her boot catching him in the chest. Crumpling leaves absorbed none of his weight as he fell to the ground.

Standing over him, Ri Ur Tol said, "You lie. All others improve except you."

Nicole joined Ri Ur Tol's side and offered her hand to pull Derek upright as he winced from the new injuries. "What were you saying about preventing bodily harm?" Somehow Nicole's facial expression conveyed both a sneer and pained sympathy from also knowing every curve of the bottom of Ri Ur Tol's boot.

The right words failed Derek. He brushed the back of his neck, where he intentionally didn't count how many twigs fell from his sweat-matted hair. "I'm working on controlling my powers," said Derek, "which is much more important than increasing my raw power."

Ri Ur Tol drew a dagger in each hand so suddenly it was as though she had teleported them. "Nicole is correct. You do not try. Fight me now. If you still refuse to devote yourself to the task, you will not survive."

Staring at either edged point made him lose the nerve to ask her for his planned favor. "You're going to kill me?" Derek asked with shock in his voice.

Ri Ur Tol spun her daggers in a flashy motion. "Better for us if you die now, at my hands, than fall when we rely on you during the hunt."

Nicole's eyes went to her feet, unwilling to defend Derek or defy the person instructing them to fight. Softly, Nicole hummed a classic tune from a movie he couldn't place.

Ri Ur Tol flicked her wrists, and Derek struggled to raise his telekinetic shield in time.

The two daggers ricocheted from his shield. Unexpected fathoms of power bubbled to the surface. Every breath enriched Derek's muscles. Like a sprinter crouched in the starting block, he wanted to unleash this new overflowing power.

Derek restrained his abilities from launching a counterattack. His Beast was out there, somewhere, waiting for him to slip and use his powers in anger so he could, in turn, feed his Beast his power.

Ri Ur Tol caught one of her rebounding knives, flipping it forward to strike Derek's shield. She used her full weight to press the point deeper.

He adjusted his telekinetic shield to sag around the blade like a deflating balloon.

Her eyebrows raised, a rare moment of surprise, to witness the depth of his controlled manipulation.

He sent more power to hold off Ri Ur Tol's attack. The palm of her free hand struck her blade's pommel. Under the strain, she flexed her muscles, revealing the tight cords of someone well-versed in combat.

She was no longer advancing; his protection held.

Her head shook from side to side in disapproval. Derek had made a mistake.

Snap.

Rippling air disturbances came from behind.

He spun too slowly, unable to reform the telekinetic shield behind him. Ri Ur Tol's blade stopped an inch short of piercing his eye. She pulled her dagger back, allowing Derek to let his racing heartbeat return to normal. He stumbled back from her to increase the gap separating them.

Ri Ur Tol did not advance. "You pooled your defense to the point of your attention, drawing from everywhere else and leaving your back exposed. Do not fall for my simple deceit again."

"How do I fix it?" asked Derek.

"Learn from your mistakes. This was more or less what Tracy told me to do to beat you after she used a similar trick."

Derek recalled Tracy's paint balloons, which got through his telekinetic shield in the initial days of discovering his powers. He realized his worse mistake: allowing thoughts to wander beyond this battlefield. Ri Ur Tol renewed her attack, her dagger becoming a blur of stabs and thrusts.

All he could do was parry by forming small telekinetic shields over his hands. His powers had faded over the drawn-out training fights, too weak to fully enclose himself in a protective bubble.

Mindful of his growing exhaustion, Ri Ur Tol didn't draw a second blade. Their duel was already unbalanced in her favor. Derek stepped back to gain breathing room. Ri Ur Tol pressed forward to steal his respite.

The faster adversary slapped his unprotected forearm with the flat end of her blade.

"Pretend it was severed and use your arm no longer. You should have stopped the attack."

"Sorry."

"Do not apologize. Seal mortar in the hole allowing your thoughts to drip out."

The slight lull in conversation gave him a moment to regain his breath and the possibility of asking Ri Ur Tol his planned question. Under her determined gaze, he decided to wait until after he was done failing her training.

Derek adjusted, putting his hand behind his back, and losing it as a means of balance.

She slowed her stabbing motions, returning this to a lesson rather than an all-out fight. He set a small telekinetic shield between himself and the point. Ri Ur Tol stabbed faster. Derek sped up to match, forming the protective wall in front of him. Leaping to the side around his defenses, Ri Ur Tol slashed in a wide arc. He leaned away from the attack and set a new barrier to absorb the blow.

Together, they danced, Ri Ur Tol leading by the point of her dagger.

Derek lost ground until his back bumped into a tree.

He used his abilities to spin around the tree as wide as his wing-span. Landing on the balls of his feet, he fired a telekinetic slash. His attack nicked the tree, held at bay from doing harm by Ri Ur Tol's blade.

"Good," she said. "You finally fought back."

He sent another mental slash in her direction. It scattered the leaves on the ground where she had stood. A blade appeared at his throat, Ri Ur Tol having swung around the other side of the tree to catch him unaware.

"Never doubt your magic and don't be afraid to move in close to strike."

For the first time he had ever witnessed, her mouth opened, and its sides lifted into a toothy smile. To Derek, the end effect cast her face in a menacing grimace. "I have learned what a minute is, and despite what you declared to Nicole moments ago, you lasted longer than a sixty count in this fight."

"That's what I tell my Derek, too." Nicole raised her hand for a high five. When no one smacked her waiting hand, she lifted Ri Ur Tol's and used it to slap her own in acknowledgment.

Ri Ur Tol withdrew, defeating Nicole with a mere icy look. "Come, we shall see how the others progress."

They returned to Mr. Marshal's mansion. From the outside, it looked like one of those southern refurbished restaurants where a new wing cropped up right when you thought you finally walked to the end. Aside from its size, the unassuming exterior appeared normal, proof that appearances were deceiving shells.

A trail of smoke rose from the metal grates above an open grill, carrying smells of lunch. Derek wiped the drool rolling from the corner of his mouth from the cooking burgers.

"Back already?" Mr. Marshal asked.

He flipped the burgers, adding life to the fire as grease dripped below and burned.

Nearby, Tracy and Rachel sparred. Heavy breathing and smacking sounds came from their heated fight. An arm's length apart,

Tracy threw a punch Rachel knocked aside. Their back heels leaned against a wall that stopped at their knees, prohibiting either from retreating without falling.

"Switch!" Flint barked.

The pair paused, alternating their forward arms and legs. Tracy gazed longingly at the cooking food, pleading with her eyes for help from Derek.

"Begin," Flint commanded.

Rachel swung for Tracy's head, only for Tracy to deflect it by spinning her arm upward. Neither used their powers, bending the advantage in favor of Tracy's agility and reach. Years of video games had paid off by raising her hand-eye coordination off the charts.

Rachel dodged and countered, instincts saving her more than once from a Tracy punch. Once blocking became too much effort for Rachel or Tracy, they threw punches at one another, not caring where they struck.

Uncertain who to cheer for, or even if he should cheer, Derek wanted to cover his eyes from the brutal training. He longed for the early days of these powers, where Tracy threw paint balloons at him and invented whimsical games by comparison.

Rachel shielded her face, leaving her stomach and shoulder exposed. Her body absorbed each hit with a grunt. "Don't be lazy," Rachel said with the wheezing effort of a ninety-year-old woman who still smoked a pack a day. "You hit me harder than that an hour ago."

Rachel's punch caught the side of Tracy's face as Tracy turned from the hit, reducing the knockout punch to a glancing blow.

Tracy's eyes narrowed. Her back foot kicked off the wall, throwing herself at Rachel and disregarding the fist fight altogether. Tracy's tackle sent them both to the ground. The short wall intended to hold Rachel in place tripped her at the back of the knee.

They both hit the ground hard. Tracy rolled to the side, panting from the exertion. She sat up and shook her head. "Sorry. I don't know where that came from."

Derek ran forward to help, but Tracy had already picked herself up.

Together, Derek and Tracy got Rachel upright as she said, "You did what I told you to. I'm fine." Rachel dusted herself off with a laugh, but her stiff-set jaw said that was a lie.

Mr. Marshal ran over, worry forming creases on his forehead. Derek's guidance counselor likely checked to ensure he didn't need to make a hospital run with a minor. "In the end, that's all there is."

"What did you expect?" Rachel challenged Mr. Marshal's babbled nonsense. "We aren't fighters."

Flint pulled a marker from his pocket. "Your enemies won't be wielding these coloring toys. They'll be coming at you with real weapons, which is how I learned to fight."

"My training was more intense than this, and I was less than half your age when I started," added Ri Ur Tol.

Tracy made her way to the lunch table, calling over her shoulder, "We aren't in the past you grew up in. We don't need to train for war."

Mr. Marshal stared into the woods, gazing far from everyone present. "What you face has proven to be dangerous. You need to train harder."

Derek, Rachel, and Nicole followed Tracy to the spread of food for lunch. Their three instructors talked closely together. Despite his beckoning stomach, Derek leaned on the cool wooden porch railing, trying to hear what they were saying. Too far to grasp anything useful, Derek went to the food and layered his hamburger patty between sesame buns with lettuce, a sliced tomato, cheddar cheese, and ketchup. Done with their conversation, Ri Ur Tol and Flint walked to the table to make their meals.

Nicole pushed a hamburger into each of Tracy's and Rachel's hands and said, "Those were quite some moves you both threw at each other. Is anyone else worried about injuring ourselves training here before we take on the next monster?"

"That is a concern. Keep in mind, our combined efforts defeated the shadow monster, yet we did no more than hold the Beast at bay," said Ri Ur Tol. "We have much room to improve."

She looked at Derek, seemingly with hope of supporting what she said. She had been with him for the final punch to stop his Beast. Ri Ur Tol knew how narrowly they avoided dying. That was precisely why he held back in these training exercises; to prevent his Beast from chowing down on morsels of his power.

"I agree," said Nicole, faster than Derek could respond.

Everyone turned to her.

"Well, we can't go home until we clear the shadow monster from the void."

"Aren't you on some quest to find the other Derek first?" Rachel asked.

"That was implied in the 'we.' I'm not going home without him. Finding Derek and returning home require us to move freely through the void. Then, *you*-Derek can take us back to the point where we left so that I can pick up my life from there."

Tracy prepped a second course on her plate. "You may want to rethink that last point. We hoped for the same thing and wound up losing five weeks when Derek got us back. Time had moved forward relative to our travels."

Mr. Marshal hovered over Derek's shoulder. "You treat your abilities like a wall to smash through."

Derek added a fistful of potato chips to his plate. His mind was juggling far too much to spend lunch on self-reflection. "You sound like my dad."

"He must be a smart man." In the same breath, Mr. Marshal faced Rachel. "You leave too many openings. Enemies are not your friends."

She nodded, but then said, "Not everyone's an enemy. Besides, who says enemies can't grow to one day become friends?"

"My experience tells me otherwise," replied Mr. Marshal. "Although I admire your naive optimism."

When Mr. Marshal rounded on Tracy, she made a *stop* motion with her raised palm. "I already know I'm flawless."

Mr. Marshal didn't laugh or otherwise acknowledge her comment. "Recklessness is your downfall, particularly when triggered by frustration."

Mr. Marshal left them to go inside. His words acted like a thundercloud steadily moving farther into the distance, its light flashes growing dimmer and its sounds fading to nothing.

The three friends fumed, lost in their individual worlds until Ri Ur Tol and Flint started the afternoon training.

Derek walked back to the tree line with Nicole and Ri Ur Tol.

Flint followed the trio. "I wish to speak with you," he said to Derek.

Ri Ur Tol whispered to Nicole and sent her on ahead. Ri Ur Tol moved out of earshot, giving Derek and Flint privacy.

"Why do you insist on traveling into the void where my master fled?" Flint asked.

"I have a promise to keep. What's the big deal? I went in once since coming home from the past and learned my lesson not to do it again by myself."

Flint placed his hand on Derek's shoulder and held him in place. "Have you opened the doorway to the void more than once since returning from my time?"

Derek tried to slip from Flint's grasp, but the man held firm. "No. I went in and came out. Those were the only times."

Flint looked Derek over, searching for something. "I have sensed multiple hand's worth of crackling magic from doorways opening to the void. I do not get to them until long after they have sealed on their own. Most proved to be unfinished, though I fear my master's hand and his desire to break into the time I am in."

"I haven't sensed any more of the void's disruptions."

"You are not adept at sensing magic, nor do you search for what you do not expect." Flint unwound and wound the chains wrapped around his upper body, the metal clanging together. "We cannot wait. We must find my master within the void and destroy him."

"Did you not hear what Nicole said? The void isn't safe with that shadow thing free inside. I won't be entering the void again without a plan."

"Then I will continue to train you all until we can travel into the void safely." Flint leaped into the trees, his thick boots landing on a low branch. Using his chains, he swung back toward the house.

A shudder crept over Derek at the thought of anyone who could rile Flint and consume him so completely.

"Ready for your afternoon exercises?" Ri Ur Tol said, seemingly pleased at how high Derek jumped at the sound of her voice.

His heart rate cartwheeled inside his chest. More than from the sudden shock, his body refused to slow now that it recognized they were alone. This was what he wanted. He calculated the number of steps in his head until they rejoined Nicole. That number halved in their walk through the woods, yet he remained silent.

I can't ask her to risk her life on a chance, but I won't survive without her.

The usual sounds of a breeze rustling leaves or a squirrel's claws scurrying across bark were absent. The woods held their breath. He looked at Ri Ur Tol. She opened her mouth to say something but stopped.

The number of steps to their destination halved again.

He opened and closed his hands, feeling blood roaring under his skin.

"Next weekend, do you want me to take you on a tour of this present time?" Derek blurted out, practically shouting the words. Far from the favor he wanted to request, he settled for this stalling tactic to find the right moment to ask her to risk her life with him.

The smile on Ri Ur Tol's face seemed to be formed from an inside joke where the punchline was at his expense. "Sounds better than teaching you to hunt."

13

Green and Gold

Derek

A day later and Derek's world remained crumbling beneath his feet, no sturdier despite his night's rest. His twice-snoozed phone alarm insisted on starting the Saturday morning.

Wishing his bed were quicksand to swallow him whole, Derek lifted his head from his pillow. The minimalistic bed was soft, but not in the right way, having yet to mold to the curvature of his body. His plain room held none of the trappings of home, caught in the transition of becoming an extended hotel stay in Mr. Marshal's training mansion. On the one hand, the room begged him to add his own flavors to the decorations. On the other, an outer coating of posters and pictures would remind him how, underneath it all, this room wasn't his bedroom.

His cloud-white IKEA desk clashed with the futuristic orbital station metal motif of the walls, floor, and ceiling.

Someone knocked at his door, and before he could open it, Tracy and Rachel entered. Tracy pushed aside the textbooks and incomplete homework on his desk to make room for her plate of food. Rachel wheeled in her chair from a few doors down.

"I woke up to your message," Rachel's smile was way too broad for his discomfort. "Tell us all the details."

He was already regretting telling them about his date with Ri Ur Tol next week. "I didn't intend to ask her out. The words slipped out."

"There's your problem right there, Derek." Tracy leaned back in Derek's chair so far he now stared at her upside-down face. She pressed a finger to her temple. "A lot got lost in the space between your brain and your mouth."

Tracy spun in the seat and took a bite of her pancake doused in syrup. "What did you think would happen?"

Watching Tracy chew the syrup with a dash of pancake made his teeth feel like they were rotting. He settled for one of the strawberry Pop-Tarts he kept in his nightstand, afraid to walk to Mr. Marshal's dining room on the off chance Ri Ur Tol was there. "That wasn't what I was going for."

Rachel piped up, consuming her pancake stack enthusiastically, and repeated Tracy's question. "What were you going for?"

"All I wanted was help exploring the void," Derek admitted. "Not some date."

Rachel leaned forward, her energetic go-get-'em morning attitude dissolved. In its place was a stern mom hovering over his bed, telling him he wasn't sick and needed to get his ass to school. "I know you're smart enough not to go into the void with that shadow thing inside, right?"

The light from his desk played tricks on Tracy's face to make the bags under her eyes appear to be lengthening. She licked her lips and looked at him like he was her next meal, skewered on the end of her fork and covered in sugar. "Open it! Open it! Open it!"

Derek shrank beneath the covers. "Aren't you afraid of the shadow monster?"

Tracy's expression settled back to normal, and her attention returned to her last piece of pancake. She spun the fluffy carb to absorb the remaining syrup on the plate. "Of course."

"With Ri Ur Tol's help, I can snap past the shadow and continue the search for the other me."

Synchronized beeping noises sparked from Rachel's phone. "That's my wake-up alarm to start our morning training session."

Training meant spending the day with Ri Ur Tol. Derek pressed his hand to his forehead. "Can I get an excused absence? I think I'm catching a cold."

Rachel shook her head. "Nope."

Derek extracted his limbs from the blankets, moving as though Tracy had transmuted them into iron.

In their walk to the front entrance, Derek caught a whiff of himself and regretted his every decision. Tracy and Rachel kept him from regular morning routines, and the fact he hadn't showered was plain to see, or in this case, smell.

The others were waiting for the three of them. Ri Ur Tol looked as prepared for the morning as Rachel. She stood at attention, her eyes facing forward. She nodded at him.

Derek couldn't remember if that was how she normally greeted him or if the gesture held some hidden meaning. Her look passed by Derek without him mustering a hand wave. He hadn't thought ahead to nod back.

He wiped a clammy hand on his shirt.

Derek forced his thoughts to settle. He was creating problems where there were none.

Morning training sent him, Nicole, and Ri Ur Tol sprinting across the woods. Ri Ur Tol worked them all physically, building stamina and strength within muscles Derek rarely used. In a way, it made sense. Running from his Beast in the under-construction suburbia taught him an important lesson: he was out of shape. Fighting for air while fighting for his life was a sure way to wind up dead.

Ri Ur Tol pushed Derek, but no more so than she did Nicole.

Maybe he had dodged this speeding train, and Ri Ur Tol didn't think next weekend was a date. Better yet, maybe her people didn't go on dates. No hope was too small in his mind. He wanted to kick himself at how he lugged high school anxieties into his weekend away from classes. Luckily, Ri Ur Tol kept them moving at a pace to leave him breathless. Derek couldn't speak, even if he thought of something to say.

Lunch was the same: the girls congregated together, leaving Derek stuck with Flint for riveting conversation. The man regarded him, but seemed no more interested in asking about Derek's morning than any other facet of the past ten thousand years. Derek munched on his hot dog paired with a cheese-covered baked potato, all without uttering a word.

Flint wrapped and unwrapped the small links around his fingers and shifted the bandages around his upper body. Though he looked like a burn victim, Derek knew otherwise. The few times Flint exposed his skin, it was a normal bronze shade. The power he unleashed when the bindings were undone, though, was nothing short of terrifying. He became an unnatural disaster, able to redirect lightning to burn the face off a thirty-foot bear monster.

In Flint, Derek saw his future, one in which he trapped his power inside. It was better to live with a trickle of power offered by opening the Aspect gates than power-up his Beast until one of them killed the other. Derek had scraped by in their last fight. He had done the math and recalled every second. No matter how he looked at it, he should not have survived.

Mr. Marshal stepped outside to join them. "This afternoon will be team battles. I hope you are fans of Capture the Flag."

Those born in this century let out whoops of joy. Capture the Flag was much easier than their typical exercises to push their powers and hone their fighting skills. Ri Ur Tol's and Flint's neutral faces showed how little the game's title meant out of context.

"To balance experience and power, the teams will be Derek, Rachel, and Ri Ur Tol versus Tracy, Nicole, and Flint."

Mr. Marshal handed a green bandana to Ri Ur Tol and a gold one to Flint. "Today's challenge is to take the other team's flag. They need to be clearly displayed at about head height. Ri Ur Tol, take your team north. Flint, your team goes south. Walk about four hundred paces and hang the flag."

"It's fall break," said Tracy. "You don't have to showcase our school colors over vacation."

Derek's uneasiness melted into excitement. "I love Capture the Flag!"

A rare smile cracked on Mr. Marshal's face. "Me too. Growing up, I played this game all the time."

Childhood memories floated around Derek, calling him back to simpler times. "You and every kid went who went to summer camp. My camper versus counselor matches were nothing short of epic."

Nicole let out a snicker. "I bet we could put your games to shame. We once had a hundred people racing through the woods when we got bored at a band competition weekend."

Rachel inspected the flag as though expecting it to sprout wings. "I appreciate Capture the Flag being a constant across dimensions, but are there any special rules for your version, Mr. Marshal? What about people who get tagged out? How can they rejoin their team?"

"The rules are simple. Use your powers to win. As for tagging each other out, there are no easy methods to remove opponents or regain lost comrades in fights. Tagging will not remove someone from this competition. This is all-or-nothing. Subdue your opponents if you want, but the first team to meet here with the flag wins."

"What do we get if we win?" Tracy asked.

"The team that wins earns an extra rest day, and the team that loses owes extra practice sessions. Any other questions? No? Then, begin!"

Ri Ur Tol marched Derek and Rachel into the woods. Derek kept peering over his shoulder to gauge the direction Flint's team was moving.

Looking back was easier than looking ahead. Ri Ur Tol moved with surefooted confidence for one who had never played this game. Her brown yoga pants and long-sleeved shirt combination looked much more forest friendly than Derek in his school-themed long-sleeved shirt and sweatpants. Rachel seemed the most outlandish with her light-blue sweatshirt. Discreet, they were not.

Ri Ur Tol waved her hand in front of Derek's face. "Focus."

"Focus? This game is meant to be fun." He sprang into action, looking for the best strategic location for the flag. All the while, he wished Ri Ur Tol were on the other team so he could spend the immediate future hiding from her.

Ri Ur Tol didn't relax, probably assuming Flint or Tracy were already stalking them. "This is a serious hunting exercise. No room for fun. Flint will expect Rachel or me to scout and attack unprotected flanks. We counter his move by waiting for their strike. Then we adapt to them, using our speed to hit their weaknesses."

A Derek-quality plan was coming together. "Why don't I distract them alone so you two can get their flag?"

Ri Ur Tol pointed to his wrapped arm. "With your healing injury and unwillingness to draw your full power, you will have a different role. This, you will not like."

Ri Ur Tol's explanation made Derek question whether she had an ounce of sanity left.

Rachel looked ecstatic to be the sling to Derek's stone. "It's crude, yet effective. I'm in."

"You're right," he replied. "I don't like this idea."

"Then fight better."

Ri Ur Tol's words were a kick to his gut.

Music erupted from nearby. It took a few seconds for Derek to recognize it as one of Tracy's ex-band's songs.

Derek scanned every direction for an attack. Ri Ur Tol's entire body was tense, ready to stop the other team's advance. Rachel's hand stiffly moved into her pocket, like she was pretending if she moved slow enough, Derek wouldn't notice. Her finger tapped the distinct outline of a phone.

There were too many questions for Derek to ask, so he stuck with, "That's what you chose as a ringtone?"

Rachel flicked the screen, ending the music. "Our girl has talent. It's what I set my reminder alert to. Sorry, but I have to go."

Gone in a blur, Rachel left Derek alone with Ri Ur Tol.

Snap. Derek was standing by himself.

Snap. Ri Ur Tol and Rachel appeared in front of him, with Ri Ur Tol holding Rachel in place.

"Get off me!" Rachel broke free of Ri Ur Tol's grip.

Ri Ur Tol spoke without straining her voice, as though wrangling Rachel were as simple as tying her shoes, which someone must have already taught the girl from the past how to do. "Where are you running to?"

Giving up, Rachel stayed in place. "School. I have a concert I need to play at. Will you let me go so I can get to my other obligation?"

"We hunt together. We do not abandon each other."

Rachel glanced at Derek for help. "My grade depends on my participation. I planned today down to the second, and you're making me late. I thought this exercise would be over already."

"Please stay with us as long as you can. I will return you to the bridge where we once fought the Beast when you tell me to. That is close to your school and will save you time, right?"

"You'd do that for me?"

"I do not take pride in lowering myself into an animal to be ridden for speed." Ri Ur Tol tilted her head, listening for signs of an attack or considering her next words. "I will take you."

Rachel wrapped Ri Ur Tol in a hug. Ri Ur Tol stiffened into a rigid tree. Derek knew better than to laugh at her discomfort. Ri Ur Tol gave in, swaying with the wind and returning Rachel's embrace. "You saved me a long run."

"How?" Derek asked. "It's a two-hour drive to school from here. That's too far, even with your powers."

"I was planning to try," Rachel snapped.

Ri Ur Tol looked at Rachel with a new sense of wonder. "Could you do that?"

"Until you offered to help, I didn't have much of a choice. That was the balance I struck. I don't need to worry about it anymore because you're awesome." Rachel tapped at her phone. "When this goes off, can you teleport me to the mansion to pick up my concert clothes before jumping us to the bridge where we fought Derek's Beast? That will give me time to rinse off the smell of today's training at the school showers without you needing to wait while I shower here."

"Done."

Derek searched for signs of Tracy or Flint. Thanks to Rachel's loud phone, they had to know exactly where to find Derek and the flag. "Can we focus on winning this first?"

"One more thing," Rachel said. "If I lend you my phone and message you when I'm done, can you pick me up from the same spot?"

"How long will you be there? I'll need time to recover from traveling so far and back."

"Eh... about three hours."

"Done." Ri Ur Tol's demeanor shifted, returning to their competent leader. "Though I disagree with your choice to leave, the decision is yours. That noise you made will be to our advantage, drawing them here."

Derek assumed that meant they would create a well-fortified defense. Instead, they sent him inside a hollowed-out tree to wait. His teammates were outside his line of sight. Between the opening of his hiding spot, he had a narrowed view of his team's flag and maybe ten feet on either side.

Minutes rolled by. Derek shifted his weight so his legs wouldn't fall asleep. Eventually, he craned his neck outside to see if Nicole or Tracy were sneaking their way to the prize.

A sharp pain bit into his ear from someone flicking it. Derek caught Rachel's moving blur as a gust of wind swirled leaves about. Before he could shout, she was out of sight, back to wherever she was hiding.

Heavy crunches brought Derek to full attention. The ground shook. He knew only one creature who rattled the Earth with its footsteps like this. If not for the sounds of grinding gears, he would have leaped from his hiding place to battle with his Beast. Those machinery noises told him this was something else. Derek stole a glance, peering around the corner so half his face remained hidden.

"Huh." A ten-foot-tall robot stumbling between trees was not what he was expecting.

The machine looked humanoid, with two arms and legs, although there was no head on top. Its egg-shaped body had to be where Tracy was piloting the thing from. Though she had fought with metal skeletons over her limbs to reinforce her muscles, this creation was like nothing Derek had seen her make before.

Derek crept from his hole and formed a telekinetic ball around himself to defend their flag.

He had no time to brace before he was struck from behind. Rachel rammed his shield, launching Derek's makeshift wrecking ball at Tracy's machine. Rachel's aim was true, and Derek knocked it onto its back.

Metal and plastic shrapnel flew. The robot wasn't getting back to its feet. He must have smashed some mobility control.

"I hope you aren't too dazed," Derek said to his friend on the opposite team. The thick foliage on the ground had stopped his ball from rolling too far past Tracy inside her robot.

Rachel didn't give him a chance to pop open the robot to check Tracy for injuries. With him trapped inside, Rachel pushed Derek's telekinetic wrecking ball toward the other team's side.

Seeing him glance back at the fallen machine, she said, "She'll be fine. Tracy wouldn't have gotten in it if she didn't have padding for safety in there."

Derek scrambled for balance, unable to shout anything coherent. He was thrown about inside the ball, bruising every limb, and learning how it felt to be a sock in a dryer. Resolving to hurry back to check on Tracy, he focused on maintaining his shield.

Ri Ur Tol appeared and disappeared at random, directing Rachel's mad dash to guide Derek inside the spinning telekinetic ball.

He had a split second to recognize a chain whipping at the side of his bubble before too many things happened at once.

Derek's telekinetic ball collided with Flint, moving between his defensive chains. Both parties rebounded. Under the strain, Derek's shield broke apart, making him wince at every twig on the ground that stabbed him.

He came to a stop in an open area. In an untamed forest, this clearing stood out. Past his spinning vision, Derek recognized deep holes about as wide as a tree trunk scattered around the immediate vicinity. Piles of leaves were all over, but the trees they dropped from were gone. A tremor of fear rattled him at the transmutations Tracy must have made from so much material.

Tracy sat propped against the one tree in the center. Above her, a small knife held the golden flag in place, daring Derek to snatch it.

"You weren't in your robot?" Derek called out. Not his best fighting challenge.

Tracy held up a remote control. "Nope. I was controlling it with this."

She touched a tree behind her, transmuting it into a ten-foot sealed glass dome to hold their flag.

Her eyelids sank, and she fell onto her back. Having created the robot and last-ditch defense, she must have drained the last of her power. To his utter annoyance, she refused to take this seriously and played a game using the remote's handheld joystick.

Rachel was moving as a blur, circling the clearing to look for traps.

Ri Ur Tol was falling above them, taking an aerial approach to this attack.

Once again, Tracy's band's song played. "Sorry," Rachel shouted.

"I will return," Ri Ur Tol called out in midair.

Two snaps sounded, and Ri Ur Tol had disappeared with Rachel, leaving Derek alone against the rising might of his opponent's team.

He swore and sprinted for Tracy's glass dome, ready to rip it apart. He reformed his shield on the off-chance of any traps.

A tiny click sounded from under his tennis shoes. So close to their flag, the spring-loaded trap fired him through the air and away. He hit a padded cushion in front of a tree. Tracy must have been kind enough to place it there so he wouldn't be hurt after being launched.

Ri Ur Tol appeared at the dome, holding a phone, her power's snapping sound too far removed to be heard.

Tracy struggled to rise and shouted, "Stop Ri!"

Heaving huge breaths, Ri Ur Tol moved with a stiffness to control shakes of fatigue building within her legs. She half-fell, half-dove for the dome, and stopped short. A metal chain lashed around her ankle. The chain whipped about and let go of Ri Ur Tol, sending her sideways.

Derek moved to catch Ri Ur Tol. While she spun wildly, she pointed directly at their goal. The message was clear: win or suffer extra exercises.

Turning from his teammate flailing about in midair, Derek rushed forward. At a step from his goal, leaves exploded from the ground, covering the outside of his shield. He dove for the dome. A hardened boot caught him in the side. His shield absorbed the blow, sending him rolling away.

Standing amid the raining leaves, Nicole was the other team's last bastion of hope, a longshot compared to the Flint's might or the versatility of Tracy's creations.

Nicole lunged, humming a tune that burrowed into Derek's ears.

Tired of being tossed around, Derek lowered his shield and reinforced his legs. His telekinesis helped, though Nicole hit him harder than expected. She had the decency to miss his healing-in-progress arm. The rest of him wasn't so lucky. His back slammed into the ground. He let out an "oof" as Nicole landed on top of him.

Both of them lay there, stunned.

With his ear to the ground, he felt the ground shaking over Nicole's nebulous song, like when Tracy's robot was sprinting for their flag. That might have been in his head after the rough landing.

Sounds of metal striking metal brought Derek back to his senses.

Ri Ur Tol was fending off Flint's other chain, blocking with one dagger and using the other to pry her ankle free.

Derek pushed Nicole off of him and sprinted for the other team's flag inside the dome. Renewed life flooded aches in his legs; his heart pumped blood in time with Nicole's song.

Rattling behind him acted as a warning he failed to heed.

Heavy chains hit Derek in the fleshy bits of his shoulder. The force of the blow smacked him to the ground.

Ri Ur Tol appeared at the dome, cutting through it with her dagger, revealing the golden flag. One more snapping noise from Ri Ur Tol's ability and his suffering would be over when she teleported to the mansion and they won.

A loudspeaker's cracking static spread over the forest. "Flint's team wins," said Mr. Marshal.

"Star spurned night!" Ri Ur Tol shouted, punching the dome.

"How?" Derek called out.

Tracy raised both her hands to the sky in triumph. "Booya! Enjoy the extra training." The remote control fell from her hands. "My robot you left near your flag got up and took it."

Ri Ur Tol was right. Every step of the way, Flint turned Ri Ur Tol's team's advantages against them. The winners jumped about, hurrying back to the mansion. Derek hobbled to the mansion alongside Ri Ur Tol, each bruise a reminder of a different mistake from their loss.

14

Fall Break

Rachel

Rachel power walked through the darkened school hallways. She actively restrained her powers to not work up a sweat after taking her shower. Not that she had much endurance left for a sprint. Wobbling legs regretted today's round of Capture the Flag.

She reached into her pocket to check the time, only to remember she had lent her phone to Ri Ur Tol. Rachel's eyes found the nearest circular clock hanging on the wall. Two minutes until they went on stage. Timed to the second, she was on schedule.

The one thing she didn't anticipate was her exhaustion. Ri Ur Tol saved her a trip through the woods, down the mountain, and then the long run here. Rachel was planning to have her parents pick her up near the end to give her legs and powers some rest.

That was a bad plan. It would never have worked.

From the bridge where Ri Ur Tol left her, she'd gone straight to the school's basement floor to shower and scrub the sweaty evidence of training from her body.

Rachel's thick legs now struggled to lift her up the stairwell from the school gym locker rooms. Her white, buttoned dress shirt stuck to her damp skin. The school showers were in the lonely corner of the basement. Half the lights were off during the weekend hours, giving the concrete walls an uncanny resemblance to a dungeon, albeit a well maintained one. She fidgeted with the green clip-on bow tie. Any tighter and it would cut off circulation, turning Rachel into a purple lollipop.

The side entrance to the auditorium was open. Long lines of band players stood idle, instruments supported in their arms like metallic newborns. The first chair flute player counted the heads of the other wind instruments and kept everyone focused. Another classmate held her French horn in one hand and the music sheets in the other, her eyes sprinting across the page in a last-second walk-through.

"Finally," someone said through an exasperated sigh. Lauren rushed to Rachel's side, ushering her to the lined-up percussion section. Rachel received lukewarm greetings from the other snares. Then again, the only way for anyone to greet Rachel with more excitement than Lauren displayed involved fireworks. She was bouncing around, virtually weightless now that Rachel had arrived.

Lauren stiffened, inhaling a quick breath. "Your undershirt is soaking through."

Rachel looked down and swore. In her rush from the shower, she hadn't dried fully. Blue fabric showed from beneath her band uniform. Her pulse quickened, and her brain froze. All she needed was a slow-loading website's spinning icon to complete her body's reactions.

Lauren snapped at Jason, the chimes player. "Swap shirts with Rachel."

Confusion spread over the guy's face. "What? Why?"

"You're what, a men's small? Your shirt will fit Rachel and you'll be mostly hidden on stage by your instrument."

The woodwinds were filing into the doorway beneath the green-and-gold painted wooden falcon nailed above the entrance. For a school mascot, few were more intimidating than the bird of prey.

As though Lauren was the one with the ability to move at super-human speed, she unbuttoned Jason's shirt with disturbing dexterity. Too overwhelmed and thankful, Rachel decided not to include a snide comment. Lauren wasn't Tracy, after all. Lauren thrust the shirt into Rachel's hands. "Hurry!"

Rachel ducked past Jason in his undershirt and into the dark practice room.

She unbuttoned her wet shirt with unsteady hands and put on the dry one. The buttons didn't line up, leaving the collar lopsided. There was no chance to start over. She hid the problem underneath the bow tie.

Rachel handed the wet shirt to Jason. "Sorry about this and thank you."

"No problem," Jason said with an easy smile. "Glad to save a hero."

He moved to the back of the line, buttoning her damp shirt as he went. When he hunched forward, she almost couldn't see the wet spots.

Lauren's head spun, surveying the assembled section, then she marched Rachel and the rest into the auditorium. Passing beneath the door, Rachel raised her hand and tapped her drumstick on the wooden falcon above the entrance.

Capable of holding hundreds of overly enthusiastic parents, the half-filled auditorium fell silent as they took the stage. The sound of each squeaking shoe magnified, bouncing off the walls to be heard at the back of the acoustically sound room.

Stage lights brought on a new wave of perspiration, making her borrowed shirt cling to her. The lights made it difficult to see beyond the first handful of rows. Of course, her parents found their way to those close seats. Her dad raised his tablet. Rachel knew they were recording her walking to her seat. She wanted to cover her eyes or do a somersault, anything to disrupt their video.

Instead, she took her place behind her snare drum.

Wind and brass instruments blew random notes, testing the environment and warming their instruments to the auditorium.

Rachel tapped a few notes, checking to see if she needed to tighten the drum.

The full lights came on, blinding her to everyone not on stage.

Mr. DeSantos glided across to the podium in a well-tailored suit. It wasn't quite the penguin tuxedo he wore at competitions, though this charcoal-colored suit complemented his doughy frame to make him appear more buff than usual.

With no preamble, he raised his hands and waved them in a pattern they all knew. As one, the instruments played a single tuning note. His hands spun in a circle, and the band stopped playing. Musicians made their final adjustments.

Mr. DeSantos raised his hands again. Musicians brought their instruments to their mouths and waited.

Rachel readied her hands. In her head, she counted the four-count beat. *One. Two. Three. Four.*

The band breathed in, creating a silent, invisible note.

Mr. DeSantos's baton came down.

Rachel's drumstick struck her snare, the one instrument playing on the quiet stage.

Her band director's motion had yet to reach the bottom position, signifying the start.

Lauren and the other drummers to her side were midway to striking their own instruments in agonizingly slow motion.

Rachel fought to reign in her powers which had accidentally triggered.

Lauren flinched as though Rachel's early note had caused physical harm. One of Mr. DeSantos's eyes twitched. Otherwise, he did not indicate anything had gone wrong in the piece.

Fractions of a second later, in real-time, distorted music surrounded Rachel from the start of the song. The instruments' sounds magnified until all she heard were warbling noises, her powers accelerating beyond control.

Rachel held her hands over her drums without playing. She adjusted her speed back to normal, letting the other percussionists carry the backbone of the piece without her.

Lauren smiled, gesturing her head at the silent drum in front of Rachel, encouraging her to play what they had practiced ad nauseam. Settling her nerves, Rachel rejoined her section half a page down. She ignored the *forte* designation, tapping the rhythms at a quiet *pianissimo*. She doubted the trumpets in the row in front of her could hear her playing.

Her thoughts flitted about: looking at her current spot in the music, studying the upcoming measures to prepare her hands to move, listening for the flow across the entire band, and to top it all off, fighting any tendencies which might trigger her powers.

Somehow, she made it to the end of the song without tripping over her feet again, thanks to her muscle memory.

When Mr. DeSantos cut off the band to end the song, Rachel gave in to the ingrained exhaustion in her arms and legs, which she imagined runners felt when they completed their first marathon. It took all her willpower to remain standing.

Her band director faced the audience, introducing them to the previous piece and preparing them for the next one.

Halfway through Mr. DeSantos's brief history of the English folk song they were about to play, Lauren broke rank from behind her snare drum to pat Rachel on the back. "I'm not going to say something useless, like 'everyone makes mistakes.' I want you to know you recovered well."

"Thanks," Rachel muttered. It was all she needed to say.

Rachel's insides twisted about, jumping in their own early, unplanned drum solo. Rachel had taken for granted how easy it would be to win the first percussion position back if she were to challenge Lauren. Now, Rachel was losing faith in whether she deserved the right to lead. The tightrope she was walking on to balance school, training, and life was fraying under her weight. It was about to snap, sending her into freefall.

Mr. DeSantos brought them to the next song. By the start of the third song, Rachel was playing loud enough to be heard, hitting the right notes at the right time. Songs four, five, six, and seven progressed with Rachel in a daze. She lost awareness of everything besides her hands and Mr. DeSantos's baton gestures.

When they finished their last song, Mr. DeSantos spun and made a dramatic bow. He looked like a strange lever that kept bending forward at his midsection. Then he gestured at the band, presenting them appreciatively to the audience.

The woodwinds and brass stood to join the percussionists already on their feet, and everyone bowed together. Stage lights dimmed, and the audience lights returned, showcasing parents, friends, and family in the audience, standing and clapping.

To Rachel's surprise, John was now sitting next to her parents, having joined them during the concert. He applauded with polite encouragement. No one cheered louder than her parents.

She offered a small wave, then joined the others in clearing the stage. Rachel brought her snare drum to the band room on the first trip. On the second, she returned her music stand to its correct spot in the band's practice room.

Everyone was milling about, ants in a colony performing their own tasks.

Mr. DeSantos shouted over the sounds of clanging metal and snapping instrument case buckles. "Don't forget, our main competition against the other schools is next Saturday. You all did well tonight for friends and family. I expect you to prepare between now and then to perfect the performance."

Though he spoke to the general audience, he may as well have singled out Rachel and told her outright not to screw up at the next performance. Given tonight, sinking doubts crept in; she'd be the one to let everyone down again. Rachel dropped her sheet music, the pages scattering. She dove for them, grasping for the sheets fluttering about the floor while avoiding people's shoes

Lauren handed her the last stray page. "A couple of friends are coming over to my place tonight. Want to join us?"

Rachel was caught off guard and blurted out, "Your house and parties don't mix. I missed the fun last time, but my boyfriend's still pissed about getting the drinking citation when the cops showed."

Lauren frowned. "Don't worry. It's just a few friends. No one will be drinking or anything. My parents are at home to make sure tonight doesn't get out of hand." She lightened a little. "We all did well out there tonight and deserve to keep the fun going."

A day of slingshotting about left Rachel wanting nothing more than a single night to relax around people without powers. "That's exactly what I need after messing up tonight's performance," she said, feeling like weights had latched onto her rib cage, tugging her down. "Except I have to get back to train with the others."

"Ohhhh. It's a secret superpower night?" Lauren winked. "Go on and save the world, then."

Rachel funneled out the door, her parents and John eagerly awaited her with huge smiles.

"You did great out there." Her mom embraced her in a hug.

Her dad joined in. "We're so proud of how well you played tonight."

The empty congratulations ignored how she made the most noticeable mistake of anyone during the entire performance. Her parents loved her performance out of dutiful support, rather than a musical appreciation.

John hung back, waiting for her parents to give Rachel a chance to breathe.

They gave her one last tight hug. "See you tomorrow night for dinner," said her mom. "Let us know if you're coming back early from training. You could use a break over this long weekend."

Rachel's dad had the self-awareness to let Rachel be with John and the rest of her bandmates, who continued to spill into the halls. Her dad jingled his car keys to pull her mom away and told Rachel, "Make your other superpowered friends eat your dust."

When Rachel was alone with John—well, as alone as two people could be surrounded by hundreds of others—he pulled her close. "I know what you're going to say, and trust me, everyone forgot about you entering early by the end of the first song."

He squeezed her hand. Calloused skin from hours upon hours in the gym brought gentle warmth within their touch. "Sure. I definitely don't see the way you're kicking your own ass over a simple mistake. Especially when you don't recognize how much you rocked the other songs."

Pressure eased from forearms that felt like she had been clenching hundred-pound weights for hours. "I was all set to come in without jumping the mark when my powers skewed my perceptions."

John's lips contorted into an intrigued frown. "I thought you were in control of them."

"Apparently, that goes out the window under duress."

"You must love having your precise sense of order slip into disarray."

Rachel paused, looking John over. She couldn't put a finger on it... but he looked different. His old confidence was returning. "Since when did you start psychoanalyzing me?"

"By the way," John said, changing the subject, "Louis wanted to be here tonight, too, but he had to work."

"He's starting official hours back at the Cold Snap?"

"No, he's got a real job selling shoes at the mall to offset his raised car insurance."

Rachel couldn't hide her wince from John. Mentioning Louis made her think of her other friends. If they hadn't developed powers, Tracy and Derek would have attended tonight's concert, too, cheering her on instead of spending the night training.

"Feel like taking a trip to the Cold Snap for a treat?" John asked.

Rachel bit her lip, retreating from another friend. "I already told Lauren I couldn't make her post-concert plans."

"I'm not Lauren. Can't you spare half an hour?"

"Believe me, I want to hang out." It took all her composure to say his standard painful excuse: "I can't. I need to train."

John's hazel eyes leveled at Rachel. "Has anyone else been losing control of their powers?"

"Not that I've seen."

"Aren't most of you standing on the cliff's edge, where the smallest gust carries you over? I thought that was how Derek's rage manifested his powers to cause Louis's crash."

"Powers aren't like that. They're a part of us. We can use them however we like. Sometimes your body doesn't react the way you want it to."

"Lives aren't jeopardized if I push myself too much in a lifting session and can't move my arms."

"We're using our powers to help others."

"When was the last time your team helped someone other than yourselves?"

Rachel jerked her hand to her side, unlocking her fingers from John's.

His hand clawed for hers. Rachel stepped back from his touch.

Too late, he realized his mistake. "That's not what I meant."

"I know," she replied. "You trust me, just not the friends I trust with my life."

"The giant bear was Derek's fault, and I wouldn't be surprised if he caused the shadows to appear."

Snakes crawled through Rachel's insides. "You're right," she shouted, not caring about the crowd of classmates and families turning her way. "Those were mistakes and ones we've paid for."

"You've been the voice of reason. You shouldn't have to suffer for other people's mistakes."

Rachel bit back what she wanted to say. Each additional word uttered to stem the flow of their argument instead turned sour, making things worse. She ramped up her powers and left John, speeding to the basement to change clothes.

Under the single locker room light, she threw her performance clothes into her backpack. A loose plastic button snapped, flying out. It clicked against the tiled floor and rolled along the locker's base, lost in the dim light.

Shoving her head into her hands, Rachel yelled until every molecule of oxygen ran screaming from her lungs. Splotches of black appeared on the sides of her vision.

She breathed in. And out. In. And out.

The button was gone, swallowed in a sinkhole beneath the locker. She vowed to find a matching button before next Saturday's performance so she could return Jason's shirt in pristine condition. She vowed to practice the music and not play any part out of sequence. More importantly, she vowed to lock down her powers so they didn't leak out at the most inopportune moment.

She went into the school's library and sat at a workstation. The computer monitor's glow provided all the light in the room. Rachel signed in to send her phone a message, hoping Ri Ur Tol had learned enough about modern tech to read it. "Ready. Can you meet me in ten?"

Rachel checked the two new messages. One was from Derek asking her to pick up chocolate and marshmallows to, "Show Ri Ur Tol and Flint how to actually enjoy an open fire."

The other was from John. It was a single word: "Sorry."

His message made the floor seem to fall away from her.

He owes me more than a one word apology.

She held back her tears and left both messages unanswered.

Rachel went to the parking lot, increasing her speed to get to the bridge where Ri Ur Tol said she would pick her up.

Lamp posts lit the families wading to their cars.

Rachel passed Lauren halfway to the end of the lot. To Rachel, her classmate appeared still. Caught in the picturesque form of laughter, a mist of soda sprayed from Lauren's mouth, falling in crystalline shapes, each unique as a snowflake. The classmate next to her carried her trombone in a case hanging from one shoulder, her head thrown back, laughing as hard as Lauren.

A lump caught in Rachel's throat. Lauren was the leader their percussion section deserved. She'd earned the right to hold her first position without Rachel interrupting her with a challenge.

Rachel left the bright lights for dim woods and mountain paths.

15

Campfire

Tracy

Crackling firelight cast a blazing glow on the faces of those around the camp. Tracy poked a crimson log with her stick. Sparks burst upward, their red flashes rising into the darkening sky.

Like a single furnace surrounded by scaffolding, the light from the fire emanated beyond leafless trees, banishing their largest shadows.

For every miserable idea Flint had on how to train her powers, there was one brilliant one. Those outliers usually saved her life. This campfire was better; it was a well-earned break. The only way to improve the evening was to transmute her log stump seat into a cushioned chair. The day of training left her too drained to remake the wood as a fluffy seat, complete with an extendable footrest.

Bitter winds were kept at bay by her autumn sweatshirt. She bundled her hands in the long sleeves, exposing only her face. Fire baked her, warming her skin from the top down. To complete the evening's look, she'd swapped her sweaty yoga pants for black sweatpants.

The woods were alive with night life, difficult to see in the fading twilight. Birds and insects she couldn't name shrieked, cried, and chirped, all searching for food or mates. Their calls and answers jumped around her.

To her left, Derek was lying on the ground. He stared up at the appearing stars, lost in his strange Derek thoughts. Ri Ur Tol was on his other side. For once, she wasn't oiling her knives. Her elbows rested on her knees, and she slouched forward within the folds of an oversized gray hoodie, looking like a deflated elephant.

Sharp edges on her face formed by the fire transformed Ri Ur Tol into a Valkyrie from old legends, even though the cultures didn't align with her own. Tracy waited in anticipation for her to consume mead by the barrelful and boast of spoils won. Tracy chose to ignore the purpose of Valkyries as those who brought the dead to the afterlife.

Opposite Tracy was the gruff old man section. Mr. Marshal hadn't said a word since he took his seat. His button-down shirt and slacks were out of place in the circle of workout clothes. Mr. Marshal rubbed his chin stubble while pensively looking at each of them.

Next to him was another who hardly spoke. Despite bringing them out here, Flint tended the fire and did little else. His jeans and yellow flannel shirt made him look like a woodsman dad, built for outdoor living. It helped that he used to live in the woods.

Completing the circle was Nicole. Multiple days of training wore on her face, her round features narrowing, helped along by two-a-day workout sessions and a lack of school to attend.

Buzzing came from Ri Ur Tol's pocket.

Tracy's surprise shifted into confusion, recognizing Rachel's treble clef phone case in Ri Ur Tol's hands. But Tracy knew better than to question the person doling out their training exercises.

Flint steepled his hands below his beard. Chains on his arms clanged together. Each chain reflected an orange glow, making Flint appear to be wearing thousands of tiny fires. "I wish to discuss a matter of true importance."

He breathed into the fire, adding his power to bring new life to steady embers and raise the flames above their heads. The sudden brightness nearly sent Tracy falling off the open back of her log seat. She threw her hands up to protect her face, except these flames gave no additional warmth.

When Flint spoke, his deep tones cracked along with the kindling. "Hailing from different worlds and times, we are divided. We did not fight as one against the shadow monster and it nearly felled us. Once, on the eve of battle, I witnessed far-flung tribes share our histories while sitting around communal fires. Through these stories, we came to trust those alongside us to watch our backs."

When no one else said anything, Derek rolled into a sitting position and propped against his own log. "What do you want to know?"

Tongues of flame licked the cool air. "Tell me of your lives and how you got here. I caught glimpses from some of you when I looked into your memories."

Tracy shifted in her seat, holding her tongue at how Flint had invaded their privacy by peering into their memories.

"What I know is lacking," continued Flint. "What we know of each other is more so."

Tracy slid from side to side on her log. "Bor-ing." Putting on her best old-man voice, she went for it. "In the beginning, there was heaven and Earth."

Flint blinked in resignation. The simple motion conveyed to Tracy exactly how little he thought of her antics. His expression combined a groan, disappointed head shake, and sigh, all wrapped into one. "Skip ahead to your recent history."

Derek stared into the flames. "Here's how I discovered I had powers and stopped a monster I created."

He broke into the wonder of discovering his abilities, then how he had decided to share his secret with Tracy. He held back nothing, emptying burdens of guilt at losing control of his powers to hurt Louis by totaling his car.

Various shades of red, orange, and yellow inside Flint's magic fire formed tiny images of Tracy, Rachel, and Derek acting out their parts, according to Derek's words. Although the flame counterparts seemed too bright to watch, Tracy couldn't turn from what looked like a muted television screen with green and blue colors turned off.

Tracy joined at pivotal moments, weaving her story into the living performance. When they got to the part about fighting the Beast and first opening the portal to the void, Tracy let Derek speak so she could run her nails up and down her arm to soothe the itch crawling beneath her skin.

Seeing the doorway to the void within flames was mesmerizing, a perfectly formed sparkling sphere. Vibrant, beautiful shades of red radiated from the hole, so much more than a simple gateway. It held wonders; the void unlocked the past, the present, and beyond.

Derek tapped her. "Nothing else to add, Tracy? Your idea of combining our powers saved us all and helped me defeat my Beast."

Tracy shook her head, distracted by thoughts of the void throughout his story.

Nicole stared right through Derek. "This may not be as entertaining," she said, "but it was epic for me. You're not the most talkative guy I know, in my world or this one. Three months ago, at the start of the school year, it was becoming painfully obvious something was eating at the mind of the Derek from my world. Wanting to break him out of his shell, I gathered the courage and asked him to go see a movie with me."

An image of Nicole came together at the center of the fire, along with a Derek. He looked the same, yet something in the way he moved spread goosebumps along Tracy's skin. This was not her Derek. The Derek within the flames existed within the uncanny valley, close to what a Derek should be, his likeness instead made him feel alien. She glanced to her side, reassured by the Derek sitting next to her.

Nicole went on. "Before the action movie started, I prodded Derek to tell me what was troubling him. He still wouldn't reveal anything. I kept trying while we went for late-night ice cream after the show, but he kept his thoughts wrapped up tight."

Under their stern gazes, Derek rubbed the back of his neck. Tracy knew exactly how Nicole felt. Tracy was more likely to squeeze water from a stone than convince any Derek to unburden his thoughts.

Nicole dropped her glare and continued. "We walked to his car, and I knew it was my last chance to figure out what had been bothering him. I went out on a limb to throw him off guard and said, 'At least this date let you forget your troubles.' Derek's whole body went still as he said, 'Wait, this was a date?' My heart stopped. I had to look away. I was so embarrassed. I turned back to yell at him. He kissed me before I got the chance to holler one word."

Nicole paused, staring at the images in the flames, mirroring her words.

"When it was over, he held my hand. 'I need to show you something, but you have to trust me.' He kissed me again, and I felt a rush of wind pass over me."

"We could have kissed for days or seconds. Eventually, I opened my eyes and froze. Floating leaves he ripped from nearby trees surrounded us." Within the flame images, dozens of leaves hovered by

Nicole's head. "Derek planned it as a sweet gesture, and all I did was scream in shock."

Firelit memories reflected in Nicole's eyes. Derek coughed nervously as Nicole went on. "We went to this clearing in Derek's backyard to build up his powers. About two weeks before you all arrived, he pushed beyond a breaking point and tore a hole in the universe. He quested into the great unknown, leaving me to tether him to this world. Whenever he went exploring into the void, the last I saw of Derek was his back."

Tracy looked into Nicole's face and saw her own goodbye to the Nicole of this world. "Was that the same time our Derek first opened the portal to the void?"

"From the dates you've told me, I think so." Nicole nodded, dragging her hand across her face to hide the small sniffle. "The rest of the story you know from when you crashed into my world and threw me face-first into this shitshow."

"Then it's settled," Tracy said with a start. The words spilled from her lips. Nicole deserved to be reunited. "Derek, open the void to reunite Nicole with the other you."

Derek clicked his tongue. "Not without a good plan to get around the shadow monster."

An inner fire ignited Tracy's fury. She scratched her arm to appease the irritation from sitting too close to the campfire. "You're a coward."

All eyes jumped to her, except Derek's. He stared at his feet. "No, I'm learning from the past so I don't repeat my mistakes."

Tracy paused, letting her pulse return to normal. She pulled her arms tighter to her chest to hold in her fleeting warmth from surprisingly dark thoughts. "That was meaner than what I was going for. Sorry, Derek."

"Moonless night!" Ri Ur Tol cursed. *Snap.* She disappeared without explanation.

Derek jumped to his feet, fists raised, eyes looking into the woods around them. He lowered his hands and sat back down when no one leaped out to attack them. "Does she need to do that?"

The moment Tracy became used to one less person sitting by the fire, Ri Ur Tol reappeared with Rachel.

"Sorry I'm late." Rachel pulled a log into the open space between Tracy and Nicole. She turned her face from the fire to hide wet streaks, and her stretched smile trembled. "What did I miss?"

Derek's head bobbed side to side, making a show of checking Rachel's empty hands. "Did you get my message for chocolate and marsh—" Tracy smacked Derek's leg to get him to shut up.

Tracy leaned over to put her arm on Rachel's shoulder. "Tell me who to hurt," she whispered.

Rachel hugged her back, clutching harder than Tracy expected. "It's not one person, just life as a whole."

"I'll be sure to kick life right in its hole." Tracy squeezed her friend again.

"What I meant is that it's story time," said Derek, catching Tracy's not subtle hint. "Mr. Marshal was about to explain how he ended up with powers and why he gave them to us."

"I am not wasting my time explaining my decisions. There's a reason we don't teach the nuances of grammar to someone who doesn't know the ABCs."

Consumed by a sudden urge to smack Mr. Marshal, Tracy's tongue was too tied to throw a worthwhile insult at the old man.

Flint picked up the conversation in the pause. "Tracy spoke an invaluable truth. We should venture into the portal to Somewhere Else. I will tell you my story not so you trust me, for I no longer trust myself, but so that you know why I fight. I bear my moment of weakness so you understand why I must stop at nothing to continue my hunt, lost within that emptiness."

Images swirled within the fire, faces formed and dissipated as Flint continued. "I sent so many into battle. I was wrong to assume the numbers necessary to ensure my people's survival and prosperity. Our final battle raged for days over the trampled fallen."

An ocean of dismembered bodies littered the valley shown in the flames. Some twitched, many lay still.

"Unlike the rabble of aged villagers who fought us when we left my time, this war was fueled by the will of the young." Sharpened stone points latched to the ends of long wooden staffs sought to work around shorter stone axes. One in ten wielded swords to full effect, severing wooden spears and limbs alike. Warriors stabbed or beat others to death in numbers that made Tracy regret the bowl of liquid stew sloshing in her stomach. Her latest attempt to cook meals in the mansion was soon to be undone.

Removed from the line of battle, a man sat in a hauntingly familiar pose, cross-legged with his palms angled up. The image of Flint in the fire was on the cusp of adulthood, with cheeks and chin not sprouting into the bush now consuming his face.

"The outcome was uncertain. However, it was clear many lives would be taken, whether we staved off the invaders or lost our homeland. Misguided as I was, I brought forth magic to release numerous Aspects in a single spell, believing it would slay my enemies and save my people."

A circle of fourteen men stood around Flint. Tracy's insides squirmed. These men didn't move when stabbed with sharp sticks. The blood from their bodies flowed down shallow trenches leading to Flint.

"I believed their deaths to be the trade necessary to bring a swift end to the battle. What were a few more lives compared to the widespread slaughter?"

Around the outer circle of the deceased men, dark gases swirled, wilting the grass it touched. Caught too close to Flint's power, men and women fighters fell into violent seizures, then became still. Those farther from the source dropped their weapons, ignoring foes they were pitted against seconds ago. Both armies sprinted alongside one another to flee from this new evil.

Noiseless images in the flames left Tracy to imagine the frantic shouts from those trying to escape. Warriors across this field collapsed, dying within instants in a bloodless, writhing fit. Then the truly terrible sight appeared. Wisps seeped from the dead to coalesce above their bodies.

"My master fed me lies, waiting seasons upon seasons for this moment."

In the fire, the wide-eyed Flint dropped to his hands and knees. Thousands of souls gravitated to one of the few who remained with the living. These grew brighter, blotting everything except Flint.

A figure hidden in the blinding lights of the dead carried a tiny box in an outstretched hand. From the box swirled a tremendous vortex, inhaling souls.

"My master's goal was to steal innumerable lives and harness their spirits to forge a horrid weapon."

A few of the living stumbled to flee from silent death. These, pitiful in number, scattered in every direction, tripping over limbs on the still field.

Far removed from the obscuring lights, one lone figure moved closer, hopping on one foot amid the dead bodies. They were too far away to be certain, but Tracy swore he resembled a younger version of the merchant who led the attack against her and her friends when they fled Flint's time.

Someone sitting beside her vomited. She wanted to join them. Bile rose inside, roiling at the scenes within the fire. Tracy wanted to look away, to shut her eyes and end her suffering at witnessing the suffering of so many. Instead, she watched the fire as a foot kicked Flint huddled on the ground.

The faint outline of the figure Flint indicated as his master raised the box inhaling the spirits of the dead with one hand. They used their free hand to siphon hundreds of other spirits from the box into a single point. This opened into a hole darker than anything in the world of the living. With each additional consumed spirit, it grew larger.

Soon, the tear formed completely. Shifting shadows moved on the other side.

Wind whipped across Tracy's back, revealing her sweatshirt's threads to be more of a fishnet and less of a solid cloth for the amount of cold air siphoning her body heat.

She wanted to run, to douse the fire, anything to end that horrid sight. The void spun into reality in the fire's image, beckoning with the prospect of solving life's stresses. Derek had already used it to finish his schoolwork without time passing.

Why can't I do the same?

Long, familiar arms of shadow grasped from within the void, seeking to cross into the world shown in the fire.

Flint's outline in the fire's image, difficult to see with the floating wisps of the dead, leaped at his master, sending them tumbling together toward the open portal. The box was knocked aside in the scuffle, no longer inhaling the spirits of once living warriors. Flint stopped just shy of the portal. The vague outline of master continued rolling, passing to the other side.

Younger Flint's hands moved through the air in complex gestures. The portal was snuffed from existence, trapping Flint's master with the shadow monster.

Glowing orbs of the remaining spirits floated for a moment. These sailed into the figure clambering to his feet where the portal once existed. Flint's shell of a body fell, lurching with each orb entering him. An eternity passed until every light was extinguished.

With the spirit lights gone, Tracy clearly saw Flint crawl to the box and cradle it. When he finally staggered to his feet, Flint sprinted as fast as his unsteady legs allowed, fading from view.

Flint shuddered, which rattled the chains he wore. "On the dawn of that day, many had lived. This spell consumed most of them, trapping their spirits within the Weapon. Of the rest, the spell turned my body into a vessel to contain those who deserved to be free in death."

Flint let out a long sigh, seemingly freed by unloading his burden. "I believe my mistake pulled you across the void. If true, I am ever thankful your aim was off and more focused on me, who opened the portal, rather than the portal itself. Otherwise, the shadow waiting when I opened the portal would have torn you in half."

The fire flickered, returning to normal, its glow dancing across Nicole's tear-streaked face. "Murderer," she uttered, little more than a whisper. Had even the slightest sound disturbed the air, Tracy would have missed it entirely.

Flint's voice was raw and torn as he spoke. "You speak the truth. I was trained to serve my people. Loyalty to our chieftain of chieftains was absolute. When I encouraged children to join in the war, it was so we might collectively save our homeland. I knew I was sending many to their deaths, and I wished to prevent that at any cost. My master taught me a powerful spell to ravage our enemies, sparing the blood of my people. The effects of his deception you witnessed here."

"I shared my greatest mistake with you because on that day I rebuked my master and his teachings. All I learned to consider beyond question was undone. Under his guidance, I learned to work magic by draining the lives of servants. But they were always willing participants who were likewise as foolish as me. Since this battle, I have sought two ends: to prevent that spell from ever being recast and to strive with all I possess to prevent the man I once called master from returning. When you three arrived, I was given a new purpose: to destroy the man responsible for this massacre."

Silence fell over their camp, interrupted by popping wood turning to cinders.

Some returned to the mansion, seeking electric lights and central heating to combat this chilly night and the evil terrors along with it.

Tracy whispered her only thoughts not baked in disgust. "Do you think your master teamed up with the shadow, or the shadow killed him?"

Flint gazed into the flames, having returned to a mere campfire. "I do not know. I hope my master is no more, yet I must be certain. His tongue and the power he wielded proved more than capable of bending others to his will."

Long after everyone else left, Tracy remained by the fire. Unwilling to move, she couldn't warm herself from the sensation of an icy claw holding her in its grip.

16

A Crack in the Air

Tracy

Tracy settled at her desk in the mansion and pulled the blanket tighter around her. After winning yesterday's game of Capture the Flag, she earned a full day of rest. Expect, as the last day of her fall break there were no more excuses to avoid homework. She had cleaned the campsite this morning with the others and then returned to her room to be productive.

As she got into the first few calculus questions, scratching noises from outside interrupted her thoughts. Tracy brushed aside the sounds, returning her attention to her homework.

The scratching bore deeper into her mind. *Some overactive squirrel must be trying to burrow into the mansion.*

Its abrasive scratches sent her stomach gurgling as though she were hungover. The glass of water on her desk was doing little to ease the turmoil inside. She controlled her breathing to bat down her annoyance, rereading the math question and planning the best manner to attack the solution.

The scratching made it impossible to think.

She banged her fist on the windowless wall facing the outside, hoping to scare off whatever animal was causing the noise. The cave-like sensation of being in this room and the quiet it offered were usually ideal. Today, the noises were too much. The scratches might as well be along her spine.

Tracy played music from her phone and used scrap metal on the floor to transmute a tennis racket and sword for herself, desperate to scare the outside animal into leaving her alone. Ignoring the itch inside her arm from using her power, Tracy dashed through the empty mansion to circle the building from the outside.

Though quieter within the halls, the scratching sounds carried through the metal walls. The animal must be going crazy.

Stepping through the front door, Tracy squinted against the low-rising sun peaking through the trees. The chilled air caught her off guard. Stuck in cotton pajama pants and a T-shirt, she refused to go back for warmer clothes. She didn't intend to stay outside for long, so there was no reason to transmute a tree into a jacket.

Her slippered feet ran over dew-soaked grass, absorbing the water until her toes squished with each step. She turned the corner, brandishing her weapons, ready to terrify the animal from ever coming so close to the mansion again.

Her feet stopped, the useless weapons falling from her hands.

At about waist height, a long splintering crack spread over open air, like someone had thrown the remote at an invisible television. Cold wind rushed from the crack. This unfinished portal was connecting her world to the void.

Tremors coursed along her arm, the inner itch becoming unbearable.

Whispers, too indistinct to understand, echoed around her. The noises were deafening. Her skull felt like it was flattening under their force.

Tracy's hand raised, stretching for the void.

This is my chance to catch up on schoolwork.

Derek had gone into the void for the same reason. Rachel used her powers to accelerate and finish hours of homework in minutes.

Though, we're all still far behind.

Tracy didn't understand what Derek did to open the portal, short of throwing his power at a single spot until time and space folded in on itself. There was some trick to crossing multiple Aspects, though she had never been able to use an Aspect other than the one to transmute objects.

Brushing the crack with her fingertips, static electricity sent a tiny jolt into her. Her fingers burned and chilled like being exposed to the elements on a frozen mountaintop.

Scratching sounds swelled, and the whispers called to her from within the crack. Using music from her phone to draw in power, she readied to feed the void and rip the opening wider. Desperate desires to enter the void from the deepest recesses of her mind crashed in waves against her more logical thoughts.

She clamped her free hand over her other hand still reaching for the void. "No."

Tracy knew better than to press her fingers into the crack, unless she wanted to risk losing them to the unfinished portal. This anomaly wasn't an answer to her problems. This wasn't a shortcut she trusted. Tingling fears reminded her why she avoided the void. The shadow monster was inside, breaking the barrier between dimensions, the result of which was right in front of her.

Tracy formed a pillar of dirt, raising it up to clamp down like a snake swallowing the cracked portal to the void. She dropped pillar after pillar on top of the crack until a mound of dirt rested against the mansion.

"Burying the portal won't seal it." Mr. Marshal's voice startled Tracy.

She stifled her scream, calming herself to state, "I'm not waiting for it to seal on its own."

"It may not. Clear the dirt away and I'll close it."

Tracy unmade the dirt mound, partially refilling the holes she'd formed.

Mr. Marshal brushed his hand through the air, and the crack sealed shut.

All the sounds clobbering her mind blinked from existence. She took in a long, relaxing breath and exhaled into the near silent morning. With no scratches or whispers, she could hold on to her thoughts.

Mr. Marshal eyed Tracy's slippers. "What were you doing out here?"

"I didn't create the crack if that's what you're asking."

"It wasn't, though that is good to know. I was checking in on Ri Ur Tol's training exercises when I sensed the disturbance. When I got closer, I heard scratching sounds."

"Did you hear anything else, like whispers?"

Mr. Marshal's eyebrows pinched together in question. "No. Did you?"

"No." Tracy quickly followed up with, "How are Rachel and Derek holding up this morning?"

Mr. Marshal didn't seem convinced by her change of subject but answered her. "Not great. They both seemed distracted by something unrelated to training, which is a shame given Ri Ur Tol's excitement for their extra fighting bouts." He studied the space where the portal had been, then shifted to Tracy's disheveled appearance. "Do you know who's been opening them?"

Tracy shivered, knowing what had come close to breaking into their world. Resisting inner urges to withhold from telling anyone, she forced her mouth to speak the truth. "It has to be the shadow monster within the void. Can you give me more power to fight it?"

"How would I give you more power?"

"With those chocolates you used to give to Derek. He always seemed more awake after. That's how you gave him power, which trickled down into me."

Mr. Marshal barked a harsh laugh. "The chocolates were placebos, a distraction to offset when I shared portions of my power with Derek. I'm not capable of permanently sharing my powers. I can only act as a catalyst, donating part of my power until that spark ignites in someone else. *If* it ignites in someone else."

"Why would you willingly give up power?"

Mr. Marshal gestured at the half-filled holes she had used as material for her dirt transmutations. "You've taken your powers far beyond my limitations. Individually, I grew weaker by giving power to Derek, but collectively, you all have grown into something incredible."

"So that's a no on a power boost?"

"Not one that will last."

"Okay... Then I'm going back to do some overdue school assignments."

She left Mr. Marshal standing outside, staring at the space where the crack had existed. There was no time for homework; Tracy needed to plan. The shadow monster was breaking into their world.

17

Plans

Rachel

On this Monday after school, weeks of Rachel's half-finished homework called to her through the zipped canvas of her backpack. Yet, she stared around the room of the school's library, unwilling to focus. Already this semester, another bookshelf had been removed in favor of the new octagonal station of computer monitors.

In her freshman year, this room was a solace for quiet pencil tapping and a warehouse of educational and recreational tomes. Nothing smelled more like fresh knowledge than the pungent odor of an ancient mold-crusted cover. Today, the ambiance was broken by students practicing their boxing skills by wailing on keyboards like they were weighted bags.

"I'm done with the unknowns," Derek stated to Tracy and Rachel, having migrated them to a secluded corner of the room. Secluded was a relative term, as a decent number of students were spread across the library getting their work done. Thankfully, no one else appeared to be paying attention to the three of them.

By calling this emergency meeting, he stole Rachel's evening to finish overdue assignments. According to him, this was more important.

While Derek waited for applause to his declaration, Tracy used her powers to forcibly upgrade one of the worst offending computer models to one from this decade. If the part-time librarian, part-time health teacher noticed, she kept her thanks to herself. Maybe by acknowledging Tracy's swap, the school would need to return to its previous model.

Derek leaned closer and spoke in a hushed voice. "We can't trust those old men turning us into superpowered weapons. We saw Flint's memory. Death follows him, and what do we really know about Mr. Marshal?"

Rachel spun her hand in a circle. "What do we know about any of our teachers?"

Derek started counting on his fingers. "Counterpoint one: none of our other teachers have powers. Counterpoint two: how does Mr. Marshal afford that mansion on a guidance counselor's salary?"

"Think he's used powers to amass a fortune?" asked Tracy.

Rachel didn't answer, her eyes wandering above them to an oil painting. Brush strokes of the nearby river with a backdrop of the curved bridge evoked a sense of wonder at nature, melding with the modern world. A crater, the site of the end of their battle with Derek's bear monster, was in the foreground. The monument to the day they survived by a hair's width was not an image she wanted to remember. A stylized signature in the corner declared this the work of a classmate Rachel had never met.

Derek drew on the small whiteboard sitting next to the computer. "That's why we need to learn all we can, starting with what we already know. One: Mr. Marshal arrived at our school at the start of the spring semester. Two: he has powers. Three: he gave me powers. Four: he has no social media presence."

"How do you know it's not hidden?" Tracy asked. "Most of our teachers use privacy settings or different names so they can't be found publicly. Or, does he have a partner? Anyone else on staff helping him?"

Details in Rachel's head knocked loose tiny pebbles that wanted to cause a landslide.

Derek put down the whiteboard and tapped on the keyboard to look for clues on their school's website. "No one else came in at the end of last year. A handful of teachers joined at the start of this semester. Does that mean we need to stalk them and set up tests to reveal if they have powers?"

Tracy shook her head, performing her own searches. "That's a waste of time. We've been working with Mr. Marshal for a while and still don't know the full extent of his powers."

Derek's eyes darted over the computer screen. "I don't know any of these new teachers. One teaches freshman English, another American Government, Drama, and some weird class called Television Studies."

"Hey!" Tracy looked up from her own computer research. "That class is about special effects and the art of filming shows. I loved taking it last year."

"Got it." Rachel dug deep enough in her head to grasp the golden knowledge nugget. "What if we aren't looking for a full-time teacher? What if this accomplice was a substitute who hasn't left?"

"Who?" Tracy and Derek asked together.

Rachel looked back and forth between the two, unable to understand how they missed the obvious. "Mr. Sprog."

Playing with a paper flier for the upcoming Snow Ball, Tracy gave no outward appearance she processed what Rachel had said. "He's been giving us a hard time since the world learned of our powers."

Derek's eyes lit. He turned Tracy's chair to face him. "What was he wearing in today's class?""

"I wasn't paying attention." Tracy slid back to devising new distractions. "It was probably something garish, complete with an orange tie."

"Picture him in your mind. What do you see?"

Tracy shrugged.

"What was today's lesson on?"

"We practiced balancing chemical equations."

"You don't find it weird you can't recall his face or clothes? What about your other teachers?"

Tracy counted on her fingers. "My second period teacher, Mrs. Kerlan, wore a blue blouse. Mr. Edsel was in a white button-down shirt and jeans. You're right. I remember all of my teacher's faces except Sprog." Tracy covered her mouth with her hand. "What does this mean?"

The landslide fell in Rachel's mind, revealing what the rocks covered. "Now it makes sense. Mr. Sprog's tempo is unique. It's not as dissonant as Nicole's tempo, but it is a far stretch from everyone else I've seen without powers."

Derek fell back into his seat. "Does that mean he has powers?"

Tracy went to work on the computer, searching page after page of public information on Mr. Sprog. Once she took up a cause, there was no stopping her. "Safe to assume so, unless proven otherwise."

Letting out a heavy breath, Derek wrote Mr. Marshal's and Mr. Sprog's names on his whiteboard. "The one problem is that there isn't a line connecting them. I've never seen them together."

"What fubar situation are you three handling?" asked an oddly dressed classmate. December had started this week, but you wouldn't know it by looking at her. Ill-equipped for the cold, her black T-shirt was ambitious for the season. She'd fit right in with those head-strong teenage boys who wore cargo shorts year-round. "Should the rest of us be worried?"

Like he'd never seen a pretty face, all Derek uttered was, "Fubar?"

Rachel took charge, remembering her classmate's name. "Melissa, we're not prepping to fight a monster, if that's what you're asking."

Tracy nudged her head at Melissa, trying to catch Rachel's and Derek's attention. "We're in the middle of a team meeting."

"Can I help?"

"You'll slow us down," Tracy said from the side of her mouth.

"Ouch, and inaccurate. I'm capable of more than you think." Melissa threw her arms up. "Fine. See you around, then."

"Wait," Derek called out. "Ignore my rude friend."

"I'm not wrong." Tracy stepped in front of Derek's whiteboard, blocking the names from Melissa's view. "We're looking for a connection between two people, and our new classmate appears? There are too many coincidences for us to trust her."

Derek rubbed his face, stretching his cheeks. "Your conspiracy theory falls apart. We've had three months of school without her. If she is involved with them, why bring her in now?"

Melissa's gaze jumped between Rachel and her friends. "You three haven't earned my trust either, but I'm willing to keep an eye on whomever you're watching to help our local heroes."

Derek caved under the look Tracy sent him as he spoke. "Sorry. We haven't made up our minds about letting you in on the details."

"Then I'll see you in class tomorrow." Melissa waved and walked out of the library.

Rachel waited for Melissa to step out of hearing range. "She's in your classes, too? That new girl is in my Calc II class."

"AP Chem for Derek and me," Tracy started. "See, I was right to send her away."

"Not true," Rachel replied. "You may have piqued her interest instead. It is odd how she's in classes with all of us."

Derek returned to stroking the beard he didn't have. "Not necessarily. Given when certain classes are offered, there's little choice in the schedule if Melissa is maxing out AP classes for college credits."

"That's not all," added Rachel. "Melissa showed up on the day the shadow monster attacked. I met her in the hall as I was running to the fight. She couldn't move as fast as me as I ramped up my powers, but she caught me by anticipating my movements and had the strength not to fall over."

Tracy glanced at the closed library doors where Melissa had left. "I'll pay attention to a new potential threat."

Rachel checked her phone for the time, calculating the seconds she could spare in this library and mentally prioritizing the assignments to complete. "We won't resolve anything tonight, and I'm overloaded with school assignments. Are we done for now?"

Derek looked like he wanted to say more. Thankfully, he let his thoughts go unsaid under the frown Rachel sent his way.

"There's a lot more for us to research another night," said Derek. "Tracy and I are going to the park to study the spot where the shadow first breached our world. We'll also keep our eyes and ears open for other crimes in the area, a 'Hero Watch', if you will."

"Do you know what you'll do if you find anything?" Rachel asked.

"Nope," said Tracy. "You should know by now, our best intentions fall apart at the speed of life."

Derek threw a look that was half bemusement and half disappointment. "We're getting ahead of these cracks so another shadow monster attack doesn't catch us off guard. Can you swap for Tracy tomorrow and join me in the investigation?"

A piteous groan left Rachel's throat. She'd need to pull an all-nighter and tap into her powers to make sufficient progress to make up for another Derek scheme. "What else would I do? It's not like we're being drowned by homework."

18

Hero Watch

Rachel

The next day, double the number of classmates were studying in the library after school, most likely victims of an exam cram. Clustered in small groups, the students a grade or two below her pored over the same textbooks. Every so often, a face lit up as a complex concept stuck. Others weren't so successful. A team of four had their heads resting on their hands, all looking glum and hopeless, setting themselves up for failure.

Rachel's phone alarm sounded at Derek's text. If Tracy recognized one of her ex-band's intro notes, she didn't comment. "These so-called Hero Watches are a waste of time." Rachel slammed her book shut, causing a few heads to rise above their computer stations.

Tracy was face-deep in her own textbook, an appreciated change from the amusing distractions she tended to provide. "Last night wasn't bad. Bring your schoolwork and scope out a park bench. Let Derek look for clues about the crack to the void while you spend the evening on homework. It's not like we'll be stopping someone from stealing a purse."

"Did you really spend all evening on a park bench doing homework?"

Tracy responded with a mischievous shrug. "Mostly. After I put in an hour on Calc, I wandered to that new shopping center they're building. Bad news, Louis's family is getting some competition. They're opening an ice cream parlor at the start of next year."

"Shouldn't Derek care you went off on your own?"

"I wish. Since his Beast disappeared, he's questing for a new obsession, so he stares at the space where the portal was last opened. He probably didn't notice I left."

"In this case, he's right to worry so much." Conviction hardened Rachel's voice. "At all costs, that thing cannot break into our world."

A thin thread Rachel refused to accept as resentment coiled around her insides at her previous agreement to help Derek tonight. Unlike the park, nowhere else allowed Rachel to be as productive as this contained library. The tapping of keyboards and scratching of pencils were motivating background noises. Books and notes spread across their table, allowing Rachel to pick which to pluck from for the key formula to apply. Plus, if a question gave her too much difficulty, Tracy was right next to her to work on it together.

Rachel organized her notes so she could pick right back up in fifteen minutes on a park bench. "Did you assist an old lady crossing the street or get a cat out of a tree yesterday?"

"Har, har. No, I did homework for that hour, then left."

"That doesn't sound too bad, aside from the effort of being there instead of here. Any progress on the evil teacher conspiracy?"

Tracy shook her head. "It's been a day since we started. There's a lot of disjointed lines with no direct connections. I still haven't given up on finding how Melissa relates to all this too."

"Keep at it. By the end of the week, I expect to see a creepy wall of blurry black and white photos taken from a distance, all linked with red yarn."

That got Tracy to roll her eyes. "While I'm at it, I might as well find a date to the Snow Ball. One is as likely as the other. Our new celebrity status has left everyone too scared to ask me, and there's less than a week to go."

Rachel wrapped a red checkered scarf around her neck and put on a jacket, expecting the temperature to drop with the sinking sun. "Anyone here would be thrilled to go with the amazing Tracy Wayfield, and that was before your superpowers. They're a bonus."

Tracy's face brightened. "Go support our other friend before I transmute you into a foghorn."

Rachel was about 90% certain the threat was an idle one. Still, she didn't want to push her friend to find out what inanimate object she'd be remade into.

Making her way to the front of the school and past the administrative offices, John's old words took hold of her thoughts. Derek kept making ill-informed decisions based on fear. Tonight, he was right, but her excuses on his behalf were running out.

Hero Watches were a bad idea or, at best, a distraction. The crime rate around here didn't raise a blip on police scanners. Speeding and underage drinking were all the action local police handled, and on a school night, that dropped to nil. Once Derek realized the futility of waiting another night for trouble that wasn't coming or staring at a sealed portal, she was free to continue studying.

They weren't even playing dress-up in cosplay gear to hide their identities. Since the entire world knew about the superpowered teenagers, whether they believed it or not, there was no point in wearing a mask.

"Rachel!" Mr. Marshal hurried from his office to catch up to her. Short of using her powers to leave, there was no method to discreetly speed from the empty hallways and no students to hide behind in these after-hours.

She waited in front of the school's main glass-pane entrance doors. His voice was smooth, without an ounce of strain or short-ness of breath. "I'm glad you walked by my window. I've thought about how well you balanced all your obligations this past weekend. Between your band concert and most of the full day of training, I realized how many burdens I place on you all. Don't worry about training for this upcoming weekend. You and the others have earned a break."

"A little late, but thanks for the moment of compassion. It doesn't undo my mistake at the concert when my exhaustion and nerves triggered a flash of my powers."

Mr. Marshal's face lost its harsh angles, his expression softening in what looked oddly like concern. "You still have another concert this weekend, right?"

Rachel nodded, biting back the welling surge of emotion that her friends and family were there last Saturday to watch her fail.

"I've pushed you too hard," said Mr. Marshal. "Breaking you to prepare for the future is the wrong approach. In addition to skipping this weekend's training, starting the following weekend, I'll reduce my training to Saturdays only."

"Giving us more free time won't stop us from investigating you."

Instead of surprise or guilt, she received an outright laugh. "Good luck."

"We're on to you and your accomplice, Mr. Sprog." Rachel didn't give any ground. Her heart started running a 400-yard race without her. She hoped it didn't reveal her bluff about how little they knew.

Mr. Marshal's jaw set, his nostrils flaring. "He is no accomplice, and with the exceptions of Flint and Ri Ur Tol, I only trust those with powers that I gave, directly or indirectly."

"Mr. Sprog has powers?"

"Most assuredly."

"So... he's not working with you? Care to tell us anything useful?"

A faraway look cast over Mr. Marshal. Despite the risks to her body, Rachel combined two Aspects to look and listen more fully to the man in front of her. His tempo had fallen further out of sync, moving much faster than Rachel's tempo or the tempo of lockers along the walls. A growing wedge between him and reality drove deeper.

"In the end, that's all there is," uttered Mr. Marshal, talking to himself with a brand of crazy Rachel had never witnessed.

Rachel ignored the urge to shake him. She needed answers, so she shouted his name.

Like waking up from sleepwalking, he lurched back into the present. "I thought I knew Mr. Sprog from long ago, except he doesn't remember the things I do."

Just at the point where Mr. Marshal's words might have been helpful, he returned to his office.

"Wait. What does that mean?" Rachel called after Mr. Marshal, who ignored her, lost in his own world.

Looking at the guidance counselor, she considered a dozen ways she might use her powers to force him to tell her more. Rarely one to exhibit his abilities, he knew every way to counter her, Tracy, and the rest. Understanding a losing battle, Rachel left to meet with Derek.

Late afternoon descended over the park, a far stretch from a potential scene of a crime fit for a pair of superheroes to prevent. Chilly rose-colored sunlight shone on kids running all over the plastic playground shaped like a shipwreck as they cheered and shouted at one another over some imaginary game. A tall, middle-aged man pushed a squeaky stroller, stretching to the ground to clean up the mess left by his white-and-brown spotted hound. With long ears and short legs, the unfortunate dog was about to trip over itself.

A loud pop sounded from the baseball diamond as a girl's bat connected with the baseball. She earned a long dirt stain on her pants as she slid to first base. Someone honked at the driver who illegally merged from the left turn lane across the flow of traffic to reach the park.

Wary of the holes in the fences and patches of dead grass, those in the park avoided the damage done by the shadow monster. Rachel was forever grateful the damage was minimal.

Derek crouched down to closely study the imprints of brown and wilted grass. Near as they could tell, these were the first footsteps of the shadow monster, meaning the portal was opened on this spot, or the shadow could fly. Smooth ground all around them lacked the splitting evidence of the void's entrance. Though, if the void were opened in the air, there would be nothing to find now.

Rachel shifted her perceptions, revealing a crooked line of static electricity cutting the space in front of them. "There's something here. I have no idea if what I'm seeing is from the closed opening or the start of a new one."

Derek looked up at her. "I'll check here regularly to ensure the portal remains sealed."

Rachel filled him in on her talk with Mr. Marshal. Derek's frown deepened. If it went much further, Derek's lips were at risk of falling off the sides of his face, like two earthworms dropped from a mother bird to her waiting babies.

"What's wrong with you?" Derek crossed his arms over his chest, rapping his free hand against his cast-covered arm. "You don't tell a person you suspect of being a conspiracy ringleader that you're investigating them."

"We know more now than we did. Mainly, we now know we were wrong in assuming Mr. Sprog was helping Mr. Marshal."

"There has to be a connection, assuming they both have powers. Think they're from another dimension?"

Rachel sat at an adjacent park bench, retrieving her homework. "It's possible."

"What about Tracy? Do you think she's okay? I can't pin it down... She's seemed off the past few weeks, like she's lying to us."

Rachel forced a laugh to spite him. "Someone said the same thing about you."

His brow furrowed, the mystified expression showing he couldn't understand how anyone doubted the Great and Powerful Derek or his oft misguided intentions.

The hair at the base of Rachel's neck stood upright as though a forgotten dream were forcing its way to the forefront. She lowered her calculus textbook, setting aside her homework to survey the people in the park, seeking the unnerving source causing her mind to sense that something was not right.

The outfielder caught a grounded ball. Nothing was amiss at the pickup baseball game. Kids jumped off the prow of the ship at a height she wasn't quite comfortable with. Still, they rolled and laughed at the landing. Her eyes scanned faster, looking over every person.

She settled on what was setting her off. The man with the stroller and failure of a guard dog were approaching the street corner without slowing. He was adjusting some straps within the stroller and not paying attention. Teetering toward the intersection, the man was oblivious to the stream of cars speeding through the residential neighborhood. What must have been fatherly instincts kicked in, stopping them in front of the traffic light's pedestrian button.

Too soon to exhale her held breath, Rachel watched the wrinkled pile of a dog continue walking, pulling its leash free. The man was too busy adjusting the child in the stroller to notice.

"One sec," Rachel told her friend. She turned on her powers and took off at her usual power-enhanced speed walk.

Cars hurtled along at a turtle's speeding crawl.

Rachel wrapped her arms around the dog, sparing the family pet from the dangers of the busy street.

Time shifted to normal.

The man jumped a good foot into the air. He pressed his hand against his rising and falling chest. "You scared me!" he shouted at the dog in Rachel's arms, then he regarded her. "You're one of them, aren't you? Those kids who keep saving us from alien invasions."

"The Beast and the shadow monster weren't—" Rachel stopped, accepting the compliment. "Yeah. I fought them both times. You need to be more careful when walking your pet."

She put the dog back on the sidewalk. Its goofy grin and large eyes were too pure to be angry at for walking into traffic.

Handing the man his dog's leash, he secured it to the stroller's handle with a double knot, tugging it until the rope was snug. "Normally, my husband takes care of the afternoon walk, but I thought I'd surprise him by handling it. I'm still not used to this old girl," he said, scratching the dog's back until she rolled over. "We took her in a month ago."

Rachel lifted the wrinkled folds of skin on the dog's face to reveal large, pleading eyes. She gave in and gave a nice belly rub. "She's a good dog, not the smartest, though."

"She's a bottle of lightning trapped in a loaf of bread." The man handed her a twenty, but Rachel waved him off.

"I can't accept money for saving a life." She returned to Derek before giving the stranger a chance for a rebuttal.

"Good save!" Derek raised his hand to offer her a high-five and froze. "Does it seem darker than usual for this hour?"

They weren't the only ones who noticed. The pickup baseball game had come to a stop. Everyone had their eyes raised to the sky.

Rachel followed, looking in the same direction. It wasn't difficult to find. A plume of smoke settled on the western sky, resting on the tree line.

Her body locked, remembering the monster made of shadow. "Shit! The shadow monster's back."

Derek was on his feet, fists raised. "We need to get these people behind cover and away from the open field."

Rachel adjusted her thoughts. The smoke wasn't taking a distinct form. It was a single trail climbing higher above them. This wasn't the creature within the void. "Never mind. It's not a monster. It's a fire."

Relief skipped straight to guilt. This may not be the shadow monster, but it was still a disaster, and a fire in a populated area meant lives were at stake.

Throwing her schoolwork in her backpack and slinging it over her shoulders, Rachel directed Derek. "No time to argue. Get in my car—we're helping put out that fire."

He obeyed, questioning her as they sprinted to the parking lot. "Won't it be faster if you ran and I drove your car there?"

"There's no telling how far away the fire is or how far it's spread. I'll get us as close as we can, then we'll move on foot."

People in the park were busy taking pictures on their phones. Smart enough not to risk their lives, no one was leaving to get closer to the disaster. No one, except Derek and her.

Lucky us.

19

Fire!

Rachel

Spreading gray smoke dropped visibility outside Rachel's car to nothing. Little more than red taillights from the car directly in front of her shone through.

She pulled onto a side street and parked. "I'm going on ahead," she told Derek.

He rushed outside the car, lost immediately to her sight. "Go. Save who you can." His voice sounded distorted and distant.

Rachel ramped up her powers and sped away. She was careful to only walk in case she needed to avoid crashing into someone in the limited visibility. Though she used her abilities to move as fast as a car.

Acrid fumes burned her eyes. Holding her shirt sleeve over her mouth, she made a makeshift breathing filter. It did next to nothing.

Grit and tiny particles streaked over her face and clung to her hair.

Coughing purged the thick gas from her throat, though breathing still hurt.

All she smelled was burning. Unlike the small logs of a campfire, this smoke carried noxious fumes of melting chemicals.

Smoke to the left, smoke to the right; every direction looked the same. She moved between the line of stopped cars. Those inside their cars had their phones ready to catch sight of whatever lay ahead.

Rachel slowed, relaxing her powers to return to regular time. Otherwise, she might trip or run into the heart of the fire. Glass shattered somewhere to her right, sounding muted and alien.

A figure appeared from the gray haze. Rachel braced for an attack from the monster made of shadow. A middle-aged man solidified from shifting smoke. Rachel lowered her guard. Her nerves were frayed to the point of seeing enemies where there were none. He eyed her with caution. She walked around the man, hurrying to the source of the fire, where the air was heaviest with smoke.

Without warning, she could breathe, arriving at the heart of the blaze. Fresh air felt heavenly across her skin—well, one side of her. The other was drying, heated by the all-consuming fire engulfing what had been intended to be a shopping center. Smoke billowed from the flames in waves, covering the world behind her. Until the wind shifted, she was free in the open air.

Wooden beams blazed like giant matchsticks, feeding the flames and giving them the avenue to spread. Metal shriveled under the heat, twisting into arthritic hands reaching for an escape. The under-construction parking garage was consumed in flames, as was the future home of an ice cream parlor. The dozen stores being built in the shopping center were well on their way to becoming ash.

Firetrucks and police cars blockaded the streets as gallons of water fired immense pressure at the natural monster.

"Miss, I'm going to need you to back away." Fully covered from head to toe in heat-resistant yellow gear, a bulky man blocked her path to the burning building. His ash-covered helmet obstructed his face.

Wind swept the smoke from this side of the building. Still, the hot air was intolerable this close, drying her face while pulling sweat to its surface. "Do... Do you need any help?" Rachel offered.

The man puffed out his chest. "Please move across the street for your own safety."

"Is anyone trapped in there? I have powers! I can help." She ran in a circle around the firefighter, her powers speeding her into a specter illuminated by firelight.

That gave the man pause. He lifted the visor, taking Rachel in. "Well, damn." He squinted, looking closer at her face. "You're one of those kids in that video, the fast one. I knew it wasn't fake!"

She took a step toward the disaster. The firefighter refused to budge. "That suave blond guy and his friends already came through. They got all the construction crew to safety. We professionals have it handled from here."

"Who saved the workers?" uttered Rachel. Derek was still running to get here. He wasn't blond, and he was alone. She didn't know anyone with powers who fit the firefighter's description.

"Don't worry, Chief. I can take care of this young lady," said an Olympic bodybuilder who stepped from the edge of the smoldering wreckage. The woman's long-sleeved shirt showcased arms that looked like they were enhanced by Tracy's powers to make them gigantic. Her navy-blue dress pants shifted as she walked, hinting at powerful leg muscles. Gray soot covered her black work boots. Her brown braid fell behind her, swaying as she moved.

"She's all yours, Detective," the firefighter said before wandering away to enforce the barricade somewhere else.

Rachel craned her neck back as the woman, who was strength personified, closed in. Under the dry heat, Rachel's parched throat cracked. "Did you see the heroes who saved the construction workers?"

"No. This blaze was already well underway when I arrived. They left the workers at a safe spot and ran away." The woman raised her hands toward the fire as though blind and able to read a novel written in the flames. "The firefighters assume a stray spark from a careless welder or a discarded cigarette started the fire. I'm not so certain." She gestured at the back of the building. "Follow me carefully. I want to show you something."

Rachel didn't know what to say, so she nodded as they wandered around the building. Heat carried in the air, forcing her to lift her shirt collar to cover most of her face.

She stepped lightly on the shards of glass covering the sidewalk. The adjacent apartment complex's windows had exploded from the heat, making it even more dangerous to be this close to the fire. Plastic siding on the apartment exteriors had morphed into fluid, marring the outer surface like a bad, dripping paint job. She might be able to tolerate another minute or two out here before needing to run to a few blocks away where the air was cooler.

"Since when do firefighters defer to a detective's orders?" Rachel blurted out to hear anything other than crackling wood collapsing on itself. "And are you really a detective? You don't seem like one."

The woman looked away for several seconds, staring at where the fire had yet to spread. Wistful sadness consumed her when she faced Rachel, like when Rachel's grandmother with Alzheimer's sat in front of the piano until she remembered how to play a classical piece.

"I used to be. I'm much more now. Going by 'detective' simplifies things when interacting with others." The towering woman moved in close. "Enough about me. I wanted to talk about how your actions inspire others. Please be more careful in how you're portrayed as heroes. I'm terrified my daughter will become like you, throwing herself at a burning building. She's followed you enough as it is."

Rachel laced bitterness into her laugh at the misaligned hero worship she didn't deserve. "I have no say in how people see me or perceive my abilities. As for your daughter, there are worse role models than me."

Abruptly, the woman stopped to point at the second floor, shifting the topic back to the fire. "Some kind of power is coming from in there. That's what attracted me here. Perhaps that triggered an electrical short and sparked this fire?"

Before Rachel could respond, Derek emerged from the wall of smoke blanketing the surrounding neighborhood and ran to them. Sweat mixed with ash streaked down his face. He looked past Rachel at the woman beside her. "It's you!"

The woman's green eyes studied Derek. "Derek Fen, do you have anything to add about that mysterious car accident from two months ago?"

"No," he yelped.

"No, Detective Patricia Kim," the woman corrected. "Be glad I let you go with a warning when we first met."

"You didn't warn me about anything."

"The warning was implied. I see you revealed your powers to the world. That was a mistake."

Rachel rushed to Derek's defense. "We didn't have the option to keep our powers hidden when we keep fighting giant monsters."

The woman didn't give an inch. "Have you tried wearing a costume?"

Rachel, likewise, refused to bend. "We were a bit focused in the moment on surviving."

Derek finally caught up in the conversation. "Hold on. This whole time, you knew I had powers?"

The detective faced the hungry blaze. "Among other things. I knew at the car crash that there was something in those woods with considerable power. That much power is close to what I'm sensing inside the burning building. Can you see anything?"

Firelight burned bright images into Rachel's retinas. Still, she opened herself to use an Aspect, staring at what lay behind swaying flames. The jagged outline of a crack in the air was barely visible between two melting concrete pillars. Rachel instinctively took a step back. "There's an unfinished portal in there!"

Derek swore under his breath. His eyes scanned the fire, eventually settling where an unusual wind made the flames dance more vigorously. "I won't open it to send the fire into the void. The risk is too great for the shadow monster to escape."

He waved his hands in front of him, and the crack sealed.

The strong woman clapped a heavy hand on Rachel's shoulder. "What was that?"

Rachel slid from her grasp. "A gateway to other places and times."

"Did your friends create what you closed?" Patricia asked.

"No," replied Derek. "Closing holes is easy. Opening them is difficult, and I'm the only one in this time who can do it. What do you mean by 'friends'?"

"There was another superpowered team here." Rachel leaned in closer to Derek, whispering, "Do you think that old man training us gave powers to other people as a backup?"

"I don't know what to think," he hissed back. "For all we know, Ri Ur Tol popped in to save a few lives."

"Except Ri Ur Tol isn't blond or a man. That's how the hero was described to me."

A manic gleam shone in Derek's eyes. "My conspiracy theory isn't looking so crazy now. We need to regroup and figure this out."

Rachel regretted Derek's words, thinking of all the homework she had left to do. There was another long night ahead of her.

Rachel glanced at the fire. "Is there anything else we can do to help, short of spilling the fire into the void?"

Derek chewed on his lip. "Not that I can think of, since the other superpowered team beat us here and rescued all the bystanders. My telekinesis is as likely to spread the fire as suppress it."

Together, Rachel and Derek left the odd detective at the fire as the firefighters brought it under control. The hike back through the smoke to her abandoned car was silent as both grappled with their thoughts.

20

Swerving

Derek

Derek checked his desktop computer for any new uploaded videos of the fire. He leaned back in his spinning bedroom chair, rubbing his temples. Days later, there wasn't much aside from grainy amateur footage on the superpowered B squad. He wasted his Saturday morning failing to fix blurry images of a distant blob jumping out the third floor to escape the flames. If he squinted, Derek counted one person landing lightly after falling three floors while carrying five people on their back. Three others waited outside the building to get them all to safety.

One of them might be capable of flight or super strength. Their powers were too difficult to gauge from the still shots.

He shut down his computer, needing to face the greater challenge today. Shoving clothes about, each one looked as bad of a choice as the next. A polo shirt portrayed him as pretentious. Wearing a shirt with a band's logo might lose Ri Ur Tol in the modern reference. He settled on a neutral gray fisherman's sweater, stretching the ill-used threads by putting it on.

Derek pushed aside his gathered notes on Mr. Marshal and theories about the other superpowered team to reveal his single page of discussion topics for the afternoon at the mall with Ri Ur Tol. Rachel and Tracy had zero constructive input, telling him to be more natural and plan less. He left his room, his mind tormenting him with replays of every worst-case scenario.

His mom stood at the front door, barring his exit. Dirt stained her fingers, evidence of a morning gardening. Amid beaming eyes and a spreading smile, she asked, "So, what's their name?"

The temperature in the room rose by a good ten degrees in an instant. Derek's flustered face was all the proof she needed. "Huh?"

She made no false pretense of having a reason to be there, aside from waiting for him. "You keep talking to yourself in the hallway mirror, and I've never seen you this nervous."

Like ripping off a band-aid, he spoke fast and didn't bother dodging the truth. "Her name is Ri Ur Tol. I doubt she's into me, and the idea to do something today spiraled from a favor I need."

"Ri Ur Tol sounds like an odd name." His mom's face beamed in a wide smile.

"Can't explain it now, mom, gotta run." He scrambled to put on his light jacket and shoes in world record time.

His mom pressed his jangling car keys into his hands. "Relax and remember to have fun."

Bursting from the front door, Derek ran to his recently-repaired but still-busted car. The dents to the light-red hood had been hammered into a semblance of its original form. Thankfully, their Governor declared his Beast's attack a State of Emergency, so the insurance company had to cover the damage. They replaced the engine, radiator, brake pads, tires, dashboard, and a laundry list of other ailments from when it hit a monster head-on. Though the amount spent had to surpass the total value, his insurance refused to declare the wreck totaled and buy him a replacement. His car continued to live, much less than the summation of its new parts.

A sprayed fresh car smell clung to the worn fabric, some cross between chemical cleaner and a pinecone. Vacuumed and empty of scattered schoolwork, this was the cleanest his car had been since he plucked it from the used car lot.

The cast over his healing arm made turning the ignition more difficult than it needed to be. Luckily, he was in an automatic, so once his car was moving, he wouldn't need to use his inhibited arm much. The engine flared and died. Derek cursed and turned the ignition a few more times, thrilled when it started on his fourth try. The dashboard glowed. Letters on the radio button controls were largely rubbed off by years of contact and UV rays. He set the station to DC101 and drove to school, or more accurately, the bridge near it. Alternative hits from the past three decades cracked from his sound system, making Derek feel like this drive was ephemeral, a timeless anomaly as he drove to pick up the young woman separated from her own time.

Rather than give Ri Ur Tol directions to his house or the mall, this bridge was the easiest point of reference for her to teleport to.

Derek pulled to the side of the road at the bridge.

Ri Ur Tol stepped from the park bench in the empty bus-loading area with the grace of a wolf stalking prey. Her loose yellow sweater had the space to hide maybe a dozen deadly weapons. Tight jeans limited where additional sharp implements could be stored. He assumed her black boots were steel tipped or had a blade pop out if she clicked the heels.

Ri Ur Tol inspected his car warily as she got in, looking over it like a cavern ready to collapse and trap her inside.

"Can you buckle the seat belt?" Derek asked, not wanting her to look too closely at the innards of his trashmobile. "Right! This is your first time in a car. The strap over your shoulder clicks into the piece at your hip."

"Sensible. Do these vessels go fast enough to warrant such a restraint?" Ri Ur Tol clicked herself in place.

"In theory, they go fast enough to make seat belts necessary. My car is the exception." He pressed the gas pedal, hoping his car obeyed. The engine revved and the RPM meter hit red. His car didn't move.

Ri Ur Tol started at the growling engine noises. "Do these vehicles normally sound like clashing swords?"

Derek's hands tightened around the steering wheel. He turned on the AC to chill his burning cheeks. "Nope."

"Want me to teleport us to where we are going?"

"You don't know where that is."

"Then I'll get us up for a better vantage," Ri Ur Tol said as she pointed above them, "and you can tell me where to go."

"No!" Derek shouted, surprised by the force he put into the word. "I don't like being up high," he mumbled.

"It is sensible to fear danger. You seemed fine when we fell during our first real battle together."

"I was anything but fine. My Beast trying to split me in half kept my mind a little occupied from being a mile up in the air."

"I, too, was forced to overcome my fear of heights and the new challenges present in your time."

Derek pushed the gas pedal. Once more, the car engine made a loud roar without moving them forward. An oncoming bus was growing larger in the rearview mirror.

Warning lights on the dashboard screen flickered. In a desperate attempt to move, he applied telekinesis to the trunk, pushing the ton of steel and broken parts. The wheels gave, plodding the car along. Derek's foot applied more gas. Something inside caught. The car hopped forward and then allowed itself to be driven.

Ri Ur Tol clenched the grab handle above her head until the car's acceleration smoothed from erratic to a mild jostle. Given this was her first trip in a car, and the maximum speed in her time had to peak at twenty miles an hour, she faced the newest threat head-on, controlling her fears without teleporting away.

Cursing his dad for this hand-me-down ride, Derek hoped the car held together for the next twenty or so miles.

He adjusted the volume on the radio to steady their nerves and give Ri Ur Tol a taste of modern music as one of his guilty pleasure favorites started. Even with the auto-tuned singing, the beat was damn catchy. He spared Ri Ur Tol's ears by refraining from singing along.

Her head bobbed up and down, and her rictus grin softened into the brave smile she wore into battle.

"Is this a date?" she asked when the song ended.

Derek's eyes flitted to the side, meeting Ri Ur Tol's steady gaze. "Where did you even learn that term?"

"Tracy explained it, though my people have similar customs. If this is a date, I will refrain from asking for your help in taking a difficult journey with me until another day. I do not want your decision to be influenced by an attempt to make a good impression."

He found some courage in that sideways method of thinking, enough to loosen his jaw. "Full disclosure, I have a favor to ask of you." Air left his lungs in a forced half laugh. "I'm hoping my charming personality on this date might convince you to undergo a dangerous quest with me in the future."

She nodded and made a small grunt of approval. "You think highly of yourself. We shall see how this date goes."

"Have you been on a date before?" Derek regretted opening his mouth.

"Yes, and I have assisted my mistress during many from a long line of avid admirers," replied Ri Ur Tol. "Although now that we are alone, I am more interested in your thoughts on the shadow monster. What do you think it seeks, so we might better prepare for our next battle?"

The drastic topic change almost caused him to miss a car in his blind spot as he merged onto the highway. So much for small talk.

Derek's thoughts turned to a memory of a poorly lit vault in the ancient past and an army surging to kill him. He had opened the portal to the void to escape and witnessed the devastation of the shadow monster. "The first time we fought that thing, it would have dragged warriors from your time into the void if the Ur Tol and I hadn't stopped it."

"I have seen undersea eels clamp on a fish in a similar manner and drag it back into their hole to eat."

"You think the shadow wants to eat us? When I last saw it within the void, it was hovering around a used portal into this world. Does that make it like a polar bear at a breathing hole, waiting for us seals to come up for air?"

Ri Ur Tol kept her expression neutral, though it felt like a wave of annoyance emanated at him. "I don't know those animals. The concept seems correct."

"Sorry. I've recently been doing a lot of bear-related research."

"I can't imagine why," she said, staring into the passenger-side mirror.

He let out a small, nervous laugh. "Did you make a joke?"

Ri Ur Tol's hand rose in a gesture to silence Derek. "We are being followed."

Derek stared into the rearview mirror, uncertain of what he was looking for. When his eyes peeled down from the search, he switched lanes, the cast on his arm slowing his ability to react. He signaled to return to the middle lane, looking for another car to act with a similarly erratic motion.

"Which car is it?"

Ri Ur Tol held her hand above his. "You do not need to know, as you will make it obvious we know they follow. Take no sudden actions. We want to make the hunter into the hunted. I'll watch them. You ensure we do not crash."

He didn't know where to focus his attention. A black pickup truck zoomed by, and a blue Mercedes passed him on the right, weaving between cars, speeding as though they were racing home to go to the bathroom. There were too many cars to track in his mind. How Ri Ur Tol found one to lock onto eluded his skills. "What do I do?"

"Behave as you were. I will observe."

Between sideways glances in every mirror, Derek brainstormed reasons anyone would want to follow him. They ranged from bad to worse.

Minutes dragged on, reaching double digits. He counted cars, losing track of colors and models until the red minivan tailgating him appeared to be the same as the orange sedan to his right. He looked up at the bright green sign, recognition connecting. The exit from the highway had snuck up on him.

Derek signaled and merged immediately across two lanes. Horns blared. He sped to avoid being hit in the back by a sports car. He shoved his car forward with a telekinetic boost to make it go faster as the sports car slammed on its brakes, narrowly missing a collision.

A deep-green car tried to mirror Derek's two-lane-cross maneuver, one to make any D.C. driver proud. He marked that as the car tailing them, unable to swerve and follow onto the same exit. Too far for Derek to see the driver, they sped away on the highway Derek had left.

"Not how I intended to deal with them," Ri Ur Tol's voice rang.

"Right..." Derek's heart rate slowed back to normal. "That was intentional. Go me."

"It would have been better to stop them. That way, we could discover what they wanted."

"With this clunker, the best I could do was evade, and barely at that."

Derek meandered onto Broken Land Parkway, letting the sports car he cut off go well ahead. All roads within a ten-mile radius led to the Columbia Mall. He had no interest in being verbally chewed out in a parking lot in the event the driver he cut off had the same destination as him.

After circling the outdoor upper parking lot a few dozen times, Derek found a newly available space by the movie theater as someone finally left. He turned off the car, closed his eyes, and fortified his resolve to move his mouth. "Ready to experience the best of the modern world?"

21

Modern Market

Derek

Derek opened his car's trunk. Hesitant to start this almost date too badly, they needed to be less conspicuous. "Do you mind leaving your daggers in the car? Weapons are frowned upon in public places."

Ri Ur Tol proudly dropped a six-inch dagger strapped to her waist next to his own weapon, the broken hilt of what remained of his sword. She kept drawing more needle-thin finger-length blades. Even when Derek assumed she couldn't possibly be hiding more, a final dagger appeared from beneath her sweater.

The movie theater on their left beckoned with Saturday matinee showings. Ri Ur Tol's mind was about to be scrambled when she experienced this modern marvel. First, though, he had an hour to acclimate her to the mall. A row of generic restaurants lined the outdoor parking lot. Families wandered back and forth between the movie theater and the mall.

Red and green lights spiraled around bare trees lining the sidewalk, adding holiday cheer.

They marched from the outdoor upper parking lot to the mall's entrance. Though the sun shone, it added little warmth. Derek shoved his hands deeper into his jacket pockets to keep warm. Ri Ur Tol hunkered forward, keeping her body heat close. She shivered once or twice, too stubborn to complain, walking faster and forcing Derek to race to keep up.

A pair of children ran by screaming, climbing on layered stones within a smooth fountain. Being in the midst of the fall season, the pool was drained of water. Strong winds pushed Derek back, reminders of winter rushing to blanket his home in snow. This weather held no influence over those sitting at the outside tables of Starbucks. Clustered together, people in wool jackets sipped coffee, surrounded by outdoor heaters to stave off the cold Derek was hurrying to escape by entering the mall.

Ri Ur Tol blew into her hands for warmth, then ran her fingers along the shiny black granite of the empty fountain. "Your well dried. Is your home suffering from a drought?"

Puzzled for a moment, Derek began to understand how the warrior observed the world. "No. We don't drink from that water. It's a decoration. They turn off the fountain when it gets cold to prevent the pipes from freezing."

"Freezing?"

Derek smacked his forehead. Of course, someone living in an ancient desert knew nothing about ice. This situation called for an obvious solution. The Cold Snap was too far, but there was a good runner-up. "I have a surprise for you," he teased.

By opening the glass-pane doors into the mall, Derek was greeted by his prize. Plastic covers shielded the frozen treats from the heated warmth of the mall. Hot chocolate would go down easier than ice cream, yet he wanted to show off the best modern hits.

Ice cream would have to wait; Ri Ur Tol remained stuck at the entrance, stopped in place, and partially blocking the glass doors. Her body shook as she forced down quick breaths. She reached beneath her clothes, likely grabbing for a dagger she left in his car. He needed to act fast to prevent an innocent bystander from being hurt by whatever new danger she found.

Derek did the first thing he thought of, which also was the dumbest. He placed himself next to Ri Ur Tol, ready to take on the unknown threat.

She stared straight ahead, her eyes narrowed. Derek followed, expecting to see a monster or dozens of fighters running at them with their swords drawn.

Instead, Derek saw only the indoor carousel. Simple music chimed, returning him to younger days spent riding the statuesque animals while holding his mom's hand.

Hundreds of bright light bulbs lit the landmark within the mall, a monument to a bygone era. The carousel slowed down, and all the kids funneled out of the exit.

Derek hesitated, then placed his hand gently on Ri Ur Tol's arm to ease her apparent fear of this machine. "This is entertainment, not a threat."

When her hand came free without a weapon, he brought her to the adjacent ice cream shop and ordered two vanilla cones with chocolate sprinkles. There was no sense in throwing too much modern at Ri Ur Tol with a complex flavor.

Ri Ur Tol bit into her ice cream. Immediately, she pressed her hand to her teeth. "It's delicious!"

"Lick it, otherwise you'll get brain freeze." Derek demonstrated.

She ignored him, consuming her ice cream with enthusiasm. "This is delicious. Can I have one more?"

"Leave room to sample our finest cuisines."

She may not have heard him, already moving on to study the mall. Red ribbons and bright lights hung outside of most stores, holiday decorations meant to feel like home and attract customers.

Ri Ur Tol stared higher at the glass prism roof. The mall's transparent roof doused this floor and the open floor below in natural daylight, making it feel like they were outside. "Are those glass ceilings forged by magic as they were for my home?"

"No. Magic is rare, to the point where my friends and I are practically the only ones I know of able to wield it."

"Magic was rare in my time as well. How did they make the roof and hold it in place without magic?"

"You'll need to ask an architect or engineer." Derek shrugged. "I'm not sure how, but the glass is made by super-heating and cooling sand."

They moved to the stairs and down to the bottom floor. Ri Ur Tol sprinted ahead to the decorative indoor shallow pool. Scarcely deep enough to drown in, the blue-tiled circular pool made a great place to rest. Tiny jets sprayed water up along the outer rim.

An inner light of wonder came over Ri Ur Tol's eyes. She pointed at a trio of teenagers sitting by the water's edge, lost in conversation. "Do they not realize the wealth at their feet?"

Ri Ur Tol scooped a hand into the clear water to drink, spitting out the chlorine-infused mixture. Seeing the coins at the bottom, she plucked a handful and stared at the dripping change.

Derek looked around, ready to defend them from mall security. No one approached. Her behavior got a few stares until a toddler pulled out their own stash of coins from the water.

"Please put those back," Derek told Ri Ur Tol. "People offer them in hopes their dreams come true."

"Strange ritual. Did the metal coins poison this water source?"

"Chemicals keep it clean and clear for show. We don't drink from it."

"Your kind is wasteful."

Derek rubbed his face. "So I'm gathering."

Somehow, he convinced her to leave the pool and visit the rest of the mall. It helped that the food court was in their line of sight. Still, as they walked away, she kept turning around as though the water were a mirage.

Grease, sugar, spices, and hundreds of other smells Derek was unable to pinpoint accosted him. His stomach grumbled in anticipation. Everything from Chinese food to cheap fast food to barbecue was on display, their aromas wafting about the food court to entice.

Swelled by holiday crowds, families and friends occupied nearly every open table.

Ri Ur Tol surveyed the glowing lights of the food options. "This is a suitable chance to show me whether I should mate with you."

Derek crushed his ice cream cone into pieces that slipped from his fingers. He dove to clean them up, sputtering, "Wh-wh-wh-what makes you say that?"

"My people take intended partners to the market to see how they behave. Does one know what to purchase? Will they choose taste over sustenance? Have they established favorable relationships? How are their trading skills? The most determining question for me is, how does one treat those serving them?"

"That's not what's happening. I want this to be a judgment-free zone. Wait here," he said, wandering away from Ri Ur Tol to collect himself.

His feet and hands acted on instinct, bypassing long lines by taking the offered free samples and a napkin to wipe the ice cream from his hand. He returned to her with treasures from a first pass walk: sticks of barbecued pork, teriyaki chicken, and an onion ring. He offered her one of each and split the onion ring. "Pick the one you like best, and we can get that for lunch."

"Impressive," she said. Derek's best attempt to read Ri Ur Tol's expression failed. Following his example, she returned with her own samples, choosing the tangy sweet and sour chicken and watermelon-blended smoothie.

Derek nodded in approval. "You've adapted to my present time better than I thought you would."

"Although the flavors, wares, and appearances have shifted, this is more or less the same as any market within my city." Whatever was in the tasty teriyaki chicken's secret sauce loosened her lips, and Ri Ur Tol continued. "Not far from my home were expansive forests with deep lakes fed during monsoon seasons. The Tak and Tol used their magic to find or create new water sources. We might have lived easier by building small villages a day's travel closer to the wetlands. Doing so would have defied the Great Savior's gift of forming our city."

"Your city sounds like a paradise the more you tell me about it. I wish we explored it more and pissed off fewer of its people," Derek added with his best roguish grin.

"Compared to your conveniences, mine was a harsh world, yet one I cherish." Ri Ur Tol sat heavily on an empty metal chair attached to an open table. "All of it is gone, sunk beneath waves, so deep not even the sun can reach." Water formed in her eyes, though no tears fell.

The date was spiraling from Derek's control. No sheet of conversation topics prepared him for this. "We're thousands of years removed from your people. Even the most flourishing civilizations end."

"I must know more about our end."

"Then I'll help."

Derek's hand hovered inches above hers, uncertain whether he should close the space between them. Feeling equal parts brave and insane, he patted her hand, a meager offering of comfort.

Her expression warmed, making the effort more than worthwhile. "The weight of water above my home's ruins would have crushed me had I lingered longer. Returning there will require preparation and care, best saved for another day. Show me more of your world today."

Derek took her hand and led her to the stores as a distraction.

His dad told him there was once a pet store in the mall. Staring at cute puppies was a foolproof method to raise anyone's spirit. Too bad he was a few decades too late.

Foot traffic was at record highs for the day, ramping up for the holiday season. One little boy was being led by his parents as he cried, likely overwhelmed and exhausted from a day of shopping. Everyone seemed in a hurry, desperate to buy their gifts for others. Derek stepped around one guy charging forward, unaware of those he passed, engrossed in his phone. Had Derek not moved, the twenty-something would have collided right into him. Derek missed the regular days not around the holidays, when it was easy to maintain pandemic levels of distance. Ri Ur Tol moved freely, likely accustomed to high densities of bodies within her home city.

Derek walked her a quarter-turn around the mall, past the wide corridors filled with department stores, jewelry outlets, and assorted clothing chains. Ri Ur Tol peered into the window of a Lego store, admiring the little plastic people and castle sets. The flashy electronic store gave her pause, too.

Skipping ahead in his mental list of stores, Derek went to one featuring high-end comforts containing the two best seats in the mall.

Leather thrones fitted with padding supported his back. Semicircle foam caressed his ankles. He raised the footrests and lowered the chair's back using the control panel at his side. After demonstrating that, he did the same to Ri Ur Tol's chair. She was shocked at the shifting of balance, then settled into the comfortable position.

He pressed another button on her chair's control, initiating the moderate massage. Ri Ur Tol jumped again, only to sink into the cushioned seat. She let out a small exhale of satisfaction, the first Derek had ever heard from her. "Not half bad, right?"

The pulsating seat caused Ri Ur Tol's teeth to chatter as she spoke. "Your world possesses wonderful conveniences."

From his seat, Derek glimpsed Tracy walking past the store's entrance, her chestnut hair bobbing from music flowing into her bulky white headphones. It seemed unlikely she was here for a shopping excursion, considering Tracy's abilities made her into a clothing outfitter, electronics outlet, and supermarket wrapped into one. She was likely meeting their other friends. Derek checked his phone. She might be going to meet Louis. He was still on the clock at his retail job.

If this date went sour, Derek would head in that direction, hoping his friends would support him.

While he struggled for words to fill his empty throat, Ri Ur Tol sprang to her feet and punched the air, flexing her limbs. Bending forward, she then leaned back into her full height, stretching her arms wide, like waking from a nap. "This chair is amazing!"

A few heads turned at her voice, then returned to their holiday shopping.

Ri Ur Tol pulled Derek back into the main enclosed avenue beneath the clear glass rooftop.

A bright kiosk cycled through an electronica playlist, the subwoofer bellowing electronica music with enough force to break down a kidney stone. Ri Ur Tol caressed the speaker, her arm visibly shaking with the vibrations.

Never in his life did Derek wish he knew a fraction of Rachel's musical knowledge more than now. Tracy may feel music in her bones, but Rachel knew how to speak about it in a way that made anyone believe they were a Bach or Danny Elfman.

While Derek daydreamed, the vendor listed the speaker's best features to Ri Ur Tol. Derek looked for the fastest method to extract themselves, so he wouldn't have to explain that as a student who'd abandoned his source of income, a $400 price tag was well beyond his means.

As they started walking away, the adjacent vendor offered them one of the hundreds of shiny smartphone cases. Derek held back his laugh, rather than justify Ri Ur Tol's lack of a smartphone.

Ri Ur Tol thanked the vendor politely and led Derek by the hand to the open space between the vendors, giving Derek a mischievous look. "My turn to show you something."

He recognized her look and felt a twinge of fear. An unsettling feeling rose from Derek's stomach like he had eaten something much too spicy.

Snap.

Open air rushed around them. From high in the sky, he saw miles in all directions. Derek was glad he ate only a light snack of samples. The contents of his stomach were already sloshing around. Of all the activities to engage in today, falling hundreds of feet did not break the top twenty possibilities.

Bitter cold pierced his jacket and raked across his skin. A wild shriek spilled from Derek. From this top-down view of the Columbia Mall he never wished to experience, the mall appeared as the capital letter "K." The massive stores bookending the mall seemed minuscule from this vantage, though they grew much too fast as they fell.

He slammed his eyes shut, bracing to hurl a telekinetic blast upward to steady their fall.

An inventory of the belongings on hand included a distinct lack of a parachute. Wind ruffled his sweater, air passing freely through the woven material. Maybe if he stripped and wrapped the sweater inside his pants, they might survive by using it as an improvised parachute.

A gentle squeeze reminded him he wasn't alone. "Open your eyes. Look," Ri Ur Tol ordered.

He kept his eyes sealed tight, having no intention of watching himself become a human pancake.

Ri Ur Tol applied more force. "Our fall will not stop until you open your eyes and greet your fear."

That hard-headed warrior was stubborn enough to die to be true to her word.

Derek squinted, throwing his most disdainful look at Ri Ur Tol. Her eyes were lively, absorbing as much as she could about Derek's hometown while they plummeted to their deaths.

"See, it's not bad," Ri Ur Tol shouted above the wailing winds.

Derek pointed at the oncoming end to their fall. "Until we stop moving by hitting the ground."

Snap.

Down became up, and Derek faced the sky, decelerating. Ri Ur Tol reversed their directions.

They reached a peak, hovering in place for what felt like a weightless eternity. The peaceful moment ended when he looked down, sliding his gaze from the man-made lake next to the mall with its dwindling woodlands to the suburban sprawl spiraling from the mall. Derek's organs sank, shriveling at the sensations.

Ri Ur Tol's hair drifted, undone from tight braids. Her stoic appearance faded, replaced by the embodiment of chaos. In the short time he had known her, he never had seen her so carefree.

When they picked up enough speed, Ri Ur Tol teleported them higher, and upside down, so they fell up. This second time, Derek gave in, letting out a tiny whoop at the zero-G peak and using his telekinesis to give them an added updraft, lengthening the time spent hovering.

Snap.

Ri Ur Tol teleported them back inside the mall. Derek dropped the few feet to the floor, landing on his back. The impact hurt his pride and little else. Shock and yelps surrounded them from their sudden arrival.

Someone had their phone out, calling to them, "Do it again!"

Ri Ur Tol lifted Derek to his feet.

Derek went through the motion of brushing himself off, despite no dirt clinging to his clothes. He would give anything to spend less time with Ri Ur Tol being knocked on his ass, metaphorically or physically.

Not-so-subtle people accumulated around them. Camera flashes flared at the corners of Derek's vision, and the more obnoxious of the bunch leaned in for distance selfies. Ri Ur Tol grabbed Derek's wrist and started running, teleporting them around until they appeared in an empty hallway leading to the bathrooms, having lost all the followers.

Five minutes later, they sat across from each other in the food court, two trays of French fries between them.

Derek struggled to find the words to bridge the multiple millennium gap. Next to that, describing his favorite band or top five video games was pointless. He offered Ri Ur Tol a small smile and shifted to stare at the food, aware of his flushed cheeks.

Smells of watered-down bleach carried from the table behind him. A man wearing a facemask and plastic gloves swept trash left under the tables into a dustbin, dropping the contents into a larger trash can.

"I have to know," Derek said, doing his best to ignore those around them. "You've teleported us hundreds of miles. Why didn't you do that to escape my Beast instead of going straight up?"

Having finished her starch-based snack, Ri Ur Tol snatched a French fry from his tray. She held it between her fingers, considering her answer. "I believed you would not want the creature harming others if we left it alone. From our vantage, I intended to monitor it while the rest of you recovered to finish the fight. I failed to anticipate it could follow us."

Derek scratched beneath his healing arm's cast. "Anywhere had to be better than up."

"I am not accustomed to traveling to unfamiliar places amid battle."

Over the swelling storm churning in his stomach, he asked, "Would you mind helping me with a trip into the void?"

"Oh?" Hints of amusement touched Ri Ur Tol's voice. "You think the day has gone that well?"

He hoped Ri Ur Tol didn't notice the scarlet tinge spreading over his ears. "Will you explore the void with Nicole and me to pick up the trail of the other me? Either he's still in the void or spit out of it like we were. If he left the void, we'll find that spot, look at the other side, and then come home. I need more information before we launch a rescue, so we don't lose another month of our lives." Derek spoke in one breath, words tripping over his tongue, spilling onto the table separating them.

"Ah." Intentional or otherwise, her pause made Derek's insides perform a somersault. "That is dangerous. I assume you need me to avoid the shadow creature. When we return from your favor, and you recover your strength after opening the way to the void, you shall assist me with my task."

Once his brain caught up and realized she said yes, Derek shouted, "Whatever it is, I'm there!"

She stole another fry. Derek pushed his tray of remaining fries toward her in the hope she'd accept them as a bribe. Ri Ur Tol seemed less inclined to nibble when she didn't have to reach over the table, as though she enjoyed fries best when taking them from him. "It is best to know what your prey or enemies want. What do you think this shadow creature within the void desires?"

He considered how little he knew about the shadow. "That thing has to be seeking a way into our world, right?"

"When we fought alongside my mistress, it tried to pull someone into the void."

"Do you think it's hungry?"

"It may be both seeking escape and a meal. All beings seek a home with sufficient sustenance."

"You see the shadow as a being, not a mere animal or mindless force?"

Ri Ur Tol shrugged. "It showed intelligence in the park. It should have run from the fight if it were merely after food. The shadow was far from cornered in the open field and we were stronger than it in that smaller form. We are ill-equipped for the hunt until we know what it wants."

"Well, if all goes according to my plan, when we return to the void, we will lead the shadow from the exits closest to this present world. That's my favor." Derek paused to study Ri Ur Tol's reaction. "Does yours involve life-threatening bad decisions?"

A gleam flashed in Ri Ur Tol's eyes. "I know no other way. We go to great underwater depths."

Derek's settled pulse rose at the decision to press his luck. "With all these life-threatening risks, care to have some fun on the side?"

That brought on a questioning look from her. "Perhaps."

Exhilarating dread clogged his mouth with useless words, "Well... Th-there is a school dance next Saturday... What I mean is, would you, maybe, like to join our group, if you're available?" Each word uttered siphoned what conviction Derek had until the last syllables were barely audible.

"I shall partake in your social ritual."

"Feel like searching the void in the morning and partying at night?"

"As long as we don't mix those two." A soft laugh escaped Ri Ur Tol's mouth.

Never again would he possess the courage to do something so dangerous. Derek thought his heart had sprinted when Ri Ur Tol gave him a bird's eye view of the mall. That experience was a mere appetizer compared to now. His heart thumped against his rib cage like it wanted to burst from his chest over what he was about to say. "Do you mind if I kiss you?"

"Do you normally ask? Then, yes."

He stretched across the table, its corner prodding him in the gut the closer he got to Ri Ur Tol. Everything, from sizzling rice frying at the nearest food station to the sweet cinnamon stick smells, blurred in his mind as his lips melted into hers.

Peppered flavoring mixed in at their soft touch. Uncertain whether these tastes came from his lips, Derek regretted kissing her immediately after eating. She must be thinking about how the people of the future have become slobs.

As she pulled him closer, an unearthly boom rattled the mall's foundation pillars. Their embrace broke apart.

Ri Ur Tol's pupils dilated, her head shifting from side to side.

All Derek got out was, "That wasn't in my head?"

Thick spiderweb lines spread from a single point above the distant indoor decorative pool, widening into a hovering crack in the air.

A second boom erupted, and a hole blacker than any darkness ripped into existence from within the crack. Strong, cold winds stirred from the materializing portal to the void, knocking over stunned shoppers.

Seven long fingers curled around the edges of the opening. The hand of a living shadow, larger than a grown adult, cleaved the barrier separating realities.

22

Breach

Tracy

An explosion ripped through the mall, rattling Tracy, and knocking a wall of soccer cleats off their display cases. Louis ran toward the noise, abandoning his retail job.

Tracy grabbed Louis by his checkered flag polo shirt. "I have this," she said. "We can't have your limbs break again so soon after I fixed them."

Louis opened his mouth as though to argue with Tracy, then he turned to shout at the shoppers, "Everyone out the back door! Follow signs to the exit. I'll guard the store's entrance and lead more people out."

Regretting all her life's decisions, Tracy sprinted into danger and in the opposite direction of fleeing shoppers.

A pair of women were running and holding their phones in front of their faces; bags filled from a day of shopping bounced against their hips. Unaware of where they were going, they knocked over a child, separating him from his parents. Offering a meager apology, they continued their flight, documenting the entire experience.

Tracy swam through the bodies. She still hadn't seen the child's head pop back up, which meant he was on the floor in a prime position to be trampled.

Putting on her noise-canceling headphones, Tracy silenced the crowd's screams and desperate footfalls with her fighting mix, ignoring those jostling her as they ran. She molded the floor around her feet, transmuting it into a metal exoskeleton to reinforce her muscles. Metal rods ran along her arms and legs, controlled by motors at her joints. These connected with circular pieces at her hips and shoulders, supported by a central column at her spine. Her mini-mechanized suit added power to her movements and gave her weight to throw around.

Motors spun, and she powered through the crowd.

Like minnows surrounding a shark, they gave Tracy a wide berth.

Making her way to where she last saw the child, Tracy found him on the floor, crying. Blood trickled from his nose onto his shirt. Tracy lifted him above her head and sprinted to the side of the mall's inner alley, where two people struggled against the flow of traffic, looking desperate. The kid held out his arms, greeting his relieved parents.

"Thanks," said the grateful couple, who looked barely a few years older than her.

She handed the kid to his family and pointed them to the exit. "Get to safety!"

Tracy's phone buzzed. Other phones also blared the same message through their speakers, with varying delays, creating the effect of an out-of-sync surround sound system. "Emergency. Emergency. Large creature spotted at the Columbia Mall. To those in the immediate vicinity: evacuate and find shelter."

Bodies sprinted along the sides of the mall lanes, avoiding the middle where vendor kiosks blocked the path, lest they get trapped. There was no easy way to get to the source of today's trouble without plowing through all those displays. Tracy saw one alternative to not forcing herself against the flow of traffic, granted it would be much more uncoordinated. She crouched and sprung; the exoskeleton gave her the strength to hop between the kiosks and palm trees in the middle of the wide mall path. She gained a height advantage at the jump's apex and saw the monster.

Grasping from endless depths, clawed hands were hauling the rest of the being of shadow from the void into Tracy's world. Those razor fingertips, each identical to the one that rent her flesh, didn't gleam, instead stealing the light from her world.

Shudders rippled from Tracy's pinky toe to the split ends drifting about her face.

She forgot how to move—and that she was already moving.

Some kiosk broke her fall, the impact absorbed by her exoskeleton as she hit the floor. The cart splintered, scattering packaged phone cases. A man slipped on the cases, falling face-first. Another guy picked up the man from the floor, freeing Tracy from the excuse to delay.

The sight of the shadow monster rekindled her deep seated terror, along with the itch burrowing within her forearm. Tracy's sharp nails dug into her arm. Marring her skin in red lines, her scratching was too shallow to appease the annoyance.

No one lifted Tracy to her feet. No one checked on the one person crazy enough to run at the monster.

Her legs refused to budge.

Setting her jaw, Tracy punched her knees between the gaps in the exoskeleton, ordering them to bend and forcing her body not to give in to her fears.

Several bruises later, her legs finally responded, whirring gears bringing her to her feet.

She leaped between kiosks to avoid crushing anyone in the dwindling fleeing crowd.

Skidding to a halt in front of the shallow pool, her sneakers squeaked like a mouse caught by a starving house cat. The open portal to the void beckoned in the space above, filled with the shadow creature pulling itself into her world.

Tracy wasn't the first one to arrive and fight the monster. Evidently, this monster had interrupted Derek's date. With his hands raised, Derek hurled gale forces at the creature in the void, barring its entry into their world.

Glass walls of the department store behind the portal shattered, thousands of tiny shards hitting the wall with a hailstorm's ferocity.

The opening to the void stretched wider, firing flashes of energy in all directions. Smells of smoke hit her on all sides from where the shadow evaporated as it touched the mall's solid concrete pillars.

Beads of sweat dripped from Derek's face.

Despite raging winds, the shadow hauled more of itself into the mall.

An old man stutter-stepped with the aid of a cane, inching along the second-floor walkway, ready to be the next piece of collateral damage. Ri Ur Tol removed him from danger. Snapping sounds echoed from both floors of the mall as she rescued more stragglers and deposited them at a safer spot.

Tracy transmuted concrete and stone of the stairs into a pillar she swung like a fist at the shadow. The shadow monster reared back at the contact, despite the pillar passing through it.

Unwilling to waste time collapsing the material, she left the hardened structure in place. The curved form of the pillar made it appear as though the mall itself punched this dimensional invader.

"Why did you open the void?" Tracy shouted at Derek. "Ri Ur Tol doesn't need you to flex your power to be impressed."

"This wasn't me," Derek said, his voice reaching a frantic pitch. "Maybe it's Mr. Marshal's other superpowered team?"

"What?"

"Talk later. Fight now." Derek threw more telekinetic winds to force the shadow back into the void. "Feel like reusing the bro fist attack? It worked on my Beast, and it could work here."

Tracy raised a finger. "One, not calling it that. Two, physically touching that thing hurts us a lot more than we hurt it, so no."

With a snap, Ri Ur Tol reappeared. Her hand flashed beneath her clothes, only to come up empty with a look of surprise.

"Sparse hunt," Ri Ur Tol said in what Tracy assumed was one of her odd curses.

The shadow's long arm stretched for them.

Snap. Ri Ur Tol disappeared. She reappeared instantaneously next to Derek. Shoving her hand into his pocket, his keys dangled in her hand before she disappeared with another snapping sound.

Too busy to shout at being abandoned, Tracy sculpted barriers from the mall's walls to separate Derek and her from the shadow. Her moving walls interlocked, completing the shield.

Derek fell to his hands and knees. The winds stopped.

"Close the portal!" Tracy shouted.

"I can't close it *and* protect people."

"I'll support you, so close it."

He lifted his arms and bellowed, his entire body shaking under the strain.

The void's opening stopped expanding.

Snap.

Ri Ur Tol rejoined them, daggers already flying from her hands at the shadow.

Instead of gaining a foothold into their world, the shadow's hands retreated to the lining of the portal, pulling it like a rubber band to expand its size. Crackling energy sparked from the pit of darkness, striking the pool of water, making it hiss and bubble.

Derek struggled against the shadow to seal the portal and keep it from growing.

Using material from the second-floor walkway above, Tracy fired another pillar at the shadow. The portal's boundary split her attack, half the column passing inside to fly through the shadow's hand. Losing its mass from the contact, the shadow clung to the edge of the portal. The other half of her column crashed into the walls, raising a dust cloud.

The shadow reformed and thrust its arm and a bulbous head through the portal. Its arm lifted, blocking natural light filtering through the glass ceiling from pouring into the dozens of eyes covering its head. The monster's eyes closed, returning its skin-like surface to smooth shadow.

As it shrank from the sunlight, Derek finally gained the upper hand in the battle of wills against the shadow monster. The portal collapsed in on itself, sealing the tear in reality.

Torrents of scattering energy unleashed across the enclosed mall, knocking Tracy down. Her shoulder slammed into a supporting column, or what was left of it, the exoskeleton acting as a buffer to prevent any bones from breaking.

The sealed portal severed the parts of the shadow that had climbed into this world. The creature's twitching arm was sprawled from one end of the atrium to the other. Bubbles boiled beneath the surface of the pool, reacting where it came in contact with shadow. Steam hissed from water and monster alike as if each rejected the other.

Burning chlorine fumes lit memories of her first encounter with the shadow, which she wished remained forgotten. Her throat instinctively closed at the strong smell.

Steady drips announced water leaking out of cracked seals of the pool and into the mall's foundation.

The shadow's decapitated head lay partially submerged.

Derek was on the floor, not moving after closing the portal.

Indistinct voices settled around Tracy. A light hand on her shoulder returned her to her senses. She looked up at Ri Ur Tol's knee-high boots. In her woozy state, Tracy recalled going through twenty different designs to land on the mahogany-colored, flexible fake leather she wore.

Now isn't the time to space out on my stylish transmutations for a friend. We need to run.

Ri Ur Tol leaned closer to Tracy, offering her hand. "Can you hear me?" Ri Ur Tol's voice sounded distant, like listening to an underwater shout.

The severed shadow arm spasmed, splashing them with water from the pool. Eyes opened along the creature's head, spinning until they landed on Tracy, Ri Ur Tol, and Derek. The creature's eyes narrowed, locked on the trio. Its arm curled at the joint, lifting a fist well above the second story.

Unrelenting agony split Tracy's forearm, reigniting her invisible injury with blinding pain. Tracy flinched.

From the core of her being, she craved an escape. She covered her ears with her hands and crouched to be as small as possible. Shallow breaths did nothing to slow her heart.

Ri Ur Tol disappeared with Derek's broken sword in her hand.

Striking an invisible wall a foot above them, the shadow arm rebounded into the ceiling, dissolving the support structure at its touch.

"Good save, Derek," Tracy muttered. She crawled under the second-floor awning, aided by her exoskeleton, as the ceiling caved, dropping concrete and glass on the shadow.

Incrementally shrinking with each piece of material passing through it, the shadow hammered again, forcing Derek and his telekinetic shield sliding across the floor.

Daggers ripped through the shadow from all angles. Ever moving, ever stabbing, Ri Ur Tol was a warrior in her element, already onto the next strike as her current one landed.

Ri Ur Tol spiraled, digging into the shadow arm with Derek's broken sword. Tracy lost sight of her among the steady stream of snapping sounds of her teleportations.

Tracy sought comfort in her music. Building power, she fired pillars from all sides at the arm.

Emitting a loud yell, she reformed the walkway above them and dropped it onto the shadow's head. The solid surface passed through it, though its head shrank from the contact. Smoke spewed from the crushed creature.

The daring Ri Ur Tol whittled the shadow down with every slash.

Tracy fired a pillar into and through the shadow's remains. She fired another pillar. And another, matching what the shadow had done in its frantic hammering a few moments ago against Derek's shield.

She hurled waves of raw tile and concrete, drawing material from the walls, ceiling, and floors.

I have to stop it. I... I... I... Tracy fell forward, only now realizing the shadow had dispersed into smoke already.

Derek stepped delicately as he approached Tracy before he too collapsed to the floor.

Tracy expected to hear a snapping sound of Ri Ur Tol teleporting here after their narrow victory. Instead, light footsteps announced her presence, then she dropped to Tracy's side, taking a seat with a sigh.

Over settling dust, musical notes from the upstairs carousel speakers washed over Tracy. "Where'd that last burst of power to shield us come from, Derek?" Tracy asked to keep herself conscious. "You seemed out cold once you sealed the portal."

In a voice rife with exhaustion, he replied, "You wouldn't believe me if I told you. I swear I saw my Beast's glowing eyes peeking from behind a display case upstairs. It fed me the power to hold my own so you could finish the shadow."

With the last burst of energy, Tracy unmade the exoskeleton, already missing its reinforced support for her limbs. "Go team," she yawned. Her friend's yawns joined hers, proving their contagious nature.

Not one to be left out, Ri Ur Tol asked, "Will the Snow Ball be as entertaining as today?"

"Is it too late for the shadow monster to kill me?" Derek's small laugh faded. His head rolled onto the makeshift pillow of Tracy's ankle.

Derek's eyes closed a moment before Tracy followed his example.

23

Encroaching Darkness

Rachel

Rachel used her high-powered flashlight to chase her dog's tail and keep him illuminated. The heavy metallic tool doubled as a durable weapon to knock someone out or dispel the shadows, making her recent expensive purchase well worth the price.

Rachel dangled her feet over the side of her home's low wooden porch railing.

Her dog ran past the heated pool and across her backyard. On a clear day, miles of rolling hills beyond her family's property were visible until the quarry. There, the near side of the cliff appeared to be the end of the Earth dropping away. On this cloudy night, her line of sight extended to maybe a hundred feet over the trimmed lawn. She sought the slightest sign of any unusual shadows.

A steady chirp came from a nearby bird too lazy to migrate. Rachel strained her ears and found nothing else in the still air.

Mere hours had passed since Derek called her asking for help and she rushed the police barricade to extract her friends from the mall rubble. They told her enough of the story to understand the immediate threat was eliminated. Knowing the shadow monster entered their world again left an unsettling sinking sensation in the pit of Rachel's stomach.

Thinking back to the wreckage of the mall itself, Rachel wondered if insurance covered monster attacks or if Tracy might volunteer her services to fix the damage.

Approaching footsteps sent Rachel's senses into overdrive. She ramped up her powers, shining the light about until she landed on John walking around her house.

She steadied her racing breaths as she dropped her powers and speed down to normal. She aimed the light at him to show John how irritated she was to be surprised. "Don't sneak up on me."

He flashed his smile despite the blinding light. "I'm not sneaking. No one answered the front door, so I assumed you'd be out back with Max."

John leaned against the railing beside her, resting his elbows and doing his best to exude calm confidence. He failed. His muscles were tight, flexed with tension, and his lips were pressed flat. His hands and forearms were wrapped in gauze bandages.

"Nice of you to come over," Rachel said, unable to hide the strain in her voice. "You want to tell me what happened to your hands? You ditched school and have been radio silent all week."

He looked at his hands as though for the first time. "My family did a midweek brisket dinner, but the oven tray collapsed under the weight when I tried to pull out the pan. I saved dinner, but it came at a cost." He waved his hands about.

"Does it hurt?"

"Less than expected. Louis has an idea to make me heal faster. These bandages make it look a lot worse than it is. Don't worry. I'll make sure I'm looking good for next weekend."

"And you've been ignoring me because..." Rachel left her question hanging in the air.

"I've been busy. I'm back on the wrestling team, so I need to kick my body back into shape."

"That's fantastic! Congrats!"

"You're right, though. I shouldn't have pushed you to the side. I'm sorry I let my workouts take over all my extra time and leave me too tired to text back."

"It's okay. I remember how you get during wrestling season. Don't make it a habit." She blew into her fists to warm them up and looked out to see where her dog had gotten. "Come on, Max!"

Max kept flopping on his back and rolling in the grass, happily ignoring her. She let him have his fun and stood in silence, uncertain how to clear the air between her and John.

Eventually, John spoke. "I saw the news today about the attack at the mall. Or rather, I saw what the news didn't include. You shouldn't have carried Derek out of there. He deserved to be arrested for all the damage he caused."

Rachel absorbed the verbal gut punch, knowing she did what was right. "For someone dating me, you think about another man a lot. Besides, he wasn't the one to open the portal. Not to mention, Derek, Tracy, and Ri Ur Tol saved hundreds of people."

"He didn't open *that* portal," John corrected. "It can't be a coincidence he was there to stop that monster."

"You think Derek is summoning the shadows from the void?"

"Yeah, I think he's the reason both of those shadow monsters showed up." John turned, staring at her instead of the moon poking through the clouds. "Today is another day Derek and Tracy skip any consequences for their actions. Although everyone knows they were at the mall, I doubt they'll be charged with destruction of property.

After all, they saved the shoppers and contained the damage to one wing."

Rachel didn't bother to hide the frustration in her voice. "It's not that simple."

"Aren't you pissed they canceled your band concert because of this monster attack?"

"Of course, especially since I was hoping to make up for last week's performance, where I started early. That's on me. I care much more about the fact no one was seriously injured today."

A wet sensation on Rachel's hand made her nearly leap and take off running.

Max licked her fingers, likely hoping for a hint of her dinner's burger lingering on her fingers. He nuzzled her hip, his attempt to stem her agitation. Rachel clutched the hairy mess closer. He lapped at her forehead, and she smiled at his cute face.

"Derek defended those people and doesn't deserve to be arrested." Rachel let out a long, weary sigh at rehashing their old debate. "You're right. He isn't completely innocent, and I'll concede the possibility he attracted the shadows to our world."

Reading the edge buried in her voice, John was smart enough to shift topics. "Are we all good for the Snow Ball?"

"Depends." Rachel crossed her arms, presenting a facade like her decision was still up in the air. "Feel like getting dinner beforehand, just the two of us?"

John's wide smile returned. "Absolutely. It will give us a chance to be alone together before we meet up with our swarm of friends."

"I'd hardly call five or six people a swarm."

"Your estimate is a little short." John waved off her look of surprise. "Two more are joining us: Allerie and Tony."

Rachel squeezed the flashlight tighter in her grip. Her other hand dug into the wooden railing. "Tracy is going to be pissed."

"Confronting Allerie hasn't improved things for Tracy, so I offered Allerie an olive branch to make her treat Tracy with respect."

"That's one way to attack the problem."

John flashed a bright smile. "Despite her rampant abuse of powers, Tracy's still my friend."

"She'll surprise you. Tracy won me over when the two of us fought for our lives against the shadow, initially with no other support. She's pushed herself harder than the rest of us to master her powers. Even before then, Tracy's my girl. I'd back her up any and every day."

John's bandaged hand covered her own, staving off the cold evening. "Anyone can hammer a screw into the wall, but I wouldn't want to live in a house built with shoddy workmanship."

"What's that supposed to mean?"

"Tracy isn't a doctor. Louis is too excited to move his healed legs. He isn't considering any underlying issues that could develop due to Tracy's inexperience."

"None of us do. For all we know, accelerating my body shaves time off the end of my life. Even so, I have to keep calling on my power to save others."

John reached down and scratched Max behind the ears. Rather than lean against John's leg, her dog ran to the door. Max stared at Rachel with an expectant look to return to her warm home.

Rachel surveyed her backyard, keeping the flashlight's narrow beam in constant motion. Despite finding no shadows creeping toward them, she asked, "Mind if you run me through a couple of small training exercises inside instead of out here?"

John opened the door, and Max raced to reclaim his favorite couch. "I'll make popcorn. I have some new ideas to test your powers. Get ready. This might take all night."

"When did you start acting like Tracy?" Rachel winked, closing and locking the door behind them.

24

Found a Trail

Derek

Wind rattled the rusted chain-link fence lining the bridge's pedestrian path. Derek shivered under his light jacket. The glowing morning sun crested over the horizon, warming his seat on the bus stop bench.

Car engines revved by in a hurry, both over the bridge and below on the highway. Traffic was already sizable this Saturday morning, though it was nothing compared to the weekday crawl.

Derek stretched his arms above his head and rolled up his sleeve to run a hand over the length of his cast-free arm. His exposed hairs tingled; this small sensation was missed over the past month. He flapped his arm to let it breathe in the chilly morning.

For once, he was the first one to arrive. Tossing about all night, he had given up on a good night's sleep. He woke up early enough to explain to his parents he was going back into the void. Even with that conversation, and a lot of hugs, he drove to this standard meeting spot half an hour early. After stashing his car along a neighboring side street, he was ready to face the nothingness of the void with his two accomplices.

Derek munched his breakfast hash browns. Crunchy textures held the warmth of a freshly fried batch. The guy behind the counter must have recognized Derek, as four extra hash browns rattled around at the bottom of the bag. One could be an accident, but four hinted at the intention.

"Your hometown feels so uncannily like my own," said Nicole, waiting at his side with Ri Ur Tol, who said nothing, observing the morning rituals of the modern age.

So engrossed in his breakfast, Derek had missed the signature snapping sound of Ri Ur Tol's teleportation. He banged his chest to hide the choking fit of surprise. After all her efforts to teach him combat awareness, Ri Ur Tol must have been disappointed at how easily they got this close.

"Your whole present time feels uncanny to me," added Ri Ur Tol.

Her voice caused slivers of ice to run through Derek's brain, freezing useful thoughts. The week spent brainstorming what to say to Ri Ur Tol following their interrupted kiss at the mall was wasted. "Do you want to talk before we go into the void?" Derek could kick himself for how boring his question sounded, and the lack of confidence etched into his words. Saying nothing would have been an improvement.

Ri Ur Tol waved him off. "We can wait for tonight at the dance. For now, we have the lost version of you to track."

Thinking of the Snow Ball sent Derek's pulse racing and sealed his mouth.

Nicole filled the settling gap, muttering, "That town center looks the same as in my dimension, down to the Cold Snap and that Washington D.C. art project panda."

Her easy words gave Derek a chance to unclench his jaw. "Does your town center have that red elephant and blue donkey mural on the side of Whole Foods, too?"

Ri Ur Tol glanced at his cast-free arm, stopping any reply from Nicole with her cold expression. "Stand," Ri Ur Tol instructed.

Derek stuffed the last hash brown in his mouth and hobbled up from the bench. "I'm ready for the void," he said, trying not to spew fried potato bits.

Ri Ur Tol swung at him, slower than her normal pace. He reacted without thinking, catching it in his palm.

"Good." Ri Ur Tol punched a little faster, forcing Derek to adapt. "Since Mr. Marshal canceled today's training as a reward for defeating last weekend's shadow monster, I will fill in. We warm up, then travel into the void."

Derek held most of his thoughts in reserve, knowing Ri Ur Tol would add more exercises for each complaint. She went through a series of half-paced punches and kicks. Derek caught or deflected them all.

"We're pressed for time, so this will be focused and light movements. Keep up," Ri Ur Tol said, her eyes locked on Derek.

Nicole stole his vacant seat on the bench, announcing, "Ri Ur Tol woke me up early today, so I've already done my part for light training."

Ri Ur Tol's roundhouse kick caught the side of his recovered arm. Derek winced at the sharp pinch like ten angry wasps stung him in the same spot. His arm still wasn't at full strength. He swung back in a counter with his left hand.

"You still prefer your off hand. Has your good arm not sufficiently healed?"

He flapped his arms. "It hasn't been nearly enough time to be back at one hundred percent. My right side feels weaker than the other arm though. It's like I'm not throwing as much heft into each punch."

Nicole clicked her tongue. "Makes sense. When your arm was last whole, Tracy enlarged it to ten times normal size so you could take down the Beast."

"Or I got used to wearing my cast, and dropping that weight makes my arm feel like a twig." His eyes ran over every hair and sunspot hidden for the past month. "You know, my arm gets bigger each time you retell the fight, and you weren't even there at the end to see it."

Ri Ur Tol cut their conversation short, pressing her advantage on his right side. Doing so forced Derek to use the arm that felt like it needed another two months safe inside a hard cast.

He stepped back with each hit, offsetting the impact of her strikes.

Fists and knees alternated into her attack pattern, forcing him to back up and block as best he could. His heel bumped the bus stop bench. Unable to retreat, he lifted his recovered arm to deflect Ri Ur Tol's punch.

Instead of hitting with the force to break his bones again, her fist opened, grasping his forearm. "This does more harm than good, and the day is wasting," said Ri Ur Tol.

Nicole hopped from the bench. "I'm ready to find my Derek."

Ri Ur Tol released her grip on Derek's arm. Derek flexed it, looking for signs of damage, and found none, despite the stiffness in his muscles.

"Today, the plan is to find where the other me went in the void," he said. "That's where you come in, Nicole. The void reacts to memories. It returned me here when I thought about home, and I was nearly lost forever following my multi-day cram session that left me more or less brain-dead."

Nicole gave a thumbs-up signal. "Think about Derek. Check."

Ri Ur Tol crossed her arms. "Do you have a plan so we won't end up on the losing side of a fight with the shadow?"

"Not a good one," Derek admitted. "Aside from you teleporting us past it and we act as bait to prevent it from entering our world."

Nicole was all but jumping in the air. "Good enough for me. Let's bring Derek back."

Ri Ur Tol's mouth twitched, her lips on the verge of speaking. She let out a resigned sigh. "I do not have a better plan."

Derek brought them to the spot on the bridge where he had last created a portal. He gathered his power, reopening the small spherical doorway and tearing apart their world. Sizzling pink energy sparked from around the tear's rim as it enlarged, claiming more of Derek's world for the void.

The portal barely had time to stabilize. Ri Ur Tol snapped them into the distance inside.

Once Derek stopped feeding the portal, it collapsed on its own, covering them in the void's muted darkness. Tiny streams of light shone through a webbing of cracked lines of the sealed entrance.

Another pocket of light appeared from a crack not too far from them, one of the remnants from a previous venture into the void. The shadow creature hunched over that resealed portal.

Clawed fingers dug at the closed opening. With each scratch over the surface of what was once an exit, invisible spears stabbed through Derek's ears, piercing his thoughts.

Devoted to the task, the creature didn't turn at the intrusion of light from Derek's arrival. The imposing creature stretched farther than Derek could see, encompassing all the space between in its ever-moving shadowy form.

Derek swallowed the lump in his throat. His hasty plan seemed worse and worse in the monster's presence. He fired a telekinetic blast to get its attention, distracting it from entering their world.

Eyes opened along the creature's round head, giving it a view in every direction.

It stopped clawing at the void's exit.

Dozens of arms sprang at Derek from the creature's torso. Sharp claws made of night formed at the ends of the amorphous arms, closing in on them from above, below, and the sides.

Snap.

Ri Ur Tol moved them.

The creature's hands smashed together in the space Derek no longer occupied. A concussive wave from the impact knocked into him.

He spun about, losing all sense of direction. Strands of hair covered his mouth, choking him. Harsh syllables streamed forth from Ri Ur Tol in an unrecognizable language.

A foot kicked Derek's thigh, sending him rotating backward, swinging like a ball at the end of a rope. Straining the fabric of his shirt, Ri Ur Tol's solid grip kept him from spinning out of control.

Ri Ur Tol teleported them farther into the void.

When Derek's dizzying vision cleared, Ri Ur Tol came into focus, her hand firmly gripping his sleeve. She held Nicole with her other hand, keeping them all linked.

Derek's head swiveled. The shadow monster was nowhere in view.

"Where to?" asked Ri Ur Tol.

"We follow Nicole," replied Derek.

They floated at a meandering pace, Nicole dragging them along. After moving forward for a bit, they shifted in a new direction, and another not long after.

Nicole backed into him, bumping Derek loose when Ri Ur Tol moved aside. "It's not working. You're the void expert. What do I do?" Disrupted by the void, Nicole's voice alternated from a whisper in his ear to a shout loud enough to be heard from across the non-existent street. The dissonance left a deafening ring.

"I-I-I don't know." Growing doubts settled over Derek, making his shoulders sag as he felt more lost.

Nodding at him, Ri Ur Tol gestured to Nicole and said, "Go."

Ri Ur Tol's belief in Derek lent a steadiness to his voice. He turned to Nicole and asked, "When you think about the other Derek, what comes to mind?"

"All the dumb jokes, resting my head on his shoulder, driving in his dying car solely as an excuse to get out of the house."

No wonder they were being pulled in different directions. Nicole's compass lacked a true north.

Derek continued. "Think about the last time you saw him, as he disappeared into the void."

They moved to his left. Derek thought about returning to Nicole's world, and they moved faster in the same direction.

"Now think about your Derek within the void. Derek himself, not a specific memory, and the path he traveled inside this place."

They moved straight up.

Derek supported Nicole's new bearing with his frantic memory of the chance crash with the parallel version of himself inside this void. A faint line appeared, one end leading toward what must be Nicole's world, and the other was hopefully a lifeline to her Derek's location.

After following the trail for a while, Derek checked his stopwatch, the improvised canary in a coal mine. No more than an hour or two seemed to have passed since they entered the void, yet the stopwatch read fourteen hours since they started. He was tempted to chuck the device. Even as he stared, the seconds rolled by at a record pace, then came to a halt like ticket numbers at the deli counter.

Ri Ur Tol tapped him.

Small streaks of light seeped into the void. Like a cracked circular window, they had arrived at an exit portal.

"This must be where the other Derek went. One quick peek to scout the other side, then we go home," Derek announced.

"Why can't we keep searching until we find him?" Nicole all but whined at his side.

Derek rubbed his forehead. Expecting this debate and convincing Nicole they were unprepared were vastly different battles. "Two words: shadow monster. That thing almost got us, and we have no idea if an army of them are waiting beyond this portal. There may not even be breathable air on the other side, or it might not be where the other Derek exited."

"We're looking, but not leaving the void." Derek didn't wait for an argument. He stretched the existing tiny crack into a full breach to the outside world. The portal formed and widened, bringing with it dry air of another world. Dirt clouds swirled into the void.

The contents of his stomach stirred, risking the release of his hash browns. Fallen skyscrapers blocked the view. Steel spines of the buildings were warped from their collapse. Shattered glass littered the crusted earth where no grass grew. No sounds came from outside the void; no animals, no machines, nothing.

Covering his mouth to keep from screaming at the desolation, Derek closed the portal.

Nicole lunged for the opening before it sealed shut, only for Ri Ur Tol to restrain her. "Get off me!"

Ri Ur Tol lifted Nicole's face until their eyes met. "I taught you to hunt. You know the risks are too great when entering a new hunting ground, and that was a hostile wilderness."

Derek supported Ri Ur Tol. "We'll come back to that exact moment when we have enough gear, food, and support."

"Fine." Expecting a bigger argument, Nicole surprised him when all she added was, "I can't open the portal out. Take us back to your home."

* * *

Daylight clashed with Derek's void-adjusted eyesight. Unable to see clearly, he focused on the footsteps and cries of shock around him.

Blinking and rubbing his eyes, eventually his hometown became more than a blinding light. He let out a sigh of relief to see the distant town center still standing. Imagined visions of his home being wiped out by the shadow monster had haunted him across the return trip within the void.

He checked his phone. Less than an hour had passed since they left the boundaries of planet Earth, reaffirming how his sense of time was warped the moment he entered the void.

A stranger's squeaky voice called out to them, overflowing with excitement. "Oh! It's you kids."

Clicking noises of phone cameras followed.

Derek covered his face with his hand, straining to see past his fingers.

The guy who'd spoken leaned in close to Derek, his bushy beard brushing Derek's face. "Mind if I get in the shot?"

Without waiting for a reply, more clicking noises sounded.

Already sealed on its own, the portal, a clear path for the shadow monster to enter his world, leaving no lingering distortions in the air.

Meanwhile, the shadow monster in the void had seemed engrossed in scratching the other portal near the exit they used, neither turning nor attacking them as they left.

The few people along the pedestrian path were less willing to approach. A family holding grocery bags smiled in their direction. Another group of kids stared wide-eyed at Derek's trio, who appeared from a hole in space and time.

Leading his friends from the crowd, Derek wanted them to teleport away at a more secluded spot. They were all becoming too brazen in showcasing their abilities.

Throwing his best angry expression at those following them, Derek stopped more strangers from taking photos. "Leave us in peace, or I'll transform you all into toads."

"You can't do that," whispered Nicole.

"They don't know that," replied Ri Ur Tol, nodding to him in approval. "I performed similar jests when getting crowds to step back from my Ur Tol."

The crowd settled back and let the trio walk to Derek's car without chasing them.

He yawned, which spread to Nicole and Ri Ur Tol. Derek's feet grew heavier, his steps slogging. Despite how much Nicole wanted to, Derek had no intention of opening the void to continue their search until he slept for a full day and packed a week's worth of supplies for that dead world.

"See you tonight," Nicole interrupted Derek's daydreams of a pillow and soft bed with too much cheer in her voice.

Derek tilted his head and stared at the sky, unable to recall tonight's importance. "What am I forgetting?"

"Tracy invited me to your dance."

"Oh." Derek's stomach dropped into the void. The Snow Ball. He looked to Ri Ur Tol, trying to gauge a reaction on her neutral face. Derek's thoughts zigzagged on their own pathways, getting lost and coming up no better than when he started.

Nicole stepped in front of him. "With Ri Ur Tol going with you, I'll be stuck and bored at Mr. Marshal's training site with him and Flint. Not that either of them are around most nights. They each keep to themselves and leave me with nothing to do and no one to talk to. I don't want to be sitting alone all night after how close we came to picking up Derek's trail."

"Fair enough," Derek said with encouraging cheer. "I want you to know, we don't think of you as a replacement for our Nicole."

Nicole glanced back toward the bridge, her round eyes full of longing. "Likewise, for you and my Derek."

"I'm glad you'll be there tonight," he replied.

Nicole elbowed him in the ribs. "Don't you have anything to add, maybe to your date?"

Words spilled from Derek before his brain thought them through. "I'm glad you'll be there, too."

Ri Ur Tol let him squirm for a second or two, glaring at him with her neutral expression. Then her smile broke, and she spoke. "I'll see you this evening."

"Can I meet you on the bridge at a quarter to seven, so we arrive together?" Derek asked.

"Sure," Ri Ur Tol replied, snapping herself and Nicole to another location.

25

Tying a Tie

Derek

Derek's hands failed to mimic the diagrams on his phone. He turned to the mirror in his den, disappointed at his handiwork. The narrow end of the tie protruded like an unseemly tail from behind the front which sat high above his belly button. Plus, the knot itself was far too large.

"This is impossible." He tossed the misshapen knot. Still dangling around his neck, the green striped tie went nowhere.

Tracy placed her video game controller on the coffee table. She undid his atrocity and laid the tie's ends on her shoulders. "How have you never learned to do this?"

Derek looked at his friend, a glimmer raised in his voice. "Have you?"

"My little bro needed help for a slew of B'nai Mitzvah a year or two ago, so I learned and taught him."

"You're not Jewish."

"Victor was a popular kid when he was in middle school. My first drive after earning my license was to take him to a golf club for a post Bat Mitzvah celebration."

"What a nice sister that makes you," said Derek. Tracy wove one tie end around the other twice and slipped the perfect Windsor knot on him, tightening the tie until it squeezed his neck, eliciting a response of, "Can't. Breathe."

"It's supposed to be that tight. Don't be a baby." Tracy stepped back, eyeing Derek from his black leather dress shoes to the crisp light-blue dress shirt. "You clean up well."

"And you..." Derek faltered.

Wearing yoga pants and a baggy shirt, no one would consider her ready to go. She had straightened her hair and put on makeup while Derek was showering and getting dressed upstairs. The amount of concealer Tracy applied was a little more than usual to cover the small bags forming under her eyes from their extensive training sessions. Without proper attire, she would be barred from the dance, celebrity or not.

"You look comfortable. We need to leave in ten minutes," he reminded her.

"Tell me when it's down to five." She picked up the controller and folded into the den couch.

Derek fiddled with his collar, pulling it to return airflow. He uncapped the gel container to tame his hair.

"Don't," Tracy called from the side of her mouth, her attention unwavering from the TV. "You don't want to end up with a stiff case of helmet head. You're pulling off the mildly unkempt and wild style, so leave your hair alone."

"That might mean more if you looked at me instead of your game."

"I'm right, though."

Derek returned to the mirror. He lifted the broken sword leaning against the wall. He leeched all its power to replenish what he had spent during this morning's trip through the void. Despite the tie choking him, the extra power coursing inside allowed him to easily filled his lungs.

Tracy paused her game. "You still keep that thing around?"

"It reminds me of the cost of my overconfidence. Not to mention, I'd prefer this sword over you in a fight."

"You don't mean that."

"Of course not." Derek's voice softened, so she knew he was only partially serious. "But my sword won't make us late to the Snow Ball."

Having missed Homecoming due to getting stuck in the distant past, it had been half a year in the present since he last attended a school dance. There was no way of knowing for certain how long that equated in time relative to Derek with the number of days he spent unconscious. He hoped dancing wasn't like a forgotten carton of milk with defined expiration dates, after which his skills turned putrid.

"You have five minutes until we leave to meet Ri Ur Tol," he told her.

Tracy shut down the game and went into the bathroom. Clattering and clinking sounded through the walls. Another round of noises made Derek concerned Tracy was remodeling his bathroom.

"Did you say something?" Tracy asked through the wall.

"Nope. I'm waiting on you, hoping the bathroom is still intact when you're done."

It was worse when everything went silent. Strained ears heard nothing. Derek wondered at what point he needed to knock and check on Tracy.

The door swung open, thudding against the doorstop.

A young woman wearing a tight-fitting strapless black dress emerged from the bathroom. Tracy carried her sparkling high heels for later, walking around in plain slip-on shoes instead. A trail of tiny embroidered white snowflakes at the top of her neckline enlarged to the size of a fist by the dress's bottom. Like a sudden blizzard, Tracy made it difficult to see anything other than her. A dash of silver eyeshadow underplayed the stunning outfit.

"I take it you appreciate my work?" Tracy batted innocent eyes at Derek. "Wait until you see the dress I made for Ri Ur Tol."

Immune to Tracy's charms, Derek released a groan. He escaped the clutches of the shadow monster today to be caught in his best friend's machinations.

"By the way," Tracy said, her smug grin growing. "You need new towels in this bathroom. It took a few tries to transmute this dress right... so I used them all as material. Ready for tonight?"

Derek rubbed lingering weariness from his eyes. "My afternoon nap didn't do much, but it was better than nothing after going into the void."

With her lip quivering into a look of distaste, Tracy bit into her words. "I still wish you had brought me on the trip for support."

Derek backed away, waving his hands to show he meant no offense to whatever he had done to upset Tracy. "You're better off. I'm only on my feet because punching portals into and out of the void was much easier when those spots had been opened."

Tracy's wide smile returned, as flashy as her dress. "If things go well tonight, you might end up off your feet," she winked. "Stay awake, otherwise you might miss your chance."

Derek's cheeks flushed. The doorbell interrupted the half-formed comeback on his tongue.

Muffled sounds filtered through the wall into the den.

"Derek!" his mom shouted, excitement raising the pitch of her voice. "Come here."

Derek held his head in his hands. "What did you do now?" he asked Tracy.

She shrugged, looking as bewildered as he felt. "This wasn't me."

Derek's mind sprinted through scenarios waiting at the front door, from a rampaging monster who waited to be invited in to Mr. Marshal rescinding the free weekend and forcing them to train. Derek's heart fluttered at the chance of an excused absence from the dance. His ideas became more extravagant as he and Tracy filed from the addition to the main house.

What he found was worse than he could ever imagine.

Ri Ur Tol stood with her back pressed to the door, accommodating his parents' steady barrage of photos. Expecting a conservative ankle-length dress, she instead wore a dark dress ending at her knees. White crystal snowflakes dotted the top of the dress, a wintry night to Tracy's storm. Reconciling his assumption of how the people in the past might dress for a dance left Derek reeling.

A pang of jealousy burrowed inside him at Ri Ur Tol's comfortable white tennis shoes to tie off the outfit. His leather dress shoes pinched his toes and would leave blisters on his heels by the end of the night. He considered dressing to match her footwear, but decided against looking like a kid borrowing a suit.

Ri Ur Tol spun, the hem expanding to look like an umbrella. While Derek was coming to terms with a version of Ri Ur Tol he never witnessed, she smiled politely, accepting his parents' attentions. In the short time she had spent in Derek's world, she already understood the dreaded purpose of their cameras.

Derek's dad brandished a framed picture showcasing an eight-year-old Derek hanging upside down on a jungle gym.

As though Tracy transmuted his lungs into stone, Derek stopped, unable to breathe.

Ri Ur Tol let out a small laugh at his expense.

"Your hair looks lovely," said Derek's mom, clicking away on her phone.

Ri Ur Tol ran her fingers over the line of braids. These met in a bun at the back of her head. Her remaining hair fell in a single short twist. "Flint did this according to the warrior traditions of his people."

"You prepped for a dance like you were going into battle?" Tracy laughed, thriving on Derek's misery. "I wish I had that much foresight."

"I thought you were meeting us at the bridge," Derek squeaked, turning the statement into a question. He wanted nothing more than to shout how sorry he was for ever thinking tonight was a good idea.

"I was bored once I got into this dress."

Derek swallowed, the tie constricting the motion. "How did you get here?"

Ri Ur Tol clasped her hands in front of her, turning her focus to the hardwood desk next to the door. "Mr. Marshal gave me your address and I studied a map to teleport here. It was slightly dangerous teleporting to a new place, so I first went to the sky above before touching down in front of your home."

"You're the teleporter?" Derek's dad called out, shaking a surprised Ri Ur Tol's hand. "Thank you for bringing my son home from that horrid, nothing place today. He told us all about it."

Derek's mom beamed at Ri Ur Tol. "In case our son didn't say it, thank you for saving his life in the void. From what I've heard, this wasn't the first time."

Tracy smacked Derek's arm. "Don't *you* have anything positive to tell Ri Ur Tol before your parents do it for you?"

Derek fought to loosen his tongue, finally able to utter, "You look... nice."

Smacking his arm again, Tracy admonished him. "Nice? Nice! She's wearing the best dress of the Tracy line, patent pending. Its rhinestones accent her bronze skin and highlight her natural beauty. I even fit a pocket or two for her knives, which, if your clumsy mouth keeps taking over, you'll find exactly where she keeps them."

Derek's dad adjusted Derek's tie; his quiet words intended for Derek alone. "I don't tell you this enough, but I'm proud of you." Water welled in his dad's eyes. "I'm glad you've returned to the present and that I'm alive for days like today."

Rather than risk turning a yet undiscovered shade of red, Derek rescued Ri Ur Tol from a threat more dangerous than a thousand shadow monsters. Derek pushed his mom's hand down to point her phone's lens at the floor.

She took the hint, yet her boundless excitement didn't shrink in the slightest. "How did you meet your new friend, Ree Ur Tool— am I saying that right?"

Ri Ur Tol nodded, her chin held high, giving his parents the same respect she would for Ur Tol's siblings.

"Remember when I told you I celebrated with royalty?" Derek gestured at Ri Ur Tol. "She was there for that escapade."

Derek's dad dropped his smile, returning to his default stern glare. "That wasn't a lie?"

"When the truth is so fantastic, I stopped needing to lie."

"Mr. and Mrs. F, as fun as it is to embarrass Derek, we need to get to the dance." Late afternoon sunlight illuminated Tracy. In all of Derek's life, she had never appeared to be more of a legendary knight adorned in magical armor.

"One more photo?" his mom begged.

"I'm fine with it," said Ri Ur Tol, who adjusted to modern hindrances like cameras with grace.

Tracy positioned Ri Ur Tol to lean on Derek.

His mom took several quick shots as Tracy jumped in and out of the photos. Once his mom checked no one was blinking, she gave the "all clear" signal. Derek raced to the door, tripping on the way. He tugged the handle hard enough to risk ripping it clean off.

Ri Ur Tol grabbed her puffy jacket from the banister. She may have dressed for the dance to dazzle onlookers, but her jacket was practical to combat the cold evening rolling in.

Remembering his own outerwear, he ran into the den for his winter jacket to throw on top of the full suit.

Tracy and Ri Ur Tol were already in the front seats of Tracy's car. Derek jumped into the back, eager to leave his home and his waving parents.

Ri Ur Tol twisted to face him. "Do you want to ditch this dance and go back inside the void to find the other you?"

Tension seeped from Derek in a euphoric laugh. "I had the same thought, except my powers are too spent to open a portal."

"I'm in for the void!" Tracy shouted, hurting Derek's ears in the enclosed space. Lowering her voice, she added, "I mean, I could use a party in Ri Ur Tol's time to pregame."

"I'd take a fight for my life over this dance any day," he admitted. "We deserve a night off, so no more void trips for today. Onward to the dance."

For a second, venom seemed to shoot from Tracy's eyes as she glared at him. She shook her head, then her expression was gone. When she spoke, her voice oozed with cheer. "The pair of you are too high-strung. It will do you good to unwind once in a while. That's my challenge for the night: to make you relax."

Ri Ur Tol's frown matched the horror he felt.

26

Star Shrouded Night

Tracy

Tracy emerged from her car in the school's parking lot, swapping the slip-on shoes she had driven in for her high heels.

Whatever playlist the DJ planned for tonight, there was no way it came close to amping her up like her solid car mix. That, and the fact she was done being the third wheel for her silent passengers.

Tracy had an excuse not to drive the conversation, given she was driving the car. She couldn't be expected to also carry both ends of Ri Ur Tol and Derek's conversation. She had tried. Through Tracy's poignant questions, Ri Ur Tol opened up about life in the ancient past. Whenever she uttered the Ur Tol's name, a hairline waver rippled in her voice like she was swallowing a gnat, and she would go quiet or shift to one-word answers. Derek was equally unhelpful. Having traveled through time and fought monsters on a disturbingly weekly basis, he failed to do something as simple as add to the conversation.

Derek and Ri Ur Tol stepped from her car like they were waking from a dream. They both opened their mouths to speak, and nothing came out. Nervous laughter fell from the pair walking to the well-lit school.

Tracy knelt, careful not to topple over in her tall heels. Pretending to fix the straps, she offered Ri Ur Tol and Derek a chance to get ahead.

"Clouds shroud the stars," Ri Ur Tol said to the sky. "Beware."

"What does that mean?" Derek asked.

"Tonight brings ill fortune for hunting and is better spent inside our homes beside a warm fire."

Derek hid twitching fingers by clenching his fist. A canyon filled the gap between his hands and the adjacent Ri Ur Tol.

"Do I have to do everything for you, Derek?" Tracy muttered to her car key.

Taking the initiative, Tracy draped an arm around Derek and Ri Ur Tol's shoulders, bringing them closer together. Ri Ur Tol slipped from Tracy's loose grasp to halt in front of a green Pontiac.

"This was the car that followed us on the way to the mall," Ri Ur Tol said to Derek.

Derek went rigid mid-step. His head moved to either side. "This car was already parked when we got here. They couldn't have followed us tonight." He took a picture of the license plate, though Tracy doubted he knew anyone willing to run the tag to trace the owner.

"I'll be on the lookout for anyone unusual," said Ri Ur Tol.

Derek clicked his tongue. "After all we've been through lately, anyone and everything seems unusual."

"Maybe it's more people hoping to get pictures or steal our powers," offered Tracy, striding past her friends.

Derek and Ri Ur Tol crossed the parking lot, looking around every car like they expected to catch someone spying on them. All they did was startle a handful of other seniors walking to the dance.

Tracy made her way to the school's front entrance, attempting to force her friends to walk faster by example so she could get to dancing. She waited for the pair to catch up.

A white stretch limo pulled into the empty bus turnaround.

Three teenage boys tumbled from the open car door with the grace of forty clowns exiting a car built for two. Two teenage girls followed from inside the limo, stepping delicately around the pile who fell from the car. A final guy left the car to pull his clumsy comrades up. He linked fingers with one of them, making the caring act seem as simple as breathing. Tracy was tempted to shove Derek their way and ask for pointers.

Once standing, the two guys not holding hands leaped to cover their dates' flashy dresses in warm jackets for the short walk inside. The girls' upturned faces appeared cold, with or without their added clothing.

Derek and Ri Ur Tol made their way to Tracy, watching the other students' antics along with her.

"Just because we go to a school with some rich kids doesn't mean they need to flaunt it." Tracy clenched her teeth. "I should transmute their dresses into paper bags, or better yet, remake that limo as a pumpkin."

Derek tapped her shoulder before Tracy realized she was moving toward their classmates to do what she claimed. "They have as much right to enjoy tonight as we do. You can tell them off later. Besides, you're rich yourself, and that was before you gained the power to make infinite money."

His words pulled her back. There was no reason to start a fight tonight. Tracy shook her head to clear it of murderous frustrations, fearful over how easily her desires to hurt those around her bubbled to the surface.

A long shadow extended toward Tracy. Streetlamps lengthened Louis's outline, tripling his actual size.

Louis made a show of looking up at Tracy, eyeing her heels, then craning his head back, putting him at risk of toppling over. "Did you really need to add to your height?" he asked.

"Grow up and grow a pair," she retaliated automatically, filled with an unusual rage as her arm felt like it was on fire. "Like you have room to talk with your getup?"

Louis tugged at the golden-colored lace creeping from beneath the suit cuffs. More puffy lace hid the line of buttons on his golden shirt in a style not popular since pirates sailed the seven seas. Though by far, his greatest wardrobe catastrophe was the green suit jacket and matching pants.

"Two questions," Tracy began, raising two fingers to make a show of the count. "One, where did you find this mess? Two, why did you ever think of wearing it?"

Louis's smile didn't falter in the slightest. "Because you healed me so I can dance tonight, I'll go easy on you and simply state: you wish you looked this good." He made a show of brushing his shoulder and delicately tugging the lace at his wrists.

Louis acknowledged Derek with a nod and stopped in front of Ri Ur Tol. "Who is this stunning lady, and what horrid fate aligned you with Tracy and Derek?"

Ever having a way with words, Derek asked, "I thought you were gay?"

"I can recognize beauty in someone of the opposite gender without wanting to bone them."

Derek turned to Ri Ur Tol, lowering his head. "I'm sorry about my less mature friends."

Ri Ur Tol extended her hand in greeting, having learned modern manners by observation. "My name is Ri Ur Tol. Pleased to meet you." To Derek, she added, "I have dealt with many in my time whom you might deem immature. This man seems like a step up from most."

Louis shook her hand. "Your name was Ree? Am I saying that right?"

"Close enough," she replied.

"Hi, I'm Louis." Louis's eyes popped wide. "When you say 'my time', do you mean the age of dinosaurs, or are we referring to our recent present?"

Ri Ur Tol shifted her gaze to Derek and Tracy. "Dinosaurs?"

Louis tried again. "Are you the one they rescued from prehistoric times?"

"They did not rescue me. I chose to leave, and yes, I come from your past."

Louis leaped in the air, clapping in excitement. "You just became my favorite person of the night. I don't recognize any language roots in your name. Does it carry special meaning?"

Ri Ur Tol stood taller, glowing as she spoke confidently, though a slight waver carried in her voice. "It marks me as the first maid of the fifth daughter of my home's glorious rulers."

"Do you go by something other than your title?"

Though shorter than him, Ri Ur Tol's presence loomed over Louis as she smiled with the force of a night's star. "I was born to serve my mistress for all nineteen harvests of my life and thus became nameless. Earning the title of my new name bestowed great honor to me."

Louis jumped up and down at each detail Ri Ur Tol added. "Then, by all means, I won't shorten your honorific."

A chill breeze sent a shudder rippling through Tracy, dropping the temperature by a good ten degrees. All around her, voices buzzed. Too many people were talking at once, varying between whispers and shouts. She clenched her eyes shut to drown out the noise. When she opened her eyes, none of her friends seemed to care as they carried on quiet conversations.

Tracy took charge. "Mind if we move inside? It's way too cold to stand around and talk."

She led them into the school, where construction tape arrows on the floor and walls pointed down the hallway to the Snow Ball. Bass thumping vibrations shook the floor and carried to her ears.

Louis nudged her as they followed posted signs to the dance. "Not to bring down the night, but are you sure you healed my arm right? I've been having some trouble playing my sax, even the easy songs."

Tracy's stomach lurched at the thought of doing more harm. "I don't know. I'll look at it tomorrow for you."

"Thanks. I might have lost some of my skills from the month in a cast. Don't worry. Let's have fun tonight."

They turned down the hallway to see thick paper covering the cafeteria's glass walls, preventing outside light from invading the makeshift dance hall. She couldn't see inside, but swelling cheers from her classmates passed through the glass without issue.

Warmed by heated air blasting inside the school, Tracy removed her jacket and handed it to a volunteer at the coat check. The middle-aged man, likely a student's parent, hung her jacket on the coat rack and waved her to a table filled with snacks.

Tracy dropped two dollars in the donation bucket to select her sugary treats. Her hand drifted over shiny green apples and oranges to swipe two chocolate chip cookies. She bit into one. Its warm, gooey center collapsed perfectly in sweet flavors. The quick sugar rush gave her much needed sustenance. She handed her spare cookie to Ri Ur Tol.

In less than a second, a dot of chocolate stuck to the outside of Ri Ur Tol's lip was all that remained. "Mmmmm. These are delicious! What do you call them?"

"Chocolate chip cookies. Another night, I'll have to take you out for some modern cuisine and blow your mind," Tracy said.

As she opened the doors to the cafeteria-turned-dance-hall, loud music hit her like a tidal wave.

Manufactured fog leaked from inside, cooling her exposed toes.

Beams of red, green, and blue lights flashed from the DJ booth, coordinated with the Top 40 hit currently playing. Recognizing the DJ the school always hired, Tracy respected the choice, knowing he might throw some interesting, borderline risqué songs into tonight's mix.

A crowd of a hundred students jumped along with the music in the center of the makeshift dance floor. Another three hundred or so milled outside them, working up the courage to join in.

Two stories above them, ribbon streamers were taped to the ceiling. They ended in paper snowflake cut-outs to create the illusion they were in a classy winter dream.

Able to do more with less, Tracy was a little insulted. None of the students and staff who constructed the decorations had asked her to add to the snow-themed transmutations. Considering the ice sculptures and ten-foot-tall animatronic snowman Tracy pictured in her head, maybe the dance was better without her meddling

Flowery fragrances melded with thirty variations of Axe body spray. Like mixing colors of Play-Doh, they joined into an unappealing singularity, choking Tracy in smells found at a festival where showering was optional.

Smaller circles had opened within the large congregation of bodies shaking their asses and jumping up and down. Her classmates cheered those willing to step into the center and show off their dance skills. Tracy politely clapped for the guy shifting from doing the worm to spinning on his back. Only then did Tracy recognize him as her brother.

"Who knew the kid had moves?" Derek's shout was nearly lost beneath the music.

"He's on a roll," Tracy agreed, impressed by how Victor rolled his hips to pop from the ground and stand without using his hands.

Ri Ur Tol joined the outlining circle, clapping along with everyone else. She stomped her feet in time with the music, proving that dance was a universal language.

Rachel's short figure emerged from the crowd. Her knee-length dress hugged her shoulders and thick thighs. She didn't shy away from the tight clothing but embraced the body she showed the world —and looked good. The dress's black and white diagonal pattern shifted with each movement. Her high heels matched the pattern on her dress and added a noticeable inch to her height. She dabbed a light line of perspiration on her face with a handkerchief. Springy hair bounced as she twisted to return the cloth to her date, John.

John folded it into a flower in his suit's breast pocket. In the least surprising occurrence of the night, he looked handsome. His three-piece charcoal suit was cut to fit, allowing the flexibility to move and highlighting the toned body underneath. His feet drew Xs on the tiles in time with the music, proving that extracting him from the heart of the dance floor in no way stopped him from continuing to groove. John's polished brown leather shoes were going to get a lot of use tonight.

His bright eyes engaged everyone, high-fiving the four of them, ending with Derek. He returned John's gesture, giving Tracy hope the Derek/John quarrel was laid to rest. Ri Ur Tol seemed uncertain of the gesture but followed by example and introduced herself.

Tracy caught Rachel's eye and tugged her wrist, leading her back to the dance floor and away from Derek and Ri Ur Tol. John obediently followed, linked by Rachel's other hand. Though Louis was still with Derek and Ri Ur Tol, Tracy had tried her best to give the pair some alone time. She dragged Rachel and John into the depths of the dancing mob. Once they were close enough to the stage to lose their hearing, Rachel backed into John and started dancing. Tracy slid in front of Rachel, shaking her limbs to the fast beats billowing over them.

One song melded smoothly with the next and the next.

Warming up to her best moves, the faces of Tracy's classmates and the rotating DJ lights blurred in the dark room.

A pair sidled up next to the trio. Hoping for Derek and Ri Ur Tol or Louis and a new plus one, Tracy was disappointed by those who had joined. With no teacher's asses to kiss, Tony appeared normal. His hair was slicked upright to defy gravity as though someone continually ran their hand through the hundred-dollar haircut. Some might consider his new muscular body type attractive, especially when he wore a long suit. Oddly enough, it did make him appear taller. Tracy knew better; she had known the person wearing the suit for too many years.

Matching Tony's height, Allerie led him as they moved in unison. Her pastel teal dress accented her brown skin, even under the poor lighting.

"How are you an inch taller than you were yesterday?" Tracy confronted Allerie. "Even without those heels, you've grown and your skin looks more flawless than I've ever seen it."

Allerie shrugged, her straightened hair sliding to cover her face. "Jealous much? I'm honored to be the source of such devotion and observation."

"Play nice," John interjected. "This is a chance for you two to get along and appreciate one another."

Allerie's eyes glinted at John. She didn't look like she wanted to hit him, but her expression was in the relative ballpark. "This is nice me."

Tracy stretched her lips into a smile, hoping it didn't appear to be the grimace she wanted to send. Still, she had no intentions of letting petty annoyances hinder the night.

Fast-paced music wrapped her in its blanketing comfort. She shook her feet, hips, and arms under the guidance of the rhythm.

Soon her world faded into songs and dancing.

The bright lights above the DJ stand combined into a wide circle, blinding Tracy to the endlessly large room's darkness.

Rachel folded into John's arms and Allerie spun like a kid's toy top to end with her head on Tony's shoulder.

Dimly aware of the new slow song's tempo shift, being alone at this moment made Tracy feel like hands squeezing her lungs.

Exposed animalistic fears mingled with an emptiness inside as she idly scratched her arm. Her stomach growled, the cookie all but forgotten. Ravenous hunger, as though she'd never eaten, took hold. She scratched her arm, digging into her flesh to draw a tiny streak of blood.

Her starved form longed for claws to tear open the bags of meat dancing around her and consume the life essences within.

27

Dancing

Derek

Left alone with Ri Ur Tol and Louis, Derek bobbed his head in time with the music, feeling pathetic. He knew how uncoordinated and tone-deaf he looked. Seeking a glimpse of Tracy to inspire him, he wished he were as brave as her to dive headfirst into the music and dancing.

Cheap smoke effects added an ethereal quality by hiding the floor and the soles of his shoes.

Techno lights drew stars on walls and blinded Derek when he caught them the wrong way.

His classmates proved to be burgeoning fountains of confidence. None of them were dancing the same, each with their own unique flair, yet somehow, all of them seemed coordinated with the music. A guy in his English class swirled his hands as though washing a car. The girl he danced with moved her shoulders and hips to complement the layered rhythms of the song.

Following his friends into the heart of the human thicket would tangle Derek's feet.

"What did you do for entertainment?" Louis barraged Ri Ur Tol with another question about the past.

Though curious, Derek couldn't hear her reply over the booming music. He led the other two to the edge of the cafeteria behind a supporting pillar near the back wall separating them from the dance floor. Large glass windows let in little light from outside on this cloudy night.

Folded twenty-foot-long lunch tables lined the wall, with more rows of tables extending inward. There was no way to sneak out the two doors for extracurricular activities without rolling the tables aside.

Once behind the concrete pillar, the blasting music was dampened to a low roar.

One chaperone walking the perimeter eyed the three of them with suspicion to ensure they weren't about to have *too* much fun. Derek held back from laughing in the teacher's face for not knowing their audience.

"That's better," said Ri Ur Tol, finally able to be heard. "For fun, we hosted competitions and feats of strength. It was a boring night if no blood was lost."

Louis gazed at Ri Ur Tol and shook his head. "I can't tell if you're serious or making fun of me."

Subtle signs of a smile started at the sides of Ri Ur Tol's lips. "There are tastes of both in my answer."

Louis groaned. "I see why you're hanging around Derek. He likes to make me miserable, too."

"Hey!" Derek shouted with indignation. "What did I do?"

"What did you do? How about trash my body, to say nothing of my car?" Louis's look chilled Derek, the guilt of crippling his friend dragging Derek to someplace well below the school floors.

Louis spun his healed arm in a windmill motion and patted his leg. "Though that's been forgiven, mostly, since Tracy healed me. My bigger concern is that you were right where the portal opened for the shadow in the mall."

"I didn't help that monster if that's what you're suggesting."

"Not at all. But rupturing holes into another world *has* to be shining beacons to catch that monster's attention."

Derek paused, the music fading from his thoughts. "I never told you that much about the void. Where are you getting your insider info from?"

"Everyone's seen you. Wherever you go, live recordings and theories follow."

His words made sense, though they didn't sit right. "You might be right," Derek admitted. "The fight in the mall also caught my Beast's attention. It was there that day. It gave me the power to fight the shadow monster. By the way, Ri Ur Tol, you've fought my Beast up close and saw how it looked after we sent the shadow back into the void. Do you think my Beast is no longer an evil monster?"

"Your Beast?" She took a long breath, and Derek's throat clenched. "Are you a better person now? Your creature is tied to you."

He sank into his thoughts, wincing at all the times he had abused his power. Since defeating his Beast with the help of his friends, he refrained from unleashing his full abilities, lest he feed his Beast.

Ri Ur Tol clenched his arm and pulled him back toward the loud music, giving Derek little choice. "Follow."

Happy to avoid saying something to Louis that he might regret, Derek thought of ways to recover the dance and get it back to how he envisioned tonight. Louis joined them, likewise willing to leave the past where it belonged.

They waded through the outer wall of bodies, his classmates grinding together to a bouncing song being mangled by the DJ.

"Derek!"

He turned to see Nicole walking up to him.

Damn, another interruption. Tonight was supposed to be all about dancing and proving to Ri Ur Tol I possess skills other than fighting.

Nicole shouted something at him, though the background cheers and deafening music made hearing her nearly impossible.

Nicole tried again. "Have you seen Tracy?"

Her red hair brushed her shoulders while she searched faces lost within the crowd. Nicole's frown deepened, likely from recognizing this world's versions of her classmates and remembering the full life she left behind.

A lead weight wrapped around Derek's chest at the thought of this world's Nicole. For a moment he was transported to last year, when life was whole and his five closest friends roamed this school together, unafraid of bears and shadows.

This Nicole wasn't the one he grew up with, he forever reminded himself. Derek's discomfort tightened into a lump lodged in his throat.

"Look who I found. It's our good friend, who I've known for a long time." Nicole's smile was strained as she pointed at Melissa behind her.

Melissa gave Nicole a questioning look and offered a small wave as she sidled up to Louis and Ri Ur Tol. While Melissa wasn't paying attention, Nicole stared at her with a troubled expression, conveying her confusion, which Derek caught onto.

Derek pulled Nicole to the side and out of Melissa's earshot, which wasn't difficult with the DJ actively trying to make the crowd deaf. "You don't have to pretend. Our Nicole didn't know the new girl. Her name is Melissa."

"Phew," said Nicole, her expression relaxing. She rejoined Melissa. "Nice to meet you, then. I'm Nicole."

"I'm Melissa. Glad to meet you."

Melissa nodded at Nicole while her eyes studied every facet of the cafeteria. The way she stared, it wouldn't be surprising if she could draw detailed schematics and mark all the exits.

"I thought this was a Ball, so why are you standing around?" asked Melissa.

For her first dance at this school, Melissa made an entrance. Her purple long-sleeved dress swished about her knees. She lifted her black combat boots above the generated fog with each step. Anyone else in the same dress would be out of place, yet her confidence made the outfit feel right.

Nicole singled out Ri Ur Tol. "I just got here, thanks to this one leaving without me. I had to borrow Mr. Marshal's car and speed the whole way."

Panic flooded Ri Ur Tol's features as she froze in place. "I'm sorry. I was too nervous about the night and forgot my former commitment. I swear I will make it up to you."

Nicole's hands fled into the pockets of her cinched faded-blue dress. Fabric bunched around her drooping shoulders, making it look like it was frowning from the guilt trip she was sending Ri Ur Tol's way. Nicole held her glare for a few seconds, then smiled and waved off Ri Ur Tol's concern. "It was an accident. Just don't leave me behind again."

Yawning loudly, Derek's eyes sank. The dark room was getting to him, leaving him feeling like a wet sponge; strength, endurance, powers—all of him was being squeezed out.

"None of that," said Melissa, closing Derek's gaping mouth. She turned on Nicole. "As for you, showing up late isn't an excuse. That means you have to make up for lost time."

Melissa strode deeper among those dancing, carving a path for the rest to follow.

Derek shrugged at Ri Ur Tol's cryptic face. He had run out of stalling tactics and excuses. Ri Ur Tol was about to learn he had two uncoordinated left feet.

"We need to warn your Nicole," Nicole began as she passed Derek. "I've been tagged in photos and caught up with people I don't know. Please, don't let your Nicole think I'm some creepy clone."

"I'll do my best, though she hasn't replied to our messages."

Nicole, Louis, and Melissa set into their own series of dance steps, looking like they had practiced in unison for months. Nicole raised her arms over her head, waving them about. Louis crisscrossed his legs with fancy footwork. Melissa remained collected, moving no more than needed.

Ri Ur Tol and Derek were left standing there. She squeezed his arm hard enough to cause pain.

"Are you afraid to dance?" he joked with a musical ring to his voice.

Ri Ur Tol's lips pursed. "You aren't dancing either."

"Sure, I am," said Derek, pointing to the fact he nodded his head along with the fast bass.

"Moving your head doesn't count."

"Who made that rule?"

To prove her point, Ri Ur Tol mocked him with exaggerated nodding. "I dance... differently than your people."

"Music and dance are a shared experience across cultures and times. Who cares if you aren't from now?"

"You tell me not to show my differences."

Derek bit his tongue to not send a telekinetic fist directly at his face for being an idiot. He held her hand, feeling the strength of the person who saved his life on a regular basis. "I meant that for our powers. Using them where other people can see means they'll only see us for what we can wield. As far as anyone knows, you're my plus one from another school. Tonight's your chance to be you."

All his pent-up anxieties over the night melted under her smile. Ri Ur Tol brought her knees high, stomping the ground. Heads turned their way, some confused, one or two, perhaps, feeling revolted.

Derek brought his legs up to follow the same steps, clearing the light layer of man-made smoke with each stomp.

Kick. Heel slide. Stomp. Other leg. Repeat.

Derek's heart charted its own course, sprinting ahead regardless of what his feet wanted.

Ri Ur Tol took his hand, spinning them around in a tight circle. Someone short and blond shouted as Derek bumped into her, but he had lost sight of everyone other than Ri Ur Tol.

His partner led comfortably, as though she were born in the present time, and this was *her* school's dance, not the other way around. Certain of her well-placed footsteps, she never looked down at her legs crossing, alternating her front feet.

Almond-colored eyes, alight under the limited DJ lights, gazed back at Derek. Tilting her head, she whooped, her voice blending with other cheers.

His right foot lifted before the other foot was steady. He stumbled. Trying to regain his footing and move faster, his feet refused to obey. Ri Ur Tol grabbed his arm, preventing him from falling and adjusting to match his slower pace.

An apology was on his lips when a loud yawn took over.

Louis clapped Derek on the back and said, "Those are some of the most impressive moves I've ever seen you pull off."

Louis's contagious broad smile spread.

The last notes of the current song faded fluidly into the next one's intro.

From the first guitar riffs blasting out of the speakers, Derek knew this classic rock song in his bones.

"I love this song!" Nicole cried out. She sang along, a beautiful rendition calling to Derek from every past party with his friends, regardless of the good times or the disasters of those nights. He stood taller, no longer relying on Ri Ur Tol for balance. Buzzing energy inside spread warmth from his fingertips to his toes.

Louis added his vocals, rounding out Nicole's higher pitch. Derek came in at the chorus. The second time through, Ri Ur Tol added her voice to the mix. Neither she nor Derek were of the same caliber as Nicole, and they lacked Louis's conviction. That didn't matter.

Melissa shook her head at Derek and the rest making fools of themselves. Her judging look made him shout louder. Weights from the trying day melted into the carefree now. Derek rested his arms around Ri Ur Tol and Louis, belting out lyrics to bring the song to a close.

I want more of these moments where I can live and let someone else be the next hero.

Memories of today's trip into the void beckoned, shackling Derek once more to his obligations.

The DJ blended his mix into the next song, and, one by one, their singing stopped.

Under returning waves of exhaustion, Derek's legs gave out; Ri Ur Tol and Louis became his human crutches.

"Hmm," said Melissa. "Nicole, sing some more. I want to see something."

Nicole wavered on the new tune, less sure of the words than the song that crossed dimensional borders to be their group's favorite.

Her voice made Derek breathe deeper, fatigue abating from his limbs. As though he sat in a hot tub, his muscles loosened, weeks of knots unwinding in a matter of seconds.

He wasn't alone. A handful of seniors jumping to the song were getting two feet of air with each leap. A dancing teenage girl advanced from spinning her partner to tossing her into the air and catching her.

At Melissa's signal, Nicole stopped.

Weakness spread over Derek like a disease, and those around him went back to dancing normally. He wanted nothing more than to find a corner to curl into a ball and fall asleep.

Nicole's smile spread wide across her face. "It's official. I have powers!"

Despite drooping eyes, Derek smiled back, basking in the warm pride emanating from Nicole's expression. "Makes sense. The last time I was this drained was when I gave my powers to Rachel and tore open this world."

"Are you sure that's why you're so tired?" asked Louis.

Derek shook his head. "No idea. I've already pushed myself today in going in the void, though I haven't felt a sudden rush of exhaustion like this since I shared my powers."

Nicole's head tilted at an angle, regarding Derek. "I think I've had these powers long before tonight."

Building excitement from the last stretch of songs plummeted into a slow, softer melody, allowing everyone to catch their breath. Dazzling lights went from jerking patterns to swaying like midday tides on an isolated beach.

"I promise we'll figure out your new gifts later," said Derek.

Melissa looked hopefully at the people dancing around her. When no one approached, her expression sank, and she filtered off the dance floor.

Louis slipped from beneath Derek's arm, leaving Derek draped over Ri Ur Tol before he knew what happened.

Nicole stayed near, humming along with the music. She grabbed Louis's hand, and they spun. With their arms extended high and to the side, they looked like they were dancing a waltz.

Derek twisted around Ri Ur Tol, lowering his hand from her shoulder to her hip. Ri Ur Tol mimicked others on the dance floor and lifted her hands to rest on the back of his neck. She nestled her chin into the fabric of his shirt, her light breaths warming his chest.

Dark hair brushed his nose, bringing scents that reminded Derek of picking strawberries on a mild summer day.

He stopped counting beats; he stopped staring at his feet.

In this precious moment, Derek stopped thinking. There was only steady music, Ri Ur Tol pressed against him, and his speeding heart refused to recognize this was a slow song.

Ri Ur Tol leaned her head back, meeting his eyes.

Derek lowered his lips and she raised hers.

Their soft mouths met.

This kiss awakened him more than the double shot of espresso from Nicole's singing.

Smooth fabric shifted beneath his fingertips, exploring the space from Ri Ur Tol's hips to her lower back. Ri Ur Tol danced her fingers to his ear, down to his chin, and along his neck, tingling every hair she touched.

He wanted to hurl. He felt like he could climb to the roof and take flight. He hoped this moment might never end.

His phone vibrated. He spared on hand to shut off notifications, but it kept going. Moving the phone to his back pocket, he prayed that whoever was calling him stopped.

A tug on his suit's sleeve beckoned him from Ri Ur Tol's embrace.

Behind closed eyes, bright lights came on. The tugging continued, pulling him from Ri Ur Tol.

Music severed, emitting a loud pop from the speakers.

Booing bore into Derek's eardrums from every direction, and he opened his eyes, ending their kiss. Without the slightest filter, he said the first words popping into his head. "Was the kiss that bad?"

He looked at Ri Ur Tol's furrowed brow.

Her eyes shifted to those around them, and she braced her legs, entering a fighting stance.

People were looking around and up at the bright cafeteria lights, turned on far too early in the night. Their booing stretched into chants to return to the dance.

Derek spun to the person interrupting him, looking to lay blame for what ruined his moment.

"I feel wrong," Tracy shuddered, letting go of Derek's sleeve to scratch her other arm.

Perspiration dotted her forehead, undoing her styled hair. Her glowing vigor from this afternoon was gone, revealed by the bright lights.

His pocket vibrated again. Without music to drown out the alert, he heard the electronic voice of his phone. "Emergency. Emergency. Large creature spotted near Rabbit Run and Cedar Street. To those in the immediate vicinity: evacuate and find shelter."

Derek's gaze jumped to the tall windows, a barrier keeping the night at bay. "Those cross streets are a mile away. We need to gather the team."

An air gap formed as classmates took a collective step away from Derek and his friends, isolating them on an island within the dance floor.

28

Lights

Rachel

Cafeteria lights turned on, dispelling the Snow Ball's winter ambiance. Glow-in-the-dark glitter on the snowflakes hanging from the ceiling dulled with the brightness.

"Not now, not now, not now," Rachel pleaded.

Mrs. Strata ran to the stage to whisper something to the DJ. The other teachers sprinted about the room, but with no clear purpose. The semblance of order they presented crumbled, utterly out of their control. High heels clicked across the linoleum floor and leather shoes squeaked. No one wanted to speak first. If the teachers waited much longer, there would be a stampede.

"What do we do?" one student shouted.

"Where do we go?" came another voice.

Amid their restless cries, the crowd expanded and contracted. Her classmates must be weighing the options of sprinting for the exits or huddling closer together.

Rachel removed her diagonal-patterned heels, dragging her feet over the cool tiles. "I have to help," she told John.

John looked out the windows, trying to see into the dark night. "Good luck." He wrapped her in a hug and kissed her forehead. The tight embrace he had used to hold her close throughout the dance now turned cold.

Rachel's fingers took an eternity to detach from John's. She hoped her doubts were misguided, overactive in sensing what wasn't present. She searched his eyes for answers and found none.

Rachel used her powers to speed to the raised DJ platform. The floor stuck to her bare feet from someone's dropped soda, giving a sickly ripping sensation as she moved up the steps to join Mrs. Strata.

Mrs. Strata gestured Rachel to the front of the stage, telling her, "I knew you were a hero."

"Please don't turn tonight into a physics example for our next class," Rachel said. "I never wanted to be a hero."

"The best never do." Mrs. Strata directed Rachel to the students waiting for anyone to take charge.

Rachel picked up the microphone from the DJ stand and projected across the cafeteria using her marching band voice. "Don't worry. My friends and I are here to protect you. We'll stop whatever is threatening our school."

Outcries from students blended into a single mess. A handful of them ran for the side exit.

Rachel rounded them up in less than a second and guided them back to the crowd. Returning to the DJ booth, she applied a different tactic. "The best thing to do is find shelter until we know more details. Can everyone calmly walk to the library in the center of the school? For those who still feel unsafe there, go to the workout room in the basement. The worst thing we can do is clog the parking lot so no one can leave safely and expose everyone outside."

"Follow me." Mrs. Strata organized the students and directed them into the hallway. To Rachel, she mouthed the word, "Thanks," before directing students into the hallway and organizing lines to leave the cafeteria.

From above the crowd on the DJ booth, Rachel had a clear view. Tracy was already with Ri Ur Tol, Nicole, and Derek.

Rachel ran to her friends, prodding the stragglers unwilling to listen to reason. The line to leave had already slowed to a stop as people cut the line or formed new lines at an angle.

"How hard is it to walk?" Beating sense into her classmates was a losing battle, so Rachel took comfort in the familiar: monster slaying. "Ready for a fun night?" she asked Tracy.

Tracy backed up, pressing against one of the room's central columns and picked at her arm with her nails. "Not tonight."

Derek's phone buzzed again. Jealous of his pockets large enough to carry a phone, Rachel glanced at her purse across the room, knowing her device was blaring alert messages too.

"Emergency. Emergency. Large creature spotted near Rabbit Run and Cedar Street, heading east. To those in the immediate vicinity: evacuate and find shelter."

Tracy went rigid. "We're in that thing's path!"

Rachel positioned her friends between the exiting crowd and the glass wall of windows. When she spoke, uncertainty crept into every word. "There's no way to know it's heading for us."

Tracy hugged herself. "That shadow is bringing the fight to us."

"Then we fortify." *Snap.* Ri Ur Tol disappeared. *Snap.* She re-appeared, strapping on a belt which overflowed with daggers. "I stashed this at Derek's house in preparation for such an occasion."

Shock laced Derek's voice. "You did what? When?"

Ignoring him, Ri Ur Tol muttered to herself. "Is the training facility too far? I would be drained to go there seeking bring more help. But two more people could turn the tides of battle in our favor. *If* I can find them fast enough and *if* they are ready to fight." She shook her head and faced Derek. "There are too many unknowns. We hunt with those already present."

"What's the plan?" squeaked Victor. Tracy's gawky brother emerged from the line of students leaving the cafeteria.

Ri Ur Tol acknowledged the crowd of students hurrying to shelter. "I'll stay and save others."

"I want to help," said Victor.

"Absolutely not." Tracy's harsh voice caused her younger brother to flinch. She shoved her high heels into his hands and pushed him back to the line. "Follow them and go where it's safest. It's my job as your sister to protect you."

Nicole put her arm on Victor's shoulder. "Monsters are danger-ous—you need to find a place to hide."

He ducked out of Nicole's reach. "I can rally the troops, organize people to fight."

Tracy's voice was absolute. "You aren't a soldier. We aren't fully trained for this either, but we can live through the night."

Victor bit his lip but gave in as Nicole led him to the long line to leave.

Nicole rejoined the team at Rachel's side, for all the good her power-deprived friend might do in a monster fight.

"Uh, I have a question," started a pale-faced Derek. Sweat dripped down his face, seemingly from the effort of standing in place. "Wouldn't there be a delay between when the monster is reported and when the alert is sent?"

Rachel applied her abilities to her vision, plunging into the world of music. Static appeared over the quieted DJ equipment as a dull single repeated note.

Outside, there was nothing.

Each of her classmates' footfalls behind her was as unique as the person making the noise. Their conversations were too far to overhear, but musical notes from their voices let Rachel guess the broad themes of the fear in what they were saying.

Normally, trees, birds, hell, even cars could be seen as music. Beyond the windows, no music sprang into existence within her power-infused vision.

No music floated nearby; only emptiness was in front of her, as though what she saw didn't truly exist. Trembling from her fingers to her toes, Rachel stared at the first thing she witnessed with no music. She wanted to run to the basement locker rooms and bathe this unclean sight from her memory. "Shit! It's here."

Her vision returned to normal. She saw the muted streetlamps along the sidewalk through the translucent form of the shadow creature, their lights appearing like dying fireflies. The shadow monster passed through the school's glass and brick wall. Glass bubbled and melted, pooling on the floor. Trails of smoke rose from the green-painted bricks.

The top of the creature almost reached the ceiling. Rachel had to lean back to see the entire thirty-foot creature. What passed for its skin festered, having passed through the wall. This shadow appeared humanoid, with two arms and legs, though their proportions were wrong. The arms were too long, the legs too short, and the middle connecting everything was too narrow. It looked like a giant human had been stretched and compressed by some grotesque machine. A round bump existed where the shadow's face should be.

Piercing screams called to Rachel. Her classmates begged for help or prayed for the line to move faster. Distinct sounds of bodies shoving and slamming one another into the walls left a bad taste in her mouth. Rescuing classmates would distract Rachel and expose her to any of the monster's incoming attacks.

The shadow blocked the outside exit, though she could see the door's outline through the creature, taunting Rachel with a false escape route.

Her classmates funneling out the door to the hallway blocked their best exit. She didn't want to send people into the kitchens to seek another back door. Dividing the line Rachel and her friends were holding could easily backfire in searching for alternative exits. They could spare one person to help with the evacuation.

Rachel grabbed Ri Ur Tol and pointed at the hundreds still in the room. "Save them."

Ri Ur Tol disappeared with a snap, taking two students within her reach somewhere safer than here.

The shadow stepped forward, its head knocking aside the paper snowflakes hanging from the ceiling. These fluttered to the ground, dissolving into black ash.

Two long shadow arms reached for both of Rachel's friends and the mob of people hurrying to leave. Any semblance of the organized line disappeared with the shadow's arrival.

Melissa ran from the hallway, forcing her way through the crowd to the monster, throwing her arms wide to protect those too slow to get out.

There was no time to think about the sharp fingers coming to pierce flesh. Rachel pulled in power. She used her speed to shove her friends out of the shadow's reach and then raced over to move the foolishly brave Melissa to another part of the room.

The shadow raked over Rachel as she slid her and Melissa under its closing fingers. Thick as trombone oil, the shadow's slick touch across Rachel's back was icy, then burned like no fire had done to her before. An involuntary shudder escaped at the sharp pain, throwing her off balance and causing her to stumble as she brought Melissa to safety. Rachel's speed carried them forward. Depositing the human weight, Rachel ran back to her friends.

Tracy slipped an earbud in her ear, the other dropping from shaking fingers. She stretched a wall of stone between two pillars, shielding Rachel and her friends from the creature's flailing claws. Stone crumbled from the transmutation, crashing in front of them. Holes widened in the collapsing walls as they became little more than mosquito nets.

Tracy dropped to the floor, scrambling for her missing earbud while her phone called out an alert.

"Emergency. Emergency. Large creature spotted at the Colesville Memorial Bridge, heading east. To those in the immediate vicinity: evacuate and find shelter."

"There's another one now?" Rachel called out.

"That's the bridge where I first opened a portal." The anger held in Derek's voice surprised Rachel.

Derek levitated trash cans and metal chairs, launching them at the shadow. Junk entered and exited the monster, leaving small pieces of its skin smoking.

Rachel sped about and picked up Tracy's earbud, handing it to her friend.

Spires of concrete launched from the school's structural pillars, impaling the shadow with Tracy's full might. Her attacks stabbed through the creature, where the transmutations remained, the creature's form dissolving faster where she made contact.

The shadow craned its head back. It emitted no sounds, yet the force of its silent wail made Rachel's brain feel like it was swirling through a blender.

"There's not enough material to break down the shadow unless I want to bring the school down on top of us," panted Tracy.

Derek lifted Tracy to her feet and said, "We took it down before. We can do it again."

The shadow moved closer, ignoring the fact her pillars had pierced it.

Nicole stood her ground without flinching, all the while her wide eyes screamed that she wanted to join the herd migrating to a safer room.

Rachel threw herself in front of the monster, dodging the massive claws seeking to rip her apart. She kept running, keeping its focus on her and away from her classmates.

She leaped over the tables at the side of the cafeteria, catching parts of another emergency message announcing something about the Columbia Mall and southwest.

For all her effort wasted moving around the tables, the shadow had no such limitations. It passed through the solid surfaces uninhibited. Touching the tables caused the shadow to smoke and disperse, but at too slow of a rate. Rachel was going to trip or have her powers give out well before the shadow unmade itself.

Gale forces flung at the shadow, hard enough to break the glass windows behind it. Cold evening air flowed into the cafeteria through the broken windows.

Outside of the brunt of the storm, the gusts were still strong enough to push her against the back wall. "Knock it off, Derek!" she shouted. "You're doing more harm than good."

"I'm pushing it outside so Tracy can work with more raw material to transmute." Derek jumped forward, throwing his hands up and calling down a cyclone aimed at the shadow.

Derek swayed, sweat dripping down his cheeks.

From behind, a table sailed into and through the shadow's long claws, shrinking them from the contact.

The creature reached for Derek, inching closer despite the savage winds pressing against it.

Ri Ur Tol appeared, teleporting her and Derek elsewhere. The shadow's fingers closed around empty air.

Nicole lined up next to Rachel with a recycling bin and a fire extinguisher. She threw the bin at the monster and handed the extinguisher to Rachel. "Use your speed."

Rachel's quick tally showed maybe half of her classmates were out of the cafeteria.

She sprinted in an arc, spraying pressurized chemicals at the creature.

Shadow arms swung. Rachel moved around and beneath, dodging claws carving the floor apart.

"Emergency. Emergency. Large creatures spotted near Highland View High School. To those in the immediate vicinity: evacuate and find shelter."

Tempted to smash every phone, or throw them at the shadow monster, Rachel shouted, "We know! The shadow monster's already here."

"No." Tracy's skin turned chalk white. "*Multiple* shadows are here now."

The shadow ignored Rachel to grasp for Tracy.

Rachel ran to save her frozen friend. A shadow arm barred her path. She slid to a halt and backtracked to avoid passing through the shadow swinging for her.

The shadow's other arm was bearing down on the frozen Tracy. A tall boy with the same lanky arms and legs as Tracy ran in front of her.

Too slow to stop it, Rachel watched the shadow pick up the flailing Victor. Nicole lunged for Victor, clasping his hand as the shadow lifted them both. Nicole couldn't hold on. She dropped five feet to the hard floor, her legs buckling.

Tracy's brave brother shouted a war cry. "My sister will kill you!"

Victor's skin turned red where the shadow held him, burning from its touch. He released an impressive string of curses, his voice cracking while he endured the pain.

As though on a hinge, the shadow's midsection split, revealing its gaping mouth.

Derek hurled wind into the shadow. The forces unleashed ripped open the cafeteria and scattered everything not bolted to the floor. Even though she wasn't the target, Rachel was tossed against the cracking wall. The impact made her wince, yet she didn't care about bruises, so long as Derek's power freed Tracy's brother.

More winds pushed her and the shadow creature back.

Weakened by the shadow's touch, the outer wall collapsed onto the sidewalk.

Despite the force thrown at the shadow, Victor remained captive in the creature's grasp. The shadow's arm bent, positioning Victor above the mouth that had formed.

Ri Ur Tol surrounded the shadow by repeatedly teleporting, throwing daggers to disperse it.

Though the shadow was shrinking, they weren't cutting deep enough to cause lasting harm.

A moment of hope fluttered in Rachel, knowing Ri Ur Tol could catch Victor in the split second when the shadow dropped him into its mouth.

Such meaningless wishes were squashed. The shadow's mouth closed around its own arm, consuming it, along with the trapped Victor.

Like sinking in the deep end of a lake, Victor dropped lower within the shadow's bulk. Through its shadowy form, Rachel saw her friend's brother floating in the center of the creature.

A new arm sprang from the shadow's body. As though it were a scorpion's tail, the new arm curled back to strike at anyone who dared to get close.

Victor clenched his eyes shut. He opened his mouth in a scream Rachel couldn't hear. Red welts formed on his arms and face, his dress shirt melting.

Her friend's brother took his final breaths, unable to gulp fresh air. Unless Rachel ditched her friends to run outside and never stop running, she would suffer a similar fate.

29

Shadows

Tracy

That thing swallowed my brother.

Heavy metal music flowed from Tracy's earbuds, summoning her power even as it dug a channel of pain inside her arm, like her skin was being peeled to the bone.

She wiped aside her tears, smearing dark mascara on the back of her hand.

Challenges and curses at the shadow erupted from her lips.

Her brother floated within the shadow monster. His head bobbed and his eyes bulged, losing the battle to breathe.

Daggers flew through the shadow from multiple sides. Ri Ur Tol's best proved ineffective.

"Ri, teleport Vic out!" Tracy shouted.

"I don't know if I can teleport inside without getting trapped." Ri Ur Tol threw more daggers at it, chipping away at the surface without splitting the shadow apart.

Tracy pounded the ground. The world felt like it was collapsing on top of her.

Derek was at Tracy's side. "You've hurt that thing the most. Hit it hard with your biggest transmutations. We'll cover you." Warmth spread from her back, where he pressed his hand and sent her more power.

His soft comfort eclipsed the sensation of glass shards flowing within the veins of her arm as Tracy wielded her ability.

I have craved a meal for so long. Pressure from the vast other voice in her head stopped Tracy, holding her firmly to the ground. She shook the distracting thoughts free, needing every second to save her brother.

Rachel retreated to the mass of fleeing students, no longer in organized lines. "I can't help against the shadow, so I'm getting more people out before they're eaten, too." She became a blur moving within the crowd to get them out faster.

Tracy's knees grew weak. *I'm alone. I can't save him.* "Shit!"

A cafeteria table soared overhead, passing through the shadow to land on the collapsed brick wall. It skidded into the empty bus drop-off zone.

Tracy breathed a little easier. "Thanks for distracting that thing, Derek."

"Wasn't me," Derek coughed. "I'll thank whoever they are if we survive the night."

"Wait, there's another superpowered person out there? Think they could loan me some more power? Your donated boost of energy won't last long."

Derek sank to the floor. "I gave you as much as I could. I'm going to need to sit out for a few minutes."

"Is that how little Derek the Magnificent has left?"

"Something's been leeching my power all night and my battery sword is stuck at home."

A ball of white light bounced off a column and struck the shadow. It detonated in a flash, forcing Tracy to turn away.

The shadow folded its body around the explosion, leaving it untouched and free of harm.

For a split second, Victor's head was free. Sounds of him gasping in a full breath spurred Tracy.

The shadow reformed, engulfing her brother once more. Blisters appeared across Victor's body. These popped, splattering his blood into the shadow, where it dissolved.

Anger swirled inside Tracy. *I'm supposed to protect him.*

Another table flew into and through the monster, spearing the school's grass lawn beyond.

The shadow drew its arms back and braced to capture its next victim.

She pulled in more power from her music, and the itch in her arm expanded into a throbbing icy pain.

Gathering material sent ripples coursing over the broken bricks and glass, the former wall of her school, Tracy's school, which this creature dared to attack. Her brother wanted to help, despite not having powers.

Her arm burned, further fueling her fury.

She transmuted the school walls into giant concrete scythes, dwarfing the shadow.

She guided her weapons into a horizontal slash that split the shadow in half.

Two downward slashes severed the shadow's arms.

Tracy's power cut the creature over and over, like an ax hacking through a tree trunk, inching closer to freeing her brother.

The shadow reformed, unwilling to relinquish its prisoner.

She cut it again, aiming for its extremities.

Those were distractions.

Tracy launched a pillar from the tiled floor at the shadow's stomach. Transmuting the end of her speeding pillar into a cushion, she knocked her brother out of the shadow.

Tracy formed a cushioned mat on the ground outside to absorb Victor's fall. He landed and rolled to a stop, his arms scraping across the sidewalk and broken bricks. Sputtering breaths showed he was at least still alive.

She left the pillar inside the monster, letting her world eat away at the horrid creature.

Relief at freeing Victor flooded her. She bared her teeth at the shadow creature in a hate-filled grimace. She lifted more scythes to carve up the thing that had dared hurt her brother.

You're going to pay for every ounce of pain he suffered.

An arm made of shadow sprung from the stomach which had contained her brother.

Tracy reformed the scythes into a defensive shield and used the leftover material to fire a spire at the shadow. The shadow arm folded itself around her attack, dodging it, advancing for her.

She wrenched new material from the columns and floor, solidifying layered walls between her and the shadow. The shadow kept coming. Its claws aimed at Tracy, passing through her barriers, which made its skin turn to smoke, accepting the loss of its size, so long as Tracy ended up as a gutted fish.

She scrambled backward while creating more walls.

Her head knocked into a brick column, halting her escape.

In desperation, she threw up her hands and sent a pillar from the floor in front of her into the shadow's arm, cutting it from its body.

Widening the pillar, she pushed it higher until her transmutation struck the ceiling with a crashing pop. Her attack hit the shadow arm with enough material to disperse it.

Bits of ceiling tiles battered the floor and Tracy alike. Broken glass from a crushed long light bulb fell on top of her, cutting her skin. A long pole of broken rebar clattered a few feet from her, ringing like an instrument.

Out of weariness, Tracy leaned on her knees to stay upright.

She felt the impacts of composite tiles and glass, but any pain paled compared to the shredding sensation inside her arm.

Tracy hobbled around her handiwork of the reformed room. Any semblance of a cafeteria was lost amid the transmuted pillars and barricades. Shiny poster boards depicting winter wonderlands and cardboard letters spelling "Snow Ball" lay on the ground, torn, crushed, and covered in fallen dust and debris. The DJ's sound equipment lay on its side, sparks flying from the main board.

The shadow remained still, though its skin smoked where Tracy's transmutations stayed embedded.

"Help! More shadows are here." Victor's shouts from outside caught her attention. He frantically pointed over his shoulder before running out of view and hopefully to safety.

Darker than the cloudy night, two other giant shadow creatures loomed over the bus parking lot. Blotting out Tracy's view of the football field and the distant hills, the sentinels from the void shook, their humanoid forms becoming insubstantial.

They stretched, bodies distorting like tentacles linking those creatures to the one Tracy had reduced to half its original size. Together, the creatures swelled into a single being.

The reformed shadow monster's short legs ended in four pronged toes, three facing forward, one back. Hooked talons dug into the floor to give the massive shadow more stability. Its arms lengthened, reaching the floor while its torso climbed to the ceiling. Each of the seven fingers stretched into long claws. Nubs on its back appeared to be misshapen wings. The round head on its shoulders elongated into a cone.

The creature of shadow shifted, its form molding as though it hadn't fully set.

Tracy wiped the sweat from her forehead and stumbled, cursing the shadows. Drawing material, she reinforced the inner lining of her dress with a metallic mesh for her protection, getting ready for the next round.

Two shadow arms lunged for her, claws outstretched.

Tracy leaped to the side, transmuting a wall from the floor as the last means of defense.

The shadow all but ignored her power, catching a tight hold on Tracy's arm and lifting her.

Chilling burns seared her arm inside and out from where the vile creature held her in midair.

Tracy swung herself in pendulum motions, worthless attempts to slip free. It held her, a contradiction, being insubstantial one instant and gripping her the next.

She couldn't hear the music over her wild shrieks, which left her voice hoarse. Without clear music, her power refused to flow. Fear ballooned inside, suffocating her, until it popped, spreading toxic thoughts of panic and hopelessness that paralyzed her.

New arms had sprouted from the shadow, swinging across the cafeteria well away from Tracy, occupying her friends or anyone who might free her.

Another hand of shadow crept closer to Tracy. Its single pointed claw opened a deep line along her arm. Blood oozed from the wound, sliding down to her back.

Her severed flesh barely clung to the bones beneath her skin. Tracy clenched her stomach to hold on to her latest snack, in spite of her innards on display.

The claw prodded deeper. Pressing skin and muscle aside, its icy touch left her numb.

A foot-long sliver of shadow writhed inside her wound. Drenched in red, the tiny piece of shadow slithered from within her exposed muscles, onto the larger shadow's claw, up its long arm, and burrowed into the protruding shape where the shadow creature's head belonged.

Far above her, thousands of eyes opened along the head and body of the creature, which had risen above the broken ceiling and exposed rebar.

A seam appeared in the center of the shadow instead of along the part Tracy mistook for its head. The toothless mouth that had swallowed her brother twisted, grinding from side to side until it creaked open.

"FINALLY, I AM WHOLE." Hearing the booming voice out loud, which she had only ever heard inside her head, made Tracy want to cut off her ears rather than feel her brain boil inside her skull. "I HUNGER."

30

Stalwart Shields

Tracy

Dangling ten feet above the floor, Tracy steadied her uneven breaths. Her skin made the shadow monster's form disperse where it held her, even as touching it burned her. Smells like a rampant tire fire brought stinging tears to her eyes.

Her bleeding arm and the searing sensations running over exposed nerves kept her conscious and aware.

Free of the bit of shadow inside her arm, choking pain no longer limited her full music-enhanced abilities. Power ignited inside Tracy.

Pulling material from the hem of her dress, she reformed muscle and skin to seal her wound. Through gritted teeth, she challenged the monster. "You're going to regret ever slashing me in the desert."

The shadow pulled her closer, its mouth chomping in anticipation of a second meal from the Wayfield family tree.

As little more than a blur, Rachel moved close to the shadow's feet, aiming at it with a fire extinguisher. She pulled its pin and squeezed the lever, sending gases billowing forth, reacting with the shadow's skin. The creature shifted to reform into its humanoid shape and adjust to the amount of its body lost.

For all the harm Rachel caused, Tracy moved closer to the shadow's open mouth.

Someone's solid body collided with Tracy, freeing her from the shadow monster's clutches. The person's taut muscles gripped her close as they landed on their feet, Tracy lying in their arms. Having passed through the shadow, parts of the person's suit were disintegrating, but their exposed arms carrying Tracy were unharmed.

Tracy got a good look at his face, a face she knew. John had saved her from becoming the shadow's dinner. The same John who sat next to her every day in class, who also possessed the power to touch the shadow without his skin blistering.

"Huh." The unintelligible word fluttered from Tracy.

She hopped from John's arms, prodding his biceps to ensure he was real.

The one Tracy had expected to be her rescuer, Ri Ur Tol, snapped in front of them, bringing Derek with her. Rachel held her position, putting her speed to good use to harass the shadow. Its arms followed in her wake as she chipped away at its size by throwing trash through it.

"Thanks for saving me," Tracy said to the friends who let her suffer, who were about to let her die.

Ri Ur Tol had the good grace not to meet Tracy's eyes. "I saved those of your village too weak to save themselves. I was not prepared for the speed and savagery of the shadow, nor did I know its intended target."

Sweat streaked Derek's face. His cheeks paled and drained of their flush coloring. "That shadow's arms kept blocking my way to you."

"It's a wonder the cafeteria hasn't collapsed from this fight," said John.

An energy ball bounced against a wall and into the shadow. It exploded, though the shadow expanded around the human-sized blast to limit how much of it burned away.

Tracy released a yelp and formed a wall for cover from the sudden explosion.

Rachel retreated from the energy blast, then returned with her fire extinguisher to sting the shadow's legs and continued distracting it.

John's eyes darted about the room, steady on his feet despite the ball of light that hit the shadow. "My team will work with you now that we got the rest of our classmates to a safer place."

"Your team?" Incredulous tones flavored Tracy's question. "I'll never hear the end of how I owe you my life from tonight."

John's reply was instant, filling Tracy with dread. "I'll make it worse than that if we survive. Keep that thing's arms occupied so my team can get a clean shot."

"About time someone took charge." Melissa appeared beside them. She lifted a table above her head and threw it through the shadow monster.

Nervous laughter burst from Derek. "Does everyone in our school have powers?"

"Are you another person they stole from the past?" John asked Melissa.

Melissa shook her head. "I'm here to save lives. All civilians have escaped and are accounted for, including Tracy's brother. What's your mission's op?"

Tracy winced under crushing guilt. In fighting for her life, she lost track of her brother when he was stuck between three living shadows. "Thanks for saving my brother, but mission what?"

The combined shadow contracted, its limbs shrinking into its lengthening form, a giant beanstalk climbing higher. It used the thinner frame to dodge around Tracy's constructs, the few of them left intact.

"Do you have an operational plan?" Melissa said, condescension mingling in.

Tracy understood the general meaning of the odd question. "Yeah, ripping that thing apart."

Melissa stared at the shadow shifting its width to add to its height. "Great objective. One question: how?"

Tracy reached for Ri Ur Tol's and Derek's hands. "Can I have more power from you? The shadow can't hold its form outside the void. I dispersed smaller versions of this big boy by hitting it with solid objects."

"Good to confirm what I observed about its weaknesses. Cover me." Melissa hoisted a folded lunch table above her head without so much as a grunt of exertion. Though it outweighed her by three-to-one and was nearly twice as long as she was tall, Melissa looked like she was holding a piece of cardboard. Rather than throw it, she ran at the shadow with the giant fly swatter.

Small chunks of the shadow dispersed into smoke with every swing of the table. A handful of swings later, the table was eaten away. Melissa tossed the corner she was holding. What remained of the table broke apart on impact. She retreated before the monster's arms could grab her.

The wide column of shadow stretched higher into the night. It contracted, the circular base shrinking, then exploded outward in black spears. These lashed about, weaving around every Tracy-made transmuted obstacle.

Icy aches spread from Tracy's legs before she even knew what was happening.

Red liquid spilled from where the spears made of shadow had punctured her. One pierced her leg clean through. The other stopped at the bone, her power-enhanced dress absorbing some of the impact.

John leaped in front of Tracy, acting as a human shield to prevent more spikes from stabbing her. Several spears rebounded off his skin, swerving to strike him again. John swung his arm, cleaving the shadows stabbing her, dissolving them into smoke. The snaking shadow claws buffeted against him, their repeated blows breaking through his protection to carve long gashes across his chest and back.

A ball of light struck the shadow's arms and exploded.

Shock dissipating, Tracy gagged at the blood pouring out of her, to say little of the clear hole in her leg. The world spun, dizzying lights fluttering about her head. Without the shadows to hold her upright, her legs gave out.

More flexible shadow arms launched to finish the job of dismembering her.

Derek raised his hands. Shadow arms rebounded off his telekinetic shield.

Louis rushed to Tracy's side. "Damn, Tracy. Can you heal this?" Without waiting for a response, Louis held his jacket against her legs, using his clothes to absorb her blood. He tore strips from his fancy dress clothes and used them to bind her wounds. "What do you need? Are you okay?"

Gasping pain rippled throughout Tracy, her legs slow to respond. She would have passed out were it not for the adrenaline coursing through her veins. "I've been better, but you need to stay safe. Get behind a wall."

Tracy brushed Louis and his makeshift bandages away. She pressed her blood-drenched hands to the wounds. As she had done to repair Louis's legs and her own injuries, she pulled in nearby material, rebuilding her muscles. Luckily, the shadow's claw stopped at her bone, without splitting that, too.

Drawing in her full power invigorated her, her arm no longer burning when using her abilities. Aided by her music, she regrew deep muscle layers in both her legs and worked steadily outward to her skin.

Tracy trusted her friends to hold off the creature while she healed.

Fire raced within Tracy, spreading from newly forming musculature as sensation returned. Coughing in pain, she swallowed her scream.

Louis's touch chilled her forehead as he stayed by her side amid the shadow arms lashing about. Blurry, feverish vision rescinded, though Tracy's power fell further from her grasp.

She healed enough to rejoin the fight, saving the scraps of power she clung to before they faded.

Gratitude flashed from Tracy to Louis before she pushed him behind a pillar for cover. Driven to action, her head cleared. She turned up her music and power returned.

Rachel and Ri Ur Tol moved fighters about like game pieces. Aided by the pair, Melissa hurled a steady stream of tables through the air from every corner of the cafeteria.

John threw himself in front of the shadow's arms when they broke through Derek's shield. "Out of my way!" John shouted at Derek, knocking him over.

Derek stood, shakily regaining his feet. "We're on the same side!"

"You and Tracy lured those things here."

Derek's mouth opened to form a rebuttal. Nothing left his lips.

"Don't you dare lie to make it seem like you didn't attract the shadows here to feast." Spit flew from John's toxic rant.

"Not on purpose," Tracy countered, furious at her supposed friend for distracting them while they fought for their lives.

Struck by several shadow limbs, John still found the strength to continue arguing. "How does that help our school, or victims caught in the monster's path?"

Tracy ignored him and studied the field of battle. For all the havoc caused by the shadow's arms whipping in every direction, it could be doing much more damage.

"Wait. The shadow isn't focusing on us. Why?" Tracy asked anyone reasonable and willing to listen.

She traced the outline of the shadow above the open ceiling and outside the range of fluorescent lights. Shifting clouds revealed the moon briefly, indirectly highlighting the shadow's form by the sky it blotted out.

Its top bent, curling down, but not aimed at her.

"Derek! Telekinetic wall, now!" Tracy pointed through walls where the ceiling above the library would be, hoping her friend understood. "It's aiming for our classmates."

He raised his hands above his head. "I won't let it hurt any more of us."

The impact shook the roof as the shadow became the world's largest mallet, striking the bass drum that was Derek's telekinetic shield. Ceiling debris crashed down on them.

Derek collapsed at the shadow creature's second impact, the reverberating strike carrying into the shaking ground.

Tracy pulled material from the supporting columns, the school grounds, and lunchroom tables to make two pillars, each over thirty feet tall. At its current size, enclosing the shadow as she had in their first fight was no longer an option. She slammed the pillars together into the base of the shadow.

Its roar twisted thousands of rusty screws into her eardrums.

Hers wasn't the only body to hit the ground. Ri Ur Tol clutched her head as she sank to her knees and Derek rolled around like he was on fire.

Melissa somehow found the strength to lob the nearest table at the shadow. It fell short, hitting Tracy's pillars which covered the shadow's base, with a loud crash.

"LET ME FEED ON THE OTHERS," began the rumbling thunder of the shadow's voice, "AND I SPARE YOUR LIVES."

"Never!" Tracy stood with the force of her words.

"What she said." Derek rose a moment later.

Tracy's friends regained their feet.

"THEN DIE."

Tentacled claws sprang from the shadow, aimed at Tracy and the rest.

The claw hit the tile floor to Tracy's side.

Each of the other claws inexplicably missed their intended targets.

Grateful for a little luck, they came together. Rachel, Ri Ur Tol, and Derek's hands latched onto Tracy's shoulders, donating their power to her.

Soil, concrete, and the Earth itself surged; she transmuted her pillar into stone, sending it climbing higher within the shadow.

The shadow screeched, the sound ringing in Tracy's ears and boring into her mind. Above the missing ceiling, the shadow squirmed. It pulled and stretched, struggling to free itself from the pillars she pressed into its base.

Tracy faltered, unable to build her construct higher. Her power was fading, the shadow shifting itself through her physical anchors, the solidified pillars.

Derek recognized the problem. "We need to topple that tower while we still have the bottom of the shadow trapped inside. Anyone with power left, please help us."

Wind rushed past from Derek's telekinetic fist.

Melissa and John ran full speed at Tracy's pillar, making it wobble.

Rachel circled the room and hurled herself at the solid cylinder holding the shadow.

Looking like a tall rotten tree, the mess of shadow enclosed in her transmuted stone fell.

With the might of an earthquake, the ground bellowed from the impact. Tremors rattled Tracy. She took cover, crouching to feel the safety of a solid floor, and found none. Cracks ripped apart tiles, and the floor opened. Concrete foundation split, lengths of concrete pushing to the surface while the rest sank deeper.

A cacophony of falling pans clattered from behind the kitchen doors.

The long shadow looked like a flailing arm with the rest of its body trapped beneath Tracy's cylinder pillar.

Rachel sprinted among Tracy and everyone else, lifting them. "It's not over."

Tracy piled tons more material on top of the creature, burying the shadow under rolling waves of soil.

The tip of the shadow, no larger than her car, tensed and stretched in its efforts to escape. She dumped another layer of earth on it.

Tracy wiped her face on Louis's loud green jacket she had used to mop her blood. She tied a sleeve around each leg to compress her partially healed injuries until regaining the strength to transmute her body to finish sealing all her open wounds.

Dredging up her power, she transmuted the ground beneath the shadow monster into a pit, then dropped a mountain of earth on top.

Too tired to yelp in triumph, she exhaled in a long, drawn breath. Cheers carried from her friends. Needing to see what she wrought,

Tracy limped to the fallen outer wall for a better view of the buried shadow. She teetered, holding herself up by leaning on broken bricks, careful to avoid touching the shattered windows.

Scraping together her tiny, lingering power, she opened the giant pile of dirt she dumped on the shadow monster and removed her transmuted pillar that had covered it.

Nothing was inside except the burning smell emitted when the shadow faded into smoke.

Precious silence spread over the wrecked cafeteria.

31

Crumbling Lives

Rachel

Metal rebar pipes clanged to the ground in an impression of a B flat scale. More ceiling collapsed in the wasteland of the Highland View cafeteria, thankfully far from anyone. Half the room was now an outdoor patio with the forecast of a high likelihood of raining debris. Rachel shivered, exposed to the cool night.

Stale smells of stagnant water sifted through the rubble from untouched maintenance rooms and cracked foundation, leaving the taste of moldy bread in her mouth.

Rachel rubbed dust from her hair, lamenting the countless tears in her dress. "Can I have one night that isn't ruined by monsters?"

Ri Ur Tol looked up from retrieving who knows how many of her weapons. "We hunted no monsters last night or the night before."

Rachel groaned, too tired to explain to Ri Ur Tol how she missed the point.

John grimaced with each step he took, his movements stiff and full of aches. He wandered over to check on Allerie and Tony.

Rachel slid her tongue across her teeth, processing her thoughts about John.

That liar *is making sure two people he barely knows are fine instead of me and our closest friends?!*

She wanted to yell at her boyfriend, shout until her throat ran dry and he felt as betrayed as she did. Rachel had revealed her powers to John at the first chance. He hadn't done the same for her.

Mentally tossing and turning, she refused to go to him. She looked across the wreckage for her other friends.

Sprawled on the floor with his arms stretched wide, Derek looked ready to make angels in the remains of the Snow Ball. He let out a single barking laugh. "Guess I'm the only one who thinks fighting the shadow was an improvement over the dance."

John finally bothered to look at his old friends. "You don't mean that."

"Of course not," Derek snapped. "It was a bad joke from the surprise at being alive."

"You shouldn't be this arrogant, considering my team had to step in and save you," John said, gesturing to the two people at his side. Having spent most of the fight hiding, Allerie and Tony didn't so much as have a bruise or cut on them. It was near impossible to believe Allerie could kick exploding energy balls, though Rachel had caught sight of her bouncing them around to strike the shadow.

Allerie rose from Tony and John, her face wracked with uncertainty and confusion as she walked to Nicole. Nicole had done well for her first battle with a monster, shepherding classmates from the shadow. She rested with her head in her hands at one of the few intact tables. Tony made a beeline for the snacks table out in the hallway, protected from falling debris and dust by thick glass panes and closed cafeteria doors.

John approached Rachel with a strained smile. He reached for her hand as though that selfish prick hadn't kept a massive secret from her. She pulled away.

"You've lied to me for weeks." Her bone-weary statement came out as feeble croaks.

John had the grace to seem bashful. "Good thing I showed up, though."

She didn't like it, but he was right. The shadow would have killed them without John's support. Rachel voiced her displeasure, but held back from releasing her full-blown anger by resorting to yelling. "We have a lot to talk about. In private."

"Okay," John said nervously.

Fear-filled faces poked around the cafeteria entrance doors. "Is it safe?" asked one of Rachel's classmates, his suit disheveled from the earlier race to the library.

Leaning on the one part of the collapsed wall that was still upright, a ghastly pale Tracy lifted her head, failing to speak. Sweat-soaked hair clung to her face, retaining little of the elaborate shape it held during the dance. She adjusted a green jacket tied to her legs to reveal two large, blood-soaked holes in her dress, making it an act of wonder for how she was able to stand.

Tracy needed two tries for anyone to hear her frail voice. "I slayed the shadow, if that's what you're asking." She pointed to the open ceiling and added, "Stay clear of here, though."

"Bye, then," said their classmate. He sprinted for the school's entrance.

Teachers openly gaped at their bad remodeling job. Rachel's injuries and those of her friends went unnoticed next to the chunk removed from the school building.

"You all were amazing! Thank you for saving us." Mrs. Strata's face faded back and forth between horror and awe. How will we repair this damage?"

"Put it on the monster's tab." Tracy nodded at the large, exposed pit outside, the grave and death trap for the shadow. "Wait for me to sleep for the next month. Then, I'll take care of the renovation work. Think you could convince my teachers that either this fight or using my powers to reconstruct our cafeteria would be worth extra credit?"

"That is the exact attitude we need to fix," John muttered to Rachel.

Mrs. Strata's brow furrowed, though a bemused half smile graced her lips. "Of course not. Consider any repairs you make as worth-while community service for college applications."

Tracy snapped her fingers. "So close."

Screeching tires and car lights speeding from the parking lot showed what happened to the classmates who were more cautious than curious. Those who stayed marveled at Rachel and the rest, pointing and taking pictures, making her feel like an exhibit in a museum. They remained at a distance from their superpowered classmates, an imaginary wall separating the battle-weary from the normal people.

Putting her stewing anger at him aside, Rachel squeezed John's hand to feel another's touch.

Allerie pulled Tracy upright and gestured at Nicole. "What the hell did you do?"

Rachel sought her powers to interrupt the new fight and found none.

A ball of light formed in Allerie's hand, held inches from Tracy like a blazing fire to scorch her face. "Did you clone my ex-girlfriend? This Nicole clearly isn't the one I dated."

Tracy's head tilted until she faced Nicole. "You look amazing, by the way. Sorry we didn't get a chance to dance tonight."

"Shut up!" Allerie dropped the ball of energy and kicked it. The ball exploded, illuminating the empty bus lot. "You cloned my ex!"

"I didn't clone anyone," said Tracy, exhaustion dragging out each word.

Nicole's voice cut across Allerie as though it were a thrown dagger. "I'm from a parallel world."

"You're into some weirdness, Tracy." Allerie dropped her hold on Tracy, whose legs shook. Tracy's flailing arm missed the wall behind her, and she collapsed to the floor.

Nicole lifted Tracy to her feet and said, "I'm sorry not everyone appreciates the sacrifices you made tonight."

Nicole checked the deep wounds on Tracy's legs.

From a distance, Rachel saw a mass of tender, scarred flesh beneath Tracy's smeared blood. "Does she need to go to the hospital?"

"No," Nicole said as she glared at Allerie, her eyes carrying the same fury Allerie reserved for Tracy. "She patched herself up decently enough. Also, I'm not into girls, and you could have really hurt the one who saved us by defeating the shadow."

Allerie flinched, berated by someone she likely couldn't help but see as her ex.

Rachel squeezed John's hand tighter. As pissed as she was with him, she couldn't imagine an alternate world where they weren't dating.

John nudged Derek with his foot. "When you go into the void, do you make it a job to kidnap people?"

Stretching across the floor, a yawn escaped Derek's mouth and carried into his reply. "Does she look like a victim here? I might as well mention Ri Ur Tol is from the past. That doesn't change the fact that you have powers! You could have helped us sooner tonight."

"We were busy protecting our innocent classmates while you attracted those things here."

"We didn't know I was the one they wanted," Tracy cut in.

John's voice boomed, halting all other responses. "Shouldn't you assume everything wrong is Derek's and your fault?"

"That's not fair!" Tracy shouted back.

John held up his fingers, counting. "One: Louis's car crash. Two: the demon bear. Three through eight: those shadow things. Those are only counting problems I know about."

Rachel glanced between each of her friends' faces, scrambling to find a way to use her speed or musical sight to prevent someone from uttering words they could never take back.

Derek backed up Tracy. "We stopped the shadows tonight."

John turned his ire back on Derek. "Fixing a problem *you* caused doesn't make it not your fault. You know what? You're unfit to have power, and the world was safer when you were nothing more than a regular student."

A bitter smile cracked Derek's red-flushed face. "Not much we can do about it now."

"Not quite." John waved his hands at Louis. "Take Derek's powers."

Condensation formed from Rachel's exhaled breath as she gaped in surprise, too shocked to move. The cold night turned colder.

A downtrodden Louis shuffled to Derek. "I don't want to do this. You left me no choice when you used your powers to cripple me." He placed his hands over Derek's heart. Light passed from Derek into Louis.

Derek grasped Louis's hand, and the light stopped. The temperature rose from frigid to merely chilly.

The wide-eyed Derek pushed himself away from Louis, swaying half a step back.

Rachel looked between Louis and John, not wanting to believe they would rob anyone of their powers, least of all, one of their friends.

John moved between Derek and Louis. "You can either willingly give up your powers or we can take them."

"What will a fight prove? I spent all my power already defending our home."

John's eyes burned with a hunger Rachel had never witnessed before. "That will make it easier to take power you so readily abuse. Continually sinking to this helpless state isn't doing you any favors to prove you're responsible enough to have powers for when the next threat attacks."

Derek raised his fists. "Fine. Let's finish this."

As though speaking to a child, John's condescending tone was appalling. "I'm not a monster. We aren't fighting here, where by-standers will be hurt. See? Even the basics of responsibly using our gifts are beyond your understanding. Follow me. I know a more fitting location."

Too stunned to speak, Rachel looked at Tracy and Nicole, hoping for a voice of reason that would stop the fight, except they were equally speechless.

John stepped over the wreckage of the school walls, along with Louis, Allerie, and Tony. John didn't look back, knowing Derek would never run from this fight.

Derek checked over his friends still in the cafeteria, his face fuming in boiling rage, then he started for the parking lot. "Don't stop us."

Tracy jerked her head at Derek's back as she spoke to Rachel and anyone willing to listen. "Come on. We need to make sure they don't kill each other."

Ri Ur Tol wrapped Tracy's free arm around her shoulder, and together, Nicole and Ri Ur Tol helped Tracy limp to the car in Derek's wake.

Rachel raced ahead of Derek to chase after John. No matter what, she was stopping the twin headstrong tempests from colliding into a superstorm that would destroy them both and everyone nearby.

32

Long Drive

Rachel

Rachel slumped into the passenger seat of John's black Mazda. The overabundant smell of pine trees swirled from the air freshener dangling behind the rearview mirror. It attempted to disguise the general smell of John's sweat permeating the seat cushions—and failed.

She stepped into an old pair of her sneakers rolling around on the soft car mat, her dress heels lost during battle. Her dress, for that matter, had more tears than threads. She crossed her arms to cover the most egregious holes at her sides. Blood boiling, she wanted to hurt something for ruining her night. Of course, the shadow was no longer of this world, leaving Rachel fuming beneath her skin, with only one person close enough to vent at.

She slammed John's car door shut. She considered opening the door again and giving it a good power-infused slam to break it altogether. "How long have you had powers, sweetie? With your skills fighting the shadows, it's been weeks, if not months, right?"

John started his car and tilted his head back at the three passengers. "Do we have to do this in front of everyone?"

Rachel caught Allerie's face in the side mirror. The three extras were mute statues, wary of suffering from Rachel's rising fury. "Allerie and Tony aren't my friends, and sorry about this one, Louis." Rachel offered Louis an apologetic half smile before rekindling her ire for John.

Louis was careful not to make eye contact. "I thought you told her a while back."

Rachel cut off any response by berating John. "Nope. How long have you had powers, you asshole?"

With his eyes set forward and mouth practically in a grin, John didn't appear to be nearly as concerned about lying as he should have been. He started driving when Tracy's car pulled behind them, following to where John intended to fight.

"You're not wrong," he said matter-of-factly, as though Rachel was the one being unreasonable. "I'm an asshole, but I was right. This was the second major threat Derek and Tracy caused."

"Don't twist this around. When did you know you had powers?"

"The day after your fight with that bear monster."

A month! Consumed by anger, Rachel forgot what she was about to yell at John, settling for, "The minute I returned to the present, I told you I was safe and that I had powers."

"I thought you saw us when we saved those people in the burning building. It wasn't *that* far of a stretch to assume you figured it out based on all the reports about terrible drivers we've stopped."

Hairs on her neck bristled. "And what? I said nothing about you having powers all the times we've been together since then? You know me. Do I seem like the type of person to keep quiet about powers emerging in anyone? I told you everything. You told me nothing."

"I guess it was too much to hope that you didn't want to talk about it. Does that mean you're siding with Derek?"

"*Both* you and Derek need to put your dicks away and skip the measuring contest."

The car screeched around a turn John took too fast, leaving streaks of rubber on the road. Rumble strips shook the car. John regained control without spinning them down an embankment.

"Mind easing that accelerator?" squeaked Louis. His olive skin turned another shade paler with each mile per hour John took them over the speed limit.

John heaved a sigh and brought them to a more reasonable, legal speed.

"Wait a minute." Rachel considered John's past month in a new light. "Is this how you scrounged your way back onto the wrestling team? What did you do, blackmail your coach?"

John had the grace to look insulted. "Of course not. I demonstrated the strength in my powers and showed how much more of an asset I am."

"In other words, you pulled a Derek move by behaving as the villain you claim he is."

John let out a frustrated bark. "You're not getting it. I was already a top pick to win State."

"In what world is guaranteeing yourself a victory not an abuse of powers?"

"I deserve to be wrestling, and I don't use my powers during matches. I win on my strength alone. My powers were nothing more than to show Coach how outstanding I could be."

"Derek's powers slip, especially when in stressful situations. What makes you think you're any different?"

John banged his thumb into the car's console, blasting them with hard rock.

His avoidance was the last straw. "I never should have confided all my doubts in these powers with you," Rachel muttered. It was the least harsh tone she'd taken, yet the force of the statement startled her.

"That hurts."

Once spoken, she could not take back her words. Still, she pressed on. "You've been lying to me this whole time. As if that wasn't bad enough, you used me for information on our friends."

John tightened his grip on the steering wheel, crushing the plastic to match the outline of his fingers. "I'll concede that I was a shitty boyfriend from my lie of omission if you concede that Derek and Tracy with powers is dangerous and wrong."

"Who gets to decide right from wrong? You?"

"I'll be better than Derek."

"Congratulations. You're making all new mistakes."

"Mr. Sprog told me to be wary of anyone who fought alongside Derek."

"Mr. Sprog?" Even as she spoke, her brain connected the dots within Derek's web of paranoia. "What, did he train you or give you powers?"

"The second one. He gave me power from the excess energies spilled when Derek fought that giant bear, which I then shared with the three in the back seat here."

Rachel's attempts to curb John's anger made him hurtle faster into the brunt of the storm, dragging them all with him. "You're choosing to trust a teacher you've known for mere months over friends you've known for a decade?"

"This goes beyond a lifelong friendship or two. I don't fully trust Mr. Sprog, but everything he told me has been right so far. He explained that if Derek and Tracy keep abusing their gifts, they will tear our world apart. Seeing Derek's bear and Tracy's shadow monsters, I agree."

Rachel pointed at Allerie and Tony. "Why bring those two into it? You don't even like Tony."

"Hey! That's harsh," Tony called out from the back. Any more of his thoughts were kept to himself by Rachel's glare.

"I gathered those I could trust to not run to the resident heroes." John's final words brought them to silence.

Rachel couldn't think of anything to add to avert John's bad decision of challenging Derek. Too soon, the caravan of cars following them turned onto John and Derek's street, only to speed past John's house.

"You're not fighting in your yard?" Rachel's voice trailed off as they continued down the street.

"I never intended to bring this mess to my front doorstep."

"That's a dirty move, especially since Derek's dad is still recovering."

"I'll make sure Mr. and Mrs. Fen stay inside and safe. Derek's sister, too, if she's home for the weekend."

Derek's house sat at the end of his long driveway, a glowing jack-o'-lantern sitting in the middle of the woods. Light reflected off the dark-red wood panels and caked the house in the color of blood.

Smaller lights of neighbors' houses appeared through the trees, visible only because most of the leaves had fallen.

John left the car to piss off someone else. Tony, Allerie, and Louis stepped out, leaving Rachel alone, watching enemies gather.

The two immature boys sized each other up like two dogs about to fight over a discarded bone. Their suit jackets were in disarray, Derek's being little more than tattered fabric. Derek's face was drawn in the limited light offered by the cars and exterior house lights, his skin pale. John shivered, sweat having worked outward through his undershirt, torn dress shirt, and suit jacket, which was now more of a vest.

Rachel was powerless to stop Derek and John from tearing the other's limbs apart.

She screamed, binding her frustration to her voice, a voice whose valid arguments no one listened to. Louis jumped in surprise as the car could not contain her yell.

Her breath spent, she emerged to join her friends and stop the bloodbath.

33

Battleground

Tracy

Car lights shut off, letting darkness close in on the crowd of eight bedraggled high school students and the plus one of Ri Ur Tol. Moonlight crept from behind clouds, brightening the night ever so slightly. Derek's outside house lights cast long shadows to the edge of the woods encircling his house.

Out of habit, Tracy wandered closer to the light. The leg muscles and tendons she repaired with her powers pinched her nerves like they were misfiring robotic appendages, making walking difficult. Still, she was able to shamble about without relying on Nicole and Ri Ur Tol to carry her anymore.

Everyone milled about their cars except for Derek and John. Each stared at the other, ignoring the dim light hiding half their features.

Fifteen minutes removed from John's heated challenge at their school, Tracy was hopeful cooler heads would prevail. She imagined Derek inviting everyone in where they would spend the rest of the night playing video games and raiding his pantry.

"This is too close to my house for our fight," said Derek, dissolving the opportunity to make peace.

John's lips twitched. "Then don't go overboard. Otherwise, your house will be caught in the crossfire."

"We're doing this in the woods. I won't hurl my family into one of my battles again."

"That's my point. You know you can't control yourself and endanger everyone when you fight."

A green Pontiac pulled up, drawing Tracy's eyes. The car parked and Melissa stepped lively from it. She walked to the Derek and John staring match and dropped her hands on their shoulders. They noticeably leaned in from the force she applied. "I hope this wasn't an invite-only post-dance party. Mind if I join?"

Derek finally broke his staring contest with John. He looked from Melissa to her car and back again. "Why have you been following me and why did you tail me last weekend to the mall?"

"To determine how much of a threat you are and eliminate you if necessary."

Derek's mouth gaped open. "Eliminate? Who do you work for that would willingly kill us?"

"What was the verdict?" asked John.

Melissa looked around at everyone with an intense gaze that was hard to read. "You all have stopped multiple monster attacks and averted disasters. However, the extent to which you influenced, or outright caused, those incidents is unknown. Your public declarations tonight were very interesting."

"Enough talk," barked John. "I know what Derek's done, and we are finishing our fight now."

Tracy cut in. "Not yet. I'm warning Derek's parents their home is now a war zone. Also, anyone who doesn't want to go traipsing through this cold night in their ruined dresses can come inside, and I'll make you some new clothes."

Everyone except Derek and John followed her through the den's side door. The bright indoor lights momentarily blinded Tracy. "There's a bathroom up ahead to the right. The clothes I make won't be flattering, but they'll be warm."

Allerie approached Tracy and asked, "Would you really make some new clothes for me?"

Tracy considered refusing. Though she would feel satisfaction by the petty act of spite, it would do nothing more than pour gasoline on the simmering fire. Tracy grabbed a towel from the closet and turned on her music, transmuting the soft material into gray sweatpants and a sweatshirt.

"Don't break anything," Tracy declared to Allerie, handing over the new clothes.

Allerie's cold eyes flashed in anger. "My fight's with you, not Derek's family. I'm not that disrespectful, you racist ass."

Heat flushed Tracy's cheeks. "I'm not racist. I don't trust you."

"I never should have trusted you around my girlfriend."

Allerie disappeared to change her clothes, leaving Tracy frozen in place, words rattling in her mind.

Only a full bear hug broke her stupor. Mrs. Fen held Tracy close. "Thank you for being all right," she whispered. "I heard about the massive destruction at the school. I'm so glad you're safe."

"The night's not over yet. John and Derek insist on hashing things out with their fists." Tracy formed new gray clothes and handed them to Ri Ur Tol. Unlike with Allerie, she made them the proper size, rather than slightly too tight.

Mrs. Fen frowned at the destruction of their spare towels, though her face truly soured when she spoke. "I thought you all were friends. I remember visiting his house when his family first moved to our street. Why would my idiot son ever agree to a fistfight?"

Tracy leaned in close. "John has powers, too. So they might hit with more than fists."

Allerie appeared from the bathroom. Her shirt's sleeves stopped halfway up her forearms while the sweatpants looked more like capris stopping around her knees. Rather than seem embarrassed, Allerie flaunted the ill-fitting ensemble with her head held high.

Mrs. Fen opened her mouth, likely to offer some baked good or leftover dinner, but Allerie breezed by to step outside. "Who's your friend who can't say hello?" Mrs. Fen asked Tracy. "Was she also attacked by that terrifying shadow thing?"

Ri Ur Tol shuffled into the bathroom with the clothes Tracy made for her.

"She's no friend." Tracy chewed through her words. "She's here to support John."

"Let me talk some sense into him. I've known John since he was in diapers."

Mrs. Fen started marching, but Tracy grabbed her arm. "The boys are well beyond rational thoughts. The most we can do is reduce the fallout from their explosive personalities."

"That's *my* boy, and he could get hurt," Mrs. Fen begged. "I have to try."

Mrs. Fen walked past Louis with a quick warm greeting. Her loud shouts erupted outside, muffled by the door, but distinct enough to hear the intention behind the words.

Ri Ur Tol appeared in the bathroom doorway with twin daggers strapped to her belt. Tracy could only guess at the number of blades hidden beneath the outer layers. Ri Ur Tol approached the outside door as the shouting match between Derek and his mom grew louder. Without opening the door, Ri Ur Tol rejoined Tracy and the others waiting in the hall.

"I see the source of Derek's fighting spirit," muttered Ri Ur Tol.

One by one, Nicole, Melissa, Louis, and Tony changed into comfortable sweatshirts and sweatpants. Hardly the combat gear they may have dreamed of wearing, but Tracy's powers were stretched too thin, having spent her greatest flash of fashion inspiration on her torn dress.

A glint of metal shone from the closet. Derek's broken sword lay propped against the wall. She wrapped the broken blade in the discarded clothing her friends handed her, feeling the dwindling power within her rekindle at its touch.

"I may be able to smooth everything over with Derek's family," Tony said, surprising Tracy to hear his voice without raising his hand first.

Bad enough John insisted on bringing Allerie into their group. Tracy had no intention of trusting the slimeball that was Tony. "Whatever trick you have planned, don't do it."

"I don't have a trick," Tony grumbled with the fake look of innocence he regularly wore in class.

The outdoor shouting match died down.

Sounds of heavy footfalls crunching on gravel approached. Mrs. Fen wrenched open the door and slammed it shut, knocking a picture frame of Derek and his sister from the wall. "I can't reason with them."

"I'll do what I can," Tracy promised, playing music from her phone. "As for you and your home, I'm on it." Tracy pointed outside. She raised a wall of earth at the far end of the projected light. As strength drained from Tracy, she clutched Mrs. Fen for support. Tracy applied the finishing touches and reinforced the barricade to withstand blasts of energy.

Mrs. Fen sighed, her eyes watering. "Thank you." She left for the kitchen and returned with a package of cookies. "If you keep our home safe from the fight, I'll have more waiting when common sense returns."

Tracy left the warmth of the Fen household, finding her way to Derek's side. "Your mom is pissed."

Derek caught the transmuted clothes Tracy flung at him, stripping to his boxers, and changing into sweats in clear view of everyone. "Let her be. John dragged us here to keep me in line, using them as unspoken hostages so I don't explode over everything unfortunate enough to be within a mile radius."

Tracy looked John up and down. His dress clothes were mostly intact, aside from the tears along his arms where the shadow monster's claws had shredded the material. "I'll make you new clothes if you stop the insanity of this fight and come inside to relax."

John grunted, ripping off his tattered shirtsleeves. "I'll pass. I like my formal wear."

To occupy her hands and thoughts, Tracy ripped open the package of chocolate chip cookies and munched an entire row. She was too worried for her friend's safety to taste the sweetness. The cookies might as well be dry cardboard for all she enjoyed of them.

Ri Ur Tol grabbed a row of cookies for herself, loudly crunching as she chewed.

Derek turned on his phone's flashlight and led them into the woods.

Except for Ri Ur Tol, everyone had their own light. Tracy brought her phone closer to Ri Ur Tol so they could see, moving the wrapped sword beneath her armpit. The born hunter thanked Tracy, then stepped from the group, traveling alone, parallel to Tracy in near darkness.

They walked past the bare harvested pawpaw orchard to pass beneath towering trees, silent obelisks standing watch over tonight's folly.

Bugs buzzed about, irritating her hands and face.

Passing up and over a hill, Derek's house and its lights sank from view. Tracy lifted her phone higher to spread her shred of light farther. Together they moved as shadows, wandering the dark woods, guided by tiny phone lights. By no means were they quiet. Plenty of swears flew freely when a branch caught someone's shirt, or a root tripped the careless.

Nicole broke out into a hummed tune. It was a melody that reminded Tracy of times long past and a future worth fighting for. Tracy's steps lightened, stumbling on fewer outstretched roots. Even Derek carried himself higher. His slouched posture straightened, new resolve replacing the exhausted husk from after their last fight.

Meanwhile, Nicole looked like she had fought dozens of shadows single-handedly. She yawned mid-song and much of the surge of energy ebbed from Tracy. Melissa put her arm under Nicole's shoulder, supporting Nicole as they kept walking.

"Good job on the much-needed power-up, but I think you recharged more than just your friend," said Melissa, nodding her head at John, who was leaping over fallen trees.

Nicole nodded, her head sinking forward until she snapped back upright and forced her eyes wide open. "Even if I accidentally replenished a little of everyone's powers, Derek needed to recover some to stand a chance. I can't direct where it goes."

Rachel approached their friend. "How long have you known you could do this?"

"I've thought I could for a while," explained Nicole, "but was never fully certain until tonight. I recharged you all during your fight against the shadow, and what I gave now was the last of it."

Breaking from the tree line, they entered the open meadow, the opposite side's edge lost beyond Tracy's phone's beam of light. Shifting clouds offered glimpses of the night sky. Under the limited moonlight, the meadow seemed alien. For all she knew, the scramble from the woods transported them to a foreign planet.

All the familiar markers looked different in the dark. Trees they had knocked over loomed larger than she remembered. Tracy ran her fingers along carved bullseye targets she knew were on the trees but had trouble seeing with her limited phone light.

She unwrapped the bundle held to her side and tossed the broken sword to Derek's feet.

"I already drained this earlier." Derek handed it back to Tracy and set himself into a fighting stance. "No weapons, no powers."

John punched his own palm for an intimidating smacking noise. "Fine by me."

Rachel nudged Ri Ur Tol. "Can't you teleport them far apart and end this fight before it starts?"

Ri Ur Tol looked between the two men and shook her head. "Stopping tonight will do no more than delay these two. Their paths are set to cross. Look no further than their eyes."

"Don't you owe Derek your life? Shouldn't you protect him?" Rachel pressed.

"Protecting Derek would dishonor him in this fight." Ri Ur Tol's voice carried an edge that sent a shiver through Rachel. "You would do well to know that I no longer owe a blood debt to Derek for when he first defeated me. That ended when I saved his life."

"Which time?" muttered Tracy as her attention returned to the two childish boys within the clearing.

"I stopped counting," replied Ri Ur Tol.

Derek and John stared each other down, unwavering as they walked in a circle, a few paces separating them.

"Come on!" John yelled, raising his hands and challenging Derek to attack.

Derek balled his hands into fists, bringing them in front of his face. He looked more confident trying to dance earlier tonight than in this fistfight. "We don't have to do this."

Derek's words gave Tracy hope one of them was starting to come to his senses.

"You didn't have to kidnap my girlfriend for a month."

"What?" Derek paused. "When we went into the void for the first time? Nothing happened."

"Of course not. That's not the point. She's still suffering from all the time she lost. She'll be finishing this semester's assignments well into the spring."

"We're all struggling to make up our schoolwork. Besides, opening the void was an accident."

"Isn't that worse? There was no guarantee of ever returning home."

Derek rotated his shoulders to loosen them. "Worse than staying on the bridge to be ripped apart by the Beast? We made the right call to jump into the unknown. Seems I have more faith in my abilities and our friends than you do."

"That thing was *your* monster." John pulled back his fist, his feet planting firmly. His fist moved so fast it seemed to disappear as he brought it forward.

Derek ducked, and John's right hook sailed over him.

A second jab from John's off hand caught Derek below the eye with a resounding crack.

34

Bloody Fists

Derek

Stars flared over Derek's vision, melding into multicolored flashes. He reeled from John's punch, catching himself on a tree trunk lining the meadow. The semicircle of phone lights held by his friends left John as little more than an outline.

Tapping his cheek, Derek felt a tender bump forming.

John dove for Derek's legs.

Derek jumped to the side and kicked John in the stomach. Air escaped John's mouth in a combination of a wheeze and gasp. John recovered and rounded on Derek before he could back away from reach.

They fell into a series of punches, each unraveling another year of friendship, tearing memories of their triumphs, their joys, asunder.

Derek swiped his arm to deflect John's fist. John's wide follow-through kick caught Derek in the side, knocking him down.

Choking for air, Derek's arms and legs shook as he struggled to rise. "They teach you that sneaky move in wrestling?" he sputtered.

John closed in on Derek, separating him from his friends. All of them stood still at the edge of the meadow, watching, refusing to humiliate him by offering to help.

"I wouldn't know. I missed half the season," said John. He kicked Derek in the same spot as before, compounding knots of pain burrowing deeper.

Derek rolled over mounds of uneven earth, his abs burning. For a moment, he wanted to stay down, to give in. Derek grabbed a fistful of grass, wrenching it free of the ground when he got to his knees. Somehow, he stood.

Dancing farther from their friends, Derek kept the tree line to one side to limit how John could attack. Derek led with a quick series of punches before John was ready. Each hit collided, John's head recoiling. John's fist found its way between Derek's arms, hitting him in the jaw.

Blood dribbled down Derek's chin, his tongue licking a busted lip. A clicking noise sounded when he opened and closed his mouth. He leaned on a tree for support, catching his breath.

John spoke through clenched teeth. "Give me your powers. You've caused so much suffering to those around you simply by having them."

John hit Derek in the shoulder, sending numbing needles spreading down his arm like it had been dunked in an ice bath. Derek shifted his weight, testing which of his limbs were still obeying him. "You're causing plenty of suffering without my help."

An angry gurgling sound spilled from John. Rushing wind announced his punch.

Derek dodged to the side, swiping John's arm to redirect the blow as it passed. The force of John's follow-through sent a thundering crack over the meadow as he struck a tree and lodged his arm in it up to his elbow.

Words spilled from Derek. "Fuck you! So much for not using our powers. That would have crippled me if you hadn't missed."

John pulled his arm from the tree, his skin unscathed. "Like you haven't been? There's no way you could keep up with me in a fight."

"Shows how little you know." Derek grasped for his powers, knowing his inner fire had dwindled to embers thanks to fighting the shadow monster. He chose a different tactic: stalling. "I trained my ass off to hone my skills, with or without powers. What have you done to deserve your power upgrade?"

John didn't take the bait. His fist hit the telekinetic shield Derek barely formed. Derek's shield flickered and held, though the attack sent him flying onto his back.

Aching muscles strained to lift Derek to his feet.

His friend's faces were too difficult to make out, though more than one person cringed to see him standing once more. Somewhere over there, Ri Ur Tol had a great view of the amount of her training he had forgotten.

Derek pressed his words further. "Seriously, how did you get your powers?"

"From you."

Intelligent words failed to form on Derek's lips. "When?! How?!"

"Much like that alcohol citation, you never pay attention to how your choices affect others. So much of the power you and your monster tossed around to destroy our hometown was collected and given to me. By the way, thanks to that citation, my parents search my backpack every day for drugs."

"That's over the top and shitty, but I have nothing to do with how they treat you. Kind of like how I didn't cause you to get the citation."

"You dragged me down with you." John's fist struck Derek in the chest, knocking the wind out of him.

Derek caught the next blow in his palm, using his power to keep his body from breaking. Acute pain bore into his recently healed arm; it shook, holding John's force in place. Derek spun away to place a tree between him and John.

John kicked through the thick oak trunk, coming an inch short of knocking out Derek's teeth. John brought his leg into a sideways kick, splitting the tree. It toppled with a crash that trembled through Derek's legs, leaving nothing separating them. John took in a few heavy breaths of exertion from his unnecessary show of strength and hopped over the stump toward Derek.

The newly fallen log blocked one of Derek's means of escape. He ripped branches free with his telekinesis to fling them at John. Though he wanted to lift the entire tree and swing it like the world's largest baseball bat, he knew better than to waste his power showing off.

The sticks bounced harmlessly off John's body, as though he were protected by his own personal telekinetic shield.

John lunged, grasping Derek by the shoulders. Derek threw up a small telekinetic shield, but John broke through it, headbutting him on the bridge of his nose. Blood poured like a faucet, splattering the forest floor in thick drops.

Derek cried out, unwilling to touch the blinding pain.

Blinking until his vision slowly returned, he saw John waiting with a smug grin.

John kicked at Derek's head.

Derek formed a telekinetic bubble, stretching the shield around John's foot, absorbing the force like a rubber band. The shield snapped to its original shape, launching John back into a tree.

John's body hit and crumpled to the ground.

Derek snorted out blood and ran forward, extending his hand to help John. "I won't let you take my powers, but I'll still be here to help you."

"Get away!" bellowed John, knocking Derek's hand aside. John used the tree to support himself as he stood on shaking legs. He swayed, then caught himself, his hand covering his face and massaging his forehead.

"Fine, you want a confession?" Derek yelled, fighting to suppress his rising fury so it wouldn't tinge his attacks. "By going into the void, I opened the way for the shadow to break free. The shadow creature was still out there whether or not I entered the void. If I hadn't opened the doorway, it would have discovered another way out into our world or one like it. In hindsight, I'm glad it came through. We stopped it and prevented it from hurting anyone else. That's why I'm holding on to my powers: to save even one more person!"

John spat at Derek's feet. "Tonight, your choices threatened everyone we love, you self-righteous trash."

Hardened resolve billowed from the depths inside Derek. "We stand a better chance of protecting everyone by working together. I'll fight you, tooth and claw, to keep my powers."

Derek wiped the blood leaking from his nose on his raised fists. He drew in what little of his power remained, readying for another round.

35

Erupting Power

Tracy

Tracy looked away, revolted by the messy fight between her two friends. Thankfully, her earphones muffled each hit from Derek and John. Her limited phone light caught dark specks of red sprinkled across tree trunks, grass, and disturbed dirt.

John panted, heaving deep breaths, ready to inflict more pain on Derek. Dirt and sweat riddled the once fine fabric of his button-down shirt. Derek looked no better. The clothes Tracy had made for him were already stretched, torn, and filthy. Derek rubbed a line of sweat dripping from his forehead.

Tracy started forward, only for Ri Ur Tol to pull her back, unleashing Tracy's fury. "I don't care what those boys want. We're friends, and this shouldn't be happening."

Allerie's face twisted into a grimace. "Maybe if you all didn't force us to clean up your messes, it wouldn't have come to this. Monsters don't attack every day, but every day someone runs a red light or dangerously weaves through traffic. We've stopped those selfish drivers from putting other people's lives at risk. What have you done to protect your home?"

Tracy discarded her pride, pleading to Allerie's decency. "You're right. I'll be better in the future. Right now, though, you don't like this fight any more than I do. We can put a stop to it. Maybe tonight wouldn't have happened if we had worked together from the start!"

Ri Ur Tol shook her head. "You are wrong. Either we let those two fight to a decisive end now, or they will do so when they are alone."

Ri Ur Tol raised the phone in her hand higher, offering a better angle for the light.

"Can you dim the light on my phone?" Tony asked Ri Ur Tol. "The battery's about to die."

Ri Ur Tol regarded Tony. "I will light the fight for as long as I can."

Tony lunged to get his phone back, but Ri Ur Tol swatted his hand aside.

John sprawled forward, hit from behind by a force Tracy couldn't see.

"Good. Derek learned from my lessons," said Ri Ur Tol.

For all her battle wisdom, Ri Ur Tol was blind to the irrevocable damage Derek and John were causing to one another, mentally and physically.

John careened to the side, hit by what must have been another telekinetic punch from Derek. John fell to the ground, where he lay still. Derek stood beside him, loud rasps escaping his throat.

A cheer rose inside Tracy, which she silently held tight between her lips. Rooting for Derek meant sacrificing years of friendship with John, and likely Rachel and Louis. Either way, Tracy was going to lose.

Tracy shivered, caught by a sudden chill. She wasn't the only one. Melissa rubbed her hands together and blew into her fists. Everyone's breaths came out as fog. Tracy looked around, uncertain where this cold attack was coming from.

Tony and Louis broke from the crowd to run toward John, frost forming on the grass Louis touched.

Tiny glints of metal flashed, daggers landing in front of Tony's and Louis's feet.

"Stop," said Ri Ur Tol with more small blades clenched between each finger, ready to be thrown. "That's your warning."

Tony pushed Louis on ahead. Dozens of daggers split the night sky, all of them missing the two runners.

"Stop them!" Tracy yelled.

"I'm trying." Ri Ur Tol bit through her words, yet her thrown weapons never hit either Tony or Louis, plenty missing by a wide margin. Ri Ur Tol disappeared with a snapping sound, reappearing next to Tony. She swung her dagger in the opposite direction from where Tony stood. Ri Ur Tol teleported all around, continuing to miss Tony and Louis as though she were drunk or intentionally helping those they fought against.

Ri Ur Tol's curses echoed against the surrounding trees with each miss.

"Fine. I'll do it." Tracy turned on her music and formed pillars from the ground, which she launched at Tony. He dove around her attacks. She formed walls to stop Louis, though her friend seemed to always be ahead of where she aimed.

Tracy directed the ground, yet she struck well behind where she was aiming the pillars of earth. Large piles of earth smashed together without so much as touching Tony or Louis.

Louis didn't stop running until he placed his hand on John's back. Bright yellow light passed from Louis to John. The meadow returned to its normal cool night, rising from the frozen temperature of a moment ago.

John sprang upright, launching several feet into the air before landing smoothly on his feet. He punched a nearby log, effortlessly splitting it in a single motion, rejuvenated mid-fight.

"Louis must have given John more power." Tracy looked on in horror at the twisted smile John flashed at Derek. "That's not fair!"

Allerie returned Tracy's verbal shots. "Derek received a boost of energy on the walk to this arena."

"John and the rest of us benefited from that as well. If John can get help, then so can Derek." Tracy used the ground beneath her feet as material to transmute a giant skeletal brace around her legs, back, and arms. Above her shoulders, robotic arms formed. The exoskeleton supported her limbs, giving her the strength to carry the large metallic arms stretching above her. Rather than create individual fingers, she made the hands into metallic spheres, like boxing gloves. Tracy stepped around the hole she used as material to form her weapons.

"You're not joining him," said Allerie, stepping in front of Tracy to block her path to Derek.

Allerie's limbs of flesh and bone were a paltry match for Tracy's metallic transmutations. Tracy rotated the robotic arms on her shoulders, ready to shove Allerie aside.

"You don't stand a chance," Tracy started. "Thank you for saving my brother's life tonight, but don't think that will stop me from hurting you."

A ball of light built in Allerie's hands, so bright Tracy needed to cover her eyes. "You saved my life, too, back with the bear monster. Tonight makes us even. Now I can kick your ass without any guilt. Better yet, I'll enjoy some well-earned payback from when you tried and failed to steal my girlfriend."

"You treated her like shit, and she was a willing participant when I kissed her." Tracy brought the two robotic fists clanging together. Gears whirred as the arms flexed.

Allerie wasn't intimidated by Tracy's stunts. She dropped the ball of energy and kicked it at Tracy.

Tracy punched the ball with a robotic arm, using the other to shield her body.

The explosion smashed in the robotic hand that punched it, crushing the skeletal structure holding the arm in place. Compressed air escaped from cracks in the side of the pistons controlling the robotic arms, though they held. Sparks flew from the crushed robotic arm as it moved, slow to respond to her commands. She rotated the other arm to prove that it still worked well enough.

Tracy lunged for Allerie, shouting, "Nicole used to confide in me after every one of your fights."

Allerie dodged to the side, kicking a ball of energy at Tracy. "Nicole used to tell me all the trash you said, too, princess." The word curdled on Allerie's lips, thrown as an insult meant to disarm Tracy.

Tracy deflected the exploding energy with her breaking robotic arm and wound the other back to pulverize Allerie.

Allerie moved behind a tree as they circled one another, her crisp voice striking Tracy. "You've wasted your gifts, bending the world around your entitled ass, serving you and your friends' wants, exposing the rest of us to unimaginable dangers."

Allerie stepped into Tracy's range. Tracy's fingers twitched above the console for her robotic arms, unwilling to punch Allerie. Limited light shone over the long line of Tracy's healed skin where the shadow monster tore into her flesh. "That's not... true?" Tracy's inflection turned all conviction in her statement into a question, doubts creeping into her thoughts.

Over the sounds of her robotic arm's gears, Tracy heard a tree crash to the ground, another casualty in John and Derek's ongoing fight.

Tracy's robotic arm remained poised behind her shoulder, held back from hitting Allerie.

We're no better than those boys.

A ball of light as bright as the sun formed in Allerie's hands. She dropped the ball and kicked it at Tracy, the small popping noise of the kick barely audible over the crackling air around the ball of energy.

Tracy lowered her guard, refusing to strike or raise a defense. She dissolved the brace holding the robotic arms on her shoulders, sending them crashing next to her.

I'm done fighting.

At the last possible second, Tracy lifted her regular arms to protect her face.

The ball of light exploded in front of her.s

36

Open Wounds

Rachel

Rachel ran forward to protect Tracy but was too slow to save her from Allerie's exploding energy ball. It detonated, blinding Rachel and sending all of them flying backward.

Rachel skidded over thick grass to the sound of Tracy's wild scream.

Regaining her senses, Rachel rushed over to Tracy, holding her phone's light close to her friend. Red and pink flesh littered Tracy's arms, burned skin seeping with blood.

Allerie crawled to Tracy. "You were supposed to block that. I never thought you'd willingly drop your guard. You're lucky I was able to detonate the blast early so it didn't blow up in your face."

Tracy nodded toward the crashing sounds from Derek and John's fight. "We were acting as bad as them."

Allerie held the one part of Tracy's hand that wasn't burned. "Why do you handle life in the worst possible way?"

A groan escaped from Tracy. "Because I'm me."

Louis scrambled to their side. "John told me that no one would get hurt! Taking Derek's powers was supposed to be for the greater good."

Louis removed his sweatshirt and wrapped Tracy's arms to protect them, shivering in the open air. It grated over her exposed flesh like sandpaper. Tracy tensed, suppressing a whimper. Red soaked through the layers, her blood tingeing the evening air with the smell of copper. "Thanks."

She drew in power to heal herself, and nothing rose from inside except more pain. *I'm too spent.*

Tracy bit her lip, struggling over the words she needed to tell Allerie. Taming her somersaulting stomach, she said, "Nicole isn't in our lives anymore. Her shadow shouldn't hang over us like this."

Allerie closed her eyes and sniffled. "I know, and neither of us caused her family to move."

"I should never have thrown myself at her in a last-ditch effort to somehow get her to stay."

"I knew we were over when she had to move. Our relationship wasn't built to last over such a long distance. It was so intoxicating to blame you."

Tracy tried to sit up, only to sink back to the ground, her face scrunched in pain as she groaned. "I wanted her to know how much I loved her before she was no longer a part of my life."

"She cared more about losing you as a friend than dating me." Allerie's voice wavered. "That's what hurt the most."

Rachel pulled Louis away to give Tracy and Allerie some privacy. "We're ending this *bellicoso* shattering of Derek and John's friendship," she told him.

Louis nodded, then paused. "For those of us who don't speak music major, what do you mean?"

"We're stopping those boys from fighting as soon as I figure out the how of it."

Derek and John were out of sight with the encroaching night. With Allerie and Tracy on the ground and everyone else running around, there were fewer raised cell phones to light the area. Repeated crashes and thuds announced that Derek and John were continuing their battle. Ri Ur Tol was overpowering Tony's trick to make her miss by applying a sheer volume of thrown weapons. She collected knives and threw them again, faster than Rachel could follow. Ri Ur Tol held Tony at bay, preventing him from joining John and helping him in his fight against Derek.

Rachel pulled Louis to Melissa and Nicole, the two people smart enough not to pick a fight. Melissa held Nicole upright while standing in front of her, shielding Nicole from wayward blasts.

"How can we keep Derek and John from tearing each other apart?" Rachel asked Melissa.

Rather than answer, Melissa took stock. "What are we working with? What powers do you and Tony have, Louis?"

Without hesitation, Louis replied, "I absorb energy from the world and can redistribute it into others. Tony can alter people's perceptions, making them appear where they aren't or, as he's been using it, make himself appear more handsome. Does that help?"

"It's better than nothing," replied Melissa.

Rachel's eyes wandered as she brainstormed ideas, landing on two white glowing eyes hovering not too far beyond the tree line. Using her power of sight, Rachel pierced the darkness, revealing the great four-legged bear shape, her abilities showing that the Beast's tempo matched Derek's in his fight.

Her body went rigid. Pulling in power, Rachel's voice caught before she could sound the alarm.

Though formidable at about fifteen feet long, the Beast was a far stretch from the fifty it had topped out at during their last battle. In both previous encounters Rachel experienced, the creature had attacked without hesitation.

Now, it watched.

Here, it waited.

37

Expired

Derek

Derek panted, struggling to stay upright. He broke through John's guard and landed a hit to his chest. John absorbed the weak force without budging. Derek's muscles were spent, providing no force behind his blows.

Derek reached for power, pulling nothing from the trickle he had been relying on. Empty. He scoured himself deep inside.

A fist hit him in the gut, stealing his breath.

Falling to his hands and knees, Derek gasped, his breaths coming in high-pitched wheezes. His eyes drooped, though pain throughout his body kept his senses clear.

John circled his prey, for once benevolently refraining from kicking Derek while he was down. John clenched and unclenched his hand, flakes of skin dropping from his fingers like sand emptying from an hourglass.

Lurching to his feet, Derek swayed. "You'll keep scorching your hand if you infuse your hatred into every punch. I made the same mistake."

"You don't know what I'm going through."

An uppercut to the chin toppled him. Coppery tastes rolled beneath his tongue. He spit out a stream of blood.

"Stay down," John ordered.

Derek looked toward his friends, unable to see more than outlines through the night's darkness. Nicole and Ri Ur Tol were over there, watching and supporting him. They had upheld their ends of the bargains by helping him search the void for the other version of himself. He could do no less than strive to uphold his promises. Derek stood. "If this were just about me and my powers, I would."

"Now you care about others?" John spat. "Where was this compassion when you almost killed Louis? Why not go back further to when you nearly crushed Tracy with a tree?"

John punched sideways, breaking a tree's trunk, sending the tree falling beside Derek. Its smaller branches broke over him, scraping his shoulders and ripping what remained of his bloody shirt.

Derek choked, fighting for air. "I'm the first to admit that I'm not perfect."

John struck down another large tree. Derek's legs trembled at the impact as the fallen tree blocked another escape route. "Rachel told me about all your adventures, and each story was worse than the last. How you didn't rip apart time when you attacked those people in the distant past is beyond me."

John's words were a heated knife stabbing Derek's chest like butter, both melting and cutting his insides apart. Derek spat blood onto the grass and spoke, feeling his jaw loosen from being beaten too many times. "You're right. I learned my lesson, though. Because

I abused my powers, my Beast went on a rampage. That's on me, and I was willing to sacrifice my life to undo my mistakes. Yet I—"

John cut him off with a roundhouse kick, bouncing Derek off the unyielding bark of a collapsed tree. Derek dropped to the ground, limp limbs catching none of his weight. Lying on his back, blood spilled from his nose, coursing down his chin onto what remained of his shirt.

Derek stared upward, trees circling in his spinning vision. Rolling onto his hands and knees, he struggled to rise and flopped back down. His shaking body could not hold himself up under the strain of the rotating world. "I need my powers to help those I care about."

Steadying his breathing, every muscle aching, Derek's body rejected the motions to stand. Warm tears fell. Still, he pressed on, bending his knees, inching himself upright until he faced John, steeling his voice to continue. "I'll travel the entire void and return the other me to where he belongs. Once I fix the final problem I caused, you can take my power."

John strode forward, fists at his sides. Bloody tears streaked John's cheeks despite not hitting him in the face. "That won't undo your past sins, and there's no guarantee you'll come back from the void. Taking your power here and now, I'll protect us from what may come in the future, be it monsters, aliens, or the void itself, all without endangering our friends."

Wobbling on shaking legs, Derek summoned what minimal strength he possessed to move his tongue. "I won't fight you anymore. You're my friend!"

John clutched at his heart, sucking in shallow, uneven breaths. He wound his other fist back as visible static charges sprung from the ends of his power-enhanced knuckles. "That's why I need to stop you."

38

Sides

Rachel

John's fist was mid-swing, though, to Rachel, he was stationary, one bloodied statue punching another. And like a statue, Derek was going to shatter into pieces on contact. Light around John's fist cast a tiny glow over the woods, shining across the red already soaked into Derek's clothes and leaking from John. Crimson lines ran from John's eyes, nose, and ears, places Rachel was certain Derek hadn't struck him. Fresh scars marred John's hands, where sizzling energy burst from him.

Rachel opened up her powers to accelerate even more. Her vision blurred and her legs nearly went out from under her. She exhaled a measured breath, regaining control of her body.

There was no plan, yet she sprinted ahead.

Rachel leaped in front of John's strike and pushed his arm to the side.

She returned to a normal speed, watching John spin in slow motion. His punch sailed wide of Derek, striking the fallen tree next to him. Even the force from the missed hit sent Derek toppling.

Meanwhile, John's fist crushed the bark, the impact crater bursting through to the other side of the log. John looked from his hand embedded in the wood to glare down at Derek.

Rachel stepped between the two idiots, yelling at the top of her lungs, "Are you insane?"

"Why'd you stop me?" John shouted back, wiping his face and smearing blood along his arm. "I was about to end Derek's powers."

She helped Derek to his unsteady feet. "You were about to kill Derek, if not yourself, too."

"Then I'll hit him lighter." John pulled back his fist, stumbling around Rachel to reach Derek.

Rachel accelerated to stay ahead of John's unsteady step, gripping his wrist. "You've made your point. Being the strongest person in a room doesn't make you right."

John looked back and forth between Derek, her, and his own clenched fist. Between heaving breaths, he managed to say, "He came close to killing two of our friends, and who knows what he did to our timeline."

"I was there, too, for the trip to the past. Why don't you punch me while you're at it?"

"That's not what I meant, and you know it."

"Then you're lying to yourself. You look awful. How many more punches can you throw? You're bleeding as badly as Derek is."

John leveled his voice. "I'll be fine. I know my body's limits."

"Not that you need another reason not to hit Derek, but look behind you." Rachel pointed over John's shoulder at the large creature approaching from the woods. Its eyes, solid ivory in color, seemed to glow. "If you insist on fighting a Derek who's been pulling his punches these last few rounds, then you'll have his Beast to contend with."

Under the limited light passing between the trees, when the Beast moved, it appeared to be a snow-covered mountain rolling across the land. It exhaled and almost blew Rachel over. Rather than tremble in fear, she stood tall against the full bear-shaped creature.

It could have attacked at any moment during this fight, but instead stood to the side like his friends.

Derek lifted an outstretched hand toward his Beast's white fur, falling forward in the motion. With a great swell of crunching leaves, Derek's Beast moved its head to catch Derek, his hand clinging to its thick neck.

Having blocked his bloody nose with a torn piece of cloth, John stood ready to resume his attack. "I knew you were working with that monster. For what, unearned fame?"

"You're wrong," Rachel said. "Yes, Derek accidentally created the Beast and fed it when his unchecked emotions drove his powers. Then he learned a little thing called control. Look at his Beast now. It hasn't grown or transformed into the savage monster Derek and I destroyed together."

"What does that have to do with anything?" shouted John.

The Beast nuzzled Derek's face.

Rachel looked on nervously as the monster embraced her friend. Through her powers, she watched a steady stream of musical notes pass between Derek and his Beast, returning Derek's fading tempo to normal. "From what I saw of this fight, Derek never lashed out in anger, unlike you. Had this Beast been linked to you instead of Derek, it would have twisted into something vile all over again."

Fury blazed within John's eyes, his gaze shifting between Derek and the Beast to their friends hobbling over to them. He faced

Rachel and sank to the ground. He reached for her hand, but she brushed it away.

"I thought you were on my side," said John.

Rachel refused to bow or break on the surface, hiding the weight tugging on her heart. "I was. Somewhere along the way, you lost what you were fighting for. Did you ask Louis if he forgave Derek, or are you leading a charge only you believe in?"

"Our lives have capsized since Derek first caught powers and spread them to the rest of you. It's been one crisis after another until I can't remember what we used to have."

"Living our lives, surviving school, planning for our future... everything becomes exponentially more complicated with powers," Rachel admitted. "We all need to find a balance."

"John has a point, though," Derek interjected. "I've made too many mistakes and deserve to be punished."

Rachel let her own anger blend into her voice. "Don't get me started on your self-righteous bullshit! You two deserve one another for your thickheaded arrogance and the way you ignore those around you."

Friends and enemies circled Rachel, John, Derek, and the Beast, hanging back at a safe distance to ensure the fighting wouldn't erupt once more.

Derek pushed off from the Beast, finally able to stand on his own, though the Beast lifted its paw behind him in case he fell. "You're both right. I may not deserve these powers, but I won't give them up. Not yet. I need to see a promise all the way through." He pointed to Nicole. "Her version of me is lost somewhere in the void. Once I return the other Derek and Nicole to where they belong, I'll freely give my full power to all those with abilities."

John's lip twitched. Rachel recognized that he was tossing thoughts about in his head, discarding ideas left and right. He tensed his legs to stand, but fell back down. "Fine."

Derek shivered in his tattered clothes, hugging his arms to his chest. "If no one else wants to pick a fight, then I'm heading home. It's a miserably chilly night and everything in me hurts."

39

Waking

Rachel

Battered and bedraggled, Rachel picked her way through the woods to Derek's house along with everyone else. Down to three working phones to light their way, each step risked twisting an ankle.

Despite bad limps and shuffling steps, only Derek and John needed help walking, except for Nicole, who climbed on top of the Beast's back and promptly fell asleep. Derek leaned partially on his Beast and put the rest of his weight on Louis, who seemed to be trying to make amends. A few minutes in, and they already needed to rest.

Ri Ur Tol studied Derek. "How badly are you injured?" she asked.

Derek let the smallest smile grace his lips. "I think I've been worse, but I can't remember when."

Ri Ur Tol stood on her toes to press her forehead into his. "Rest up. I've learned much about your weaknesses, which I plan to fix."

"Can John kick my ass all over again, so I don't have to train more?"

With a yelp, Louis went down, bringing Derek along with him. Prodding his leg, Louis grimaced. "Ow! My leg's acting up again."

"I got you," said Melissa. She scooped him in her arms and carried him as though he were as light as a pile of clothes.

Rachel replaced Louis, helping Derek get upright, and they started walking again. This kept her close to the Beast and far from John, who insisted on maintaining a respectable distance from the creature.

Looking at John's face made her want to ramp up her powers to punch him before he knew what hit him. Supported by his two cronies, they straggled behind the rest. John coughed a viscous spray of blood onto the forest floor, making Allerie and Tony stumble.

"What's wrong with him?" Tony shouted into the darkness.

John glanced at Rachel, blood dripping from his lips as he mouthed the words, "I'm sorry."

Like drinking poison and expecting someone else to be hurt, Rachel fed into the empty sorrow gnawing at her, allowing it to worsen with John's apology. "This fight spent too much of your power. We need to transfer some back or you'll die."

Allerie let out an aggravated sigh. "None of us have anything left."

Everyone was covered in swelling bruises, deep cuts, and scrapes; no one had the means to save John. Rachel swore, her worry building. "Did all of us burn ourselves out? Even for all the misery he caused, I can't lose John."

Derek's clothes had become rags of dirt and blood-stained fabric. Revitalized temporarily by his Beast, his head sank lower into his chest, eyelids failing to rise. "I'll do it," he said behind closed eyes.

"Like hell you will," John croaked, his throat raw.

"It won't only be me," Derek replied. "Once we get back to my house, we all need to come together to save you. Flint and Rachel did the same thing for me when they pulled me back from dying after I first opened the way into the void."

Rachel looked to those around her to stop him from doing something stupid again. "You're too weak, Derek. The rest of us can do it without you. Saving John won't turn back the clock and make us all friends again."

Derek forced his eyes open. "You're right. Except, we need John, along with Allerie and Tony. They're the reason we survived tonight. More monsters are coming. We need everyone together. I'm making sure John lives through the night, even if it kills me."

"I don't want your pity." Under another bloody coughing fit, John's grumbling quieted.

"It's not pity," said Derek, letting out a spreading yawn. He shook his head to stay awake and returned to marching out of the woods.

Tracy limped past Rachel and muttered. "I'll keep Derek awake. The worst thing he can do right now is pass out before we check the damage John did." Nodding her head at all of those injured, she added, "If your parents were upset before, Derek, they're going to be livid now."

Derek let out a long sigh. "Especially with my Beast joining us."

Rachel gathered her power with each step, all to save the man she once cared about. "No one appears to have broken any bones, or at least no one is screaming in pain if they did. That makes us better off than our last encounter with that thing."

"Speak for yourself," said Louis. "My leg hurts like it's been broken again."

Melissa lowered Louis, and Tracy lifted his foot as everyone stopped to rest again.

"No one hit you there, and I thought I fixed it," said Tracy.

Louis looked surprised at Tracy's inspection of his ankle. "It's been acting up. The ankle you healed doesn't feel as strong as my other one."

Tracy lowered Louis's leg with a delicacy Rachel didn't think possible in her exhausted state. "Be careful with it. We're almost at Derek's house. I'll look at it under decent lighting there."

Melissa lifted Louis and left the woods with him in her arms. A long row of cars were parked in front of Derek's house, far more than had been there before.

Mr. Fen ran to greet them, only to shriek as Derek's Beast stepped from the edge of the woods, as it and Rachel supported Derek. Mr. Fen looked ready to bolt for cover, though he would never willingly leave his son. "Derek, get away from that thing!"

"This big monster's with us now," said Derek, petting the Beast's side.

Mr. Fen stepped back, uncertainty etched on his face. "Are you sure?"

"Yes," said Derek's Beast, in a voice that was more growl than word.

Mr. Fen let out a small yelp. Rachel couldn't blame him. She flinched when the Beast first spoke in front of her, too.

One of the parked cars honked, shaking Mr. Fen into action. He waved Rachel and the rest on. "I called your parents and updated them on what was happening. Those I reached sped here as fast as they could. It took a lot of convincing to keep them from running blindly into the middle of your fight, especially with all the loud trees falling. I'm glad you're all still standing. Where's Nicole? I had an awkward chat with her parents because apparently she's with them, at home and across the country. Clearly, she can't be here, right?"

The Beast lowered its back to reveal Nicole still asleep.

"So this is the Nicole of a different world?" Mr. Fen stammered.

Rachel took charge. "There's a lot to fill you in on."

Mr. Fen shook his head in confusion, then faced Melissa and Ri Ur Tol. "I didn't know how to reach your parents, so let me know, and I'll smooth this incident over somehow."

Ri Ur Tol barked out a laugh. "You missed mine by thousands of years, we think."

Derek's dad's eyes widened so much they looked ready to pop out. He opened his mouth to say something, probably to make sure he'd heard her right, then closed it.

Rachel's parents' car was parked near the back of the long line. Seeing them standing there, waiting for an explanation, made sprinting for the woods behind her look all the more appealing.

"Mine know I'm here," said Melissa. "I'll send them a mission report of the fight soon."

Derek noticeably struggled to swallow. "Report? Mission? What are you, a fed?"

Melissa brushed twigs from her clothes. "Close. After publicly showcasing your powers, did you really think the government wouldn't keep a close eye on you? Don't worry. My first impressions were way off. You aren't as bad as you initially seemed to be."

Rachel's mouth ran dry at the thought of anyone analyzing her mistakes.

Allerie left John clinging to Tony and barreled over to Mr. Fen. "You had no right to tell my parents!" She sank her head into her hands and muttered, "I'm so grounded."

Mr. Fen stood his ground. "You had no right to pick fights among yourselves, or to do so on my property. Even though you have powers, it doesn't mean you're exempt from rules of human decency."

"You're right, but can you hold the lecture?" Derek's weak voice was little more than a whisper. "We need to keep John breathing."

"What happened?" Mr. Fen asked. "What do you need?"

"Room to work," Rachel replied. "Preferably with a way to reverse time."

They all headed into Derek's home, followed by the collecting mass of worried parents.

* * *

Dawn crept in through the window. Rachel crawled from the sleeping bag, stretching sore muscles after her night on the floor. She'd convinced her parents to let her sleep at Derek's house, along with everyone who fought last night. Friends and foes lay sprawled over his den.

John snored on the couch, having stabilized somewhere around two in the morning.

When he wakes up, we need to have a long talk. If Derek's past burnouts were any indication, John will be unconscious for the next week for how much power he expelled. That's plenty of time to figure out what I want for us.

Looking at his snoozing face, the crushing weight inside made it hard to breathe. It was nothing more than wishful thinking to consider staying together.

She stepped over the bundles of slumbering people on her way to the kitchen. The person closest to the door rolled over.

"Help me up." Derek's voice cracked, in desperate need of some water.

Rachel almost fell over getting him upright. Together, they limped to the kitchen.

She scrounged around his cabinets, looking to eat everything in sight. Derek sat at the table, his nodding head resting in his hands.

He sipped the glass of water she poured for him while moving as little as possible.

The sight of the Beast staring at her from the outside porch made Rachel drop all the energy bars and boxes of cereal between her arms. A few groans and sounds of stirring came from the den where everyone was still sleeping.

Not being afraid of the creature was going to take getting used to.

Derek went outside, leaning on walls and tables as he moved. Rachel followed, despite her better judgment. She regretted not bringing a jacket to keep her warm on this bitter morning, the type that stole the air from her lungs.

The Beast shook itself. Dew droplets trapped in its fur sprinkled over the porch, a mini rainstorm.

"Thanks for reviving me yet again." Derek patted the Beast's paw, which was half as large as Rachel. "You were ready to fight John with me last night. Why didn't you help us against the shadows?"

Derek's Beast covered its muzzle with its free paw. "Fear." Like the rumblings of a volcano before it erupted, the Beast's voice made Rachel recoil. "I was afraid of the creature like me. When you fought the fragment of shadow in the mall, I arrived to share our power." Derek's Beast curled into a ball. "Too much of the shadow was there last night at your school. I hid."

Derek faced his Beast, creases forming on his forehead. "The shadow thing was like you? It's another creature torn from someone?"

"It is like me," replied his Beast.

"Could I have created the shadow, too?" asked Derek.

His Beast's shoulders lifted in a two-ton shrug.

The door from the kitchen eased open and Ri Ur Tol joined them on the porch. "Why so gloomy? You both saved your home last night. No one has died. Celebrate!"

Derek shook his head. "At every chance, I forgot the fighting lessons you instilled in us."

Ri Ur Tol clapped him on the back, sending Derek cascading perilously forward before he caught himself on his Beast. "Quite the opposite. Your form was rusty, yet that's to be expected after two major battles in a single night. No amount of training prepares one for those strains. I've seen more capable warriors than you fail when given similar trials. I will train you to hunt better."

"Thanks." Derek slid from his Beast to face Ri Ur Tol. "Speaking of trials, ready to venture back into the void? When my body recovers, I'm returning the lost other me and Nicole to their rightful home dimension."

Ri Ur Tol brought Derek in close. "I'll search the dead world we glimpsed to find the other you."

Morning light climbed over the bare trees, beating back the chilled air and instilling new fortitude in Rachel. "Whatever we face, we're doing this together."

ACKNOWLEDGMENTS

If I have learned anything in publishing this second novel, it's that there are far too many people to thank for bringing my ideas to life. Once again I am humbled by all of you who have supported me in this journey.

Were I to thank each of you individually and explain how much you mean to me, this book would double in size.

Thank you for those who have followed the Into the Void series and cheered me along the way. I am ever appreciative of those who have devoured these books not once, but multiple times. Thank you to my friends and family who encouraged me and showed up in astounding numbers to get copies of this book's prequel.

Thank you to my talented wife and alpha reader, Adriana. No one has read this book as many times as you, with the exception of its author. Thank you to my parents, Mom and Steve, Leandra and Phil, who have expressed overwhelming pride and support for these stories. To my siblings, cousins, aunts, and uncles, thank you for reading my novels and offering honest feedback. I appreciate the positive comments as much as the valid criticisms.

To everyone in the AuthorTube community, thank you. I would have given up on this dream long ago were it not for the support I experience everyday. Thank you to those who champion my works, including Richard Holliday, Shanon (S.D.) Huston, Morgan Lee, Barrett Laurie, Martin Lejeune, JM Celi, Margaret Pinard, Lauren

ACKNOWLEDGMENTS

Adele Wheatley, Nicole Wheatley, Adrian Santiago, Amy Rosenfeldt, Natalie Locke, Nia the Vixen of Fiction, Benjamin Baggett, Eva of Bookend Lane, A.F. Stewart, A.M. Molloy, and there are still too many more to name.

Thank you to my Discord writing group. Those frequent check-ins with Brennan Bishop and Marc DeGeorge keep me motivated to finish this novel.

Thank you to all my additional beta readers Jordan Effron, Max Saperstone, Greg Roberts, and Greg Taylor. Thank you for continuing with these stories and helping me to close the plot holes and grammar issues.

I am thrilled to continue this series and my thanks to all the characters in my real life who inspire me on a daily basis.

Ben Pick is an avid runner and application security analyst who enjoys writing character-focused stories in his spare time. He also posts weekly videos on YouTube about the writing process on his channel, Running2Write, where he compares writing to the struggles of running. He loves getting lost in worlds, from the books and games he enjoys to the stories he creates. When not writing, running, or gaming, he takes care of the laziest Plott hound in the world.

Did you enjoy the adventures of Rachel, Tracy, and Derek? Sign up for the Running2Write newsletter via the QR code to get updates on future books!